I0757879

THE MOON TRAVELERS

K.E. DAVENPORT

The Moon Travelers
Copyright © 2021 by K.E. Davenport

All rights reserved.

No part of this book may be reproduced in any form or by any electronic or mechanical means, including information storage and retrieval systems, without written permission from the author, except for the use of brief quotations in a book review.

www.kedavenport.com

For Hoppy & Jumpy
I love you to the ends of the universe and beyond.
Thank you for inspiring me every day.

&

In Memory of Jason
Thank you for your friendship, my dear Mad Hatter.
I will miss you always.
-CC

INTRODUCTION

One of the greatest errors humans have made throughout history is failing to listen to the echoes of the past—the same melodies ricocheting off freshly painted walls in the long corridor of time.

They'd be wiser to remember that the melodies of joy, love, trauma, and heartache that they experience are only a few notes in a symphony written billions of years ago, on a musical scale more complex than any one generation of mortals could ever comprehend.

PROLOGUE
THE YOUNG WOMAN WHO COULDN'T REMEMBER

Lovely, young Maude sat on a hill, staring at the blue and green planet that spoke to her in inaudible whispers. Like a faraway voice calling to her through a dream.

She'd left the lunar wolf pack days, maybe even weeks earlier. They had taken good care of her when she first arrived. Yet her longing to set out on her own had grown strong as it became evident that she was not who they thought she was.

Her memories were almost non-existent. An empty void filled the space where they belonged. She remembered water and waves, an entire sea crashing down on top of her. She could hear a deep voice yelling, "Hold tight!" and "Don't let go!" But that was it. There was nothing before, and what followed barely made sense.

She was all alone now, though she knew she could return to the wolf pack if she chose. She hadn't ruled it out, but she hoped that by spending time in solitude she would recapture her lost memories. Nothing about the dusty, gray landscape felt right. It was desolate, and unwelcoming, and not at all like the planet that sang to her from across the black sea. Nevertheless, the Earth had offered her neither muse nor inspiration for reclaiming her memories, and she was beginning to lose hope.

Before she gave up, Maude decided to challenge the Earth to a battle of wills. She would use her mental prowess to bend the planet into presenting a key that unlocked her past. If, however, it had offered her nothing by the time she was spent, she promised herself that she would drop the obsession over her forgotten past and return to the pack.

Maude made herself comfortable, crossing her legs and relaxing her torso. She worked on concentrating her mind. She had to find the right balance. Too much concentration and she'd burn out quickly; too little and she might fall asleep. Soon she sank into a meditative rhythm that felt sustainable.

There was no way to know how long had passed when it happened. Minutes, days, and weeks had become foreign to Maude in this new place. It wasn't exactly that time *didn't* exist; it was that it didn't exist in the way she'd understood before.

She thought her eyes were playing tricks on her when she noticed a flickering light at the top right quadrant of the Earth. She had chosen to blink as little as possible during the *battle of wills*, and therefore, she dismissed the twinkle as nothing more than an optical nerve misfire. A visual fabrication caused by overstressed eyeballs. At least that's what she told herself at first. Eventually, the little light grew into a golden fireball, and Maude's heart began to flutter.

"A shooting star!" she exclaimed. "The planet is sending me a message!"

Maude's thoughts raced with anticipation. She stood and analyzed the path of the celestial dispatch to calculate where it would land. Without giving any thought to how she knew these things, she estimated the object's velocity, acceleration, and angle at which it was hurtling towards the Moon.

Remarkably, she projected that the object would land only a couple hundred yards from where she stood. She raced down the slope, careful not to fall as she tracked the incoming rock. Maude worried the fire would fade as it drew closer, and she didn't want to risk losing sight of it. She reached the bottom of the hill and bounded across the land as the meteor approached. There was no way she would be able to beat it to its destination, but she'd be close behind.

When the meteor had nearly reached the point of approach directly above Maude's head, something unexpected happened. The fireball stopped moving and hung in place. Then its fire dimmed, and it began to plummet. A few more flares erupted from the object, though, before it hit the ground.

Maude didn't understand how this was possible. What force could have acted on the shooting star to prevent it from completing its flight? Without hesitating, she ran in the direction of the fallen meteorite. Unfortunately, when she reached the vicinity where the rock should have been, all she found was a tall, young man wearing a backpack. His eyes twinkled at her, and he smiled.

Maude frowned at the young man with the dark tan skin. "Did you see a message…I mean a shooting star fall over here a short while ago?" she asked. "It's fine if you picked it up, but it's mine, just so you know."

Seemingly amused by Maude's curtness, the man laughed and said, "Well, that's about the weirdest greeting I've ever received. But, no, I haven't seen a shooting star. On the other hand, I just arrived, so I might not be the best person to ask. Say, are you up here all alone?"

Maude didn't like the man or his question at all. "No, there are others. Not humans, but—"

"Really!?" the man interrupted. "So you've been by yourself? For how long?"

Maude snapped, "I didn't say I was by myself. I told you there are others."

The man looked confused. "But you said there aren't any other humans."

"Has anyone ever told you that you don't listen very well?" Maude stared at the man crossly.

The young man laughed again. "As a matter of fact, I've been told that a lot. My name is Bob, by the way. I'm sorry if I've upset you, but is it okay if I ask you another question?"

Maude shook her head. "No. Look, I don't mean to be rude, but I've really got to find that shooting star."

Bob looked disappointed. "I see. Well, let me ask you this at least. Did your shooting star drop straight down from the sky right about where we're standing?"

Maude's eyes widened. "You did see it!" she exclaimed. "Where did it go?"

"I'm sorry to have to tell you this," Bob said, "but that wasn't a shooting star. It was me."

Maude put her fingers to her temples and pushed down. "That's impossible. How would you have looked like a shooting star?"

Bob turned around to show her what was strapped to his back. It wasn't a backpack at all but two cylindrical tubes that were fastened together. "See! It's a rocket-pack," he said, pointing behind him. "It creates propulsion by shooting ignited fuel from the bottom of the rockets."

Maude moved closer to Bob to inspect the rocket-pack. After she'd looked it over, she shook her head and said, "I don't believe you. I saw the shooting star come all the way from Earth. There's no way you made it all the way here from Earth using *that*."

Bob laughed and said, "To tell you the truth, you may be right. I can barely believe it myself. One minute I was in the ocean, trying to figure out how I was going to get home, and the next minute I was here."

"Ugh!" Maude grunted in frustration.

"What is it?" Bob asked.

Maude combed her fingers through the hair on the top of her head and then clenched her fists. "I told you! I thought you were going to be something important. I thought I was *finally* going to remember my past."

Bob looked at Maude sadly. "I'm very sorry. I didn't realize you had amnesia. Do you remember anything at all? Like how you got here?"

Maude avoided Bob's sympathetic gaze by looking back towards Earth. "No. I don't. Only that I thought I was drowning. Then I woke up here."

Bob's face lit up again. "Hey! What do you know! I thought I was going to drown too before I found my way here. Maybe there's something to that! Maybe the Moon offers shelter to people like us, people who've been stranded at sea."

Maude snickered. "Well, I'd say that's a stretch, considering there's only the two of us, and I'm pretty sure the others have always been here."

Bob shook his head. "No, you don't understand. There's lots of others like us, but they're trapped on the other side of the bridge."

Maude was confused. "Bridge! What bridge?"

Bob raised his hand to his mouth. "Holy smokes! You don't know about the bridge either. Well, I guess that makes sense, seeing as how you don't remember how you got here. Plus, those folks down there are right in front of it, and *they* can't even see it."

"What are you talking about?" Maude asked.

"Right! So once I got out of the ocean, my rocket-pack kind of grew a mind of its own. I thought it was broken, but then, somehow, it was turning on by itself and shooting off into the sky—taking me with it. If I'd thought of it fast enough, I would've unfastened the belts and dropped back into the ocean, but by the time I realized I was in trouble, it was too late.

"It took me up to the very top of the atmosphere, faster than I ever thought it could go. I thought surely the rockets would falter at such a high altitude, but you know what? They didn't. They kept going until we got to outer space, and that's when things got *really* weird. Once I passed into space, I saw a bunch of people—probably two or three dozen—trapped on this tiny platform together. They looked scared. I wanted to stop to talk to them, but the rocket-pack wouldn't slow down. In fact, it was only a few more seconds before the whole thing started to shake. And then, suddenly, it was going even faster than before. To be honest, I actually *felt* like a shooting star.

"After I reached the Moon, I worried I wouldn't be able to stop. Then I caught sight of you, and that's when the rocket-pack sputtered a few times and dropped me down to the surface. I know it sounds goofy, but I think whatever brought me here wanted me to find *you*."

Maude's expression had softened. It dawned on her that maybe this tall, young man named Bob was a message from Earth after all. Maybe there was something he knew that would be the key to unlocking her past. "But what about the bridge?" she asked.

"Oh, right! There's a bridge that runs all the way from the Earth to the Moon, but it's so dark you can't see it. The only reason I noticed it was because it was reflecting the fire from my rocket-pack."

Maude threw her arms around Bob and kissed him awkwardly on the chin. Bob smiled as his face flushed. "Do you know what this means?" she asked.

Bob shook his head. "No, what?"

"It means we can go back! We're not stuck here! I can find out who I am! I can find my family!"

Bob's face sunk, and he looked away nervously. Maude's smile faded. "What is it?" she asked.

"You don't understand," he replied. "Those people are *trapped* on the platform. There's no way for you to get back down to Earth, even if you made it across. And honestly, I don't think it's supposed to work that way."

Maude had had it. She was beyond frustration. She screamed as loud as she could and banged her fists against Bob's chest. "You don't know that! If they were able to get up there, then why wouldn't there be a way down? And what about your stupid rocket-pack? Huh? That could take us back, right? Just think about it! You're not even trying to help!"

Bob wrapped his arms tightly around Maude to calm her down and prevent her from striking him again. At first, she tried to push him away, but eventually she went limp and broke into loud sobs with her face buried in his shirt. "I hate it here!" she cried. "Nothing about this place feels normal."

Bob patted her on the back. "It'll be okay. We'll make it better. I promise"

"How?" asked Maude. She pulled away from Bob to look him in the eye. She wanted to believe his promise, but she had no reason to trust this stranger.

He smiled at her reassuringly. "We're two intelligent people. We'll create ways to make it feel normal. We'll make it more like home.

"First, though, I think we should help those people stuck on the other side of the bridge. They looked like they were in desperate shape, but I have an idea. Do you know where to find a deep cave around here?"

Maude nodded. The idea of helping others made her feel a little better; it restored her sense of purpose. "Yes, but why do you need a deep cave?"

Bob answered, "There's a type of chemical found in deep

caves that might help us figure out a way to light the bridge. Then the stranded travelers would be able to see to cross over."

"Okay," said Maude. "I can take you there."

She began to lead Bob towards the Moon's Darkside, wondering if she should tell him about the wolf pack and all the other things she'd seen since she'd woken up there. She decided to wait, though. For the first time in a long while, she felt like she was on the right path, and she didn't want to spoil it. Besides, she wasn't sure what the others would think about the arrival of more humans.

After a while, Bob asked, "What's your name, anyway?"

Maude shrugged. "I don't know. Amnesia. Remember? But I guess you can call me Maude."

CHAPTER 1

AN AFTERNOON AT THE BEACH

Mina raced through the backdoor and burst into the kitchen. She'd run all the way home from middle school in a whirlwind of excitement.

"Is that you, my love?" her grandfather called from the living room.

"Yes, Papa," Mina called back as she kicked off her shoes, tugged her knapsack from her shoulder, and turned it upside down. Her textbooks, papers, and pencils *thudded, whooshed,* and *plopped* onto the table. She took her empty bag and walked over to the refrigerator, pulling it open with a firm tug.

Right then, Mina's basset hound, Bonkers, came racing into the kitchen to greet her. He skidded to a stop in front of the fridge and wagged his tail, eagerly waiting for her to reach down and pet him. A few seconds later, her grandfather appeared in the entryway to the living room.

"You're home early. Is everything okay?" he asked in a concerned tone.

Without looking at him, Mina nodded. She grabbed some carrots and sliced lunchmeat from the bottom shelf of the fridge and dropped them into her knapsack.

"Yes, Papa," Mina responded while scanning the contents of the refrigerator once more. "I always get out of school early on the last Wednesday of the month, *remember?*"

Mina slammed the refrigerator door shut and turned her back to her grandfather. She searched the countertop until she found the last of the homemade cookies her mother had saved from the night before. Mina tossed them into her bag too.

"Oh, that's right. How could I forget?" Her grandfather laughed.

The words stung Mina. She knew how he could forget. He forgot all the time; it was the reason he lived with Mina and her parents in their small cottage. When he moved in, her parents had said it was so he could keep her company at home while they worked their busy schedules at the hospital. But Mina knew that wasn't the real reason.

Her grandfather had been forgetting important things. Like turning off the stove and how to get places, or even worse, how to get home. But it wasn't until he began to regularly mistake Mina for his own daughter, Mina's mother, that they finally decided to move Grandfather in with them.

Mina filled a tall thermos with water and stuffed it into the side pocket of her knapsack. She fastened the clasp on her bag and in one quick motion heaved it over her shoulder.

"What's this you're doing now?" her grandfather asked.

Mina paused and forced herself to make eye contact. She was ashamed of how frustrated these conversations made her feel, but she resented having to spend so much time helping her grandfather make sense of things. "I'm going to take Bonkers down to the sea, Papa. It's a beautiful day, and Mom and Dad said I could have a picnic if it was nice out." She stopped herself from saying, "You know, like I *always* do when I get out of school early?"

"Oh, I see," said her grandfather looking disappointed.

Mina knew she should invite him along, but she didn't want

to spend her whole afternoon babysitting him. She wanted freedom. To get out of the house on her own for a while and enjoy some time away from her studies. Avoiding his sad gaze, Mina ran past him out of the kitchen. She scooted across the house in her socks while Bonkers bounced along behind her, sliding into the walls. His nails tapped rhythmically on the wooden floor and provided an upbeat tempo for their short journey across the cottage.

Before they reached Mina's room, they glided down a tiny hallway covered in framed photographs. The pictures were mostly of vacations her family had taken over the years. Brief jaunts when her parents hadn't been too busy to spend time with her. Unfortunately, since both her parents were doctors who pulled long shifts at the hospital, they were almost always too busy to spend time with her.

Mina jumped over the threshold to her room and scooped up a thin, checkered blanket that was bundled and tied. She stuffed it under her arm and ran back to the kitchen. Grandfather was taking a seat at the table as Mina and Bonkers raced back into the room. Mina sweetened a little when she saw her grandfather accepting his fate. She walked over to where he sat and wrapped her arms around him from behind.

"Bonkers and I will be back in a few hours, Papa. I'll sit with you in the living room and do my homework then," she said as she pulled away from him and headed for the backdoor.

Grandfather smiled. "Don't worry about me," he said. "I'll be waiting for you right here when you get home. You two have fun and be careful."

"Thanks, we will!" Mina replied, sliding her shoes on.

She looked down at Bonkers and opened the door. "Now, Bonkers, I won't make you wear your leash if you promise to be on your best behavior." Bonkers stared up at Mina and cocked his head from side to side. Then he let out a loud sound that was half yawn and half grunt, which Mina assumed was basset hound for "It's a deal!"

"That's a good boy," she said, and she let Bonkers run out ahead of her before giving her grandfather one last wave goodbye and shutting the door. Bonkers pointed his nose to the ground, sniffing his way into the tall grass on the side of the house. Then once he'd reached a particularly overgrown spot, he flopped onto his back and rolled around in pure delight. Mina giggled at his silly behavior.

Bonkers pulled himself back to his feet. He was covered in grass and sprinkled with tiny purple flowers that had blown across the yard from the front garden. He panted happily at Mina with his tongue hanging out of his mouth and drool dripping from his jowls. "Why, Bonkers, I've never seen a hound dog fairy before." Mina laughed.

She walked over to him and bent down to scratch his ears. The portly basset hound returned her affection by nuzzling his head against her leg. A moment passed, and Mina stood up with a burst of energy. "Tally ho!" she cried, punching the air above her with her fist. "We're off to discover where the land meets the sea!"

She took off running towards the tall trees. They stood like wooden soldiers guarding the little cliff that rose above the shore. Bonkers trotted along behind her. His back two legs sprang up and down in unison, working hard to keep up.

Mina paused when she reached the cliff and waited for him. She looked down at the sand dunes that butted up against the cliff's edge. Then she looked across the secluded beach below, and the rest of the world melted away.

As soon as Bonkers reached her side, Mina leapt onto the sand dune in front of her, just like she'd done a hundred times before. Her legs knew exactly what to do. She leaned back, and her heels pressed deep into the hot sand. With each step, she could feel the warmth of the dunes bleeding through her canvas shoes a little more.

When they reached the seashore, Mina dropped the bundled blanket onto a dry spot and let her knapsack slide off her back. She knelt down and untied the blanket while Bonkers ran along the edge of the tide, flirting with the water and searching for sea creatures to chase. She spread the blanket over the sand, revealing its hidden treasures. Two short novels, a pair of blue sunglasses, and a pack of fruity gum.

Mina picked up the items and moved them from the middle of the blanket to the side. She walked over and lifted her knapsack from its sandy spot, dusting it off before dropping it onto the blanket. Then she unlaced her shoes, and peeled off her socks, and tossed them into the sand nearby. Next, she opened her bag, reached in, and pulled out her lunch. She unscrewed the top of the thermos, tilted her head back, and took a long swig of water while feeling around blindly for her books. Her fingers grazed the top of one of the novels, and she grabbed it and pulled it up to her face.

Mina screwed the lid back on the thermos and examined the novel's cover. It was a comedy about a pirate crew that discovered a talking treasure chest. Only, the talking treasure chest believed itself to be a person trapped inside of a treasure chest. Mina flipped through the book until she found the page she was on and began to read, breaking now and then to take bites of her lunch. Bonkers, who hadn't found any sea creature friends to chase, lost interest in the water and returned to Mina's side to patiently wait for the occasional scrap of food to be tossed his way.

After all the food was gone and Mina had spent a long time immersed in her book, Bonkers began to whine. Mina understood this to mean he was bored and wanted her attention, so she put her book down and stretched her arms out above her head. Then she stood up and ran playfully to the wet sand. As she waded into the sea, she turned around, expecting to see Bonkers following along behind her. Bonkers, however, was right where she'd left him, and he looked anxious.

Mina worried that he might be hurt. She hurried back and knelt down in front of him. Bonkers was pressing himself into the blanket, as though he were cowering from something above. She placed her hand on top of his head for comfort and asked, "What's wrong, sweet boy?" Without lifting his body, he dragged himself as close to Mina as possible and dropped his head in her lap, whimpering softly.

Seconds later, the ground began to shake, and suddenly, the beach around them shifted every which way like they were riding a turbulent wave on dry land. Mina leaned over Bonkers and wrapped her arms around him. Tiny pellets of sand flew up in all directions. They stung her skin like tiny arrows. She knew it was an earthquake, but it wasn't like the little ones she'd experienced before. This one was big and angry, and Mina prayed for it to stop.

It took nearly forty seconds, but the shaking did stop. Mina waited a few more moments, not sure if she could trust that it was really over. The ground stayed still, though, so she lifted herself up and breathed a deep sigh of relief. She looked around. The blanket they were sitting on was folded on top of itself several times over, and parts of it were buried in the sand. Her knapsack, books, shoes, and other items had been thrown ten, fifteen, even thirty feet away.

Relieved it was over, Mina couldn't help but laugh. "It's a good thing that thermos didn't land on my head!" she said. Bonkers looked at Mina and wagged his tail frantically, the way he did whenever he was in trouble. Glancing past her at the water, he let out a deep, rumbling bark and then turned and hurried towards the dunes. His tail swished back and forth across the sand, practically sweeping a path behind him.

Mina called after him, "It's okay, boy! It's over now. We

might have to tidy up, but we can still enjoy a nice day at the beach. There's no sense in going back to the boring, old house. Papa's probably fine, and Mom and Dad won't be home for—" She stopped. Something wasn't right. She turned around to face the water, and her jaw dropped. Two hundred yards from where she stood, a gargantuan sea-monster in the form of a three-story wave was barreling towards her. It rose high into the air as it closed in fast, preparing to swallow everything in one gulp.

Without wasting another millisecond, Mina turned back and sprinted for the dunes. Unfortunately, with every leap, her feet sank into the sand, making it impossible to get good traction. It gave Mina a terrible feeling that something was holding her back.

She turned her attention to Bonkers as he climbed up the sandy hill to the tall trees. She had almost made it to the base of the dunes when Bonkers reached the top. He jumped onto the low cliff and out of sight. The rushing water came roaring up behind her. She leaned forward and began to climb when, all at once, the wave caught her. It grabbed ahold and lifted her halfway up the sand hill, slamming her into the side of it with crushing force.

The front of Mina's body was buried in the sand while her back was pummeled by the raging water. Her lungs were full of air, but she had no way to relieve herself of the burden. It made her feel as though her chest might explode. She could feel the heavy water running over her like a roller coaster pushing her down as it raced upward. In her mind, she saw herself trapped under water, enslaved by the fierce current that engulfed her. She imagined her dark hair floating towards the surface, desperately trying to show her the way out.

Strangely, Mina had grown peaceful. Though her situation was dire, she had reached a state of serenity. Her body relaxed, and the pressure from the wave subsided. Her imagination faded into the shadowy recesses of her deepest self, and she waited to see what would happen next.

The answer came quickly. The water reversed course, ripping her away from her sandy, sloped bed. With the change in tide, Mina's euphoria disappeared, and her survival instincts kicked back into high gear. She used all her strength to swim up. At one point, her feet hit the beach as the water rushed away from the shore. Her head rose above the surface for a split second, and she was able to gasp for breath before being dragged under again.

She was towed farther and farther away from the shore. When she was able to open her eyes, Mina could see all sorts of debris caught in the current, bound to the water's mercy just like her. Besides the plethora of dirt and plant matter, there were schools of frightened fish; tattered fishing nets; a scuba mask; a table lamp; a board game with all its tiny pieces and colorful scraps of paper; a teakettle; and a ship's steering wheel. Some of them floated lazily by. While others, like the teakettle, zoomed past her like torpedoes, forcing her to bend out of their way.

Eventually, the current lost its momentum, and Mina was able to swim to the surface and take a deep breath. She treaded water as she turned in a circle to get her bearings. She turned and turned, but there was no sign of the shore in any direction. Her stomach sank. It didn't seem possible she could have been pulled so far from the beach—*so* far that she couldn't even spot it. She knew, however, if this were true, then she must be a very long way from where she needed to be. And without knowing which direction to swim, she worried she might drown before finding her way back to shore.

Suddenly, she felt very small up against such a gigantic problem. In an attempt to keep her wits about her, Mina forced herself to think about which way she should swim. She looked to see where the sun was in the sky because she knew her home was on the south shore. However, the sun was directly above her, which meant it would be a couple of hours before she could tell which direction it was going to set. Her eyes began to fill with tears.

Then, without any warning, a tree popped straight out of the water a few meters away. It towered high above the surface. Mina gawked at the surreal sight until she saw that it had started to lean, and she dove back under the water and swam away.

The tree did a giant bellyflop into the ocean. Mina's body tightened with fear. She was certain the tree had crashed down on top of her. Once she realized that she was still in one piece, though, she calmed down and pulled herself together. When she raised her head above the water, she found the tree floating on its side. She swam to it, breathing hard and thanking her lucky stars. *Now that I have a tree to hang onto*, she thought, *maybe, just maybe, I won't drown after all.*

CHAPTER 2

THE DARK EXODUS, PART I
THE UNRAVELING

N othing was written down, but the memory of what happened still remains. The bryobane possessed three-pronged hooves that were soft and weak and lacked the dexterity needed to use a writing tool. Not that the idea would have ever occurred to them anyway. They existed only in lunar nighttime, but this wasn't by choice. The bryobane, being the completely unimaginative monsters they were, never thought to wonder if there was any other part of the Moon than where they lived. For generations they lingered in the dark until, by accident, they discovered the lunar wolves. And that's when everything changed.

Before going this far back, let's begin again by jumping forward. When the Moon Travelers first started to arrive, they went right to exploring every inch of every crater, mountain, valley, and hill on the Dayside of the Moon. This was perfectly normal behavior for the humans. As per usual, it was their attempt to gain knowledge about their new habitat and, even more importantly, to assert control over it.

While the humans were exploring, they came upon a tunnel filled with bones from giant, horned creatures that had walked upright on three-pronged hooves. The discovery was tantalizing. Right away, the explorers started making assumptions about who the remains belonged to and how they'd ended up in the cavernous tunnel.

"*Well, this explains everything,*" said one very unlikeable pseudo-archaeologist. "These were Maude's ancestors. They must be the ones who started all the wolf colonies on the Moon—probably to keep away the vermin. How awful they had to suffer such a terrible end. Most likely, they died of some dreadful disease that Maude was lucky enough not to catch."

Several people, including Maude, pointed out how preposterous this theory was. Surely Maude couldn't have descended from these giants if for no other reason than the extremely obvious fact that she resembled a human and not a horned monster. However, the amateur archaeologist, backed by several other pretend scientists, gave a perfectly reasonable explanation for how this came to pass. "The creatures' odd deformities," he said, "were a symptom of the disease that ultimately led to their demise. Since Maude was somehow spared from the illness, she didn't develop any of the abnormalities that it caused."

Maude hated this theory with a passion. It was true that she didn't remember where she'd come from, but she thought it was more likely she had simply apparated into existence, than had descended from these strange beasts. It wasn't the nightmarish appearance of the reconstructed remains that made Maude so opposed to the man's theory, though. It was that the pseudo-archaeologist didn't have one shred of evidence to support his assertion, and yet he went around espousing his theory as though it were science-based fact.

Even more upsetting was that many of the Moon Travelers willingly accepted the amateur archaeologist's belief without any evidence at all. And pretty soon, they were expanding on his hypothesis with no proof to stake their claims on either. With each new idea, the story of the remains grew:

"These honorable men faced great adversity when settling the Moon, but they overcame it and created a utopian society."

"These heroic alien men fled persecution from an advanced civilization that was out of control. They crash-landed on the Moon and built beautiful inventions. Unfortunately, their inventions are all gone now. The climate was disagreeable to their fragile systems, and they fell ill and died. But before the illness wiped them out, they destroyed their creations and hid themselves away in the tunnel so that those who oppressed them would never know what had become of them."

"The aliens were magical. They could move mountains and seas like gods. They planted discs below the ground to create a permanent Dayside. They built the glass bridge between the Earth and the Moon so they could learn about humans and bring us knowledge of their advanced technology. When they realized they were going to die, they gave the glass bridge the power to rescue humans lost at sea. They wanted us to discover their remains and continue the important work of settling the Moon."

"They were our saviors! They rescued Maude before they died and passed their story along to her. But Maude's mind was too weak to possess such powerful knowledge, and now their story is lost forever."

Though ludicrous, the tales continued to evolve until they became legends. Of course, many Moon Travelers understood how absurd it all was. They knew that this so-called history was nothing more than a bunch of mythical stories, yet they didn't see the harm in letting the others play make-believe if it made them happy.

Whenever a believer recounted one of the legends as truth, the non-believers would just smile and nod to be polite. After all, the non-believers knew they had a leg-up on the believers when it came to intelligence, and most of them didn't see any reason to rub it in.

Others, however, like Bob and Maude, were much more outspoken about the dangers of presenting these stories as truth. They worried that people's ability to tell the difference between fact and fiction was eroding more and more as the tales grew. They tried to warn the believers that if they willingly put their faith in unfounded claims, they'd become an easy target for those who wished to manipulate them.

Unfortunately, it made no difference. People's minds had already been set in stone on both sides of the matter. If Maude and Bob had only known how prophetic their message would turn out to be, possibly they would've done more to make the Travelers understand the peril they were putting themselves in. At least, if the events that followed hadn't turned out to be so personal for the couple, they might've recognized sooner what was going to happen.

Alas, by the time they began to suspect what was going on, it was too late. There were already statues and shrines devoted to honoring the giant, hoofed beasts, and *nobody*—not even Maude and Bob, the first two Moon Travelers—dared to question the stories about the revered creatures, once known as the bryobane.

∞∞∞∞

JUST AS PLANET Earth's forces help to create life, the stubborn yet delicate force of planet Theia worked for ages to bring back life to the Moon. The life it brought forth was not the same as

Earth's masterpiece, however. It would have been impossible for Theia to produce such an array of beings since its potential for life came nowhere close to matching that of Earth's. But this hadn't always been the case.

Eons ago, the barren planet, Earth, stalked the thriving and fruitful planet, Theia—once, twice, a million times around the sun on nearly the same orbital path. To say that Earth was attracted to the lush planet would have been a gross understatement; it was more than lust, envy, or obsession that fueled the sterile planet. Earth chased Theia with a psychopathic desire to snuff out every last morsel of her beauty.

When Earth finally overtook Theia, the violence that ensued was enough to obliterate both planets. Earth crashed into Theia, intent to destroy her, but Theia fought back with everything she had. She battled Earth while clinging to her life-giving properties, but Earth outpowered her and stripped them away. Quickly, it became evident that the only way for Theia to preserve anything she held dear was to let Earth take what it wanted and escape with what was left.

Once it was over, Theia pulled away from Earth before the energy that had built up between the two planets caused them to explode. Yet sadly, Theia suffered one last blow. She had become so weakened by Earth that when she broke free, she didn't have enough mass or momentum to escape Earth's gravity. Therefore, she became its lone satellite. Forever buoyed to her tormentor. Forced to watch what had once been her own joyful destiny play out from afar.

Theia went into a great period of mourning for what she'd lost, but when she recovered, she became determined to use the little energy she had left to create life again. This is how the Moon Walkers came to be. The Moon Walkers were higher life forms like the ones that had existed on Theia before. They were sensitive and wise beings; however, because they'd been created with such little energy, they couldn't exist on Theia's surface for very long.

To make up for this weakness, Theia gave the Walkers the power to create their own life forms like the lesser creatures that were evolving on Earth. In this way, the Walkers became like a fire with a weak source; their flames would never grow strong, but their spark could ignite a more robust fire.

To ensure that life continued after they were gone, the Moon Walkers used their power to create two new life forms: the lunar wolves and the bryobane. One to strengthen Theia with intelligence, love, and loyalty, and the other to guard her with ignorance, hatred, and brute force. Very quickly, the wolves became the Walkers' treasured companions. They were shown the Moon Walkers' ways and taught how to use Theia's energy, or the *Great Energy* as it was often called. But the Moon Walkers' strength continued to wane, and they knew it was only a matter of time before they would have to leave the lunar wolves behind.

Before they left, they showed their friends how to make the journey to the Darkside in order to honor the Great Energy. The Walkers told the wolves it was important to connect to Theia's energy on the Darkside because this is where it was strongest. It was so important, in fact, that the Walkers made the wolves swear an oath that they would continue to make the journey every year.

The last thing the Moon Walkers did was warn the wolves never to go near the bryobane dens. The dens were setup to guard the border of the Darkside from intruders, but the bryobane didn't even know the wolves existed. And the Moon Walkers told the wolves it should always remain that way. To make the journey to the Darkside, while avoiding the bryobane dens, the wolves built tunnels underneath the border that allowed them to move safely back and forth between the two sides.

For ages, the lunar wolves traveled to the Darkside to worship at Crystal Crater—a deep, wide hole at the top of the Moon that held the most powerful crystals. Here, the wolves sang songs, performed ceremonies, and gave thanks for the gifts bestowed on them by the Great Energy, just like the Moon Walkers had taught them to do.

Time passed and the number of wolves grew. Eventually, there were so many wolves that they began breaking off into separate packs. Each pack had its own name, a pack leader, and a head healer. Over time, there was some fighting and competition between the different packs, but mostly the lunar wolves got along and shared generously with one another.

Every cycle, the lunar wolves made the pilgrimage to Crystal Crater. Each pack journeyed separately because the pack leaders had decided early on that it would be safer if they traveled through different tunnels—just in case the bryobane ever discovered one of their passageways. Overall, the wolves were content with the leaders' decision since it was convenient for the packs to take whichever tunnel they lived closest to.

A problem arose when the Lesego pack—the second oldest and largest of all the packs—outgrew their home in Deep Valley. The valley had provided the Lesego Wolves with shelter since the first Lesegolese broke from the original pack to create a new one. It was a sad day for the Lesego wolves when it became apparent that there was no more room in the valley for the pack to grow. They knew that the younger generation would be asked to split off into a separate pack, as was normally done when a pack became too large.

But Fego, the pack leader, decided that this isn't what he wanted. Without consulting the others, he made the decision to relocate the entire pack, rather than ask members from the younger generations to leave.

To begin the massive undertaking, Fego appointed three prominent Lesegolese to the task of finding a piece of land.

The only criteria that he gave them was that the land had to afford the pack with plenty of space to expand into an ultra-pack. The three wolves toured other valleys but were unable to find a valley larger than their own that was unoccupied. Next, they searched the craters because they knew a crater would give them plenty of vertical space in which to build their caves.

The spot the three finally settled on met their needs for space. It was located inside an enormous crater and surrounded by tall cliffs on all sides. Fego, however, wasn't so sure about it. "You've brought me a strange choice," he told his appointees. "I wouldn't have expected you to pick a crater right next to the mountains that border the Darkside. I'm sure you're aware that the bryobane dens are just on the other side, are you not?" Fego asked. The appointees were prepared to defend their decision, though.

"Yes, it's near the border, but the crater is so massive that we can build a switch-back entrance on the opposite side. We'll never have to get within striking distance to the Darkside," the first wolf reasoned.

The second chimed in, "The bryobane can't climb or tunnel. We don't need to worry about them reaching the crater any more than we worried about them reaching Deep Valley. It's not going to happen."

It was the third wolf, however, that made the most compelling argument. "There's a narrow tunnel only a mile from the top of the crater's northwest side. It runs under the mountain and is an offshoot to a larger tunnel that leads to a safe spot on the Darkside. If we widen the narrow tunnel, we can use it to travel to Crystal Crater in less than half the time that it takes us now."

This was all Fego needed to hear. Not only was his pack going to have a larger area to call their new home, but they were also going to have the easiest access to Crystal Crater. Their travel time to get there and back would be far shorter than any of the other packs'. Fego thought that, surely, this was the wisest decision any leader had ever made for the long-term prosperity and well-being of their pack.

The Lesegolese got right to work, planning and then building their new home in the crater. Everything ran smoothly until halfway through the project when Fego ordered that eight of the builders break off from the crater's construction crew and begin widening the narrow tunnel to the Darkside.

Fego had been boasting to the other pack leaders about his brilliant plan to build the Lesego pack's new home so close to Crystal Crater. But many of the pack leaders questioned his plan. They thought that it was a bad idea for a pack to live in such close proximity to the bryobane. Fego felt that he'd been shamed by these leaders. He told himself they weren't actually concerned, only jealous, and it made him even more determined to show off. But to do so, he had to make sure the tunnel was ready for the upcoming pilgrimage.

The head of the builders, a wolf named Belo, warned Fego that taking so many workers off the crater project would undermine the speed at which they could finish their new home. Fego thought he knew just how to handle this problem, though. "That's a simple fix, Belo. Move the less experienced builders to the tunnel project. It doesn't take a genius to dig up rocks and dirt, and certainly you won't miss these less skilled laborers in the crater."

Belo didn't like this plan, however. "Widening a tunnel isn't only digging up dirt and rocks," he argued. "There's skill and technique involved, just like when we build a cave in a rock wall. Understanding the structure and stability of the tunnel is important, and less skilled wolves don't have that kind of knowledge yet."

Fego was unfazed by Belo's attempts to persuade him. "I know you hold your work in high esteem, but you're not going to convince me that a tunnel is a complex structure. It's just a hole in the ground. I mean *really*, Belo. Consider yourself free to oversee the tunnel work if you'd like. But only after you've finished your shift in the crater each day."

Belo was furious, but he knew there was nothing more he could say without crossing a line. So he did his best to oversee the work in the tunnel, even though the double shifts kept him exhausted. He was positive that there were many things he might have missed or overlooked, but he was stretched so thin that there was little he could do to make it right.

When the day came for the pack to join the others in the pilgrimage, Belo confronted Fego again—this time pleading. "The wolves did their best, but I can't ensure it's safe. We need more time to build supports in the tunnel to protect against cave-ins. I'm begging you, Fego. There could be catastrophic consequences if the pack uses that tunnel too soon."

Fego shook his head. "Belo, Belo, Belo. You don't give your team enough credit. They worked very hard to get our tunnel ready for the big day, and now you come here to tell me that we can't use it? Please, stop this nonsense. There's enough credit to go around. Nobody's forgetting how hard you worked, watching the builders create our new home."

Belo had become livid. "How can you call yourself our leader and yet be willing to lead us to our deaths? You think this is my pride speaking? I *warned* you not to put inexperienced wolves on that project alone! But you dismissed my concerns because you're too worried about what the other pack leaders think of you!"

Fego snarled at Belo. "That's enough!" he snapped. "You will go out there right now and tell the pack that the tunnel is safe! And I don't want to hear one quiver in your voice. There are young and old depending on that tunnel to make this journey."

Belo snarled back. "I'll do no such thing! My family and I are leaving. We can no longer stay, knowing what kind of leader you are. You're a coward, and yet you show no shame! You hide behind the young and the old in a pitiful attempt to pretend that you care for members of this pack. When in reality, you completely disregard everyone's safety!"

Fego stammered, "Y-you can't go! I-I'll tell the other pack leaders you betrayed us. They'll never let you join them!"

Belo, who'd already turned to leave, looked over his shoulder. "Do what you must. We'll form our own pack if we have to. Even if we fail, at least we'll have shown more courage than you ever did!" And with that, Belo was gone.

Fego was consumed by rage. He spat after Belo, "Good riddance, Belo! And don't you *ever* come back, you traitor! You and your family are banished forever!"

Fego wanted to run after Belo and tear him apart, but he forced himself to calm down. He was going to have to think fast to keep the plan for the pilgrimage in play. He couldn't let Belo's abrupt departure change anything. Like a madman, he raced to where the pack was beginning to form a line outside the newly widened tunnel. As he approached, he thought he saw some of the wolves eyeing him and whispering to each other.

They're already talking about what happened, he thought. He couldn't wait a second longer. He had to take control of the moment before it got away. "Let me have your attention everyone!" he shouted to the other wolves. "As I'm sure many of you know by now, it's a sad day for our pack. Belo and his family have been exiled. I can't go into any specifics, but I can tell you that it's not something you need to worry about. The actions Belo took were ones that affected only him and his family. I have taken great pains to ensure that nobody else will suffer for his misdeeds."

The wolves looked around at each other in astonishment. Not even the oldest wolves among them had ever heard of a wolf being exiled before. From *any* pack. Instantly, an unspoken sadness and uncertainty began to grow within their ranks. One of the wolves who'd just arrived at the back of the line yelled, "I heard that Belo thinks the tunnel is unsafe. Is that true?"

Fego was so quick to get his next words out, he nearly choked on them. "No! That is absolutely false, and any wolf who says otherwise will be reprimanded for such nonsense!"

Fego ignored the looks of disbelief he was getting from the crowd. Instead, he pressed forward with his plan, although if someone had asked him in that moment to explain why, he wouldn't have been able to give them an answer. He was like a force in motion with no sense to deviate from the dangerous path he might be setting them on.

"Now, please everyone. While our journey will be much shorter than before, it's still a long journey. We need to get going."

Someone from the middle of the line shouted, "But not everyone's here! There are others still on their way."

Fego laughed awkwardly. "That's okay. We'll start slow so they can catch up. And I'll lead the way to prove that there's nothing to be worried about."

Fego moved towards the entrance to the tunnel. He could hear the wolves talking behind him in hushed tones, and suddenly, it occurred to him that they might not follow. He'd fully committed himself to his big charade, though, so without giving it any further thought, he leapt down into the dark tunnel.

The drop took longer than he'd expected, and Fego wondered for a second if he might be falling to his death. Finally, he hit the ground, and after regaining his composure, he called back up, "Mind the drop, everyone! It's a greater fall than you might expect!"

He moved ahead, anxiously awaiting the sounds of the other wolves entering the tunnel. Much to his relief, the sounds came a few moments later, and Fego marched happily on. The wolves entering the tunnel behind him began to sing the ancient songs, and all around them, the crystals embedded in the walls came to life in a deep reddish-orange glow.

It was one of the first practices the Moon Walkers taught the lunar wolves—singing praises to light their way. By singing the songs that honored Theia, they summoned her energy and brought light to all the dark places where the crystals were found.

Though many were hesitant, the entire pack eventually made it into the tunnel, minus a few stragglers who didn't arrive until after the pack was already gone. Fego was finally able to relax, and privately, he praised himself for what he'd accomplished. He thought about how, in a very short time, he'd not only found the pack a new place to thrive and prosper but had also given them the best route to Crystal Crater.

He couldn't understand why Belo had refused to take part in celebrating such grand accomplishments. But he decided it must be that some wolves just didn't have strong constitutions like the pack leaders. Belo only understood minutiae, which was why he worried so much. Fego thought that if Belo could have understood the bigger picture, then maybe he would've made a better leader. Not for the pack, of course, but for the builders at least.

Boom! Boom! Boom! The front of the line had nearly reached the connecting tunnel when Fego heard three explosions from far behind. The sounds were followed by a commotion that echoed down the walls. The singing had stopped, and the reddish-orange lights from the crystals faded in and out, leaving the tunnel in complete darkness at times.

Fego heard a male voice shout, "The tunnel collapsed! There are wolves back there! We have to save them!"

Then a female voice yelled, "Don't stop singing, everyone! We have to keep the lights on!"

Immediately, Fego's brain began to swim in circles as he

tried to calculate his next move. It didn't take long. He had to deflect blame, and quickly. "Belo sabotaged the tunnel! He knew more about it than anyone! That means he knew its weaknesses too!"

A few of the mothers and pups had started to sing again, which brought the light back to full brightness. Fego could see that there were large gaps in the line; many of the wolves had run back to help the others. He glanced around at the wolves who were singing. Several of the women were staring at him in disapproval.

Fego didn't care for the women's boldness, and he pointed his nose in the air to show them he wasn't interested in their opinions. Though nobody was in his path, he ordered, "Clear the way, ladies! I need to get back there to check on the others."

But before Fego had passed the chorus of singing wolves, there was another series of explosions. This time, they were much closer. The tunnel went dark. Fego heard several pups wailing, and someone cried out, "Oh my god! It's the bryobane! We're under attack!"

Fego panicked. In every direction, he heard wolves screaming in terror. He was hit by a wave of bodies that pushed him backwards towards the other tunnel. He knew he had to get himself turned around before he lost his balance and was trampled to death. But he never got the chance.

He saw a dark red flash as the tunnel's ceiling caved in on top of him. He tried to continue going backwards, to get out of the way. But the heavy dirt pounded him into the ground until he could no longer move. The rubble had him pinned. Fego couldn't see, but he could hear groans coming from all around; it was the other wolves who had tried to escape. There were other noises, too, coming from above them. Noises that sounded like squealing grunts.

Time passed, but Fego was too dazed to know how long.

Every once in a while, he would feel the dirt shifting nearby. Always it was accompanied by mumbling and then gasping. Always, *always* the terrible sounds of gasping. Fego couldn't make sense of it.

Soon enough, he felt the dirt being scooped away from around his neck. His fur tickled, and something slid over the top of his head, dropping down right above his shoulders. It tightened hard around his neck and cut off his airway. Fego choked and gasped as he was lifted out of the dirt. Suddenly, he could go no farther. His left back leg was buried under heavy debris, unable to escape. The tightness around his neck increased, nearly strangling him, and he felt his leg snap in two as he was pulled up by a mighty force. Fego's eyes bulged from their sockets, and searing pain coursed through his entire body. He wanted to cry out, but he couldn't muster even a tiny whimper through his compressed trachea.

Finally, he was dropped onto a pile of fur, and the grip around his neck eased. Fego could feel the pile of fur moving beneath him. He was lying on top of the other members of his pack. The bryobane had rescued them from their dirt graves, but Fego suspected that whatever the bryobane had in store would make them wish they'd stayed buried.

Belo had been right, except that Fego hadn't led the others to their deaths. He'd led them to something far worse. And with this thought at the forefront of his mind, Fego laid on top of the pack and willed himself to die.

CHAPTER 3

THE PATHWAY

Mina spent a while catching her breath. A hard wind swooped in like an angry spirit blowing across her wet skin and clothes. Shivering and exhausted, she lay on the tree, considering her options. Though she knew it was unreasonable, she hoped that if she rested there long enough, the tree would magically float her back to shore.

After much contemplation and going nowhere, Mina decided to stand up. Doing so would give her a better vantage point from which to spot the shore or, even better, a rescue boat. With great effort, she lifted her torso into a seated position and pointed her legs down like she was straddling a horse. Slowly, she leaned forward, bracing herself with her hands while pulling both legs up on the trunk so she was in a kneeling position.

She was nervous. She knew she would have to calm down for this to work. She pretended she was in the gymnasium at school. She wasn't a castaway trapped in the middle of the sea. She was simply practicing her gymnastics by raising herself up on the balance beam. Soon she learned that this was much more delicate work than she'd expected because, unlike the balance beam, the tree didn't stay still. Instead, it tried to spin underneath her feet—forcing her to make constant adjustments to keep from falling off.

She stood up all the way and turned her head slowly from side to side, searching for land. Unfortunately, there were no signs of the shore, which meant that her only hope for the time being was to see if the shore was behind her. However, to turn around, she had to kneel down again. Carefully, she lowered her torso towards the tree, but halfway into it, she lost her balance and flopped sideways into the water with a stinging splash. She paddled back up to the surface, but before she reached it, a crackling blast of sound ripped through the water. It threw Mina forward, and she panicked, certain it was the beginning of another earthquake. Without thinking, she raced back to the tree for safety.

She pulled herself over the top of the scratchy bark and looked down at the ocean. There were no giant ripples or waves. She took a deep breath and sat up slowly. And that's when she saw the most unusual thing she'd ever seen. Mina's mind began to do somersaults. She knew that what she was looking at defied logic, yet there it was anyway—a colossal, glass pathway, curving out of the water's surface and reaching high up into the sky.

Mina knew the pathway hadn't been there a moment ago, and though she had no explanation for how it was possible, she decided that the path must have shaken loose during the earthquake, fallen from somewhere above the clouds, and crashed into the sea. Of course, it made no sense, but after everything she'd been through, Mina was willing to lump it into the category of mysteries she could solve later.

Well, I suppose this is good. I mean, there are very few things I need more right now than an elevated place to stand, she thought while lowering herself into the water and doggy paddling over to the behemoth structure. When she got there, she bobbed her head under the water to see how far the pathway descended. Surprisingly, she found that it sloped to the sandy sea bottom ten yards down and didn't stop there, for it looked as though it had knocked a large hole into the ocean floor and tunneled into the ground.

Mina was curious where it would take her if she followed the path that led below, but she decided she'd had enough underwater adventures for one day. Besides, she needed to hurry and figure out which direction was home. She didn't know for sure how long it would take her to paddle the tree to shore, but she was certain it would be long enough for her grandfather to become worried.

Mina grabbed onto the translucent path. It was six feet across and two feet thick. It felt extremely sturdy but was slippery due to her wet clothes, and she had to shimmy back and forth to keep from sliding backwards. Once she was able to stand, she found that it was actually quite easy to walk on, and so she began to climb.

She knew she wouldn't be able to see the shore until she'd reached a high enough point on the path. But having no way of knowing how high up that might be, she made it a habit to turn around every twenty steps to see if she could spot anything new. She stared through the thick glass as she climbed, hoping she would see some flash of color, besides blue, to indicate that the shore was up ahead.

She climbed over forty feet into the air when, suddenly, she heard a familiar sound coming from far away. It was Bonkers! She spun around and looked way out in the direction he was calling to her. By squinting hard, she could make out the shoreline and, in the center of it, a tri-colored speck sitting on the beach, howling. Mina was so relieved she began to cry. "Bonkers! Over here, Bonkers! Wait for me! I'll be home soon!" she shouted.

Mina extended her foot to begin taking the path down but

was shocked to find that she was about to walk right off the end of it. She raised her arms out to each side and thrust her weight backwards, landing awkwardly in a seated position. Her heart was pounding. She looked towards the sea and realized that the entire way down had disappeared. A tingling sensation took hold of her as her anxiety kicked into high gear. She pressed herself against the bridge, afraid she would fall if she relaxed.

She stared forward at the vast sea beneath her. She wondered if it would catch her like a soft net if she fell, but the very thought of this made her dizzy. She was aware that crashing into the sea from this height would more likely be like crashing into blue asphalt, and suddenly, she became aware of a terrible truth. There was nowhere to go but up.

Her pounding heart sank inside her chest. "How could part of a solid glass pathway just vanish?" she asked out loud, though she knew the answer couldn't be any stranger than how the whole thing had appeared in the first place.

She wondered if possibly she just couldn't see the path anymore, and she tested this idea by tapping her foot in front of her where the pathway had been. But there was nothing there; her foot dipped into the air below where the structure should have been. Then a sickening thought popped into Mina's head. *What if the pathway up had disappeared too?*

She turned around quickly on her hands and knees and looked up. Much to her relief, the path was still there. Mina knew that she didn't want to go any higher, yet for some reason, it was more frightening to think of being trapped on a tiny piece of vanishing glass than on a solid glass structure.

For the longest time, Mina sat, hoping that the path down would reappear. She suffered as she hoped, and she hoped as she suffered. Her heart ached to return to the land, to Bonkers, to her mom, dad, and grandfather. And to her little cottage by the sea. She sat and waited for a solution, any solution at all, that would change what she feared was the inevitable. Mina knew it was far too dangerous to jump, but it nearly broke her to face the uncertainty of going up.

More time passed before Mina finally stood again. Cupping her hands around her mouth, she yelled, "I can't get home yet, Bonkers! I'll do everything I can to get back, though." She paused a minute. Her voice felt tight, and tears slid down her face. "Take care of Mom, and Dad, and Papa! Make sure to love them extra while I'm gone!"

Then wiping her tears away, Mina turned back to face the glass pathway. She craned her neck. The path ahead stretched like a bridge to the sky. *This could take forever,* she thought, but she took a deep breath and began. She climbed, and climbed, and climbed some more. She climbed past a v-formation of mallard ducks that looked at her quizzically when they passed nearby. She climbed through several puffy, white clouds that smelled refreshing like a rainy day. She climbed and climbed until the sea no longer looked like water but a painted blue canvas instead.

The higher Mina climbed, the more she felt like she had entered a dream. Her mind wandered, but she blamed it on the thinning air. She knew that, eventually, if she climbed high enough, there would be no more oxygen left to breathe. She hoped she would reach her destination before then. Wherever that might be.

At some point, she realized that she had no idea how far she'd gone or how long she'd been climbing. She turned to see how high up she was but immediately became woozy when she discovered she was tens of thousands of feet above the Earth. She wanted to sit down to regain her composure, but she didn't dare give herself a second chance to look down. She turned back to the path and exorcised her fear by allowing her mind to roam as she climbed some more.

∞∞∞

"Hмм…нмм….нммм…" An old woman with dark eyes and purple hair stood behind the counter of her wooden booth, humming to herself as she pressed a pencil into the paper in front of her. She was writing a note to a dear friend, although at that moment, she was completely unaware of this fact.

In actuality, the woman had fallen into a trance, and the note that she was writing wasn't from her. The old woman was merely being used as a medium to transfer information, which in this case was a farewell letter.

All around her, there were sounds of men and women shouting at each other in raspy, old voices. "Horace, you old fart, if I catch you trying to steal one of my repeat customers again, I'll knock you into next week!"

"Gale, keep your bunion-riddled hooves off the counters! What're you trying to do? Scare away the shoppers?"

The old woman didn't hear any of the ruckus, though. She was completely oblivious to the world around her. She continued to hum as she wrote, "…and don't hold it against Ruth. She only did what she knew was best for me. Keep me close to your hearts, but please don't try to find me again. This is the way it must be. The way it was always meant to be. With all my love forever…"

Crack! Suddenly, a cabbage the size of a cannonball slammed into the wooden booth next to the old woman. It awakened her from her spell. She looked around at her surroundings, as though she didn't trust what she was seeing. Then she looked down at the note and read the last few lines.

She sighed deeply and looked to see if anyone was watching her. When she was certain that no one was paying attention, she picked up the note and pressed it tightly against the crystal hanging over her heart. She whispered, "Oh, Helen. It shouldn't have to end this way."

CHAPTER 4

THE SUN, & THE EARTH, & THE MOON UP ABOVE

Time was passing much differently than what Mina was used to. For as long as she could remember, she had quantified time with beginnings and endings. Now, though, it seemed as if there had never been a beginning or an ending to anything. Stranger still, was that despite the non-stop climbing, Mina didn't feel the least bit tired.

In no time at all, or possibly in all the time that had ever existed, Mina found herself approaching the end of the path in quite a daze. Hard as it was to fathom, there didn't seem to be anything remarkable about the end, except that it leveled off and vanished into the sky. *Maybe it's a mirage*, she thought.

As Mina got closer, she noticed that the pathway was glowing a bright neon blue. She tried to think back to the beginning, to remember if the path had always been glowing. But her memory on the matter was entirely blank. Baffled about what to do next, Mina walked all the way to the end when, abruptly, she became aware of a large hole directly in front of her. Surprisingly, she hadn't even noticed it until she'd nearly climbed right through it.

She walked the last few feet and poked her head into the

hole. "Unbelievable!" she gasped. She had discovered that the hole was an entryway into outer space. *That's amazing. I never realized that the border between Earth and space was so definite. I always assumed it was more like a gradual fading away of Earth's atmosphere,* she thought.

She decided to try an experiment. Pulling her head back through the hole, Mina looked around until she found the sun. It was big and bright and surrounded by blue sky. Slowly, she moved her head back through the hole and looked in the exact location that she'd seen the sun on the other side.

"Incredible!" she exclaimed. She had found the sun right where it should be, only on this side of the hole, it was surrounded by the black void of space and thousands of stars that had been invisible in the blue sky. The sight made her ponder. *How odd that something as grand as the sun could seem so different when viewed from two separate places only a centimeter apart. And stranger still that those stars go completely unseen when they're always right here, hiding behind a curtain of atmosphere.*

Then with a shake of her head, Mina pulled herself away from her thoughts. She knew she should focus on the situation at hand, which was that she had no idea what to do next. Her eyes had been slow to adjust to the darkness of outer space. She held out her hands and tried to see by touch. Instantly, her fingers landed on a platform at shoulder height. She spread her arms out wide across it and realized it was big enough to stand on.

"Here goes nothing," she said, hoisting herself up and sliding her torso onto the platform. Then, with one last push and a shimmy, she heaved the rest of her body onto the dark ledge and was greeted with a face full of feathers.

"Ptooey," Mina spat as she jerked her head back and realized she could suddenly see again. She sat up to inspect her surroundings. The platform was so dark that it could have been part of the emptiness that surrounded it. However, laying in front of her on the dark platform was a pair of beautiful wings, bound together by a small feathery harness.

She was stunned. Never in her life had she seen feathers like these before. They were as white as fallen snow, but when they moved—even from the slightest touch—a delicate gold hue shimmered across them in a diagonal wave. Mina wondered where on Earth there were birds that possessed such magical-looking feathers. While she thought it over, she noticed a piece of twine wrapped around the wings with a thin, metal note attached. "Maybe this will explain where the wings came from," Mina said as she reached for it.

The small metal piece at the end of the twine had words engraved in calligraphy across it that read:

> *Be strong of mind and fair of heart*
> *If you wish to fly.*
> *Your temper must be long in length,*
> *And you mustn't fear to die.*
> *Try these on and sing a song.*
> *I advise it that you do.*
> *For going up is option one.*
> *Falling down is option two.*

Mina wondered if there was an option three or four, though she doubted it. She couldn't understand why, but she knew these wings were what the long glass pathway had been wanting her to find. Soberly, she looked down at the spinning Earth below. The hole had vanished, just like the path that had led her to it, and the grave reality of what she was facing gripped her. She sensed that the chances of ever making it home again had become very small.

Her entire being ached for her family, and though she knew it wasn't right, she wished that Bonkers hadn't made it up the sandy hill. That he'd been swept away with her instead. *At least*

I'd have had a friend by my side, she thought. Her eyes filled with tears as hopelessness reared its ugly head. But before it completely took over, she remembered the first few words in the note. "Be strong of mind." She pushed the despairing thoughts away and worked to regain her composure.

She grabbed the wings and began to slip her arms and head through the shimmering harness. As she worked, she thought more about the note and wondered if she would really be able to fly. She felt sure she had a strong mind, but she wasn't certain what it meant to be "fair of heart." She liked things to *be* fair and hated when people cheated or lied, but she knew the note might mean something entirely different.

As far as having a temper "long in length," Mina assumed that this was the opposite of having a short temper, and she was pretty sure she didn't have one of those. However, what she was most uncertain about was the part that read, "you mustn't fear to die." After all, didn't everyone fear death? At least a little?

I guess it's time to see if I pass the test, she thought as she pulled down on the straps to the feathery harness. Once the wings were fastened, she stood tall on the dark platform, waiting to see what would happen next. A buzzing sensation poured over her that felt like electricity traveling up and down her spine. But nothing happened after that. She remained firmly in her spot.

Wondering if she'd failed to meet the note's requirements, Mina picked up the piece of metal and read it again. Right away, she realized her mistake; she'd overlooked the part about singing a song. She shoved the note into her pocket and straightened herself out. Then without even thinking about which song to choose, Mina began to sing a tune that her mother often sang to her about gray skies and sunshine. In her mind, she could see her mother leaning over her bed, singing her the song.

The lyrics and tune carried a message of love, but they also hinted at sadness and the unknown. Mina's heart broke as she sang. The image of her mother faded, and large tears rolled down her cheeks. The wings on her back stretched out wide behind her. They began to beat softly back and forth. Mina fought hard to sing through the tight lump in her throat, and her voice went off key. Suddenly, she was lifted off the platform and out into the void, farther and farther away from everything that had ever mattered to her.

Mina closed her eyes and concentrated on bending the wings to her will. She told them to take her back to Earth, back to her home. When that didn't work, she kicked her arms and legs in an attempt to change their direction, but that was no use either. Feeling disgruntled by the control the autonomous wings had over her fate, she rebelled in the only way she could think of—she stopped singing.

Instantly, the wings folded back together, and Earth's gravity pulled her in once more. She cried out in horror as she tumbled towards the great big planet. She knew she had no choice; she belted out the song again, desperate to stop the dizzying free fall. Much to her relief, the wings burst open and halted her descent. This time, however, instead of lifting her up gently, the wings flapped frantically like there was suddenly some great urgency to their journey. Within seconds, Mina was rocketed away.

The acceleration pushed the skin on her face back and pried her lips open. She was no longer able to control her jaw or tongue, which meant she was no longer able to sing. Fearful of what might happen if she didn't continue the tune, Mina forced herself to hum through her teeth. Luckily, the soft dental vibrations seemed to do the trick because there was no discernible change to the terrifying speed or to the trajectory she was on.

Please take me home. Please take me home, she thought. A vision popped into her head. She stood above the sea just as before, only it didn't look so far down this time. She imagined jumping into the water, plunging deep below the surface, and floating back up with ease. She wished with all her heart she could go back and take that risk, knowing now where her other choice had led. Over and over, she played out all the different scenarios that might have come from diving into the water. But no matter how many times Mina pictured reliving the moment differently, her situation remained the same. She flew deeper and deeper into the darkness, away from Earth and into the unknown.

∞∞∞∞

Bob could feel the excitement of what was about to happen. He'd known this day was coming for a long time.

The soldiers had been getting restless. They'd been showing up one by one, four or five times a day for months so that what had once been a small band of renegades was now a sizeable army. Bob kept telling himself this was good. It's what they needed to execute their plan. There was an obvious downside, however; with every new recruit that arrived, there was less work to go around.

This meant the jobs that had already been delegated were now shared between several men and women. It wasn't enough to keep anyone occupied for very long, and so the soldiers spent much of their time asleep, bored, or fretting over the future. This led to lots of fighting, and Bob quickly realized they needed more to focus on while they waited for the real fighting to begin. He had his officers put together some games for the soldiers to play. Still, there wasn't much else for them to do in the form of recreation. Not when they had to stay hidden.

The base camp had been set up in a mile-deep valley on

the Moon's Darkside, a location that never saw sunlight. The site was strategic because it was near Black Ice Glacier, their eventual target, yet completely out of sight from its surroundings. The never-ending darkness, however, only enforced the angst that many felt. The soldiers who'd been there the longest were just beginning to get used to the eternal night, even though they'd been at it for over two years. Bob sympathized. He understood, all too well, the painful process of adjusting to the darkness that existed there. It wasn't just the eyes that had to be recalibrated. It was the mind as well—an entire overhaul of a person's psyche, and not everyone got through it with their wits intact.

Bob had set his alarm for thirteen-thirty Lunar Central Time, a time zone located on the Moon's Dayside. The soldiers used this as their primary time zone because it was a reminder of where they'd come from, a place where hours and days were easier to keep track of. Not because they were less ambiguous, but because everything just seemed to make more sense in the light.

Bob's captains and top aides knew the plan. He had ordered them to stay awake and guard the camp while the lower ranks slumbered. The others were not to be woken until an hour after Bob had departed. However, since only the lower ranking soldiers were assigned to guard duty, there was some clever rearranging that had to be done.

In order to relieve the assigned soldiers of their watch without suspicion, a couple of the captains had cajoled them into a friendly game of horseshoes. "To make it interesting," said one of the captains, "we'll wager you a night of guard duty against a week of keeping the army's equipment log."

Eventually, the captains threw the game just like they'd planned, but they had a difficult time in doing so. It turned out that the rookies were terrible at horseshoes. The guards' horseshoes landed almost everywhere, *except* near the stake, most often on top of the mess tent, which had infuriated the cook and almost led to a fight. It was a demoralizing exercise, but after fifteen games, the captains finally managed to stoop to the right level of mediocrity to hand the rookies the win.

The plan was all set. Bob had dressed the night before so that all he had to do was grab his gear and set out for Sharashka Mountain when he arose from his cot. The mountain was a mile-high peak just south of camp, a location that was off-limits to the troops but that would give Bob the view he needed.

He had almost reached the halfway point of his climb when he looked at his watch for the first time. Soon, the captains and aides would be telling the troops that Bob was ill and was to be left alone in his tent until further notice. The lie was regrettable, but it was how they'd chosen to avoid all the questions that would have to go unanswered. Only a select few knew about the secret operation, and it was important to keep it that way.

As Bob climbed, he thought about what a relief it was to get away from base camp for a while, especially since it afforded him the opportunity to do something he loved so dearly. When he was a boy, he spent most of his time outdoors, climbing to the highest point around, whether it be a rooftop, tree, or hill. It kept his poor mother in a constant state of worry. One time after he'd fallen off the cement wall behind the neighbor's house, his mother marched him in front of his father and ordered, "Franklin, *do* something before your boy gets himself killed!"

His father had laughed, and with a knowing smile, he said, "Should've named him Billy instead of Bob. Guess we'll just have to call him 'Bobby goat' instead."

His father's solution hadn't sat well with his mother, and she'd made her dissatisfaction known for weeks after. Nevertheless, from that day forward, the nickname stuck, and justifiably so. Bob had never found anything that made him feel as free as climbing did. No matter how high he climbed, he always longed to go higher—to break free from the planet's gravitational constraints just a little more.

When Bob reached the top of the mountain, he untethered the long telescope that was tied to his pack and set it up on its stand. Then he checked the location points on his wristband. Looking through the scope, Bob rotated the telescope towards the south and tilted it upward 62.254 degrees. After a few more adjustments, he pulled away from the scope and looked in the direction of the Dayside. He knew it was just a matter of time now *if* his calculations were correct. But this thought made him nervous. He began to obsessively check and recheck the numbers until his senses drifted away.

His mind conjured visions of his wife whenever these Darkside daydreams appeared. He smiled. He could see her exactly as she was the first time he ever laid eyes on her. She was beautiful. Tall and thin, just like him, but with strawberry-blonde hair that flowed to her waist and skin so smooth that it looked like porcelain. The vision floated in the ether for a long while until, inevitably, it faded.

Once Bob had fully returned to the present, he scolded himself for being so self-indulgent. He knew better than to allow his daydreams to take over. He had to stay sharp up here all by himself; there was no one to save him if he got lost in his daydreams. To stay lucid, he forced himself to sing songs that he could only remember parts of the words to. It was a trick he'd figured out many years earlier to keep the darkness at bay. Trying to remember song lyrics or making up new lyrics to familiar tunes helped him remain grounded.

Time passed. Impatiently, Bob began the fourth verse of his fifth song, *"A wise old frog, the big blue cow..."* When finally, he spotted what he'd been waiting for. High above the horizon, way out in space between the Earth and the Moon, was a tiny, glittering light moving at an extraordinary velocity. Bob looked through the scope. Then while making some modifications on the fly, he adjusted his telescope so he could see the object better.

It was a girl strapped to the wings, the last of the two pair he'd worked on so painstakingly. And now there was no more of the synthetic materials left for a new pair. This was it. Just as Ruth's prophecy had stated, a girl—*this* girl—would set the final stages of their plan in motion.

Bob knelt down. He had to get a message to the market fast. He grabbed a small, mechanical bird from his pack and pushed his thumb and index finger down firmly on both sides of the silver bird's stomach. The round part popped open like a tiny, swinging door, revealing an empty hole inside. Bob took out a slender engraving pen from his pants' pocket and gently pushed the point of it into the top of the hollow bird's stomach while pulling it towards him at the same time. A curved magnifying glass, three centimeters long and one centimeter wide, slid out.

He took a tiny piece of metal from his pocket and clipped it to the flat part of his pack. Holding the magnifying glass above the piece of metal with his right hand, he used his left hand to grasp the engraving pen, carefully etching tiny letters into the metal. When he was finished, he held up the metal piece and whispered the short message aloud, "Operation Eclipse is a go."

CHAPTER 5

THE ARRIVAL

Hours passed before Mina realized where the wings were taking her. She'd watched the Moon growing larger as she flew in its general direction, and it seemed as if she might zip right over it. However, this all changed when, suddenly, the wings repositioned themselves, and Mina began to fall headfirst, straight towards the glowing, white rock.

Her body stiffened as she braced for impact. The land below rose quickly to meet her, leaving her barely enough time to contemplate her chance of survival. Yet seconds before she reached the ground, the wings curved up and spread out wide. Mina was pulled upward with a strong tug, as though an invisible parachute had burst open above her. The motion slowed her descent, and soon she was gliding high over the bright, lunar surface.

She was spellbound. The wings had taken her to *the Moon*. All sorts of thoughts swirled around inside of her head. She wondered why she'd been brought to the Moon and by whom; she wondered if this made her the first non-astronaut to visit the lunar world; and most importantly, she wondered how she was ever going to get home. Realizing that she was powerless to answer any of these questions, though, Mina focused on the landscape to calm herself down.

It reminded her of a ghostlier version of the Wild West, a place she'd never been but was the setting of many of the films her grandfather liked to watch on Sunday nights. Sunday was the day that both of Mina's parents worked overnight shifts at the hospital, and without any serious adult supervision, Mina and her grandfather broke the rules and watched movies while they ate dinner. This was time that Mina still enjoyed spending with her grandfather. His memory never seemed to fail when it came to old movies, and he had taught Mina all about American cinema, especially the old westerns.

She marveled as she soared over deep canyons, scraggily shrubs, and dry tumbleweeds, just like she'd seen in her grandfather's favorite films. *How different the Moon is than I'd imagined,* she thought. *And how big too!*

As her flight continued, Mina suddenly spotted some bright lights and a wall that looked like it ran along the outside of a village. The sight was shocking. Mina was positive she'd never learned anything in school about the Moon being colonized. Then a thought occurred to her that made her nervous. *What if this is some sort of military secret that one of the governments on Earth is hiding?* If they found out she'd discovered their covert base, they might not help her get home, assuming they let her live at all.

She thought about this idea for a moment but then dismissed it. She knew there were only two superpowers on Earth that were capable of creating a moon village. And she was certain that if either of them had pulled it off, they would have announced it to every square inch of the world until even the termites were aware of their great achievement.

The wings lowered Mina to the ground, and as she descended, she saw over the top of the large wall that cordoned off the village. Except that it *wasn't* a village. It appeared to be an outdoor market filled with colorful booths that were aligned in rows. A multitude of people walked between the rows, and thousands of vibrant lanterns dangled from crisscrossing wires high above their heads. Mina thought the wires looked like a giant spider web from above. She drifted closer to the ground until she could no longer see over the wall. Her feet made contact with the Moon's surface, sending up a thick cloud of dust. She took a deep breath. Her nostrils were invaded by the stench of gunpowder. It tickled her nose, and she let out a giant sneeze.

She wondered if there had been some great battle that had left the awful smell behind, but the notion of a moon battle seemed so preposterous that she immediately dismissed it. Curious about her new surroundings, she reached down to feel the grit and dust that made up the Moon's surface. She scooped up a handful and let the grains sift between her fingers. The dust that was mixed in with the dirt was so fine that some of it floated away from her hand in twisted strands of smoky powder. She blew at the spiraled strands, and they spread apart and vanished.

She stood up and examined the terrain while taking her first steps. She was surrounded by flatlands covered in gray and white rocks. The dirt beneath her feet was unexpectedly thick in some places, which made it feel padded like walking across the Earth's tundra. Away from the market, in the distance, she saw long chains of shadowy hills.

Mina looked around a bit more and finally came to the conclusion that none of it looked real. The light from the sun illuminated the world around her, but there were shadows everywhere. Even in the air it seemed. Without a daytime sky, none of it felt right. It was like watching a play with a well-lit stage but no backdrop; you had to ignore what was missing in order to believe any of it. Mina did her best not to think about it. She knew it would drive her crazy if she didn't look beyond the strangeness of the place. Besides, she had seen PEOPLE walking up and down the rows inside the market, and she was anxious to go explore. She wanted to find out who all these people were, where they'd come from, and if they could help her get home.

Mina walked towards the market but came to a dead stop almost immediately. The giant wings were dragging on the ground behind her. *Oh right*, she thought, *I better not cause a scene.* She reached for the harness to pull the wings off, but she couldn't get her fingers underneath the feathery straps. She looked down and saw that the harness had melted into her clothing. There was no way to take it off without removing her shirt. She took her arms out of her sleeves and pulled the back of her shirt in front of her so she could get a better look at how the wings were connected to the harness. She thought maybe she could untie them, but the wings had been stitched into the harness with a hard wire that she knew would be impossible to break.

Mina turned her shirt back around and looked longingly at the market up ahead. She assumed that the people there had the same social conventions as the people back on Earth and would find it objectionable if Mina walked around with no shirt on. She wasn't as certain whether it was socially accept-able to walk around winged, however. *Maybe the wings will be a good ice breaker*, she thought. *I might as well give it a shot. After all, I'm going to need all the help I can get if I'm ever going to get home.* She took a deep breath and garnered her courage as she walked towards the bazaar.

When Mina got closer to the outside wall, she began to smell the delicious aromas from the food being sold inside. She hadn't thought about eating since she was back on the shore, polishing off her lunch. She didn't know how much time had passed, but it surprised her that these potent smells were failing to trigger any hunger pains after everything she'd been through.

A few more steps and she began to hear the festival noises spilling over the wall. The loud murmur of hundreds of voices mixed with the up-tempo beat of music playing somewhere off in the distance. She angled herself towards the left corner of the market where she spied a slight opening in the wall. As she drew near, she saw a man and a woman sitting behind a metal desk near the entrance to the marketplace. Each was dressed in a gray uniform like a security guard. They even had shiny bronze badges pinned to their shirt pockets.

The man greeted Mina. "Welcome to Waldoff Market. Please show your papers."

Mina pulled her head back in surprise. She didn't have any papers. The woman picked up on this and said, "If you don't have papers, you'll have to acquire a visitor's pass before entering."

"I see," said Mina. "And how do I get one of those?"

The woman eyed Mina from head to toe. Then she replied, "You say, 'pretty, pretty please, with a cherry on top, may I have a visitor's pass?'"

Mina laughed. She was sure the woman was joking. This couldn't really be the way to get a visitor's pass. But the woman didn't waver from her serious expression. She nodded her head at Mina as if to say, "Get on with it."

Mina stood silently for another moment. She couldn't believe she was being forced to say something so ridiculous just to go shopping. Nevertheless, she went ahead and did what was expected of her. "Pretty, pretty please, with a cherry on top, may I have a visitor's pass?" she asked, feeling humiliated.

The woman said, "Of course, but first you'll have to fill out this form and get approval." She reached under the table and pulled out a tall stack of thin, metal sheets and dropped them on the desk in front of her. It had become clear to Mina that the woman guard was on a power trip. "Why did you make me say all of that if it has nothing to do with getting a visitor's pass?" she asked the woman.

The man snickered. "What makes you think it has nothing to do with getting a visitor's pass? We don't just hand out passes all willy-nilly to anyone who can fill out a form, you know. We want to make sure you're capable of being polite, too. Otherwise, maybe we don't want you visiting our market. Savvy?"

"Fine," said Mina wearily as she picked up the top sheet from the large stack. It looked just like the engraved note that had been attached to her wings, only bigger. "How am I supposed to write on these?" she asked.

The man and woman glanced at one another with a look that Mina recognized well; they thought she was a moron. The lady looked back at Mina, and in a huffy tone, she said, "What do you mean *how*? You use a pen, of course."

"Okay. Then may I have a pen?" Mina asked.

The two guards looked shocked. "You mean to tell us you came all the way here without bringing your own pen?" the woman asked.

Mina was exasperated. She blew a puff of air towards her forehead as a way to release some of her frustration. "No. I didn't even know I was coming here, so why would I have brought a pen?"

The man ignored the question and reached into his shirt pocket for a pen. "Well, I suppose if you haven't brought your own pen, then mine will have to do."

Mina was relieved. Finally, someone was being reasonable. "Thank you," she said as she reached for the guard's pen.

"What are you doing?" he asked disdainfully, staring at Mina's outstretched hand like it was a cockroach.

"I'm going to fill the form out with your pen like you said."

"Don't be absurd!" exclaimed the guard. "You can't just

steal my pen because you were too lazy to bring your own. I'll write down the answers for you."

"You're serious?" Mina asked.

"Quite serious," said the man in a superior tone of voice. "Question one. Your name. Oh, that's easy. It's Cornelius." The man began to scribble his answer on the metal sheet. It made a high-pitched scraping sound, and Mina winced.

The woman guard nudged the man with her elbow and said, "It's not asking for *your* name, Neil. It wants *her* name."

"Oh, right. Of course," responded the man as he began to scratch out what he'd just written.

The woman rolled her eyes. "Oh, for goodness' sake. Give me those!" she said, and she reached over and slid the stack of metal sheets towards her.

The woman read the first question. "What's your name?"

"Mina."

The woman yanked the man's pen from his hand and scribbled across the top sheet.

Then she asked, "Where are you coming from?"

Mina was nervous to answer this question. She didn't know if the guards would believe her. Hesitantly, she responded, "Earth."

The woman glanced up from the form and shot her an annoyed look. "*Uh, yeah,* we know you're from Earth. Obviously, that's where we're all from. What part of Earth?"

Mina wasn't sure how specific she should be, so she said, "The northern part." She was happy to see the guard jot down her answer.

"How do you feel about the market?" the guard asked next. Mina looked puzzled. "What do you mean? I've never been to the market before. How could I feel anything about it?"

The guard looked down at the form and spoke out loud as she wrote, "Subject has no feelings."

Mina interjected, "About the market. I think you should

specify that I have no feelings about the market. I mean, if you're going to put it that way."

The guard looked at Mina with a raised eyebrow and then looked back down at the form. "Subject has no feelings about the market," she said as she made air loops with her pen an inch above the form.

With agitation in her voice, Mina said, "I can see that you're not actually writing that down."

The guard didn't look up from the form but said, "Great! Next question. What items do you seek to buy during—"

But Mina interrupted her. "Don't you think it's important to write down my answers correctly? Otherwise, you might change the meaning of them."

"Nope. I don't see how it matters. Can we continue now? This is going to take forever if you get hung up on every question."

Mina knew the guard was right, but she couldn't let it go. "I understand, but I'd just like to know that you're putting my answers down properly. I might not get approved if you make me sound crazy."

"Yes, you will."

Mina crossed her arms. "How do you know that?" she asked.

"Because you don't look like the type we reject," replied the male guard.

This statement didn't sit right with Mina. "And what does that type look like?" she asked.

The male guard smiled. "Oh, you *know* the type."

Mina shook her head. "No, I *don't*."

The guards looked at each other for a second, and Mina thought she saw something sinister pass between them. Then the female guard looked back at Mina and said, "What he means is you don't look like some of the shady characters we get here. I'm sure you've seen them before—goatee, red horns, pointed tail, and a pitchfork."

The male guard who'd been taking a sip of water from a tiny cup spit it out all over the table as he began to laugh and choke. The female guard chuckled at this and leaned back in her chair with her hands clutched behind her head. Mina couldn't believe how unprofessional they were being, and she began to wonder if getting into the market was really worth all this trouble. She glanced towards the entrance. Judging by the number of people going by, she guessed that there were thousands inside.

She looked back at the guards. The woman was still smiling smugly as she watched her partner pull himself together. Mina asked, "Well, if I'm going to be approved anyway, then how about we save some time and skip all of this?"

This snapped the man out of his laughing fit. He sobered up and put his serious face back on, though he didn't sell it very well. "No can do, little winged thing. The rules are the rules, and the rules say that all visitors have to complete one of these forms before entering Waldoff Market."

"Ugh! Fine. Let's keep going then." Mina sighed.

Ignoring Mina's tone, the woman guard began to ask questions again. "Have you ever shoplifted before?"

"Never."

"Have you ever been a member of a circus or traveling band of gypsies?"

"Wait, what?" Mina asked, but then thinking better of it, she replied, "No, I haven't."

"Do you own, or have you ever owned an exotic bird or reptile?"

"No."

"Do you own, or have you ever owned, one or more plague rats?"

"Plague rats?" asked Mina. "What's a plague rat?"

"It's a rat that has fleas infested with the bubonic plague," replied the male guard.

Mina stared at the guard incredulously. "Why would anyone ever want to own a rat with a bubonic plague infestation?"

The male guard scoffed, "For protection, of course. Nobody's going to mess with you if they know you can unleash the bubonic plague on them. Do you *realize* how many people the bubonic plague has killed?"

Mina couldn't believe the level of absurdity behind the guard's thought process. "But wouldn't you be more likely to catch the plague if you keep plague rats as pets?"

"*Pets?!*" cried the guard. "Shows what little you know. You don't keep plague rats as *pets*. Those things are killing machines! Obviously, you have to keep them locked away in cages."

Mina shook her head in disbelief. "But then how would anyone know you had them?"

"They don't," said the guard. 'Everyone just assumes that everyone else has them. Then it's less dangerous, overall."

"It's *less* dangerous?!"

The guard nodded. "Exactly. It keeps people in check if they think you can give them the plague. Do you *realize* how many people the bubonic…Oh wait, I asked you that already. Well, anyway, the only thing you have to worry about once everyone has plague rats is if some madman decides to let a slew of them loose in a densely populated area."

Mina retorted, "*Yeah*, but that seems like something to actually worry about!"

"Well, maybe," said the guard, "but that hardly ever happens."

"*Hardly ever?!*"

The woman guard shrugged. "If you two are finished, can we continue with the form? We still have 3,355 questions to go.

Mina hung her head but nodded. The guards went on and on. There were questions about Mina's previous shopping history, questions regarding her preferences in food and plants, questions about favorite types of spiders, and how many ears, legs, and eyes she preferred animals and insects to have. None of the questions seemed relevant to being vetted for a visitor's pass, and most of them were so ludicrous that Mina couldn't help but wonder if it was all part of some elaborate hoax the guards played on hapless guests.

Then partway through the stack of metal sheets, the guards began to argue over a multiple-choice question that read, "If there's an alien invasion while you're shopping for stew, do you: a) run and hide, b) make friends with the aliens by offering them a fresh pot of stew, or c) make alien stew."

The dispute arose when the male guard suggested that there should also be an "option D" that involved protecting the mayor of Waldoff. The female guard responded, "Nonsense, Neil. The mayor is a tough guy. He doesn't need some little girl protecting him."

The male guard raised his voice. "You're missing the point, Becky. The question has nothing to do with that. It's a question to figure out where the visitors' loyalties lie, and I'm just saying there ought to be more questions like that in here."

Becky replied, "Don't you think that might be making too much out of one question?"

"No, Becky," said Guard Neil, "and I'll tell you another thing…" But Mina didn't hear the rest of the exchange because at that very second, a round, silver object whizzed right over the top of her head and flew through the entrance to the market. It stopped and hovered over the people walking by, and Mina could see that it was a shiny metal bird, half the size of a sparrow. Its tiny, metal wings were beating at a miraculous speed, but nobody even seemed to notice it. Mina stared at it in awe until it darted off to the right of the entrance and out of sight.

Mina looked back at the guards who sounded even more contentious than before. She attempted to interrupt them. "Did you guys see that thing that just flew by? It looked like a metal bird, but it was much faster than any bird I've ever seen." The guards didn't acknowledge her, though. In fact, it seemed like they'd completely forgotten she was there. Their fight had become a screaming match, in which both of them were trying to drown out what the other was saying.

Mina looked at the entrance and then again at the guards. Slowly, she crept towards the moving throngs of people while keeping her eyes locked on the guards. Once she'd gotten close enough to slip through the opening in the wall, she went for it. She leapt across the threshold into the crowd. Then she listened carefully for any sound that could indicate the guards had noticed her disappearance. She knew she was probably safe, however, when she heard the male guard yell, "At least I didn't waste the best years of my life making a stupid quiz that EVERYBODY hates!"

Phew, thought Mina, relieved to have finally made it inside the market. She walked quickly through the crowd, doing her best to fit in. She wondered if the guards would search for her once they realized she was gone but decided not to think about it for the time being. All she needed to worry about now was finding someone who could help her get home.

CHAPTER 6

THE WELCOMING COMMITTEE

The two women sat together inside of Ruth's booth. Ruth, a petite old lady with a light tan complexion and purple hair, was pushing a small magnifying lens back into a hidden compartment inside a silver bird's stomach. Then she latched the little door back into place and flicked the bird's left wing. The wings sprang to life, and the bird flew out of the booth into the air above them.

"Thank you, Ruth," said Maude, a tall, old woman with silvery white hair. "I should've had Bob sending these to you instead, but I didn't want him to know how bad my eyesight's gotten."

Ruth took her friend's hand. "Oh, sugar, don't fret. Bob's a smart man. I'm sure he already knows how much you've aged, and truth be told, I bet it doesn't bother him one lick. After all, he loves you something fierce."

Maude shrugged. "I'm sure he suspects it, but I promise it's not my vanity I'm concerned with. You know how Bob is. If he finds out I could lose a vision contest to a possum, he'll spend every free moment trying to invent some new gadget to help me. And he's already got enough on his plate as it is." Maude laughed, letting her playful spirit shine through her tough skin for a moment.

Ruth laughed too, but then her laughter faded. "Do you really think she'll be able to pull it off?" she asked in a serious tone of voice.

Maude looked at Ruth sternly. "Yes, I do. The Theian Frequency has never been wrong before. It's why Bob worked so hard to make the two sets of wings. He trusts it. We both do."

Ruth smiled a bit nervously. "But are you sure this is the right way to go about it? I just don't know that sending her after those blueprints is such a good idea. There are other ways, you know."

Maude stood up, clearly annoyed by what her friend was saying. "Ruth, we've been over this a million times. Like I've said before, I trust the information we have. The information *you* gave us, by the way. Plus, there aren't many other ways to skin this cat. It's the only plan we have that brings everyone back safely."

Maude suddenly realized she'd been talking too loudly and leaned out of the booth's side entrance to see if anyone was within earshot. When she didn't see anyone looking in their direction, she pulled herself back inside the booth.

Ruth stood up too. "Alright, sweetie," she said, squeezing Maude's arm. "Then this is how it'll be. We'll do what we must, and we'll pray for everyone's safe return."

"And you promise not to interfere?" Maude asked. "You'll go along with the plan?"

Ruth nodded. "If you and Bob trust the plan, then so do I. You know I always do whatever you ask anyways," she said, giving Maude a big grin.

Maude smiled back. "I know, Ruth. You've been wonderful."

Maude leaned in and gave Ruth a hug. Then she turned to

leave, but before she did, she looked back and said, "Oh, and please don't let anyone give the child a cucumber, Ruth. We don't want things to get out of hand."

Ruth laughed while shooing her friend away. "Of course not. Now get on with you! You gotta get back to your booth, and you ain't as fast as you used to be."

Maude laughed. "Now, isn't that the truth! Oh, and don't forget to start heading for the center as soon as she leaves!"

Ruth pushed Maude gently out of the booth. "I know. I know. Now get!"

Maude heeded her friend's instructions this time and headed down the aisle. Ruth walked back to the middle of her booth and began looking over the mound of vegetables that were piled high on the counter. She reached in towards the bottom, thrusting her hand below several lettuce stalks. Then she rummaged around for a moment before pulling out a smooth, green cucumber.

"Here we go," Ruth said out loud as she rested the ripe cucumber on top of the pile. Then she sat back down, humming to herself. Ready to begin the long wait.

∽∽∽∽

MINA REACHED the first row of booths without anyone seeming to notice anything different about her. At first, she wondered if people were only pretending not to see her, but as she began to walk down the first aisle, she realized there was something unusual about the marketplace.

Whenever Mina had visited markets on Earth, there had been a tangible electricity in the air. The hustle and bustle of hundreds of people, the mixture of sounds, the allure of items on display. Mina detected none of this type of excitement here, however. It was like everyone was turned on autopilot.

The people who seemed most alert went about their business in an ordinary fashion but with zero enthusiasm. Many of the vendors fell into this category. They yawned and stared down at their counters, twiddled their thumbs, or fidgeted pointlessly with their merchandise. They looked bored and indifferent, as though they'd become jaded to their own reality.

Then there were the others who seemed less jaded and more lost—completely disengaged from their surroundings like they had no clue where they were. Some drifted around as expressionless zombies, devoid of normal human traits. While others maintained regular expressions but stared straight ahead like they were hypnotized by something far away.

Both of these groups gave Mina the creeps, and she almost didn't stop when one of them approached her. "Those dummies! They're coming for our water! Got no right to take it. No right!" shouted a wrinkled, old man who had stopped right in front of her. Mina tried to ask the man what he was talking about, but he didn't seem to hear her. She continued to address him and even waved a hand in front of his face, but soon she realized that he wasn't aware of her presence. He had only stopped because she was in his way. After this encounter, she made it a point to steer clear of all the people who looked stupefied.

Mina had been walking down the first aisle for a while when she spotted a boy about half her age. He was clinging to the creases of his mother's long skirt as she shopped. He looked bored, but when he saw Mina, his eyes filled with enchantment. Relieved yet nervous, Mina's heart began to flutter as she realized she was about to be called out. "Mommy! Mommy! Look! There's an angel over there!" the boy shouted at his mother.

The little boy's mother looked down at him and wagged her finger. "Now, Abner! What have I told you about crying angel? Why, there hasn't been an angel here since..." But the woman's voice faded as she looked in the direction her son was pointed and caught sight of Mina. She dropped her knitted shopping bag, and several red beets spilled out. Then she stood, staring at Mina in shock for a moment.

Mina felt uncomfortable and gave the woman a little wave, hoping to snap her out of it. It did the trick. Without taking her eyes off of Mina, the woman cried out so everyone around them could hear, "Oh my heavens! It *is* an angel. Look over here, everyone! Another angel has come to visit us!"

Suddenly, people of all different races, ages, and sizes began flooding towards Mina, forming a circle around her. People were gasping with excitement, shouting praises, and talking all at once. Mina tried to talk loudly enough for the crowd to hear her say that she wasn't an angel, only a girl from Earth trapped inside a harness with wings. But no one seemed to hear what she was saying over all the excitement.

Several young kids walked behind her and touched her wings. A rosy-cheeked girl, who was about the age of five, began tugging on one of the feathers and trying to pull it loose. Her father, who was standing close by, jumped forward and grabbed the girl's hand. He ushered her away from Mina and said, "You can't do that, pumpkin. It might upset the angel."

The little girl whined, "But, *daaaddy*, I wasn't hurting it. It didn't say 'ouch' or nothing."

The father responded, "That's not the point, darling—"

But before he could finish, a plump-faced woman pulled the girl away from her father and said, "Then what's the point, Clifford? That angel's got plenty of feathers. Why can't our little buttercup have one?"

The man said, "But she didn't even ask, Darla! You want her growing up like them fancy kids, thinking she can have anything she wants without even asking for it?"

Mina didn't hear the rest of the conversation, though. Her attention was diverted to a man and woman who were pushing their way through the crowd. They yelled, "Make way, everyone! Make way! Welcoming Committee coming through!"

Welcoming Committee? Mina thought. *I guess I really should have found a way to pry these wings off. All this fuss for nothing. Hopefully, they're not upset when they realize I'm just a girl.*

The man and woman finally made it past the swarm of people and walked towards Mina. Each had their right hand extended and a big grin planted across their face. The man grabbed Mina's hand first and shook it hard. Then he dropped it quickly and said with a thick twang, "Hiya, there! I'm Larry."

The woman grabbed Mina's hand next, adding, "And I'm his wife, Carla."

The man took this as his cue to speak again. "We're the Welcoming Committee. We've come to welcome you on behalf of Earth's Dayside."

Mina was stumped. "What do you mean, Earth?" she asked.

Carla replied, "Well dear, we're pleased to inform you that you've landed on planet Earth, the only inhabited planet in the entire solar system."

Mina shook her head in disbelief and looked towards where the actual Earth was, right above the Moon's horizon. She pointed at it and asked, "Then what's that?"

Carla and Larry looked at each other and laughed. Larry replied, "You're funnier than the last angel we had here. That there's the Sun, of course."

Mina scoffed, "*That's the Sun?*"

"Right," said Larry nodding his head. Carla nodded her head even more emphatically.

"Okay," Mina said, "then what's *that?*" She pointed to the big white ball of gas that was quite obviously the *actual* Sun.

Larry and Carla laughed again but a bit nervously this

time. Carla said, "That's a star. Didn't you already know that, though? Or are you just teasing us?"

Mina paused a moment to think. She knew that the moon revolved around the Earth, just like the Earth revolved around the sun. *Maybe*, she thought, *they're confused about their place in the solar system because they have no moon of their own.* She continued to grasp at straws of reason, *and since they have no moon of their own, maybe they don't know what a moon is.*

Suddenly, Mina felt superior to all the onlookers. She pushed her shoulders back and glanced around at the people in the crowd. It was evident from the awe that shone upon their faces that they were expecting her to offer some sort of wisdom. Armed with this new insight, she decided to try out the role that had been thrust upon her.

"Oh, yes," she said smugly. "We angels like to test people. It's a funny game we play."

Carla laughed and slapped her leg in amusement, but Larry frowned. Mina continued, "Forgive me for not introducing myself. I'm the Archangel Mina."

Larry asked skeptically, "*Archangel?*"

Mina nodded. "Yes, that's right. We're a higher order of angels," she explained.

People in the crowd gasped, and Mina looked around and wondered if she should have told the truth instead. It was too late now, though, so she continued to play her game. "Was the last angel not an archangel?" she asked.

"No," said Larry, who didn't seem the least bit impressed. "He just told us his name was Fred."

"Oh. Then, no. There are no archangels named Fred," Mina responded quickly, hoping to settle the matter. In an attempt to move away from the archangel topic, she asked, "Did Fred happen to tell you where he came from?"

Larry smiled coyly. "Where did you come from?"

Mina could see that Larry was testing her. She didn't like it, but she decided it didn't matter if she was found out. All she really cared about was getting home. With nothing to lose, she continued to play the part of the superior being, raising her arms towards the sky and decreeing with all the authority she could muster, "I traveled here from the great big sun. That is where *all* archangels come from."

Larry started to make a comment, but Carla jabbed him in the stomach with her elbow, as if to shut him up. "That's where Fred came from! You sure you two don't know each other?" she asked with a twinkle in her eye.

Mina smiled at Carla but shook her head. Carla looked disappointed, and Mina wished she could've given her a different answer.

"Well, we're happy to have you here for as long as you'd like," said Larry, breaking the short silence. "Feel free to browse the aisles or enjoy one of the music shows at the stage on the other side of the market. First, though, a warning. Don't go getting any big ideas about strolling on out of the market. There're strange happenings outside of these walls, and we don't want you to go disappearing like Angel Fred."

Mina's heart skipped a beat as a dreadful feeling came over her. Carla seemed to notice it and waved her hand at Mina, "Oh, don't you worry, honey. Fred's probably fine. Most likely he saw all he wanted to and then moseyed on along, back to the sun."

Mina nodded her head, even though she could tell by Carla's face that Larry's warning had upset her too. Mina was willing to overlook it, though. Her need to get home was weighing on her, and she felt that her opportunity to ask the crowd for help was beginning to slip away.

She looked around again at all the different faces and said, "Thank you, everyone, for your kind welcome. Before you go, I need to ask you something—" But Larry raised his hand and started to talk over her before she had finished. "Of course!

How thoughtless of us! You want a tour of the market!" he said loudly.

Mina shook her head and tried to tell him what she was really after, but Carla moved in and grabbed Mina's hand tightly. Smiling at the crowd, Carla picked up where Larry had left off, only louder. "Great idea! Larry and I'd be more than happy to give you a tour, honey!"

Then, while she continued to grip Mina's hand, she turned to Larry and said, "Alright, Larry. Tell these nice folks that there's nothing left to see here."

Larry nodded and turned towards the crowd. "Alright, everyone. Back on up now, you hear? It's time to move along and get back to your business," he said as he walked around the circle, herding people with his outstretched arms. "You can take turns staring at our visitor later, but first you gotta give her some time to get acquainted."

There were whines and groans all around. Many people didn't budge, afraid they might miss something if they left too soon. But Larry was persistent, and eventually the crowd dispersed. Once they were alone, Carla let go of Mina's hand. Then in a loud whisper she said, "Don't speak. Just wait." She wrapped her arm around the back of Mina's wing and pushed her forward gently. Seconds later, Larry joined them on Mina's other side.

Together, the three of them walked along the crowded aisle in silence. Mina was just about to ask what was going on when Larry said in a loud voice, "And over here on your right you'll see some of the finest dyed yarns, which you might enjoy if you're the kind of angel who likes knitting…"

Mina could tell that Larry was putting on a show and wondered who it was for. She didn't dare ask, though. The death grip Carla had given her was clearly a warning that there might be some danger in not playing along. So the pretend tour went on as they continued to walk down the aisle.

Finally, the trio passed the last booth and turned the corner. They made their way over to the wall where they began walking against the flow of traffic. Carla positioned herself in front of Larry and Mina to act as a shield against the oncoming crowd.

Larry, who was farthest from the wall, turned to Mina but pointed at the aisles they were passing. He spoke sternly in a hushed voice, and Mina noticed that he no longer had a twangy accent. "Look towards the aisles," he said to her, "and act like I'm showing you around still. Listen carefully, but remember to smile and nod. Got it?"

Mina was frightened, but she nodded. "Good. We know you're not who you claim to be, but it's important that you don't draw any more attention to yourself than you already have. Walk every aisle in the market and act normal. You'll be contacted when the time is right."

Mina didn't understand. "What do you mean contacted? By whom? Is it someone who's going to help me get home?"

Larry looked away from Mina towards the aisle they were passing, then back towards her again, nodding and smiling. "Yes, this person can help you get home, but that's all I can say. Just remember not to skip any of the aisles, and *don't* do anything else to draw attention to yourself. Got it?"

Mina sensed that Larry was trying to wrap up the conversation, but she had so many questions still. "What about the mayor? Do you think he would help me?"

Carla came to a sudden stop, and Mina nearly crashed into the back of her. Larry prevented the collision by throwing his arm out in front of Mina at the last second. "Keep moving, Carla. We can't stop here," Larry ordered.

Carla glanced over her shoulder at Larry apprehensively but did as he said. "Don't concern yourself with the mayor," Larry told Mina.

"What do you mean?" Mina asked, looking at Larry now

instead of the aisles. "If he's the mayor, won't he be able to help me? Or at least know somebody who can?"

Larry shook his head. "Just keep your eyes on the market, *Archangel* Mina. If you want to stay safe, you're going to have to follow my instructions."

Mina was frustrated. "I don't understand though," she said.

Larry tapped Carla's shoulder, and she returned to his side. "That makes us so happy!" Larry exclaimed, pretending again to have a conversation they weren't really having. "We're glad you liked the tour. You go enjoy yourself now, you hear? And don't forget to check out the big concert on the other side of the market!"

Then Larry and Carla turned away from Mina, but she called after them. "Really? That's it?"

Larry didn't flinch, but Carla looked over her shoulder and said, "I'm sorry, honey. We have to go now, but I reckon you'll do fine. Just remember to keep your eyes open for trouble. It'll be there even when you don't know it."

Larry looked at Carla and shook his head. "That's enough, Carla."

Without another word, he turned and walked into the passing crowd. Carla followed him but turned around once more with a sweet smile and a hint of sadness in her eyes. She looked as though she were bidding farewell to an old friend. Then she turned back towards Larry, and the two of them disappeared in front of a group of tall blonde men dressed in fishing waders.

Mina was distraught. Larry had barely given her any information at all. She wanted to scream, but the one thing she was sure about was that she wasn't supposed to draw any more attention to herself. Still, she considered doing it anyway. *At least it would force Larry and Carla to come back and give me some more answers*, she thought. But she wasn't certain if that were true, or if it might just get them in some kind of trouble instead. Larry and Carla were obviously afraid, and Mina wasn't sure she wanted to find out why.

She looked down the long row of booths beside her. They were painted bright colors: reds, yellows, oranges, and blues. All more vivid than Mina had ever seen back on Earth. Normally, the vibrant colors would have elevated her spirits, but right then, they only amplified her insecurities. The bold colors felt overpowering, just like the situation at hand.

"How am I ever going to make it through this huge market all by myself?" she whined. But upon hearing how childish she sounded, she quieted her mind and tried to think of what to do next. She hated the idea of standing there feeling sorry for herself. The best chance to get home, she decided, was to explore the giant market like Larry had instructed, although she thought it might take a couple of days to walk every aisle.

She forced herself to remember what was at stake. She thought of her little home tucked away in the grassy clearing by the sea. She saw herself inside, snuggled between her parents on the sofa; she watched herself reading to her grandfather on a sunny afternoon; she felt Bonkers' round body cuddled up against her as they fell asleep in her cozy, warm bed. Once she had finished indulging herself, she drifted back to the crowds of strange people. She looked up in the sky at the blue and green Earth. It was like a giant eyeball staring at her, reminding her that she hadn't fallen out of its scope. But despite this truth, Mina was beginning to think she could relate more to the dark void around the Earth than to the beautiful, bright planet.

Enough, she thought. *Time to get moving.*

CHAPTER 7

THE DARK EXODUS, PART II
THE DESCENSION

Blessed are the wicked...

The bryobane were horrid. Their need to conquer was so engrained that they spent their entire existence humiliating and torturing each other for pleasure. Only a few drops of compassion or guilt had ever spilled forth after their wicked deeds, and these short-lived moments had proven to be just as useful as a rain shower in the desert. The sentiment evaporated before having the chance to soak in and do any good.

If the bryobane had been granted more than an ounce of intelligence in their long-faced, boil-covered heads, maybe they would've come up with other reasons for living that were less bent towards evil. Nevertheless, they had been created as they were—to balance out the wolves' cunning smarts with brainless force. So when the bryobane discovered the wolves in the collapsed tunnel, it never occurred to them to rejoice over having found companions to share their lunar existence with. Or to exult over the chance for a beautiful exchange of ideas and survival skills.

The bryobane were much too simple for these notions. The only rejoicing or exulting they did was to praise the glowing hole in the ground for bringing them the kind of prey they'd been craving since their creation. After all, domination and power were all they truly understood. To them, everything else was weakness.

∞∞∞∞∞

"WAKE UP, THOMAS." Gertie nudged the hairless, young wolf. His light moans had turned into loud whimpers, and she worried the noise would attract the guards.

Tom's eyelids fluttered. "Let me sleep, Gert," he replied groggily and rolled over onto his other side.

Gertie didn't care if her brother kept sleeping as long as he stayed quiet. The fleshy, gray-skinned bryobane were particularly cruel when it came to nighttime discipline, and she knew she'd have to take Thomas' punishments for the time being. She wouldn't allow him to be beaten while he was already injured. He could barely walk with his gored paw, but she was sure if the bryobane were given the chance, they'd happily make his injury worse. Then he wouldn't be able to work, and if he couldn't work, he'd be executed. Tom should have been more valuable as one of the strongest young wolves, but he'd caused trouble—on more than one occasion.

After everything that had happened that morning, Gertie wasn't certain if the bryobane would allow Tom to live once he had healed. It was well known how twisted their captors could be, and it wouldn't have been the first time they'd shown mercy just to turn around and unleash hell.

Gertie couldn't sleep. There were dozens of crystal piles spread out above the quarries (the gravely pits that the separate wolf groups slept in). The crystals barely shone any light since the wolves who sang to keep them glowing always sang softly at night. She looked past the dim light and focused on the stars. Out there was everything. Out there was nothing. It was full of hope, but there was no hope to be found. It was all black and white up there. It was all black and white down here. There was no time, and yet there was all the time in the world. How long had passed?

It had been several hours since Thomas had returned from climbing the mountain alone. He'd promised he wasn't leaving for good. He just wanted to see over to the Dayside.

It had been weeks since their last sibling, Harrietta, was executed. At one time there'd been ten of them, but now it was just the two. For a while, the large group of siblings had been known as "the troublemakers" among the other wolves. They were the pups who didn't fall into line so easily, the ones most likely to start something with the bryobane. Nobody referred to them as "the troublemakers" anymore, though. Not since there'd been less than half of them left.

Months, maybe even a year, had passed since the last rescue attempt. It wasn't possible to record the attempts, but there had been some effort made to keep track of all the wolf teams, big or small, that had risked their lives to save them. Few of the attempts had ever succeeded, but there was great celebration when they did. Over time, it was estimated that a couple of dozen wolves had been rescued.

There were also many wolves who hadn't waited to be rescued, who'd gone out on their own to try and make it over the mountain before they got caught. This number was harder to keep track of since wolves disappeared all the time. Nobody ever knew for sure if a wolf had escaped or if the bryobane were just thinning out the herd in private. After all, the bryobane didn't have to make a show of killing to crush the wolves' spirit (though sometimes they did anyway). Ultimately, the monsters had rid the wolves of their dignity long ago.

From the start, the bryobane hadn't liked the look of the

wolves' tails so that was the first thing they chopped off. Then they decided the wolves' fur was too unkempt, so they forced the wolves to shave each other with the sharpened edge of a crystal. Just the process of shaving was a painful business in and of itself, but if the wolves missed even a small tuft of fur, the bryobane would set fire to it. Some wolves got into the habit, however, of leaving these small patches on purpose. They *wanted* the bryobane to burn them; the scars were a badge of honor they wore proudly in place of their fur.

It was not uncommon for the bryobane to maim or decapitate the wolves either. One time, a large group of blue-eyed wolves from the Kohlata Pack ventured over the mountains in an effort to save the Lesego children. They were captured quickly, however. It seemed that the Kohlata leaders had either underestimated the bryobane's ability to see color or had forgotten that their blue eyes would give them away next to their brown-eyed cousins. The group of Kohlata was rounded up and slaughtered, but not before the bryobane used their long horns to snatch the wolves' eyes from their sockets. The lanky beasts tied their gruesome prizes to a long piece of cloth and wore them around their necks for many years like a scarf with decaying eye baubles.

Generations. That's how long it had been since the bryobane had stolen the wolves' ancestors and forced them into servitude. For hundreds of years, the wolves had lived solely for the pleasure of these barbaric creatures. Their own will was not important. It could only get them into trouble. The wolves paid the price for their ancestors' mistakes over and over with every new generation, but it was never enough to satisfy the bryobane's lust for dominance.

Gertie thought of this now as she recalled the events of the last two days. Thomas had been telling her for weeks that something had to be done, yet he never seemed to have any ideas. The conversation had become tedious.

"They've forgotten us, Gert. We've been telling ourselves for ages that the others are going to think of a way to get us out of here, but nothing's worked. I'm telling you they don't have any more ideas over there. They've abandoned us for good."

Gertie shook her head. "You don't know that. Maybe they're working on something big. It could just take some time, right? We have no way of knowing how things operate on the Dayside."

"I don't think so, Gertie. It feels different this time. I don't think they're coming back again."

Gertie didn't like how anxious Thomas sounded whenever he talked about the rescues. She tried to change the subject. "How many crystals did you mine yesterday? Were you able to beat your all-time record? You're so strong now. Mama would be proud."

Tom saw through it, though. "Stop, Gertie. I'm serious. We can't keep living like this. We've gotta do something. If the others aren't coming, then drastic measures need to be taken."

Gertie frowned. "Like what?"

"Like we've gotta find a way out of here. We know that getting over the mountain is nearly impossible, but what if I could find us another way out?"

Gertie mocked him. "Oh, like a magic cloud of dust that picks us up and flies us to safety? That's so *smart*, Thomas. I can't believe none of the other wolves ever thought of that during the last bazillion years. I guess they just enjoyed being slaves."

Tom was hurt. "It's fine if you don't want to help, but others are going to have to take part in this too. It's going to take a lot of wolves in order for this to work."

It suddenly dawned on Gertie that Thomas was more serious than she'd realized. "You're saying you already have a plan?"

Tom looked a bit sheepish, but he responded, "Yes, I do."

"Well, what is it then?" she asked.

"Look, I want you to be a part of this, but I also don't want anything to happen to you if things go wrong. I think it's better if I keep it to myself for now."

It was Gertie's turn to feel hurt. "Why? You don't have to protect me, you know? I'm perfectly capable of—"

Tom stopped her. "I know you are, Gertie. You're more capable than anyone I know. But let me at least do the first part of the plan before I tell you everything, okay?"

"What's the first part?" she asked.

"Well, before we risk everything, I'd like to see what the Dayside looks like from the other side of the mountain."

"You can't seriously be thinking about trying to climb the mountain, Thomas. You know they'll kill you. They guard that mountain nonstop. There's no way you'll be able to get all the way up there and back down without them seeing you."

"Thanks for the confidence." Tom scowled.

"I won't apologize for not wanting you to die, Thomas. You're all I have left." She hung her head sadly.

"It's going to be okay, Gertie," said Tom. I've been watching the mountain for a while now. There's a rotation. The guards change shifts once before we wake in the morning and once after we go to bed. But they aren't careful. There's always a brief period when the mountain is entirely unguarded. As long as I can get past them during the bedtime shift change and return down the mountain before the morning one, I'll be able to make it back without anyone ever knowing I was gone."

"My god, Thomas! You've certainly put a lot of thought into this. It's not a ruse, though, right? Promise me you'll take me with you if you're actually planning to escape. Honestly, I wouldn't even care if we got caught. I just don't want to be alone in this place."

Tom shook his head and bowed to his sister. "I promise, Gertie. I'll never leave you."

TOM SET out for the mountain that night after everyone had gone to sleep. He was exhausted from hauling large crystals out of a crater all day, but his desire to begin his plan lit a big enough fire to keep him going.

Gertie worried he wouldn't even make it past the quarry that they slept in with the other wolves in their group. There were plenty of guards that roamed the pits at night, and she knew he could run into one of them easily. Her stomach twisted into knots as she watched him climb up the quarry wall. While she waited, Gertie became hyper-attentive. She held her breath and listened closely to the hushed melodies from the wolf choir. She was waiting for any change in sound to tell her something was going wrong.

Only a few moments had passed since Tom left the pit when, suddenly, all the piles of crystals around the quarries flickered and went out. Gertie's heart stopped. The wolf choir was still singing quietly. This meant they hadn't caused the blackout. She worried that something horrible had happened. Moments later, Gertie heard hooves galloping in the direction of the wolf choir, but before the bryobane reached them, the lights flickered back on. Gertie heard ghastly shrieking and knew that the choir was being punished for the blackout.

She wondered if the guards had at least heard the wolves' continual singing, though she knew it wouldn't matter. The bryobane weren't concerned with fairness, and she knew that if there was an obvious scapegoat, they'd pick the scapegoat over the complicated task of solving a mystery. There weren't enough deductive reasoning skills among the entire lot of bryobane to solve a basic math problem, let alone an actual puzzle.

Gertie held her breath almost the entire night, anticipating the worst. She watched the top of the mountain. It was easier to see than the bottom because hazy light from the Dayside peeked over the top. She hoped this meant she'd be able to see some movement when Thomas reached the peak. Eventually, though, the entire night passed, and Gertie had seen nothing but the ominous shadow of the back-lit mountain.

There were fewer voices singing the wolves' songs than when the night had begun, but Gertie didn't dwell on the grisliness of this truth. Instead, she focused on the crystals becoming brighter as the songs from the diminished choir grew in volume. It was time for the other wolves to wake. Thomas should be back.

Tom was standing in front of two very tall guards. He'd made it to the mountain base with the aid of the blackout. He'd made it up the mountain by timing his ascent with the guard change. He made it down the mountain and waited in a crevice above the base for the guards to change shifts again. When he spotted the four bryobane walking away, he ran from his shelter down a steep path. It was a quick descent over slick rocks, but Tom wasn't worried. He was filled with excitement, knowing he'd almost reached the finish line.

Once he made it down the slippery rocks, he arrived at a switch-back path that led to the very bottom of the mountain. The scraggily shrubs that lined the path were too tall to jump over, which forced Tom to make the back-and-forth journey the rest of the way. He rounded the first corner, and that's when they saw him. The two very tall guards were leaning against a wall on the other side of the turn. Tom could tell they'd been waiting for him.

The guards stood up straight. They were giants compared to the other beasts. They growled and bared their long, sharp teeth. Tom took a step backwards but was pinned against the wall. One of the guards lowered its horns and lunged at him. It scooped Tom up under his neck and forced him into a seated position against the wall. The guard leaned over Tom until its spiky teeth were just inches from his nose. Tom held his breath, trying not to gag on the foul odor that was wafting from the guard's mouth. He knew he might only have seconds to live, so with nothing left to lose, he looked into the guard's soulless eyes and did the unthinkable. He spoke.

"It's not what it looks like," he said calmly. "Let me show you."

Thomas had always had a knack at communicating with the bow-legged monsters when few others could, and now, more than ever, seemed like the right time to use his talent. He didn't want to appear to be fighting back, so he nodded his head slowly with his mouth closed to show that he wasn't trying to use force. Then he pulled his front legs in towards his chest to gesture like the bryobane sometimes did.

The guard leaning over him seemed curious. He stood tall again and watched as Tom's gestures became bigger and more elaborate. With the use of charades, Tom tried to tell them that he'd only intended to see the other side of the mountain, that he was never planning to escape. Somehow, it worked. Whatever story the guards interpreted from Tom's wild movements seemed to do the trick. Mostly.

Eventually, the guards escorted him back to the quarry where he slept but not before one of the guards rammed its left horn straight through Tom's front, right paw. Tom yelped in pain as tears burst from his eyes. He bit down hard on his tongue to stop himself from making another sound. He had to be thankful they'd let him live. The maimed paw paled in comparison to what they could have done.

Tom was marched back to his quarry. He kept pace with the guards, dragging his bleeding paw the whole way. When they reached the quarry, the other wolves were just getting ready for the day. The guard, who'd mutilated Tom's paw, kicked him into the pit. Nobody said a word, but all eyes were fixed on Tom. Slowly and quietly, the tired, young wolf crawled to the space he shared with his sister. Leaving a smeared trail of blood behind.

ALL THE STRONG wolves went to work in the mine that day, including Tom. He only got a moment of rest before he was forced to climb back out of the quarry, with the others, and journey deep underground into the crystal caves that connected to one of the large craters.

When the bryobane first discovered the wolves, centuries earlier, they also discovered the trove of glowing crystals inside the caved-in tunnel. And this second discovery gave new meaning to the bryobane's existence. The crystals brought them beautiful light by which to see, and because of this, the sparkling gems soon became the beasts' obsession.

When the tunnel collapsed, the connection that led back to the Dayside was severed. The bryobane were unaware of this, however. They had never seen a tunnel before, so they simply assumed that the wolves had been living in the underground lair where they found them. It never dawned on them that the wolves might have come from somewhere else since they were incapable of imagining anything beyond what they saw.

Due to their impaired intelligence, it took the bryobane a while to work out the details, but soon they realized that the abundance of wolves could be used for more than just a feast. They put the wolves to work, digging holes to find more crystals. The bryobane presumed that the wolves knew how to do this because, after all, they'd come from dirt.

The assignments the bryobane handed out went as so: the

stronger wolves were tasked with digging and mining, the weaker wolves were tasked with making the crystals glow, and the old and injured wolves were eaten. The bryobane were pleased. Their crystal bounty grew each day, and they found enjoyment from overseeing the wolves in their new roles. It presented them with even more opportunities to inflict pain and punishment.

The crystals were used solely for light at first, but it soon became apparent that the monsters had an unhealthy fascination with the gems. The wolves couldn't dig them up fast enough to satisfy the bryobanes' immense craving. They would mine the craters until they'd excavated every last crystal, and then they'd start work on a new crater. By the end of each workday, the piles of crystals were so large that they looked like gigantic, sparkling haystacks.

The strange thing, though, was that by the next morning the piles were always gone. The wolves never knew for sure what went on while they slept, but there were many theories. Some wolves thought the bryobane were hoarding the crystals somewhere secret. Others believed that the bryobane were eating the gemstones. Possibly, one of the strangest theories was that the bryobane were melting the crystals and filling a giant crater with the molten liquid. This one seemed unlikely, however, because of the level of know-how it would have required.

Regardless of what the bryobane were doing with the crystals, the wolves awoke each morning to find the bryobane thirsting for more. They forced the wolves to work nonstop except while they slept. There was no mealtime, and the little food they were given had to be eaten during the time they were allowed to sleep. Many of the wolves couldn't handle the ever-increasing pace they were forced to keep up. The wolves that collapsed on the job were dragged away at the end of a rope, never to be seen again. It was enough to motivate the ones who could keep going to work through the worst pain and exhaustion they'd ever experienced.

The day after coming down the mountain, Tom could feel the suffering of his ancestors—the first wolves enslaved by the bryobane. His bones were so brittle from fatigue, he thought they might break. His muscles, already tense and sore from overuse, had to endure terrible strain as he made adjustments to compensate for his injured foot. His paw still ached horribly, and pain shot through his entire leg with even the slightest touch. Overall, it was torture, but Tom forced himself to endure it.

Gertie was so impressed with her brother she could barely stand it. She wanted to find out everything that had happened, but she kept her distance. She knew better than to risk drawing attention. Even so, she kept a close eye on Thomas and was amazed to see how many wolves approached him throughout the day. It was subtle, almost unnoticeable, but she watched as dozens of wolves walked casually by him, whispering under their breath.

Gertie was happy for him. He was, truly, the last "troublemaker" in their family. She had never come close to possessing the same rebellious spirit as the rest of her siblings, which meant that Thomas was the only one left keeping their spirit alive. And just like the rest of them, he wasn't going to go down without a fight.

That night, when they returned to their spot in the quarry, Gertie hoped Thomas would stay awake long enough to give her all the details of his adventure. But he was too weak and fell asleep before he even took a bite of food. Gertie cuddled up next to her brother and stayed awake, staring at the stars.

She wondered what the other wolves had said to Thomas in the cavern that day and how Thomas had managed to escape the bryobane's wrath with only a gored paw. She also wondered if the bryobane really planned to let her brother live or if this was just one of their cruel tricks. Eventually, her wondering picked up steam and churned itself into a hurricane of worry. Gertie's mind whipped around in circles, over and over like a ferocious tempest until, finally, her exhaustion stepped in, calming the storm in the wee hours of the night.

THE NEXT MORNING, Thomas looked like a brand-new wolf. The sleep had rejuvenated him, and even his gored paw didn't look as gruesome as it had the previous day. Gertie couldn't hold back any longer. "Tell me everything that happened! Did you make it to the top? Why didn't the guards kill you? Do you realize you're famous now? I saw all those wolves talking to you yesterday. I think *everyone* knows what you did!"

Tom laughed with his mouth full of food. He swallowed and said, "Slow down, Gert. You gotta give me a chance to answer."

Gertie nodded and waited impatiently for her brother to continue.

"Yeah, I made it to the top alright, and you wouldn't believe how much wide-open land there is on the other side. You can see forever! It's breathtaking, really. There weren't any wolves, though. I'm guessing it would be at least a two-day trek to reach any of the other packs."

Gertie looked disappointed, but Tom shook his head, "It's a good thing. Trust me. This plan I'm about to put into action… well, if anything goes wrong, it'll be better if there's nobody on the other side."

"Why?" asked Gertie.

"Because I'm going to convince the bryobane to let us build a tunnel under the mountain, Gert, and once we've built it, we're going to use it to escape. I've been talking to some others who want to help. In fact, some of them already have. The wolf choir sang a new song last night to darken the crystals. That's how I made it past the quarries without being seen."

Gertie looked at Thomas in bewilderment. She couldn't believe he'd already recruited other wolves without telling her. It took her a moment to process everything, but after a few seconds, she said, "You know, a few days ago I would've thought you were crazy, but after everything that's happened, I actually believe you. If anyone can pull this off, it's you, Thomas."

Tom looked embarrassed. "Thanks, sis. That means a lot to me."

"I just have one question," said Gertie. How will we keep the bryobane from following us through the tunnel when we escape?"

Tom smiled. "We won't."

Gertie was confused. "What do you mean? Surely, you're not planning to let them come *with* us to the Dayside."

Tom shook his head. "No, we'll give ourselves a head start. Then when we make it to the other side, we'll blow the tunnel up behind us. That way the bryobane will never be able to use the tunnel again."

"How are you going to blow it up though?" she asked.

"I'm going to use the power that Mama taught me before she died. She told me to keep the knowledge secret and to only use it if I found the right way. She said it *has* to be the right way, or else the bryobane will learn that we have the power and use it against us.

"As you know, our blood ancestors were builders. They were given special knowledge of how to clear out caves and tunnels with explosions. You and I are the only ones left of all the Lesegolese builders. Each of our brothers and sisters knew the secret before they died, and now it's our turn to know. Except, we aren't just going to wait around for the right moment like they did. We're going to *create* the right moment."

Gertie was scared. Something told her that their mother wouldn't approve of what Thomas was planning to do. She could see he'd become deeply committed to taking on this problem that was so much bigger than just him, and she worried he was in over his head. Still, she was proud of what he'd accomplished so far and didn't feel like she had any right to discourage him. It took her a little while, but finally, she said, "Okay, Thomas. Tell me what I can do to help."

CHAPTER 8
THE VENDORS

Mina walked up and down the aisles, browsing the contents of the booths with the air of an aloof window shopper. Larry had made it abundantly clear that she shouldn't attract any more attention, and she thought this was a good way to avoid doing just that. Luckily, there were plenty of items to look at, things Mina would never have believed could be produced on the Moon. There were fabrics and threads, liquids and pastes, wooden beams and metal sheets. And that was just the first aisle. On the second aisle, there were pillows and shoes, cans of beans and stews, jewelry, trinkets, and so on. Nothing stood out as being exceptionally impressive, but Mina knew it was remarkable that any of it was there at all.

When she arrived on aisle six, she found little pieces of metal strewn across the ground and mashed into the dirt. The pieces reached all the way to the end of the aisle. Mina looked around to see if anyone, besides her, was interested in the silver scraps, but no one else seemed to notice them. She watched as a husky man in a light blue suit passed by, followed by a young family. Everyone walked right over the shiny pieces without ever glancing down.

Curious, Mina leaned over to pull one from the ground. It came loose easily enough, but she nearly fell face first into the dirt. She'd forgotten about the extra weight she was carrying on her back. She pushed the wings off her shoulders and forced herself back into a standing position.

Examining the little silver piece, she saw that it was another engraved note like the one she'd found fastened to her wings. It read, "The joy I've found with Gina is better than anything I dreamt of back on Earth. Happy Anniversary, G! I love you to the stars and back. -Ari"

It's a love letter! Mina thought excitedly, and even more thrilling was the note's reference to Earth. *There must be others here, besides Fred, who've traveled from Earth*, she thought. Inspired to investigate further, she bent down and dug up as many of the metallic notes as she could get her hands on. After she'd collected a few dozen, she stopped and read them. None of the others appeared to be love letters, but almost all of them contained some sort of personal information. One of the juicier ones read, "Everyone in the city knows I've got the best set of gams. The rest of you are just jealous. Tough luck! -Lillian."

Another read, "I got sick riding that dang horse over yonder mountains and spent an hour tossing my biscuits. I ain't never going to eat potato soup again, and don't y'all go telling me to get back on that rabblerousing horse. I'll walk next time. I don't flippin' care how long it takes! -Clyde"

Fascinated, Mina read them all, and when she was finished, she picked up more and read those too. There were complaints and celebrations; humor and news; personal reflections and deflections of blame; thinly veiled judgements and obtuse critiques. She found it oddly satisfying to get a glimpse into these strangers' lives, especially since she was surrounded by so many lifeless souls. However, she wondered about the habit of leaving so much of one's personal information on the ground. It seemed odd to pollute the walkways in such a manner that any random passerby could come along and learn your private business.

As she was mulling this over, she heard a voice call to her. "Whatcha got there, lovely?" Mina turned around to find a woman staring at her from inside the nearest booth. She glanced at the counter and saw that the woman was selling some type of steaming mush and chunky, green jelly out of a large silver bowl. The woman appeared to be just north of twenty, perhaps, but it was hard to tell through all the rouge and powder that was caked across her face. She wore a tight, green and black striped dress, and her red, frizzy hair was swept off her neck in an up-do. But all of this was much less noticeable than the pouty expression plastered on her face. The frown had carved deep lines into the woman's otherwise smooth skin, and the look made it abundantly clear that the woman thought the world owed her a debt it was refusing to pay.

Mina stood awkwardly in front of her without speaking. Though they were separated by the front of the woman's stall, Mina suddenly felt very exposed like she'd been caught doing something wrong. The woman spoke again in her heavy accent, "Wells aren't ye goin' to show me or ain't ye? I 'aven't got all day."

Mina was nervous to show her the notes, worried the woman might scold her for picking them up. Timidly, she held them out in front of her, but the woman raised her hand to stop Mina. "Whoa there. I don't take whatever it is ye're 'olding there. If ye want some of me delicious lamb paté and cucumber delight, ye're going to 'ave to pay with *real* money."

Realizing the woman's mistake, Mina hurried to correct the

misunderstanding. "No, I'm not trying to give these to you. I'm showing you what they are."

The woman rolled her eyes and stood up straight, taking the metal pieces from Mina's outstretched hands. Then without really looking at them, she said, "Rubbish is what these are. I don't know anyone ooe'd give ye more than 'af a piece of lent for 'em. Move along, lovely. If ye ain't got no money and nuttin to barter with, din ye'se just wasting me time." The woman thrusted the metal pieces back into Mina's hands and shooed her away from the booth, as though she were some loathsome fly circling the woman's grotesquely gelatinous cuisine.

Mina had never been dismissed in such a rude fashion before, and she suddenly felt mistreated. Her face flushed with anger. She looked down at the little messages that had been shoved back into her hands. Determined not to let the woman see the effect she'd had on her, Mina pushed the messages deep into her pockets and turned away from the booth. Slowly, she walked the rest of the aisle, doing her best not to look back at the awful woman.

She decided to refocus her attention on what she was supposed to be doing, winding through the market until her mystery person made contact. She couldn't help but wonder, though, what would happen if she reached the end, and nobody had reached out to her. What if they were busy when she walked by and didn't notice her? Despair crept in. The exchange with the woman had reminded Mina of how alone she was in this place. Surrounded by hundreds of people who didn't care a bit about her.

She couldn't stand the thought of missing her opportunity. She had to get home. Then and there, she made the decision that she wouldn't give up. Ever. No matter what. Even if she had to walk the aisles a hundred times to find the person who would help her.

Her determination made her feel a little better. She kept

walking, passing several empty booths until she came to a stall with cheeses of every shape and size piled high on the front counter. There were bries and goudas, cheddars and swisses, parmesans and provolones, havartis and fetas. Mina wasn't even able to identify many of the cheeses and was impressed by the wide selection.

She spent a moment admiring all the different cheeses when, suddenly, she became aware of a little man—barely tall enough to see over the counter—peeking out at her from between a triangle of asiago and a wheel of manchego. He was wearing a white chef's hat and a gray, V-neck undershirt that framed his hairy chest and the gold chains that hung around his neck.

Mina was startled until she noticed the friendly look in his eyes. It was completely unlike the stupefied gazes she'd grown accustomed to. There seemed to be something behind the man's stare like he believed they were sharing a private joke. Mina nodded politely at him and continued on her way. The man called after her in a French accent. "Mademoiselle, s'il vous plait, come inside for a minute and try a sample of my delicious fromages."

Mina had absolutely no appetite and therefore no desire to try the cheeses, but she didn't want to be rude like the woman selling the slimy jelly molds. So she decided to step inside for a minute to look over the assortment. It was evident that this pleased the man very much. He said, "When I saw you outside of my booth, I thought, 'aww, there goes someone with sophistication!' Your nose is so long and so pointed. Which is to say chiseled just perfectly for the delicate business of tasting gourmet fromages. Clearly, you must be more refined than these simple eaters I am all the time surrounded by.

Mina put her hand over her nose self-consciously. She had never thought of it as being particularly long or pointed, and she didn't like that the little man felt comfortable saying so. She decided it was time to go. "Excuse me, sir, but I don't have any money. So, I'll just be on my way now."

The man shook his head. "Non. Non. Non, mademoiselle. It does not matter. You must stay and try at least one. I will give you the best sample so you will have good reason to come again when you can pay." Quickly he picked up a sharp looking cheese slicer and pulled it down along the side of a moldy-looking hunk of blue cheese.

With the other hand, he grabbed a small white dish and flipped the moldy square of cheese from the slicer onto the plate so that it was perfectly centered. Wearing an expression of great pride that tensed every muscle in his face, the man bowed to Mina and held up the plate. Then in a deep, rumbling voice he said, "Bon Appetiiiiiiiit!"

Mina didn't know what to do. She would rather have eaten a soaking wet dish sponge than the disgusting slice of rotting milk that was being presented to her. Reluctantly she took the plate. She realized she was going to have to take a bite and pretend to like it, or else risk insulting the little chef.

The chef took off his hat and began twisting it in his hands, nervously awaiting her reaction. She picked up the slice and slowly brought it to her lips. She knew the chef expected her to be sophisticated, so she tilted her head forward and pretended to smell the cheese like she'd seen people do on TV with fancy wines. She took a tiny bite from the end, swished it around inside her mouth, and swallowed. The cheese tasted exactly the way Mina thought sour milk would taste. Tangy and repulsive. She couldn't think of any nice way to describe the experience, so she responded with the only diplomatic thing she could think of to say. "I'm no expert, but I imagine that's right up there with the finest of cheeses."

The little man looked aghast. "Excusez-moi! C'est terrible! How could you say such a horrible thing?" he asked, looking genuinely hurt.

"I'm sorry. I didn't mean to be rude. I think maybe you misunderstood. What I'm saying is that this cheese would likely rank among the finest."

The hairy man puffed out his cheeks and blew a few disdainful breaths of air from his lips. It appeared he was transitioning from hurt to upset. He pulled his hat back on his head with both hands until it was halfway down his forehead, resting atop his angry brow. "These," he said, swooping his arm towards the cheeses, "are not '*cheeses*' I am selling. This is fromage!"

He picked up the slab of blue cheese and pushed it towards Mina's face, as if it would help to make his point. Mina didn't understand, however, and asked, "Isn't fromage just the French word for cheese, Monsieur?"

"No!" he snapped at her. "Don't be absurd! Cheese is what vulgar pigs pour on top of their slop to make it taste *less* like slop. But fromage! Well, fromage is manna from heaven—hand crafted from the most exquisite pieces of earth. The most supreme lumps of clay you have ever had the pleasure to walk across." He tapped his heel on the ground twice to show he was referring to the Moon's surface.

Mina raised an eyebrow. "You're telling me that all your cheeses are made from *dirt*?"

The man frowned. "Yes! How is it that you do not understand something so simple?"

Mina didn't like the way the little man was speaking to her and didn't have the patience to play games with him. She responded, "What I don't understand is why someone who acts as though they're an expert on cheese would blatantly lie about how their beloved '*fromage*' is made."

The man scowled. "Do not insult me! My fromage *is* made from the finest earth. You clearly know nothing about fromage. Here! Try this, and then tell me it is *not* fromage!" He picked up some chalk-like dirt from the ground next to his feet and shoved it into Mina's face.

Mina wasn't sure that she was invested enough in the argument to eat dirt for the first time in her life, even if it did prove her point. *Well*, she thought, *I guess if I can stomach blue mold, then I can stomach this too. At least the mold might kill the bacteria that's surely floating around in this petri dish of a snack.* She took a few pieces of the soil the chef was holding and tossed them into her mouth.

Instantly, all of her saliva disappeared. The pores on her tongue dried and cracked, and her saliva glands shriveled. The only moisture that was left was a bitter paste that coated every part of her mouth. She began to spit, but the paste was too thick. Quickly, she used her fingers to pull the thick sludge from her mouth before it had a chance to block the back of her throat. It oozed down her chin and dripped onto the ground. "That's *disgusting!*" she yelled, though her words came out slurred.

The little man burst into laughter. He laughed so hard that he had to brace himself on his cheese counter to keep from falling over. Mina glared at him. She had resorted to using her fingernails to scrape the grime from her tongue and teeth. The man didn't notice, however, over all his laughter. When he finally managed to stand upright again, Mina saw that there were tears rolling down his puffy, red cheeks. She waited for him to stop. She felt she was owed an apology, or at the very least an explanation.

The man didn't show any signs of stopping, though, and Mina decided she didn't care to wait any longer. She headed for the exit, but as she did, the man regained some of his composure. Through stifled laughs, he said, "You are so gullible. Did you really think you could use *any* dirt to make fromage? That is the stuuuupidest thing I've ever seen...*you looked so stuuuupid!*" Then he broke into laughter once again, banging his fist on the counter and wiping tears away on the back of his sleeves.

Mina didn't enjoy being made to look foolish, especially when she knew she was right. On her way out the door, she turned to the little chef and said, "This place may be different than where I come from, but I'm certain that even *here* fromage is cheese and cheese is fromage. And it's NOT made from dirt. It's made from milk and other things found inside of animals. And just so you know, you'd do better to treat your customers with more respect. Good day!"

Mina stormed out of the stall and back to the walkway that ran between the booths. She stood in the aisle, fuming with anger. *What a ridiculous man*, she thought. *I am not going to get reeled in like that again.* She had become even more determined to find her contact so she could return home fast. She walked down the middle of the path, avoiding the other vendors even when it meant getting in people's way. Luckily, having wings meant that most people treated Mina like an obstacle and, therefore, moved around her as such. It made getting through the small crowds much easier, and soon Mina was able to put her bad experiences behind her.

She watched people as they passed. There were all kinds. Old couples walking hand in hand; mothers with one, six, nine, or even eleven children following behind; grandparents and their grandkids; young singles out in groups or by themselves; disheveled gypsy-types looking like they were up to no good; middle-aged men dressed in suits, looking like they were up to even less good. There were so many different types of people that, eventually, it occurred to Mina how unusual it was to see such a mix of people in one place at one time. She wondered what had drawn them to the market in the first place and if the rest of the Moon's population was made up of such a large array of individuals.

She neared a booth where pancakes were being sold, and

she moved in a little closer. The delicious smell of sweet batter reminded her of the Saturday mornings she'd awoken to the smell of her grandfather making pancakes in the kitchen. For a moment she closed her eyes and longed to be there with him.

The memory vanished when she heard the man inside the pancake booth talking loud and fast. He was standing behind a huge griddle and flipping the largest pancake Mina had ever seen. It rotated end-over-end several times. Then just before it reached the string of lanterns high above the booth, it hung in the air, and Mina could see that it was in the shape of an elephant. She was impressed. She thought the man must be an expert pancake chef and wondered how he got the pancake to hold its shape so well.

In a nasally voice, the man called out, "Step right up, folks! I've got all you can eat pancakes right here! I can make 'em any way you want 'em! Flat, round, square, bumpy, thin, heavy, or light! Flying, tiny, unbaked, half-baked, moist, or desert-dry. Giant, microscopic, soporific, beatific, or even incredulous! Any way you like 'em, I can make 'em!"

Mina really wanted to ask the man what a flying pancake was, but she decided against it. Her mouth was still dry as a bone, and she had no interest in getting tangled up in another unpleasant encounter. So she continued on her way.

On the next row, there were woolen items for sale. There were wool blankets, wool sweaters, wool purses and scarves. Everywhere she looked there were woolen items being held up by vendors or laid out for display. *There must be a large sheep population here*, Mina thought as she completed her stroll down the aisle.

She turned the two corners to the next row and stopped cold. Death loomed large as far as the eye could see. Bloody, skinned lambs hung from large, pronged hooks that poked out along the tops of the booths and the fronts of the counters. A foul smell hung in the air. It stung Mina's eyes and overpowered her senses. *I guess the sheep population isn't so large*, she thought cynically as she covered her nose, wishing she could do more to filter out the smell of dead flesh.

She began walking again while looking around. The booths were operated by big, burly men. They stood behind butcher blocks, wearing slotted, leather aprons that held various sorts of steely knives. They flung the carcasses down on their blocks and cut, chopped, flayed, and pierced the dead animals. Their brusque movements and crude mannerisms sent a chill down Mina's spine. To her, they seemed no different than blood-thirsty cavemen, and this thought made her extremely uneasy.

The most disturbing part, however, was the amount of blood splattered everywhere. The counters and animals dripped in it; the butchers' skin and clothes were saturated with it; even the dirt had clotted clumps mixed into it. Though Mina had gone on many trips to the butcher shop before, the row of dead sheep was unlike anything she'd ever seen. There was no equating it with the meat markets back home, for it looked more like the scene of a massacre than a place to buy food. She thought about turning around and moving on to the next aisle, but Larry had given her strict instructions not to skip any of the rows.

She continued down the aisle, praying it wouldn't be where she found her contact. Only a minute passed before she couldn't take it any longer, and she took off running. She knew what was expected of her—to behave discreetly and not cause a scene. But she figured that it would also create a scene if she became physically ill, and that was becoming more and more likely with every second that passed.

Relief poured over her once she reached the end of the aisle, but as she recovered, she grew nervous about what she might find on the following aisle. Fortunately, when she arrived, she was greeted by the fragrant aromas of cooked foods. The vendors on this aisle were selling prepared lamb dishes set out in pots and arranged on platters. There were mouthwatering stews; juicy braised shanks; cheesy ground lasagnas; perfectly charred kebabs; steaming roasts with cherry tomatoes, herbs, and garlic; and so on.

Mina was thankful to have escaped all the death from the previous row. She slowed her pace to enjoy the divine smells of all the delicious food. The savory air flooded her nostrils and cleared away visions of mutilated sheep. She glanced at her stomach. It seemed strange that she still had no desire to eat despite all the flavorful smells. She imagined what it would be like to sample the food but realized that the idea repulsed her.

Well, since I don't have any money, I guess it's good I don't need to eat yet, she thought. But in truth, her lack of hunger was concerning. Although she was too distracted to admit it to herself, she realized somewhere deep inside that she was beginning to change.

CHAPTER 9

THE DARK EXODUS, PART III
THE ONLY WAY OUT

…for they know not what they do.

The wolves worked on the tunnel for weeks which soon turned into months. Thomas was right. He convinced the bryobane to let the wolves build the tunnel. He showed the monsters what he intended to do by drawing pictures in the dirt of mammoth-sized crystals on the other side of the mountains and of wolves building a tunnel that led to the large crystals. Then he drew illustrations of the wolves hauling the crystals back through the tunnel to the Darkside.

He worked hard to convince the bryobane that these crystals were the source of the soft light illuminating the peaks. He drew pictures that showed a multitude of crystals shining brightly behind the mountains. And he drew pictures to explain that the giant crystals didn't need the wolf's music to glow. He made the bryobane believe that the giant crystals glowed on their own. Thomas had credibility on the matter because he'd been caught coming down from the top of the mountain, and Gertie couldn't help but wonder if this had secretly been his plan all along.

When the beasts finally understood, they were beside themselves with greed. They wanted to possess the giant crystals right away. Immediately, they transferred the wolves from the crystal mines to the mountain and tasked them with excavating the tunnel that would lead them to the other side.

Unfortunately, the work was much harder than the wolves had anticipated. They hadn't foreseen that the mountain would exist not only above the ground but below it as well. Because Thomas refused to let the bryobane know about the power his ancestors had used to clear away solid rock, the wolves were forced to dig harder than they ever had before. They used crystals as chisels to break up the biggest rocks, but the task was laborious and took much longer than they'd originally planned. What made it even worse was that the bryobane required the wolves to make the tunnel extra tall and wide so there'd be room to haul the crystals (that didn't really exist) back to the Darkside.

Every day, the bryobane watched the wolves closely as they built the large tunnel. What the bryobane failed to notice, however, was a much smaller tunnel that was being constructed inside one of the wolf quarries. Every night, the wolves in Tom and Gertie's quarry took turns staying awake to dig a narrow passageway that would lead to the tunnel under the mountain. Essentially, it was a crawl space, just big enough for all the wolves to fit through. The entry hole sloped a couple of feet into the ground and then curved into a horizontal tunnel from there.

It was nerve-wracking at times due to several close calls, but thankfully, the wolves didn't have any trouble hiding their work. After they were through digging each night, they covered their tracks by filling in the vertical entry hole with part of the left-over dirt. Then they dispersed the remainder of the extra rock and soil around the large quarry so it would blend in.

Their plan was to escape in three waves. Each wolf was assigned to a sleep-quarry based on how fast they would be able to move through the tunnels. The first wave of wolves would be comprised of the slower wolves. They were told that on the night of the escape they were to go to the young wolves' quarry so that they could leave first and get a head start.

When it was time, the first wave would make their way through the crawl space and head to the main tunnel under the mountain. Tom, Gertie, and several of the other strong wolves would lead this first wave so that they could run ahead and finish connecting the small tunnel to the larger one. Then once the passageways were connected, Tom, Gertie and the others would hurry to the end of the big tunnel and complete the work there—opening up the tunnel to the Dayside and creating their entryway to freedom.

When the last wolf from the first wave was ready to drop into the crawl space, they would give the signal that it was time for the next wave of wolves to make their move. Once this occurred, the wolf choir would begin to sing gibberish, something they'd been doing on and off for months so that the bryobane were conditioned to ignoring unusual blackouts. At this point, the crystals would go dark, and half the wolves from the other sleeping quarries would quickly make their way to the young wolves' quarry. Then when they were sure that the bryobane weren't watching, the second wave would enter the small tunnel and catch up to the first.

The same process would repeat one last time for the third wave, the wave with the fastest wolves. Again, the wolf choir would allow the crystals to darken, and the rest of the wolves would make their escape.

On this night, the wolf choir would consist of only the older wolves. The ones who knew they couldn't make the journey without risking everyone else's safety. When nobody could solve how the wolf choir would escape without giving away the whole plan, the older wolves came together on their own to discuss the matter. Several of the elders decided that they would sacrifice themselves for the other wolves. It was an action that had once been deemed by their ancient ancestors as *the most honorable deed*.

The entire plan was discussed, altered, tweaked, and re-tweaked until the majority of wolves were satisfied. They agreed that it was as flawless as they knew how to make it. Any unforeseen details would have to be left up to chance.

The day finally came when the wolves realized they were an inch away from breaking through to the Dayside. One of the wolves pierced through the rock, opening a small hole to the other side of the mountain. Quickly, he covered it back up and alerted the others. Tom estimated that they had less than an hour of work left until they could create a hole large enough for all the wolves to climb through.

Word spread that it was time to put the plan into action. That night the wolves went to their specially assigned quarries. They laid down and closed their eyes, waiting for the night to begin. But before there was time for anything to transpire, something unexpected happened.

Right after everyone pretended to go to sleep, the bryobane showed up in a large group above the young wolves' quarry. Seconds later, five of the bryobane jumped into the pit, which was something they never did unless provoked. Their shriveled skin jiggled as they landed inside, and a nervous silence fell over the quarry. The wolves didn't dare get up, but they opened their eyes to see what was going on.

The bryobane split up and searched around, clearly looking for someone. Gertie felt ill. She was sure they'd figured out her brother's plan and were there to deal with him once and for all. She looked at Thomas to see if he knew what was going on, but he didn't return her gaze. He stared straight ahead stoically, and Gertie knew that he was thinking the same thing as her.

A moment later, one of the bryobane stopped right in front of Tom and grunted to the other four who came right over. One of them produced a rope from behind its back, and Tom tensed up, steeling himself for what he knew was coming... except it didn't. Instead, the bryobane looped the rope around Gertie's neck and pulled it tight. Gertie choked and spat. "Thomas! What's happening?" she cried hoarsely in a terrified voice.

Thomas moved towards the bryobane who was holding the rope. His paw had healed weeks ago, and he was prepared to fight for his sister with everything he had. Another of the ugly beasts knocked Tom hard against the chest with its hoof, and Tom flew back. He lost his balance and fell on his side. The five beasts grunted and squealed at him as he got back up, and Thomas assumed they were mocking him. He was ready to go again. But then, all of a sudden, he realized something as he watched their animated gestures. They weren't taking Gertie away to kill her. They were taking her as leverage.

Thomas was shocked. He had never known the bryobane to do anything this clever before. It seemed that they had figured out that the wolves were getting close to the other side of the mountain. By taking Gertie, they were ensuring that Tom wouldn't lead an escape.

"Oh my god, Gert. I'm so sorry! I'm so sorry!" Thomas began to cry as he absorbed the reality of what was happening. "They're taking you so we don't try to escape. I'm so sorry I got us into this. Oh my god, I'm so sorry!"

Gertie began to cry too, but she didn't sob like her brother. For some reason, seeing Thomas fall to pieces had calmed her down, and she suddenly felt very clear headed. She spoke to him quickly as the bryobane began to drag her away.

"Remember the promise you made to me before you went up the mountain, Thomas?" she asked.

Thomas followed Gertie across the quarry to the wall, though the bryobane held him back and shoved him away every time he got close to her. "Yes, Gertie. Of course I do! And I promise it again now. A million times over! I promise!"

They reached the wall. Several of the bryobane from up top came over and lowered ropes to help the others climb up the wall. Gertie paused for a moment, and with her last free breath, she said "No, Thomas. I want you to forget. I love you, my darling, sweet, troublemaking brother. God speed!" Then Gertie flew away as she was yanked up the wall by her neck and out of sight.

Tom was shattered. He had never felt so heartbroken in his entire life. Not when the bryobane beat or maimed him, and not even when his siblings or mother had been murdered. With his little sister gone—the loving, little sister he was meant to protect—nothing else mattered anymore. It was all over. He wouldn't leave Gertie. He would tell the others to go on, but he would stay behind. He couldn't abandon her.

An older wolf named Jack, who had helped plan the escape with the rest of them, came and sat by Tom's side. "Will it bring her back?" he asked.

Tom didn't understand what the old wolf was asking. "Will what bring her back?" Tom asked.

"Hating yourself for not being able to save her. Will it bring her back?"

Tom didn't answer. He didn't want to. What Jack was asking was meaningless. Nothing about the plan made sense without Gertie. "Tell the others to go," Tom said. "I'm not coming."

"And what do you think that will accomplish? Do you think she'd want both of you to die? Because that's what will happen if you stay."

"I don't care. You don't understand how much I've sacrificed already. It's just one more sacrifice to make."

"What you're doing isn't sacrifice; it's foolishness. And your sister wouldn't want that. We've all made sacrifices, son. Your sister just made the biggest one anyone can make, and you'll ruin that by staying. There's nothing left you can do for her, but you can do a lot for the rest of us if you come."

Jack's words were beginning to get through to Tom, though it pained him to admit it. He realized, however, that he didn't have to decide whether to stay behind quite yet. He could help the others escape and still come back to find Gertie afterward. He stopped crying and stood up with fresh resolve to finish what he'd started. Nodding at Jack, Tom said, "Okay, tell the others it's time to get going."

The strong wolves got to work, digging up the entry hole to the crawl space. Then once they were finished, they darted ahead of the first wave to the end of the small passageway. When they arrived, they began to connect the crawl space to the main tunnel. Tom and the others dug faster than they ever had. They took turns, two at a time, rapidly flinging dirt behind them, and eventually they broke through to the larger tunnel. Fortunately, the passageway stretched far enough to fit a long train of wolves because by the time the two tunnels were connected, the entire first wave had made it inside the first tunnel.

Tom and his team of young wolves sprinted ahead. Several of them sang as they went so that the crystals lit their way. Tom took note of how far back the larger clusters of crystals were. The wolves had been careful to remove the clusters closest to the Dayside in case they had to blow the tunnel up before everyone got out.

At that moment, however, Tom was only concerned about two things. One, if he had given the other wolves good enough instructions so that they could blow the tunnel up without him.

And two, if he'd have enough time to make it back through the small tunnel before they did.

Not paying close attention to where he was going, Tom rammed into the wolf in front of him as they turned a corner. He looked around to see what had happened and was struck speechless. His heart sank into his stomach.

Their team had made it all the way to the last hundred feet of the large tunnel but could go no farther. A giant mound of rock and dirt blocked their way—the result of a cave-in that had occurred sometime after they'd gone back to their quarries for the night. The wolf to Tom's side stopped singing. "What do we do now?" she asked in a whisper. But Tom didn't respond. Instead, he paced back and forth in front of the pile of rubble, letting the others sing while he tried to come up with the best solution.

Only two options came to mind. They could return to the Darkside, although it would be incredibly risky. Or they could dig their way through the mess and pray it wasn't as thick as it looked. However, before Tom had a chance to carefully assess both options, the choice was made for them. One of the young wolves that had stayed behind to help with the third wave came running around the corner towards them. She looked relieved to see them at first, but as her eyes drifted to the pile of debris, terror spread across her face. She uttered the words the rest of them were thinking. "Oh my god! We're doomed."

Tom snapped at her. "Stop it! We're not doomed! We can find a way out of this."

The young wolf took her eyes off the pile of rocks and looked at Tom. "No, you don't understand. I came to warn you that the bryobane are coming. They attacked the choir, but one of them escaped and came to warn us. A whole army of bryobane is on their way to capture or kill us, who knows? But apparently they aren't taking any chances because every last one of them is headed here now."

As the wolf spoke, the first wave of wolves began to appear behind her. Many of them cried when they saw the blockade. "We have to turn around!" several yelled in panic.

The situation was grim, but Tom knew what he had to do. There was no way out, so he made a decision that was brash but that he knew in his heart was the right one to make. The messenger had spoken the truth. They *were* doomed. They had been from the beginning. Not just from the beginning of Tom's plan but from the moment their ancestors had been taken by the bryobane.

He could see it clearly now. The only way to change the wolves' destiny was to end this part of their story. They would never escape from the bryobane until they were rid of them once and for all. Tom jumped onto the pile of rubble so the wolves would have a better view of him. He could hear the faint rumbling of hooves stampeding in the distance, the sounds of the monsters storming the tunnel.

It seemed like all the wolves were making sounds too. Some cried, others screamed, but most had chosen to sing the ancient songs in this gravest of times, which kept the tunnel aglow in beautiful light.

"Please, everyone! Let me have your attention!" Tom ordered. The wolves silenced themselves, although several continued to hum softly in order to keep the crystals lit.

"I know we're in quite a tough spot here, and for my very large roll in this, I sincerely apologize to you all. It seems to me that we only have one option now, though I know it's not the one anyone wants to hear.

"During my short time on Theia, I have learned how precious life can be and how fleeting too. With that in mind, I would like to ask you this: Is it worth it to continue living these lives that are not truly our own? Do we want to forever face the terrors we've been subjected to over and over again? Will we willingly stand by and allow more lives to be introduced to these terrors as *new* generations continue to be born?"

Tom paused, and for a moment, there was silence amongst the wolves. The sounds of the bryobane were much closer now, but Tom knew there were still a few moments left. "No!" someone shouted from the middle of the pack, breaking the silence. Then several more shouts of "No!" rang out, and soon the whole pack began to chant the short reply as the tunnel went dark for a few seconds.

Tom continued more forcefully, "We're the last of the Lesegolese! In ancient times we lived with pride in our hearts. And today we will die with pride in our hearts once again! The other packs may not have been strong enough or brave enough to risk dying to free *us*, but we will give our lives now to free them. Never again will they know the unspeakable horrors of the Darkside, and because of this, the memory of the Lesego —*our* memory—will live on forever!"

The wolves cheered, sobbed, sang, and nuzzled. The older wolf, Jack, joined Tom on the pile of rubble. "You made the right decision. Your sister would be proud of you."

Tom's voice cracked, and he let out a small laugh. It was all he could do to keep his emotions from taking hold of him. He nodded to the other wolves nearby who he had taught the ancient song, a low tune sung deep from the gut. The wolves climbed onto the pile and stood next to each other.

"Everyone ready?" Tom asked. "We'll start on my command."

He waited a moment longer. He wanted the bryobane to be as close as possible before they began. It was how he would know that they were exterminating every last one of them. The pounding from their hooves echoed closer, and Tom heard cries from the back of the pack. "This is for you, Gertie," he whispered. Then he nodded to the others, and they began to sing.

. . .

WOLF PACKS from all across the Dayside felt the tremors from the explosion. Later, when it was recounted to younger generations, it was often referred to as *The Day Theia Shook.*

Deep sadness spread like dark clouds over the other packs. Though they didn't know what had happened at first, they sensed that a huge cost had been paid to expel a great evil. After they discovered the tunnel, they spent a long time mourning the brave wolves who had perished. Then when the mourning came to an end, they rejoiced in their freedom from the bryobane, knowing they would never again have to live in fear of the horrible monsters.

They vowed to rebuild the demolished tunnel so that it would serve as a place of remembrance. They would bury the wolves' remains but leave the bones of the beasts so that all who went there could look upon the true face of evil. It was done to inspire good and to keep the sacrifice of the Lesegolese alive. After a time, though, the wolves would come to regret not burying the bones of all of the dead. For eventually, the ghosts of the bryobane would return to haunt them.

CHAPTER 10

THE MAYOR

Mina had walked for an unfathomably long time when she sensed she was nearing the market's center. The crowds had grown larger, and the metal notes, buried just below the dirt, had increased in number and turned from silver to gold.

She noticed, too, that the booths were beginning to look nicer. Instead of colorfully painted wood, many of them were made of sleek metal. Some even looked like small stores with large glass windows and actual doors that opened and shut. The front displays were more intricate, and the merchandise being sold was of a higher quality as well.

When Mina turned the next corner, she was disappointed to find that the path had changed from dirt to cobblestones. She didn't think her sore feet would handle the transition well, but after she turned to the next aisle, she forgot all about her aching feet. A deep sigh of relief escaped from her chest as she realized that she had made it halfway. She had arrived at the center of the market.

A series of solid gold archways greeted her. They stood ten feet apart all the way down the aisle and curved high overhead.

The light that reflected off of them was golden, and it coated the entire aisle with a sparkling shine. Mina passed underneath the first arch and marveled at its splendor.

The entire row was dazzling. The stores were petite two-story shops, built from metal, stone, and glass, and they were crammed together so tightly they practically overlapped. In every window, artistic displays of merchandise were expertly crafted like masterpieces of mercantilism meant to draw in the masses. Protruding from each little building was a shimmering gold sign that hung above every doorway. Most of the signs were wordless and showed only picture representations of items sold within, but some of the signs said things like, "Susan's Boutique" and "Hats by George!"

Mina was blown away by the sheer size and constant movement of it all. *It's chaos spray-painted in glitter*, she thought. Every square inch of space was filled with droves of people who bumped, shuffled, and scooted along. Mostly, they traveled in a daze, but Mina noticed something different about them than before that reminded her of a children's story she'd once read.

The story began with a large group of lemmings in a single-file line. They blindly followed each other until some mishap would occur, claiming the leaders at the front of the line. Then the new leaders would lead the line until the next ridiculous tragedy took place, and the line was shortened again. Eventually, all the lemmings were dead because they'd mindlessly followed each other to their deaths. It was all quite tragic, though less so because of how avoidable it had all been.

When Mina had observed the passersby before, alone or in small groups, they had seemed mostly harmless. Nothing more than a few lost souls floating around aimlessly. But now that they were shoved together, moving as one, Mina detected something devious at play. These once stupefied people were showing signs of alertness, evidenced by the schadenfreude beaming across their faces. And Mina wondered if it was the grandiose effects of the middle aisle that were to blame.

She pushed her way through the madness and arrived in the center of the row where a large town square had replaced the walkway and storefronts. There were benches and tables all around, and each corner of the square had a multitiered fountain that was made of solid gold. In the very center of it all, was one of the golden archways, taller and wider than the rest, with the words *Heart of the Market* engraved beautifully across the top.

Water trickled from the fountains' tiers, which would have seemed tranquil if it hadn't been for all the people that surrounded the fountains. Men, women, and children pushed and shoved as they tried to make their way closer. Then, when they were close enough, they plunged their buckets into the pools of water and heaved them back out again. *How primitive,* Mina thought as she sat down on one of the benches to rest.

Seconds passed before Mina's gaze was drawn to a middle-aged man standing on a platform under the wide archway in the middle of the square. He was overweight with saggy, jaundiced skin, and he wore a dark purple and black striped suit with a matching top hat. Sweaty strands of yellow, straw-like hair poked out from beneath the brim, and Mina noticed that his hair matched his complexion in a most unflattering way.

Despite his odd appearance, or maybe because of it, Mina was captivated. She couldn't stop staring. The man had inserted himself into the busiest part of the market, forcing the moving crowd to snake around him. Yet there seemed to be no reason for it. All the man did was hurl insults, compliments, and insults wrapped in compliments at everyone who passed by. Mina decided to stay and listen for a while to see if she could make sense out of it.

"You've come to the best place! There's nowhere better. I've researched it. I wish there were somewhere better. It would be nice to have competition, but there's none to speak of. I'd tell you if there were, but you see, nobody is capable of doing what I do."

"Whoa! Get a load of this dame! I wouldn't mind trading places with her husband! Right, fellas?"

"Have you seen the outside of the market lately? A horrible place. What a dump! And don't get me started on what those lowlifes on the Darkside are doing. Hello there, sir. You're not a lowlife, are you? It's hard to tell. That tie is really ugly."

Many of the people who passed looked happy to see the man. They smiled and laughed with knowing expressions as they received their unusual greeting and a handshake. But Mina wondered if the man really knew any of the people he spoke to or if any of the people really knew him.

She was reminded of a man she'd seen on a busy street back home. He had talked a lot too, yet unlike the man in striped clothing, people had gone out of their way to avoid him. Mina had asked her parents who the man was talking to, and her father had said that the man was talking to no one. He explained that the man was very sick and probably homeless, which meant he didn't have anyone to look after him. Mina asked her parents if they could help him get better since they were doctors, but her mother said that the man needed a different kind of doctor who specialized in illnesses of the mind.

Mina had been sad that they didn't help the lonely, sick man, and the thought of it had haunted her ever since. Suddenly, Mina started to feel sorry for the yellow-haired man. She wondered if he had the same type of illness as the man on the street all those years earlier. He certainly talked as much.

After a while, a woman and her two young children sat down next to Mina on the bench. She glanced towards the woman and the little girl and boy. The woman was wearing a long, crimson dress with black, velvet trim, and a white petticoat beneath that crunched and rustled whenever the woman made the slightest movement. The children, who appeared to be twins, wore matching denim overalls and white t-shirts. Mina thought the little family looked like they belonged in an advertisement for something wholesome like canned soup.

Mina said to the woman, "Your children are very cute. How old are they?"

The woman's face looked tired, but her eyes were full of warmth. "Oh…well, thank you. I'm not sure, though. To be honest, I can't even remember if they're mine. On the other hand, they don't seem to be anyone else's, so probably they are mine."

Mina was taken aback. She didn't know how to react to such a bizarre response. Her shocked expression, however, made the woman uncomfortable, and silence ensued until Mina was able to recover.

"Oh, right. How funny." Mina laughed nervously while trying to convince herself that the woman was only joking. She changed the subject by asking, "Do you happen to know who that man in the middle of the square is? The one who can't seem to stop talking?"

The woman smiled at Mina cheerfully. "Oh yes. I know who *that* is," she said in a way that sounded like she thought it excused her from not knowing whose children she was with.

"That's the mayor. Dayside Dale. He always stands right there, talking to the shoppers. In fact, I don't think he ever does anything else."

Mina couldn't believe it. "Really? *That's* your mayor?"

The woman giggled sweetly. "Well, of course he is, silly. But he's not just mine. He's everybody's mayor. Yours too. Isn't he swell?"

Mina looked at the man again, trying to examine him differently in light of this new information. But for some reason, Mina thought he looked even sicker than before. The internal struggle she'd sensed brewing inside of him seemed to be spilling out onto everyone who drew near.

Something else the woman said had struck Mina too. "That part where you mentioned that the mayor doesn't do anything else. You mean besides sleep, right?"

The woman looked uncomfortable again. "What do you mean by 'sleep?'" she asked.

Mina replied, "You know, like lay down with your eyes closed and rest, except that you're not awake anymore?"

The woman laughed like Mina was the one joking now. "Right! Just imagine! To spend all that time not doing anything at all. Not even *thinking*! Who could possibly have time for that?"

Then, suddenly, the woman looked concerned, as if she realized that she might have said the wrong thing. "Wait. Do people like you sleep? I didn't mean to offend."

Mina smiled. "No need to apologize. Where I come from, everybody sleeps. We have to. Our bodies need it to survive." The woman looked very serious as Mina spoke, nodding along with every syllable.

Mina finished her explanation, "We need sleep almost as much as we need food and water."

"Well, then you shouldn't feel too bad about sleeping. It sounds like your type of people value it highly. Besides, now that you're here, I'm sure you won't do that kind of thing anymore," the woman said, patting the top of Mina's hand, as though she were absolving her from her transgressions.

Mina smiled again and shrugged. She could hear the condescension in the woman's voice. It would have upset her, except that the woman had no idea what she was talking about, and therefore, getting mad about it would have been pointless.

"What do people do all the time if no one ever sleeps?" Mina asked.

At first, the woman appeared stumped like she'd been

asked to solve an impossible riddle. Time passed, and Mina wondered if the woman had chosen not to answer when, finally, she spoke. "I suppose we do what we always do. Some people walk around and shop. Some people sell things, or collect water, or cook, or make things to sell. Others clean, or build new booths, or sit and talk to new people, or chat with friends. We all have something to do, though. Got to keep busy, or you might as well go live on the Darkside." The woman shivered a little at mentioning the Darkside.

Then she stood up, looped her basket over her arm, and grabbed each child by the hand. "Well, time to skedaddle. Lots of shopping to do before..." but she trailed off, and a far-away expression moved across her face like a shadow. Mina recognized it as the same clouded expression that her grandfather wore on his bad days. Days he couldn't remember who he was.

A few seconds later, the woman emerged from her fog, seemingly unaware that she'd left her last words hanging. She looked down at Mina and said, "Well, nice to meet you."

Mina nodded and waved to the children who were staring at her with timid excitement. The woman glided away, pulling the children into the crowd of people. But all of a sudden, the little girl broke loose and ran back to Mina. She threw her arms around her waist tightly.

Mina was surprised by this unexpected show of affection. She hesitated at first but then patted the girl on the head while tussling her hair softly. The little girl looked up at Mina with adoring eyes and whispered, "You're the most beautiful angel I've ever seen." Then she rushed back to join the woman and little boy, who were almost surely, but not quite definitely, her family.

MINA RETURNED to watching Dale greet the endless sea of people and wondered if this could really be his only job as mayor. If so, it seemed pointless in every way, except as a ridiculous façade for leadership. There was something else, too, that bothered Mina about the spectacle, but she couldn't quite put her finger on it.

She sat thinking about it for a while until it dawned on her. It was Dale's arrogance. For someone who was supposed to have a job helping others, he spent all his time focused on himself. Sure, he shook hands and greeted people, but he always found a way to work himself or his ideas into whatever he was saying. Plus, he never waited for people to respond before moving on. Mina had seen attention-starved children act like this, but she found it appalling for a grown-up to behave in such a manner.

Mina was sick of the show. She knew she'd probably spent too much time dawdling anyhow, so she started to go. However, before she left, she climbed up on the bench for a better view of the square. Mina thought it was impressive to watch the herd from above, all the bodies pressed together, swaying in unison.

She began to step down, but a beam of light caught the side of her eye. She looked in the direction it was coming from and saw a slender woman pinching her fingers together around a piece of gold. The woman was walking in the line of people that had just passed Dale. Mina looked ahead of the woman and saw that there were others in front of her, holding the same gold piece. Mina turned her head towards Mayor Dale and realized that he wasn't just shaking hands; he was pressing a large gold coin into the palm of every hand he shook.

Mina was curious about what Dale was up to, though she knew she should leave it alone and be on her way. After all, Larry had told her not to concern herself with the mayor. But that was only because he couldn't help her get home, right? True, she wasn't supposed to be doing anything out of the ordinary, but she decided that shaking hands with the mayor wasn't out of the ordinary since everyone else was doing it too. *Really, it's the most ordinary thing to do on this aisle*, she thought. Then out loud to herself, she said, "When in Rome!"

She walked across the square and pushed her way into the crowd that was headed towards Dale. At first, she ended up stuck between an overweight man and woman who seemed intent on squeezing her out of the way so they could walk side-by-side. She hopped backwards but almost plowed into an elderly gentleman, who had thick, white hair that was greased over like James Dean's.

Mina could no longer see Dale, but she could hear him louder than ever and knew she was getting close. "Hey there, sir! Look at this guy right here. He's a real winner. You've been shopping here for a long time, haven't you? It shows. You look good. Not like some of these slobs. You all know who I'm talking about. They go to the *other* parts of the market to shop.

"I know. I know. *It's all one market*. That's what they say, right? But we know better, don't we? Yeah, we know. This guy over here knows anyway and so does this chick. Hello, honey. You're looking very pretty today.

"Doesn't she look pretty, everyone? Give her a little whistle if you think she looks beautiful. Listen to that, honey. They think you're gorgeous. Although, and I have to say this because I can't lie, it was only the men whistling. The women are all jealous. Isn't that right? Yeah, it's true. Nobody will tell you the truth like I do. It's why everyone trusts me. I'm too smart to lie. Much, much, way too smart. I can't help it.

"Hey there, big fella! And hello to you, large lady. You his wife? Yes? Just nod. Great. She nodded folks. You ever considered the two of you dieting? Just a suggestion. I don't charge for this. Geez, lady. Don't look so sour. A smile goes a long way."

It was finally time for Dale to greet Mina. She reached out her hand and waited for him to take it, but nothing happened.

She looked up and was met with an eyeful of yellow neck skin that jiggled around as Dale talked. He wasn't talking to her, though. Instead, he was directing his attention past the spot where Mina had parked herself while she waited for her gold-lined handshake.

"Has anyone ever told you about the water we have here? It's the tastiest water you'll ever drink. Nobody has better water than yours truly! And would you believe it? *Some people* didn't want you to have water. Can you imagine? I mean just really think about that. No water? Are they crazy or just stupid? Maybe I shouldn't say, but everyone already knows the answer, don't we? Yeah, we know."

This peaked Mina's curiosity. She wondered if it was true that there was something special about the water or if it was just more of Dale's bloated rhetoric. She didn't have much time to think it over, though, before the old man behind her shoved her forward. Mina looked back at him in disgust, but he looked just as upset as she did. Mina looked back even farther and saw that Dale had his hand on the old man's back and was shoving him into her. Yet Dale wasn't looking at either of them. He seemed to be thoughtlessly herding the two of them back towards the line that had drifted on without them.

Mina didn't understand why this had happened, but she refused to be deterred. She squeezed her way out of the crowd, turned around, and got back in line to try a second time. However, when it came time again for Dale to shake Mina's hand, he ignored her once more. This time a middle-aged man with his wife and daughter shoved Mina forward as Dale swept them away, back towards the crowd.

Mina was determined, though. She returned to the line and stuck her head out to the side to watch carefully as every single person in front of her received a handshake. When Mina was the next in line, she leaned forward with her hand outstretched just inches from the hand that Dale was holding.

But instead of grabbing Mina's hand next, Dale turned his attention past Mina and used the person behind her to usher her away again.

She couldn't believe it. *Can he not see me?* she wondered.

She turned around and tried over and over, but each time the same thing happened. She got as physically close to Dale as possible, yet he didn't say a word to her. He just pushed her along by way of the person behind her. After a while, she knew it couldn't be a fluke. There had to be something about her presence that bothered him.

As Mina walked away from Dale for the dozenth time, he said to no one in particular, "There sure are a lot of angels in the crowd today. Better hold on tight to your wallets, folks!"

Mina spun around fast, nearly causing the two men behind her to topple over her. One of them was carrying a bucket of water, and as he stopped, half of it spilled down the front of Mina's shirt and pants. People cursed and grumbled as the entire crowd behind her ground to a halt.

Without paying any attention to her newly soaked clothes, Mina shouted at Dale, "I knew it! You *do* see me!"

The people around them began to back up, forming a space around Mina and Dale. "Why won't you shake my hand if you can see me?" she demanded.

Visibly annoyed by the scene Mina was causing, Dale replied, "Look, sweetheart, I don't mean to hurt your feelings, but I've never seen you before in my life. Now, turn around and keep on walking. You're holding up the line."

Mina had no intention of letting it go, though. She hated the disrespectful way that Dale spoke to people, and she didn't care anymore about causing a scene if it meant calling him out for his rude behavior. "That's garbage! I know you saw me. I tried to shake your hand every time I passed you, but you refused. You kept shoving the people behind me forward to move me out of the way. And I want to know why."

Dale smiled impishly. "Tsk. Tsk. I didn't know angels were allowed to lie."

Suddenly, it seemed that several of the onlookers had become aware of Mina's presence. She could hear them whispering about how an angel had miraculously appeared in the market. She started to reply, but before she had the chance, Dale spoke again. "Now, don't get all defensive on me. It's not just *you*. I've heard that most angels are pretty dishonest. Probably more than anyone would like to admit. Maybe even more dishonest than regular people. Who can say? We all know that angels aren't morally superior to anyone. They just act like it, right?"

The crowd around them gasped, and Mina was relieved that they were taking her side. It was obvious that Dale had gone too far. He'd have to apologize now if he wanted to save face. But while she waited for her apology, something strange began to happen. The people in the crowd started to look at one another. At first, they acted nervous, but then, slowly, as they made eye contact with each other, they grew more assured. Many even started to laugh.

The laughter was chilling. It didn't sound joyful at all. It was spiteful and cruel, and it made Mina feel weak. She knew she wasn't really an angel, of course, but that wasn't the point. Dale thought she was (or at least he knew the people in the crowd did), and he had used it to publicly shame her.

Mina sensed it would be safer to walk away right then, but she wanted to defend herself. "Do you mean 'morally superior' like how *you* act when you harass all these people and make jokes at their expense?" she asked.

The crowd gasped again, but they didn't laugh this time. Dale scowled and shifted his weight back and forth. He began to respond, but he didn't make eye contact with Mina. Instead, he stared into the crowd, as though it were a shiny mirror that he was using to admire his own reflection.

"Look, lady," he said. "Nobody here has any idea what you're talking about. Everything you're saying sounds like gobbledygook, but that's probably because you don't know what it's like to be a regular Joe. You spend all your time high in the air, looking down at the rest of us, thinking you're better. You don't understand these fine folks like I do. You can't because you're not one of them." Then, as Dale finished, he gave the crowd a big, dopey smile that made him look like a bullfrog taking a whizz.

All of a sudden, it dawned on Mina what game they were playing. Having already spent two years in junior high, she was surprised at herself for not recognizing it sooner. Mina had watched the game day after day in the lunchroom, in the hallways, in the classrooms, and especially, in the girl's locker room. It was a game played for the sole purpose of winning popularity by ridiculing your friends and enemies until you had the most power. Mina loathed the game, even though she understood it well.

It was her turn to go now. "That isn't true at all. I'm just like the rest of you. I don't spend *any* time 'high in the air.' And I can't imagine what would give you the impression that I do since I'm standing here on solid ground just like everyone else. Well, except for *you*, way up there on your little stage."

Dale frowned and took his turn. "Nope. You're different because you have wings. Nobody else here has wings. That makes you *not* like the rest of us. Maybe you aren't an angel, though. Come to think of it, none of us know where you came from. Maybe you're only pretending to be an angel to hide what you really are. A winged monster, perhaps?"

The crowd began to hiss and boo at Mina, and someone yelled, "Tear her wings off so we can see what she really is!"

Mina panicked. She could see why Larry and Carla had told her to stay away from Dale. He was clearly a loose cannon. She wanted to leave but felt trapped by the angry mob surrounding her. If only she could bring them to her side, she thought. To show them that *she* wasn't the one pretending. She decided she better give it a shot.

"I'm not the liar! I never pretended to be anything at all. You, on the other hand, are pretending to be a man of the people when all you care about is *yourself*. You make inappropriate suggestions to sway anyone who'll listen and then pretend to be ignorant of your own deviousness. That way people can believe the parts they want to and tell themselves you're only joking about the rest. They don't realize that you're doing it to manipulate them."

Mina turned to face the crowd, just like Dale had been doing the whole time. "Look, everyone! He's performing a simple trick to win you over. I've seen it done many times before, mostly by adolescent girls, but still! You have to stop paying attention to him! It's the only way to break the spell he has you under!"

The crowd was so silent that the only thing Mina could hear was the sound of the concert somewhere off in the distance. Dale's devilish expression had become downright evil, and he looked like he was thinking about all the terrible things he could do to get rid of her. Finally, he said, "Well, folks! It would seem we have a mistress of persuasion in our presence. She reminds me of someone I know. Oh, right! It's *me*!" Dale let out a forced laugh as the crowd took a collective sigh of relief and began to laugh along with him.

Then he said to Mina, "Come here, doll! I'd be happy to shake your hand."

Mina didn't budge. Dale seemed to be calling a truce, but for some reason, she felt more afraid than ever. It seemed too out of character for him. She didn't trust it. Dale kept waving for her to come closer, but she didn't move until the crowd began pushing her forward, delivering her to him.

When she was right in front of him, he asked, "Tell me, are you always this good at getting your way?"

Mina thought about it for a second and said, "Well, I'm thirteen, so I've had some practice." The crowd roared with delight.

"What's your name, darling?" Dale asked.

"Mina," she replied.

"Well, Mina, you'll be pleased to know you've made a powerful friend. No doubt you're aware that I'm Dale, Mayor of the Dayside."

Mina looked at the crowd and then back at Dale. "And they just let you be the mayor?" she asked. A few people in the crowd laughed nervously.

"Sure, they do," Dale said, bending down to take Mina's hand. He grabbed it in a bone crushing squeeze and shook it up and down for everyone to see. "You'd be amazed at what you can do when you're well-known and respected like me! Besides, someone's got to do the people's dirty work!"

Dale stood up tall again. "And who better than the smartest guy around?" Dale asked as he let go of Mina's hand. She brought it to her chest and cradled it in pain. It was throbbing so badly that it took her a moment to realize there was something inside of it.

In a vindictive tone, Dale asked, "Who let you in here, anyway? I didn't realize we were so hard up for business that we'd started letting any old riffraff through the gates."

"What gates?" Mina asked.

"It's metaphorical, sweetheart. The point is you don't belong here. Look around. You don't see any other winged creatures, do you?"

Mina responded, "I'm just passing through. Surely, I'm allowed to visit, aren't I?"

"That depends. Did you bring anything valuable to trade?"

he asked with a sly grin that implied he already knew the answer.

Mina shrugged. "Well, no. But I'm only planning to look."

Dale scoffed, "Yeah, that's what they all say. But then you find something you can't live without and bam! Am I right?" Dale directed the question to the crowd.

People nodded at each other and snickered. A few shouted, "That's right!"

Mina was lost. She had no idea what Dale was talking about. "Right about what?" she asked.

"You steal, of course," he replied with his big, awful grin.

Mina's face grew hot. "How dare you! I've never stolen before in my life!"

Dale put his hands up to Mina, as though to stop her words from striking him. "Whoa there! Calm down! I'm not saying you've done it. I'm just saying at some point everyone's tempted, and there're some people, and I won't name names. But there're some people who just can't help themselves. It's why we can't go letting everyone in the market. Otherwise, things can get very disorderly. Very *nasty*.

"I've seen it happen. And believe me! It can happen fast. Very, very fast. Faster than you think, although I don't know if you can think very fast. And you don't want that, do you?"

Mina was rendered speechless by Dale's rambling. She had become extremely aware of how careful she needed to be with her answer. For even though Dale had framed his question to sound like he was talking about order in the marketplace, she knew that he was really alluding to something else. His ramblings might *sound* absurd, but Mina understood what they really were. A way to hide—in plain sight—the rotten meaning of what he was really saying. That he didn't like outsiders.

Mina thought for a bit until, out of the blue, an idea popped into her head, and she knew just how to respond. "I'm sure everyone here would agree that they don't want a disorderly marketplace, but just because I'm a visitor from the outside doesn't mean I'm more likely than anyone else to cause trouble. Besides, aren't you all visitors too? You may come here more often than I do, but nobody actually lives here, right?"

Dale was peeved that Mina wasn't playing the game the way he liked. He spoke quickly and with heavy sarcasm. "Well, there you go, folks! You've had the good fortune of meeting the one perfect angel of the whole lot. Good as gold she is. A story to tell the grandchildren, eh?"

Then to Mina he said, "Glad to hear you aren't going to steal, honey. But I'm sure you won't mind if some of my guards escort you to the next aisle. As the mayor, I'm responsible for keeping everyone hustling in the right direction, see."

He was clearly finished with her, but the crowd hadn't quite broken up yet. Without hesitating, Mina asked loudly so that everyone could hear, "What about the Darkside? Are you mayor of that too?"

Dale pursed his lips together and slapped his hand down hard on Mina's back. "Nope!" he said with a sneer. "But nobody in their right mind lives over there anyway. Now move along. You've taken up enough of these good people's time!" And with that, Dale shoved Mina back into the crowd one last time.

CHAPTER 11

THE OLD MAN

The old man sat on the edge of the crumbling dune and stared up at the moon.

He had lived a good life. He hadn't cheated, gambled, or drank too much. He'd paid his taxes on time and had always made sure his family had what they needed. He hadn't done anything remarkable to speak of, but he was proud of the life he had.

Then his wife died. It wasn't supposed to happen that way. He'd planned to go first, wanted to go first, and now his whole timeline was out of sync. In fact, the balance of his world shifted so dramatically after she died that his memory began to fade along with her.

Losing his memory didn't hurt or make him uncomfortable in any physical way. He didn't sleep less, or eat less, or use the bathroom more or less frequently. It didn't give him a rash, or make him short of breath, or give him any worse heartburn than he already endured.

It did, on the other hand, make people look at him and talk to him in a way he couldn't stand. He was a burden, an invalid, a patient to his own family. He'd gone from being honored to being pitied, and there were many days he wished it would all end.

Living a life of forgetfulness wasn't actually so bad until you remembered, and then it got tricky. Remembering what you should've known all along was a solitary business that prompted a gut-wrenching cycle of fear, anger, and remorse.

It would have been easy to check out long ago, but the man had chosen to keep on living for his granddaughter. Sure, she'd begun to look at him more often in that way he hated, but he didn't care as much when she did it. She was young and impatient, the way all young people ought to be. He would never fault her for her youthful flare. In truth, he enjoyed it. Watching his granddaughter brought the kind of joy and excitement into his life that he'd once believed were lost to him forever.

It hurt the old man that the girl's parents didn't play a more active role in her life. Of course, they were doctors and doing important work, but the man was old enough to know that once you were a parent, there was no job more important than being there for your child. Despite his frustration, the parents' absence gave him purpose. He could fill a spot that nobody, but him, seemed to realize needed filling. Honestly, it was quite easy. All he had to do was be present for his granddaughter. He was there when she needed him and even when she didn't.

That isn't to say he crowded her any more than a normal family member would have. Yet that was the point entirely. To be the one normal family member in his granddaughter's life. He was a storyteller when he could remember; a snorer when he napped; a lover of music, and singing, and joke telling. But at the end of the day, he was someone she could rely on.

Their relationship was not entirely selfless, however. The man had also decided to continue his life in order to pass on his memories. In this way, he treated his granddaughter like a human time capsule. Sharing his stories as often as he could remember so that someday she would pass them on to her own grandchildren. But then the balance shifted again, and the timeline moved even further off course. He was robbed of something far greater than his memory. The moon had stolen his precious granddaughter, and there was no way to get her back. He felt more hopeless than ever before.

He'd never had any strong feelings for the moon one way or the other. It was just something that was there. Something he had no qualms about taking for granted. He knew that some people spent a great deal of time romanticizing the big satellite in the sky, but he didn't understand any of that. As far as he was concerned, it was just an oversized rock orbiting the Earth, doing its job of keeping the tides in order.

A few groups of men from another country had traveled there on several occasions. It had been interesting to watch the first time but hadn't made the old man feel any special way about the moon. The feat in engineering and space travel had been the impressive part, but that didn't make the moon any more impressive.

But now was a different story. The old man felt rage as he watched the big, white crescent beaming down at him. He yelled at it to send back his little girl; to not harm a hair on her head; to treat her like a princess instead of the prisoner he feared her to be.

The earthquake and subsequent tsunami had torn her away, which was bad enough. But he could have found a boat or rented a helicopter to go searching for her. His granddaughter was a strong swimmer. He could have reached her in time. He was sure of it. But then the glass pathway came for her, and he watched from the trees as she floated into the sky and away to the moon.

There was nothing left he could do. So he sat on the edge of the crumbling dune and stared up at the moon, whispering his sad story again and again so he would never forget.

CHAPTER 12

THE CONTACT

The show was over in the *Heart of the Market*, and everyone had reclaimed their spot in the hustle and bustle of the large crowd. Mina joined them, ready to move on so she could examine the piece of metal that Dale had thrust into her aching hand.

She opened her fist and saw the piece of gold indented into her palm. It wasn't a coin, as she'd expected. It looked like the silver and gold notes that covered most of the pathways all across the marketplace. But unlike the messages she'd read before, this message didn't reveal any type of personal information. It read more like an advertisement:

Shop the Heart of the Market, because NOBODY else in this place knows how to treat you like I DO!! Don't forget to drink the WATER while you're here. It's the best ANYONE has to offer. The BEST, and it's yours FREE!!! -Courtesy of Dale, Mayor with the BIGGEST brain of all time!!!!

She flipped the message over. On the back was an engraved drawing of Dale's profile with his name written underneath in large calligraphy. Mina rolled her eyes. She hadn't expected words of wisdom, but she'd thought he might at least have made some feeble attempt at it. Like possibly something out of a fortune cookie:

A branch of the tree forges its own path to the sun, but it's the power of the trunk that lifts each branch to the sky.

Dale's message, however, was like a car dealership telling people to shop at *their* lot because the air was more breathable there. Mina scratched her fingernail against a tiny bubble that she noticed on top of the engraving of Dale's nose. The gold flaked and peeled beneath her nail, revealing a rusty metal underneath. Mina laughed. Even Dale's gold was pretending to be something it wasn't. She dropped the metal piece on the ground. Usually, she was against littering, but she was happy to make an exception in this case.

Mina had walked halfway down the rest of the aisle when two men stepped in front of her. They were dressed identically in light blue suits, and Mina knew right away that they were the guards Dale had mentioned. She made a sharp turn to the side, attempting to ditch them but ran into a large arm that was blocking her way. She turned and saw two more men dressed in light blue suits right behind her. They wore sunglasses and stared straight ahead with icy-cold expressions.

Mina tried smiling at the man who had blocked her way, but his stoniness was unwavering. Suddenly, Mina was struck by a disturbing thought. She had seen lots of other men wearing these same light blue suits all throughout the market. Why would Dale need so many guards, she wondered. Mina didn't have an answer, but the question made the hair on the back of her neck stand up.

With no other choice, she continued to walk, sandwiched between the serious men. They made their way past a variety of luxury shops until they'd reached the last of the golden archways. Then they turned the corner and walked halfway to the next aisle. They stepped down from the cobblestones and back onto the cushy dirt path that ran through the rest of the market.

Mina hoped the men would leave her alone, now that they'd escorted her away from Dale's circus. However, the men showed no signs of releasing her from their formation. In fact, they moved in closer so that she was barely able to see beyond them anymore. Keeping a steady pace, they blew past lots of aisles. And the farther they walked the more frightened Mina became.

After a while, one of the men behind her said to the other, "We'll take her in the backway so nobody sees. The cage is ready and waiting for shipment."

Mina knew she was in serious danger and began to go into a full-blown panic. She leapt at the small sliver of space between two of the men, but one of them grabbed her under the shoulder and shoved her back into place. Before he let go of her, though, Mina leaned over and bit the top of his fingers as hard as she could. The man let out a blood-curdling scream, which stunned her captors long enough for Mina to break free. She hurried into the crowd.

One of the men shouted, "Don't let her get away!"

Fortunately, all of the commotion had caused the crowds of people to stop and turn towards the four men. Mina worked this to her advantage. She grabbed her wings and wrapped them tightly around her torso. Then she hunched over at the waist and darted between the large groups of onlookers, who as usual seemed oblivious to her presence.

She made it all the way to the nearest aisle when she felt somebody run into her from behind. Her heart jumped into her throat. She spun around prepared to fight for her life, but there was nobody there. Twenty feet away, she could see two of the guards moving through the crowd on their tiptoes. They were looking over the heads of the motionless crowd, searching for her, and she realized that her only chance to escape would be to hide.

She looked around for an empty stall, but instead she spotted a small opening between two booths that was hidden in the shadows. It was a tight fit, but she thought she could squeeze. Too afraid to turn back, she ducked into the tiny crevice and laid down on the ground, praying that the men wouldn't think to look for her there.

Mina lay with her face in the dirt, clutching her wings as she listened carefully for the sounds of footsteps in hot pursuit. It was hard to know how much time had passed, but Mina's breathing had returned to normal by the time she dared to look up. However, her attention was drawn to a thin piece of paper that was hanging by a pin from the top of her left wing.

Mina wondered how the paper had gotten there, but then spontaneously her mind raced back to moments earlier when she'd felt someone crash into her from behind. *That must be it,* she thought. Not ready to risk giving away her hiding spot, she stayed on the ground as she removed the paper and lowered it to a spot in front of her where she could read what it said. It was a poem written neatly in black ink:

> Jack went up to slay the Giant
> But found the Goose beat him to it.
>
> She was sick of laying gold eggs,
> So she found a noose and tied it.
>
> What goes up doesn't always fall down.
> Better find a green vine and try it.

Mina knew right away that the poem was referencing *Jack*

& the Beanstalk, a story she'd heard many times as a child. But she still didn't understand why someone would bother pinning a poem about it to her wing.

She flipped the limp piece of paper over and found a note that had been written hastily on the back. In addition to the messy scribble, the words appeared to have been written on top of another poem that had faded, leaving a ghostly imprint behind. The message read:

"You're in danger! Be like Jack!"

Be like Jack? What is that supposed to mean? Mina wondered. Was the message suggesting that she should climb a beanstalk? And what kind of danger? The men in light blue suits? Or was someone else after her too? Mina was dizzy from all the circles her mind was doing. It felt like she was drowning in her own thoughts.

Carla's words came rushing back to her: "…remember to keep your eyes open for trouble. It'll be there even when you don't know it." Mina's fear had reached a new pinnacle. She knew she had to act, but her encounter with Dale's guards had made her afraid of what might happen next. She didn't even trust her own intuition anymore. Her instincts told her that the note was meant to help her, but what if it was really a trap?

She decided that the only thing to do was to find the person who could help her get home. And fast. It was time to be brave again. She stood up and headed back to the aisle. She peeked out at where she'd last seen the men in light blue suits, but the crowd and the men had moved on. Taking a deep breath, she began to move quickly down the aisle, away from where she'd escaped the guards. She scanned every booth, looking for signs of trouble. She worried that the guards might be hiding, waiting to leap out and grab her.

When she'd almost reached the end of the aisle, Mina

spotted a stall covered in vines. *Be like Jack.* Was this what the note was referring to? Was she supposed to climb one of these vines? She slowed her pace. The stall was so densely covered that Mina couldn't tell if there was anyone inside. She took a few more steps until she was directly across from the vine-tangled booth. It was dark and still inside.

A shiver rippled through her. *There's nothing in there,* she thought. *It's just another distraction.* She began to step away, but before she turned, a dark shadow darted across the corner of her vision. She jumped back to face the booth again, certain that her fears were coming true. She searched between the shadows, ready to face whatever was back there. But nothing happened.

Just then, some teenage boys walked by. They passed between Mina and the booth, lost in their own world like all the others. Nevertheless, their presence gave her courage. She walked closer to the booth. Close enough to see the back of it through the hazy light.

"I knew it," she told herself. "There's nothing there." She spun around once more, but before she took her first step to go, her ankles were slammed together by a violent force and pulled out from underneath her. She fell to the ground, face first with a sickening thud. A muffled scream broke from her lips, no louder than a tiny whisper. It was all that she could muster through the pain.

With a spine-cracking tug, Mina was hoisted into the air by her feet and dropped onto her back atop the vine covered booth. Her head throbbed, and her vision blurred. She tried to get up, but she realized that she was too tangled up in the vines to move.

Before she had time to free herself, Mina felt something pulling at her ankles again. Gingerly, she lifted her head and saw a large vine looping itself around her feet. Then to her horror, it began to coil around her entire body like a spider wrapping its prey. Mina screamed, but in a matter of seconds, she was completely engulfed inside the cocoon the vine had formed around her.

It gripped her as tightly as a python, and Mina was no longer able to let out a breath, let alone scream. The possessed creeper lifted her into the air, even higher than before, and sent her flying over the tops of several rows. The speed made Mina sick, and she thought for sure that she would pass out. She regained her senses, however, as the long vine came to a stop, laying her down face-first in one of the last rows. It loosened its strong-hold and began to unwind. Scared and upset, Mina tried to get up right away, but her legs were still bound together.

She heard a woman running and calling to her from somewhere nearby. "Don't move! You've been nabbed by a swelter vine. They're terrible beasts when you try to fight them. Hold still for a second, and I'll go grab something to free you right up!"

Mina was relieved to have help. Something in the woman's voice put her at ease, and Mina did as she was told and held perfectly still. The woman returned seconds later, carrying a long knife. She grabbed hold of the thick vine, and with one giant swipe, she cut Mina loose. Then she tossed the front of the long, green devil vine on top of the nearest booth. Still shaken, Mina slowly worked her way into a standing position. She was excited to meet her hero but was astonished when she realized that her hero was a frail, old woman. Mina looked her up and down.

The woman was tall, though she would have been taller if it weren't for the slight hunch in her shoulders. Her skin was beautiful and would have looked youthful if it weren't for the deep lines embedded across her forehead and in the corners of her eyes and lips. She wore a tight bun on the top of her head which would've made her look stern if it weren't for the strands of white hair that floated playfully on the sides of her face.

"Hello there, dearie," she said to Mina.

"Hello, ma'am," Mina responded. "Thank you for freeing me. What a terrible mistake that was! I don't even know exactly how it happened."

"Hmm, I do. You stepped too close to a swelter vine. You mustn't ever give those things a chance to sneak up on you. If you turn your back on two of them, they'll have you hogtied faster than a twister on a Tuesday."

"I see," said Mina, not knowing what to think of this woman who, as her appearance suggested, seemed old and wise but young and airy in equal measure.

"Come to my stall. I'll check you out to make sure you haven't done any serious damage."

Mina nodded, grateful for the woman's invitation. When they arrived at her booth, however, she was surprised to find the woman's stall was covered in plants. It looked an awful lot like the stall that she'd just been abducted from.

The old woman said to Mina, "All the plants you see in this booth have medicinal properties." She pointed to a small vine with spiky leaves. "You take a bite of that one there, and you won't feel any soreness from that nasty encounter of yours for days. In fact, you won't feel much of anything for days. Come to think of it, you should probably only lick that one. Or even just a little nibble might do the trick."

Mina felt disappointed as she realized what was happening. The old woman wasn't trying to help her; she was trying to sell her something. "You're wanting me to buy one of your plants?" she asked, testing out her theory.

The old woman nodded. "Well, it's probably best to keep up appearances. Come inside and take a closer look," she said with a twinkle in her eye.

Now that Mina understood the woman's true intention, she

wished she hadn't followed her all the way back to her booth. She paused while the old saleswoman walked around and entered her booth from the side. The woman looked back across the counter at Mina questioningly.

"I've made a mistake," Mina responded. "I appreciate your help, but I don't have any money or anything to barter with."

The old lady laughed kindly and asked, "Another mistake, hmm? Well, mistakes can have meaning, you know?"

Mina humored the woman, hoping it would get her on her way sooner. She knew she was going to have to walk back a long way to cover all the rows she'd missed after leaving the center aisle. "Oh, yes, of course," she said. "Mistakes can have lots of meaning if we learn from them."

The woman laughed again even louder than before. "How marvelous! You sound just like a little schoolteacher. But no. That's not right at all. What I mean is that sometimes when you think you're making a mistake, it's really fate stepping in to put you on the right course. You just don't see it yet."

Mina liked this idea, but she still had no intention of being lured in by the old woman. She had wasted too much time already. "Fascinating. Well, I really must be going."

The woman's eyes twinkled brightly now, and she looked up towards the sky, ignoring Mina's response. "For example," she said, "the first time I ever saw a shooting star, I chased it until I caught up to it on the horizon. I thought I was being sent an important message, so you can imagine my disappointment when it turned out that the shooting star was just a man strapped to a rocket-pack. But would you believe that this memory has come to mean more to me than even a *million* shooting stars ever could have?" The woman looked back at Mina and smiled dreamily.

Mina nodded politely. "That's a lovely story. Thanks for sharing it with me," she said as she began to shuffle backwards, hoping to break free before the woman tried to tell her more.

After all, she didn't have time to waste listening to an old lady's musings.

The woman continued to grin sweetly. "I can see you're in a rush, but don't go just yet. There are several more things I need to share with you."

Mina pushed back. "I'm sorry, ma'am, but I'm really in a hurry. There's someone I need to find."

The woman nodded. "Yes, and somewhere you need to be too. You'll be hurrying off to the Sheep Spa soon enough, but you'll need to find some food before you go. I'll help you with that, but there's something even more important that you'll need first."

Mina was stunned into silence. Could this old woman be the contact she'd been searching for?

The woman pointed to the opening in the booth. "Well, don't just stand there gawking. My name is Maude. Come on around inside the booth," she said.

Mina followed her directions this time as Maude sat down in a metal rocking chair. Once she was settled, she leaned over the chair's right arm and stuck her hand down into a metal box about the size of a milk crate. Her face became very serious as she concentrated, feeling around inside the box.

Mina asked cautiously, "Are you the person I'm supposed to talk to about going home? Were you the one who gave me this?" Mina reached into her pocket and held up the flimsy note that had been pinned to her wing.

Maude looked flustered but continued rummaging through the contents of the box. "No. No note. Put that away, dearie. You don't want to go drawing any more attention than you already have. But yes, it's true. I'm the person you're meant to see. I don't know who gave you that note, but you'd better disregard it. You made some enemies when you went and challenged Dale. That wasn't too smart," Maude scolded.

"Aha! Here it is!" she exclaimed as she pulled out a large, folded-up piece of paper.

"What is it?" Mina asked.

"This, my dear, is the map you'll need to get to the Sheep Spa." She motioned for Mina to come stand next to her. Mina took a spot at the side of Maude's chair and watched her as she unfolded the piece of paper. It was about the size of a small poster. Mina could tell the map was old. It had started to yellow, and it crackled as Maude opened it.

Spreading her arms out wide, Maude held the map up in front of her. Mina stared at it confused. The paper was blank. She bent over to look at the other side, but it was also blank.

"Now, let's see what we can figure out." Maude said with excitement.

"What do you mean?" asked Mina. "That's not a map. It's just a blank piece of oversized paper."

Maude continued to gaze at the map. "Patience, dearie. You've got to give the map a chance to warm up."

Mina was frustrated. She was tired of being lured in, only to be disappointed. This woman might know a few things about her, but probably the whole market did by now. Maude was clearly nuts, and Mina was done wasting time.

"That's just great. I hope you have fun with your invisible map. But I'm off to find a real map *out* of this insane asylum."

Maude looked up from her map as Mina walked out of the booth. "Child, you would do best not to be rude. That's no way to make friends and, believe me, you *don't* need any more enemies."

Maude looked back down at the map and began to speak but this time not to Mina. "Looks like you've got your work cut out for you with this one."

Mina had just reached the doorway and was ready to bolt when the woman looked up at her again. "Archangel Mina?

That's what you told Larry and Carla your name is, huh? That's funny."

Mina didn't know what to do. Part of her wanted to run but another part wanted to find out if the old woman really was crazy or not. She nodded.

"Well, I'm pleased to make your acquaintance. As you know, I'm Maude. This map here will be your guide, Captain Key. Though I'm not sure if Captain Key is a *real* captain or just a clever spirit who knows the lay of the land well enough. Come and take a look. The map is all warmed up now."

Mina gave in to her curiosity. She returned to the woman's side, and there on the spread-out piece of paper she saw big words flashing and scrolling across the sheet—five, ten, even twenty at a time. Mina read the words as they appeared. "That was absolutely the worst introduction I've ever received. You might as well have told her that I'm a disembodied sludge monster with a compass."

Maude replied, "See here, *Captain*, you're welcome to do your own introductions next time."

More words flashed. "Fine, I will! And maybe next time you could store me somewhere other than that steel box with all your blasted knitting yarn and half-finished blankets. It smells like mothballs in there, and it's about as stimulating as you'd imagine a box of yarn to be."

Mina's mouth dropped open. "There really is someone talking to you through that sheet of paper, isn't there?"

Maude smiled and nodded. "Oh yes, honey. I may be old, but I'm not old enough to be talking to a piece of paper that don't talk back." Maude gave her a little wink.

Mina felt bad for doubting Maude, but before she could summon the courage to apologize, words appeared on the paper that were addressed to her. "Hello, Mina. I take it you're planning to go to the Sheep Spa?"

Mina hesitated and then shrugged. She felt strange about

answering a question that hadn't been asked out loud, but she didn't want to be rude. "I don't know. I've never even heard of it before. I was supposed to be looking for someone who could help me get home. Then I found a message pinned to my wing that said I was in danger."

The paper lit up with a flurry of words again. "Yes, you *are* in danger. You should never have gotten involved with Dale. I will take you to the Sheep Spa, though. It's a safe place to go when you need to get away from the market. Nobody ever ventures that way."

Mina asked, "Why? What is it?"

Maude looked uncomfortable all of a sudden, and the paper remained blank. Finally, Maude said, "I guess you could say it's an animal hospital of sorts. Or at least it's where the domesticated animals are taken care of."

"Oh, I see," said Mina, but she had a feeling there was something else that Maude wasn't telling her.

Maude didn't say anything for a moment and then asked, "Mina, dear. I need you to do something for me while you're over there, okay?"

The request made Mina nervous, but she was curious to know what Maude had in mind. "What do you need me to do?" she asked.

Maude replied, "Well, you see, ever since Dale became mayor, there have been restrictions on what us sellers can and can't sell. It used to be that we could sell whatever we wanted, and this flexibility allowed anyone with even a little common sense to stay profitable."

Mina asked, "So Dale doesn't let you sell whatever you want?"

Maude looked sad. "No, he forces us to have permits to sell anything at all, and some of us are only allowed to sell one type of product. Take me. I can *only* sell plants. I'm not even allowed to sell things that come from plants like fruits and seeds."

Mina interrupted again. "But what about all those shops at the center of the market? They seem to sell everything."

Maude rolled her eyes. "Those are the shops that Dale basically owns. He lets those sellers do whatever they want because they give three-fifths of their earnings to him. The money is supposed to go towards the market's upkeep and maintenance, but nobody actually believes he uses it on anything but himself.

"It's not just those sellers that give him money, though. Every seller has to give some portion of their earnings to pay for the market's upkeep, but I'll tell you something! If *all* of that money was going towards upkeep and maintenance, then this whole market could've been rebuilt in the purest silver five times over already!"

Mina frowned. She understood why Maude was upset and wasn't at all surprised that Dale was cheating the sellers. However, she still didn't understand what Maude wanted from her. "I'm very sorry about all that," she said, "but what does it have to do with me?"

Maude smiled sweetly. "Nothing, really. I was just hoping that while you're at the Sheep Spa, you would inquire about getting the blueprints for a greenhouse. I have it on good authority that the spa is where they were last seen."

Mina couldn't imagine Maude building a greenhouse all by herself, even if she'd been fifty years younger with ten times as many muscles. "What do you need blueprints for?" she asked suspiciously.

Maude replied, "Well, Dale has also limited how much food can be brought to market, which has caused food prices to rise so high that we can barely afford to feed ourselves. There's a group of us sellers who've agreed to build a greenhouse so we can grow our *own* food."

Mina was puzzled. "But why don't you just use the same greenhouse that you grow your plants in?"

Maude scoffed, "Don't you get it, honey? Dale has control over that too. We aren't allowed to grow what we sell. We have to buy whatever *his* people grow at an already high price, then try to re-sell it here."

Mina put her hand on her forehead. "Wow! That *is* really bad."

"Then you'll help us?" Maude asked.

Mina thought about it and asked, "Are you sure I won't get into any trouble if I bring you the blueprints?"

Maude shook her head. "Dearie, you're already in as much trouble as you can be in with Dale. But don't worry about him. Captain Key will keep you safe for now. And if you find those blueprints and bring them to me, not only do I promise to keep you out of trouble, but I'll make sure you get to go straight home too."

Mina's heart did a somersault at the mention of home. She studied Maude's face, trying to decide if she should believe her promise. After all, how was this old woman going to help Mina with something as complicated as finding her way home?

Maude seemed to guess at what Mina was thinking. "Oh, I know I don't look like much anymore, but I happen to know the inner workings of this world better than anyone. I was the first person here, so I've had plenty of time to figure it all out."

"You were the first person here?" Mina asked surprised.

Maude laughed. "What's wrong? Don't I look old enough to have been the first person here?"

Mina stammered, "Yes. Well, what I mean is, ummm, no...?"

"That's alright. I don't take offense to looking my age. I'm proud I was the first person here. It means I know all the secrets there are to know, and I promise I'll use them to get you home. All you have to do is get those blueprints for me. We have a deal?"

Mina decided to believe Maude's promise, for no other reason than she desperately wanted for it to be real. The task sounded simple enough. She would leave the danger of the market behind, find the blueprints ·at the Sheep Spa, and then return quickly so that Maude would fulfill her end of the bargain and send her home. It would be a cinch, probably.

Words appeared on the paper again. "Warn her, Maude."

"What does that mean? Warn me of what?" Mina asked.

Maude answered, "You aren't the first angel I've sent to look for the blueprints. There was another one named Fred. He went searching for them a while back but never returned."

Mina's sense of unease began to grow again. "Carla and Larry told me about Fred. What happened to him?"

Maude stared at the blank map, as though waiting to see if it would give her the answer. Finally, she said, "I don't know. Captain Key was with Fred right before he reached his destination, but a big wind came out of nowhere and blew the map away.

"We don't know what happened to him after that. Probably nothing good. But look here, if you listen to everything that Captain Key tells you, and you stay away from the Darkside of the Moon, then the captain can protect you. Understand?"

Mina had no objection to staying away from the Darkside. "Don't worry. I have no desire to go anywhere near there," she said. This new information about Fred frightened her, but the thought of going home was so thrilling that she wasn't willing to be scared off so easily.

Maude shook her head. "The problem, dearie, is that it's not a *there* exactly. The light and the dark move. If you aren't careful not to get lost, you can get dragged into the darkness without meaning to."

Mina was confused. "Wait. If the light and dark move like day and night, then why doesn't the market ever get dark?"

"Simple. The marketplace moves too. Nearly all the land here was built on top of what we call *drifting land.* Once upon a time, so the story goes, the first Moon Walkers dug up all the dirt in the best spots and installed giant metal discs deep below the soil. The discs rotate with the help of a complex system of wheels and conveyor belts.

"The drifting land was designed to keep large parts of the Moon in the light and other parts in the dark. We call these areas the Dayside and the Darkside. The whole intertwined contraption runs on a kind of timer, which means we're always being pulled very slowly away from the dark."

"Or towards it…" appeared the words on the map.

Maude smiled. "Right. Or towards it."

Mina asked, "Were you one of the first Moon Walkers?"

Maude laughed. "Oh, heavens, no. I'm not *that* old. The Moon Walkers were here before all of us and were long gone by the time I arrived. We can't get into all that right now, though. I'm sure Captain Key will tell you anything else you need to know on the way to the Sheep Spa."

Mina felt a chill run down her spine. Clearly, these Moon Walkers had gone to great lengths to keep the light and dark separate, and Mina couldn't help but wonder what they'd been afraid of out there, beyond the veil of darkness.

Words scrolled across the paper again. "Mina, I promise to keep you a safe distance from the darkness, but *you* must promise to follow my directions. If there's a decision to be made, we'll make it together. I know it's not ideal to have to communicate with a piece of paper, but it's of the utmost importance that you take me seriously and never make the mistake of ignoring my advice."

Mina felt a bit sorry for Captain Key. It occurred to her that the captain had probably had a difficult time being taken seriously as a piece of paper. She nodded her head. "Okay. I promise." It was an easy promise to make. She was relieved not to be alone anymore, at least not in theory.

Maude, who seemed to be mulling something over, added, "Look, I don't expect you'll have to worry about this, but just in case you *do* end up on the Darkside, remember to talk as much as possible and stay alert. You can sing if you run out of things to say; you just don't want to get trapped in your own thoughts. Captain Key won't be able to pull you out of them if you do."

All these warnings were taking a toll on Mina, but she still wasn't willing to back down, so she nodded once more in agreement.

"Good," said Maude as she stood up. "Now that's settled, it's time for you to get some food." She pulled out a knit tote bag from beneath her seat cushion. Then she held the map up away from Mina and smiled at it. "Okay, Captain Key. Take good care of yourself out there and watch out for our girl. I have all the confidence in the world that you two will do great." Then she hesitated for just a moment before folding the map up and placing it inside the tote bag.

Maude pointed to the end of the row. "Follow the row that way. Then head two rows over, away from the market center. When you arrive, ask anyone in the first few booths for some food. It doesn't matter which side you choose. Just show them your bag, and tell them I sent you. And don't pay any mind to their nonsense. Most of them have fewer reasoning skills than a dung beetle. Just take what you can carry, and be on your way. Oh, and make sure not to eat any of the food until you've left the market."

"You aren't coming with me to get the food?" Mina asked. The thought of asking strangers for food made her uncomfortable.

"No, dearie. I can't leave my booth. There are people

who'd notice, and someone would surely rat me out. You'll be in good hands, though. After you've picked up some food, exit the market by walking along the ends of the last few rows until you've passed them all. You're less likely to be caught going that way. There aren't any booths on the last row, so chances are nobody will see you leaving from there. Then once you're at a safe distance, pull out the map and wait for the captain to give you further instructions."

Mina's stomach churned. She'd felt safe in Maude's booth, and now that it was time to leave, she realized she didn't want to go. "But how will I know if it's okay to return? I mean, couldn't it put me in danger? What if Dale's guards find me? Then what do I do?"

"There, there." Maude rested her hand on Mina's shoulder and gave it a squeeze. "You'll be alright. Just keep moving and try not to worry so much about those mistakes of yours. They don't always mean what you think they do."

Mina sighed. She knew she had no choice but to go. She'd be letting Maude down if she didn't get the blueprints for the greenhouse. And if Maude was unhappy with her, then who would help her get home?

"Okay," Mina said as she pushed her wings and shoulders back, steeling herself for what she was about to do.

"Atta girl. I know you won't disappoint us."

Mina lingered. "But what if I'm not brave enough to do this?"

Maude looked at her sternly. "You need to stop that now, you hear? After all, a lost pocket watch is only useful when it's not lost. Which is to say, courage only works when you remember to use it. It doesn't do *anyone* any good to be brave but then never act like it. It's like being good-looking but then never bothering to brush your hair."

Maude softened a little. "You'll do fine. You've just got to believe it. Captain Key will keep you on the straight and narrow, but you need to depend on yourself just as much as you depend on the map. Got it?"

Mina thought this was the strangest pep talk she'd ever heard, but then again, the Moon was proving to be the strangest place she'd ever been. Everything seemed familiar but far away and cloudy too—like a faded memory. Maude walked Mina to the exit and patted her on the shoulder. "Good luck, Mina. I have faith that you'll do what's expected of you. Now, off you go."

Maude walked back behind the counter and propped herself up on her elbows between two small succulents so she could watch Mina make her way down the aisle. Mina looked back a few times for reassurance, and Maude smiled and nodded to encourage her along. Finally, after a few minutes, Mina disappeared from view, and Maude whispered, "Oh, dear me. Ruth's prophecy better be right, or heaven help us all!"

CHAPTER 13

THE VEGETABLE PEDDLERS

Mina found the vegetable aisle without any trouble. There were several booths on each side brimming with all different kinds of vegetables. The produce was laid out on the counters and piled high on tables inside the booths. In addition, there were giant wooden cutouts of vegetables which had been painted brightly and nailed to the tops of the stalls.

Mina glanced around at the vegetable signs. There was no denying they were creepy. They had been created as human-vegetable hybrids—vegetables that had faces, arms, and legs. What was disturbing, however, was that their faces made them look as if they had spawned from pure evil. It seemed as though someone had intended for the vegetables to have happy, smiling faces but had gotten overzealous with the paint. The result was that the vegetable people had frighteningly large eyes and exaggerated smiles. Mina thought they looked like they belonged in a horror film about healthy living gone wrong.

She stood between each side of the aisle, feeling much too shy to ask for free vegetables. While she was working up her nerve, an old, bald man, who looked like he could've been a lumberjack in his younger days, stood up inside the first booth on the right and banged his head on a low-hung, wooden carrot.

The old man roared in pain, and Mina took a few steps back, worried what might come next. The man grabbed his sore head with one large hand and ripped the carrot sign from the top of his booth with the other. He grunted angrily and flung the sign towards the booth across the way.

The ecstatically demonic carrot smashed into the first booth on Mina's left, causing several eggplants and potatoes to roll off the pile of vegetables and onto the ground. The carrot landed facedown. Mina looked at the bald man who'd thrown the carrot and saw that he was staring straight ahead, huffing and puffing while holding his head in pain.

A short man with gray hair jumped up from behind the counter that had been struck. Then several other old men and a couple of middle-aged women stood up inside their booths to see where all the commotion was coming from. The short man in the booth on the left yelled across to the bald man on the right. "What's the meaning of this, Monty!? You trying to cause a ruckus?" he asked as he walked around to the front of his booth.

The bald man, Monty, sneered at the gray-haired man. "You're the only one causing a ruckus around here, you old geezer. I can hear you just fine without you *yelling*."

The short, old man bent down to pick up the vegetables that had rolled from the counter, but when he saw the carrot sign, he ignored the potatoes and eggplants and flew towards the sign. He grabbed it with both hands and raised it above his head like a trophy. Triumphantly, he exclaimed, "It's mine!" Then he hugged the carrot to his chest and spoke to it. "I've missed you, old friend. I promise I'll never let that ugly, old coot take you away again."

Monty shook his head in disgust. "You can have it," he said. "I don't even sell carrots no more, and I'm tired of people always crying over false advertising. *Boo-hoo this* and *boo-hoo that.* I sell vegetables, don't I? And carrots a vegetable, ain't it?"

The gray-haired, old man shot back (again too loudly), "I don't need your permission. This carrot was mine, and you *stole* it!"

Monty banged his fist on his counter and then pointed at the man. "Stop that right now, Wilbur! I didn't steal nothing from you. You gave that stupid carrot to Maude when you thought you might have a chance with her, and I bought it from her fair and square after she decided she didn't want it no more."

Everyone on the right side of the row nodded in agreement and there were a few *mm-hmms.* The folks on the left side, however, shook their heads and grumbled under their breath. A little, old lady with purple hair leaned out of her booth and called over to Monty. "Why don't you just leave the man alone! Let him enjoy his carrot in peace for goodness' sake!" she shouted. But the men ignored her.

"That ain't true! Maude would never have sold this carrot. She loved it," retorted Wilbur.

"Oh, really?" Monty asked. "Have you asked her about it then?"

Mina could see that this question had made Wilbur sad. He looked away from Monty. "No," he said. "We don't talk no more. Not since she got herself reassigned to the vine section."

Feeling the need to break the tension, Mina jumped in. She held up the knit tote bag Maude had given her and said, "Excuse me everyone, but I've just come from Maude. And she told me to ask you all…well, that is to say, to ask if you could spare some of your vegetables."

The two old men jumped when Mina began to speak,

visibly startled by her presence. Monty said to her, "Good heavens, angel! Where did you come from?"

"Well, sir, as I've just stated, I've come from Maude's, but I've been standing here for a while. Didn't you see me?"

Monty shook his head. "No, I guess not."

Wilbur walked over to Mina and took her by the arm while continuing to clutch the satanic carrot to his chest. "Tell me, angel. Is Maude well? Did she tell you to come to me for all your vegetable needs?"

Mina felt bad telling Wilbur the truth since it was obvious that he harbored a deep affection for Maude. So she decided to fib a little. "Yes, Mr. Wilbur, Maude is well. She said you could help me out."

The sadness in Wilbur's eyes suddenly lifted, replaced by a brightness that Mina recognized as hope. "Well, that's just splendid! I can help you out indeed! Come over here, angel!" Wilbur pulled Mina closer to his booth, nearly stepping on one of the eggplants that had rolled to the ground.

Wilbur bent down to pick it up along with the other eggplant and potatoes, and Mina leaned over to help him. When she stood again, she began to put a couple of the potatoes in her tote bag, but Wilbur stopped her. "Oh no, you don't want those. There are plenty of clean vegetables you can have instead. If you got even a few particles of this dirt in your mouth, it would turn your piehole so dry, it would suck the enamel right off them pearly whites. And we can't have that!"

Mina giggled. "I know what you mean. I had a nasty experience with Moon dirt after I first arrived. My tongue *still* tastes like metallic sandpaper," and Mina smacked her tongue against the roof of her mouth to see if she'd regained any normal sense of taste. *Nope,* she thought.

Wilbur tilted his head. "Moon dirt? What's that?"

Mina realized her mistake and tried to cover. "Oh, I meant to say Earth dirt. Or just regular dirt. Or just dirt, I guess."

Wilbur looked at Mina funny but then shrugged it off. "Okay, well any friend of Maude's is a friend of mine. Feel free to take whatever suits your fancy over here on our side of the aisle," he said as he spread his arms out towards the booths on the left side of the row.

Monty called over, "And when nothing over there *suits your fancy*, you can come to our side and pick out some vegetables that *don't* taste like a muddy pig's hind quarters." This got the vegetable peddlers on the right side laughing and hollering in agreement.

Wilbur's face turned bright red, and he looked like he might march over to Monty and punch him right in the nose. Through gritted teeth, he said, "I'll have you know that *our* vegetables are the finest grown. They're even juicier than most fruits! And only a thick-skulled imbecile *like you* would know what a muddy swine's hiney tastes like!" Now, all the vendors on Wilbur's side snickered and laughed. Mina didn't like where the old men's conversation was headed, and she wondered if she should just take some vegetables and go.

Monty fired back at Wilbur, "Your vegetables aren't juicy *or* delicious, and the only fruits they'd stand a chance against are rotten ones. But even that's pushing it! And you know what else? Your side smells like a stink bomb went off inside of a gym sock, and I know that for a *fact* because it smelled like that when it used to be *our* side! It's the reason we swindled you into trading places!" Monty gave a firm nod.

A wicked grin spread across Wilbur's face. "Well, funny thing is that it hasn't smelled like that since all of you left. And I'm personally of the mind to think that it ain't no coincidence!"

Monty was done talking. With his giant hands, he ripped a maniacal squash and a devilish, brown tuber sign from the top of his booth and hurled them at Wilbur's head, one at a time.

Wilbur held up his demonic carrot like a shield to prevent

the deranged vegetables from striking him in the face. The giant squash flew into Wilbur's carrot shield first without incident. However, when the tuber projectile hit Wilbur's carrot, it knocked the shield back into his forehead and created a small gash above his left eyebrow.

Wilbur lowered the insane-looking carrot and brought the tips of his fingers to his forehead. He inspected his fingers, and upon seeing two tiny drops of blood, he cried out, "This is war!"

Mina couldn't believe what was happening. Suddenly, all these respectable-looking men and women were climbing up on chairs and on top of counters, ripping off the large wooden vegetable signs that decorated their booths. Hurling them across the aisle at each other, they yelled things like "Kaboom! How's an onion to that arthritic knee feel, Mildred!?" and "Suck veggie splinters, losers!" and "Pow! Eggplant to the face, Arthur!"

Watching the fight unfold reminded Mina of a terrible encounter she'd had at the zoo once when she witnessed two groups of monkeys throwing their feces at each other. It had been undignified and appalling and completely nonsensical, just like the scene playing out in front of her now. And just like the encounter at the zoo, Mina wanted to get as far away from the fighting as quickly as possible. Especially now that some of the geriatric, male warriors had begun to remove their shirts.

Mina was thinking about what she should do next when she noticed a woman exit her booth on the left side of the row. It was the woman with purple hair that had defended Wilbur earlier. The woman walked to the center of the row and raised her arms above her head in what seemed like a call for peace. "What are you all doing?" she asked in a frail voice. "Every one of you sells the *same* vegetables! From the *same* field!"

A shriveled old man, who had liver spots covering half his

face, yelled, "Lies! Our vegetables are grown in richer soil than theirs!"

Right then a spiteful broccoli hit the woman in the shins, and her legs flew out from under her. Mina was horrified. She couldn't believe someone would do such a thing to a defenseless, old lady. She quickly ran to help the woman, dodging the flying vegetable signs as she went. "Are you okay?" she asked once she'd reached her.

The woman had already started to get back up, and Mina took her hand to provide extra support. "Yes. I think so. But I'm tired of all this stupid fighting. This happens almost every day. Well, maybe not *this* exactly. Usually, they toss real vegetables at each other. They never seem to learn that it don't accomplish nothing, except to shoo away the customers!"

Mina smiled sympathetically at the petite, purple-haired woman. Up close, she could see how fragile the woman really was. She thought by the look of her that she might be in her nineties. "Let me help you back to your booth. I'd hate for you to take a hit like that again," she said as she gently took the woman by the arm and escorted her back to her booth.

When the woman was seated safely behind her counter, she spoke again. "My name's Ruth. I'm Maude's best friend. Well, more like a second mother to her really. Or even a first, seeing as how she don't remember her mother and all."

Mina tried not to laugh. "A mother to her? Really? You can't be more than ten years older than her."

Ruth smiled brightly. "Well, you know it seems that way, but when I first got here, she looked much younger. Nobody knows how old she is really. I reckon she was up here all alone for a pretty long while before any of the rest of us showed up and started trying to keep track of time."

"Hold on a second," Mina said, feeling confused. "Are you telling me that Maude really was the first one on the Moon then? I mean the Earth?"

"Oh, hon. You don't need to act dumb for me. I know we on the Moon, just like you do, but I suspect Captain Key will clear all that up for you soon. All you need to know now is that everybody up here ages differently. Those of us who traveled here, well, we had our clocks taken away when we crossed the neon bridge. We don't ever get any older. But the few who was born here, they age based on Moon time. And Maude's back to being one of them now."

Mina was fascinated. The first thing she could think of to ask was, "What's the neon bridge?"

Ruth nodded. "Like I said, Captain Key will explain what needs explaining."

All of a sudden, the leafy end of a leek grazed the side of Mina's face, startling her. Luckily, it was a real leek instead of a wooden one. She squatted to the ground in front of Ruth to avoid getting hit by something more serious like the spiky end of an artichoke.

"You'll have to forgive the lack of hospitality from these dang, old fools. Please take whatever you want from my vegetable stand. It really does all taste the same, and it ain't doing me no good just sitting there never getting bought."

Mina asked, "You mean you *never* sell your vegetables?"

Ruth replied, "Well, not *never* but almost never. People here don't really make their own food. They go to the other side of the market and buy a fully-cooked meal."

"Oh, I see," said Mina, "but then where do the peddlers on the other side get the ingredients to make the prepared meals?"

Ruth scoffed, "Doofus Dale sells everything directly to them just like he does us. Nobody in the entire market has any control over what they sell, except maybe those fat cats in the market center. Though probably not them neither. I think they just don't care 'cause they make enough of a living anyway."

Mina nodded. "I'm sorry things are so tough, but then why doesn't anyone stand up to Dale?"

Ruth smiled a knowing smile. "Maude's got you chasing them blueprints for the greenhouse, don't she?"

"Oh, I get it," said Mina. "If you all are able to build a greenhouse, then Dale won't have so much control over you anymore. But won't that make him mad?"

"I sure hope so. But look at it this way, there ain't nothing keeping him in power, except everybody agreeing that he's in charge of all of us. If we can show people that we don't need him, then maybe more people would stop thinking he's in charge. You'd be surprised how many people around here are unhappy with the way they've been treated."

Mina nodded. "Well that certainly seems to be the case on this side of the market. Nobody over here even seems like they're really trying to sell anything."

Ruth laughed. "That's 'cause we got the worst of it over here. Not only does nobody have any say over what they sell, but nobody's allowed to be creative neither. Let's say, for instance, you sell plants like Maude. Well, you'd think to help the plants sell you'd be allowed to sell fancy pots or funny garden gnomes to make people wanna garden. But nope! Over here, you sell what you sell, and you sell it the same as you buy it. We ain't hardly allowed to do anything but watch our unsold vegetables sit and rot all day long."

Mina asked, "And over there? On the other side of the market?"

Ruth slapped her knee. "Well, they've got things dandy over there, let me tell you! Mind you, they sell what they been told to also. But at least they get to do it whatever way they want. You given vegetables to sell, you can make vegetable soup. You given clay to sell, you can make pottery and jewelry. You given metal to sell, well hot diggity-dog! You can practically make whatever you want to sell!"

Mina thought she understood, but just to be sure, she

asked, "So the peddlers over there like their jobs more because they can make things to sell?"

Ruth nodded. "It's true, yes, but don't be fooled. They ain't free neither, and deep down, they know it." Ruth paused and seemed to be thinking hard about something, as if she were trying to make a decision.

Then she said, "I'll make it as clear as I can, and then I won't say no more. There are some of them—there on the other side of the market—that'd like to see them blueprints mighty bad too." Ruth smiled slyly and gave Mina a wink.

Suddenly, Mina realized she'd agreed to be a part of something much bigger than helping a few old vendors grow their own food. She felt a bit nervous, but she was excited too. She thought maybe the blueprints really would be her ticket home if they were *this* important.

Ruth gestured towards the vegetables splayed across the counter of her booth. "Go ahead and take as much as you want, dear angel. It's time you be on your way now. You have a big journey ahead and many folks counting on you. Listen to the map and you won't go wrong."

Mina took Ruth up on her offer and scooted right below the inside counter. From the loud thuds outside the booth, she could tell the vegetable fight was still underway. She slowly raised her hand up and felt around until she grabbed hold of a potato. She pulled it from the pile, careful not to cause a vegetable avalanche. Then she grabbed two more potatoes, a yam, some celery, a couple of carrots, and a yellow squash and dropped them into her bag too.

Ruth said, "Better take a cucumber. They're always good to have in case you get into a pickle. Get it? Cucumber? *Pickle?*" She laughed.

Mina thought the joke must have seemed funnier to Ruth because she was a vegetable peddler, but she gave her a courtesy laugh to be polite. Then she took a cucumber she'd seen at the top of the pile and began inching towards the door, preparing to leave. "Thank you for the vegetables," she said to Ruth before she went. "It was nice meeting you. I sure hope I'm able to bring back those blueprints for everyone."

"It was nice to meet you too, young angel. Don't fret about those blueprints. It's the rest of the journey you'll have to worry about." She smiled a tired smile, but Mina thought she detected something else in her expression—something foreboding. Ruth continued, "After all, I've never met an angel who could resist doing the right thing."

Mina didn't know what Ruth meant by this, but the way she said it gave Mina the chills. She nodded, but Ruth had closed her eyes and was rocking slowly in her chair. Then, suddenly, Ruth sat straight up and opened her eyes like she'd been shocked back to life. Mina jumped with fright.

"One more thing! I almost forgot!" Ruth exclaimed, and she pulled out a note from beneath her seat cushion. She held it up for a moment and then tossed it towards the exit where Mina was kneeling.

Mina picked up the note and opened it. It was written exactly like the one that had been pinned to her wing—on top of a faded note, printed in neat black ink. It read:

> *Dayside Dale & Darkside Dan.*
> *Alas, the two are twins.*
> *Portly and sour, they both are,*
> *But that's not where it ends.*
>
> *Gemini was in retrograde*
> *When they were being born.*
> *It made them bad and truly mad,*
> *And filled them full of scorn.*

When they were young, they pleased no one.
Not even 'ole mom and dad.
But they grew tall and destroyed it all,
Crowing, "Look at what you had!"

"Darkside Dan?! Dale has a twin brother?" Mina gasped. She shuddered at the thought of there being *two* men as repulsive as Dale. She looked back at Ruth, but Ruth's eyes were closed again. It appeared she had fallen asleep. Her head hung to the side awkwardly with her mouth slightly ajar, and snores rumbled from her nostrils like tiny trains passing through a tunnel.

Mina thought about waking her to ask who she'd gotten the note from. She was sure it had been written by the same person who'd pinned the note to her wing. However, Mina felt it would be wrong to disturb Ruth, so she decided to solve the mystery later. She crawled out of the booth backwards while tugging the veggie-filled tote along in front of her.

It sounded like the sign tossing had slowed down, and there was less shouting between the peddlers too. Mina stood up cautiously and looked around. It was clear that Monty's side had been victorious. There were dozens of vegetable signs stacked up in front of the booths on his side of the aisle, whereas the peddlers on Wilbur's side were quickly collecting the few signs they had left.

A fat, old man dressed in all white, who reminded Mina of a turnip, picked up a malevolent beet and leaned back to throw it across the aisle. Wilbur hurried over and grabbed the man's arm before he could let go of the sign. "No, Cosmo! We've lost this battle. Let's at least hold on to the few signs we still got. Otherwise, we won't have any way to advertise on our side. You see?"

Wilbur sounded sad and demoralized. Mina approached

him. "I have to get going now, Mr. Wilbur, but I wanted to thank you for your generous offer when I first arrived."

Wilbur seemed surprised again by Mina's presence. He looked at her and saw the filled tote bag hanging from her shoulder. "Oh! Well, I'm glad you were able to find something you wanted."

Mina smiled. "Yes, I did. Miss Ruth helped me out."

"Good, good. Well, I'm afraid we have lots of work to do to repair our storefront image again," he said, looking around at the splintered booths and dinged up signs. "It'll probably be ages before we get any new customers. I mean, who'd ever go shopping at booths as run-down looking as these?"

Mina didn't know if it was her place to give Wilbur a proper answer, but she felt like offering him a sliver of hope before heading on her way. "Mr. Wilbur, I don't mean to tell you how to do your job, but it seems to me that if the peddlers on your side and the peddlers on Mr. Monty's side worked together, instead of treating each other like competition, then everyone would be a lot happier."

Wilbur shrugged his shoulders and let out a sigh. "It's good of you to imagine that such a friendship could exist, but we've tried to do it that way before, and it doesn't work."

"Why doesn't it work?" Mina asked.

Wilbur said in a grouchy tone, "Because the peddlers on that side are stodgy and old and only want to do things *their* way. They refuse to listen to what *we* want."

"But, Mr. Wilbur, wouldn't it be better to listen to what your customers want? Don't you think you'd be more successful that way?"

Wilbur nodded and looked off into the distance, as if he were slipping into a daydream. "Yes, yes. The customers are wonderful and always right. We live to serve the customers. Too bad they don't know what they want. Truly, it's a burden on us peddlers to have to figure it out ourselves."

Mina could see that her attempt to help was going nowhere. She patted Wilbur's shoulder gently as he continued to stare off into space. "Goodbye, then, Mr. Wilbur."

Wilbur shook himself from his daze and looked towards Mina as she walked away. "Oh right. Goodbye, then, young angel. And safe travels to you!"

The last thing Mina heard before she turned the corner was Monty barking at Wilbur, "Who on Earth were you talking to?" And Wilbur responding, "I'm not sure, but I think it may have been a ghost from my childhood."

CHAPTER 14

THE BETRAYAL

"There is no worse lie than a truth misunderstood..."

– William James

Nothing was written down. Instead, the lunar wolves passed their history from old to young through a complex story-telling tradition. When the Moon Travelers began to arrive, the wolves decided it would be best to keep their stories to themselves. They didn't feel the visitors could be trusted with such important knowledge. Besides, it wasn't the visitors' history anyway, so the wolves told themselves that there was no reason to concern them with it.

Nevertheless, it was eventually revealed that the lunar wolves had hidden what they knew about the Moon's past and its original inhabitants. Their stories had been entrusted to a young girl named Helen. A girl the lunar wolves considered one of their own. However, the stories' existence was revealed by someone else, someone the wolves loathed. A vindictive, angry mortal who'd made enemies with the wolves.

The revelation that the wolves had been hiding knowledge

from the Moon Travelers was used as a tactic to turn the humans' hearts against the wolves. For many cycles, the Travelers and wolves had lived on the Moon with little conflict. But when the Travelers found out that the lunar wolves had kept secrets from them, they turned on the wolves immediately.

Instead of trying to understand the wolves' motives, the Travelers lashed out at their former friends. They called them "despicable traitors!" and "horrid beasts!" and barred them from entering the city's boundaries. When that wasn't enough to satisfy their new hatred, they formed mobs to hunt down and kill the wolves.

Several of the Moon Travelers tried to intervene on behalf of their old friends. They asked the people to give the wolves a chance to explain themselves. Unfortunately, most of the Travelers had already grown to hate the wolves. They'd been led to believe that the wolves had withheld knowledge that should have rightfully belonged to the humans—since *they* were the superior beings. They were told that this knowledge would confirm their fantasies about the giant bones that had been found in the tunnel.

Again and again, the lies were repeated. "The wolves betrayed us! They had no right to keep this information secret! What they've done is unforgivable! The only just punishment is death!" And once the people had heard all of it enough times, it didn't matter whether the lies were true or made any sense. The people had been conditioned to hate the wolves, and this type of hate deafens the mind to reason and blinds the heart to compassion.

Before the Travelers first arrived, the mystical wolf creatures had prospered for over a hundred thousand journeys around the Earth. Thousands of silver and white wolves had crisscrossed over the highlands and lowlands of the lunar terrain, honoring the Great Energy and practicing what the Moon Walkers had taught them.

After the visitors turned on them, there were only a few dozen wolves left. The survivors had no choice but to move underground into the massive web of subterranean tunnels on the Darkside. It was safe there because the labyrinth of deep underground tunnels was the only location on the Moon that the Travelers never dared to set foot.

The wolf executions were a tragedy on many levels, but especially because of how preventable they were. The problem was that the Moon Travelers were never given the full story. They were never told that most of the knowledge that was kept from them had nothing to do with the bones they'd found in the tunnel—and that certainly none of it confirmed their fabricated beliefs regarding the origins of the remains. Either of these truths would have had the power to change everything.

Yet the Traveler's ignorance was far from innocent. If the Travelers had stopped to question what they were told, it could have prevented great suffering. If the Travelers hadn't become so self-righteous, they might have been concerned as to why the wolves never bargained or begged for their lives. And if the Travelers hadn't been so close-minded, they might have realized that the wolves' stories contained knowledge that was worth dying to protect.

But since this is not how the Moon Travelers were, everyone paid the price.

∞∞∞∞

As Mina strolled past the last few rows on her way out of the market, she looked for the live music and cheering crowd she had heard ever since she first arrived. Larry and Carla had mentioned a concert on the other side of the market, but so far, she'd seen no signs of one. As she scanned the rows she passed, it occurred to her that no matter where she'd been in the market, the concert had always sounded like it was about the same distance away. Just a few rows off from wherever she was.

Maybe, she thought, *it's a moving stage. Like a parade float.* But that didn't seem right, seeing as how the rows weren't wide enough for even a small stage to move between. Then a weird idea crossed her mind. *What if there isn't a concert at all? What if the music and crowd noise are being played through hidden speakers to make everyone feel like they're always a short distance from something exciting?*

She decided that this had to be it, but she wondered why anyone would bother to do that. *This place is full of mysteries*, she thought as she approached the last row. *I think I could spend the rest of my life trying to figure out how it works.*

She was just about to make her way through the exit when she saw three men in light blue suits approaching her from the middle of the last row. They were creeping slowly towards her, as though they were stalking wild prey. Mina clutched the tote bag to her stomach. For a second, she thought about running back to Maude's, but she knew she'd be putting Maude in danger if she did. So she did the only other thing she could think of and dashed through the exit. The men chased after her.

Mina knew she couldn't outrun them for long. She was smaller and had a bag of vegetables weighing her down. However, this gave her an idea. She took out a yam, turned halfway around, and threw it at the men behind her. "Oof!" cried one of the guards. Mina knew she'd made a direct hit. She reached into her bag and took out a large potato. She was ready to throw it, but when she turned halfway around again, she realized she was no longer being chased. The men were retreating back to the market.

That's odd, Mina thought. *Did I really get rid of them with one little yam?* But then Mina noticed that off to the side of the exit were two guards sitting behind a metal desk, just like the two she'd met on the other side of the market. *Maybe the men in blue didn't want any witnesses,* she thought. She slowed her pace. She wasn't sure if she was headed in the right direction, but she knew it wasn't safe to stop yet. She thought it would be better to get as far away from the market as possible in case the men changed their minds.

After what seemed like a very long way, she finally grew weary and decided to stop. When she turned around to check that there was no one behind her, she was surprised to find the market at a higher elevation than her current spot. It was sitting atop of a hill about a mile away. "Well, that explains why the jog was so easy," she said to herself.

She stared at the market a while longer and noticed how it glittered with excitement. Mina thought that anyone who saw it from a distance like this would be drawn to it the same way she was when she first arrived. *Surely it has to be the most alluring market that's ever existed. It shines like a beacon of light from every angle.*

She sat cross-legged on the ground. *Too bad it's not as nice on the inside. The Welcoming Committee should tell visitors that when they arrive. Or at least someone should warn them that they're in for a rude awakening,* she thought. And she imagined herself hammering signs into the ground, all around the market, that read: "Outsiders Beware!" "Mind the Flying Vegetables!" "Keep Away from Swelter Vines!" "Crazy Mayor on the Loose!"

Mina dumped the contents of her tote bag into her lap. Potatoes, celery, carrots, squash, the cucumber Ruth had suggested for good measure, and the map. Mina still hadn't grown accustomed to the idea of talking to the map, and she felt awkward now that it was time to start again. *Better just dive in,* she thought, and she laid the large piece of paper out in front of her.

Almost a minute passed, and nothing happened. Mina wondered if she needed to say something first. "Hello, Captain Key. Are you there?"

Still nothing. Then words appeared across the page so faint they were almost illegible, "Hello, Mina. I need a moment to stretch out and get going again. It was very cramped under all those heavy vegetables."

Mina didn't understand the science, magic, or whatever it was that made the map work and felt bad for having inconvenienced the captain. "I'm sorry. I didn't realize that the vegetables could hurt you. I can place you on top next time if you'd like."

"No. It's alright. I'm only teasing. I was actually tending to something else a minute ago. However, I'd rather you keep the map handy now that we're free from the watchful eyes of the market. Do you think you could carry it from now on? We certainly don't need to talk all the time, but it would be safer if we at least have the option to communicate at a second's notice."

Mina nodded. "Of course. We can start heading for the Sheep Spa in a minute, but I think I better eat some of this celery first. I'm not hungry. I just feel like I need to replenish my energy. It's like I've been awake for days."

Captain Key responded, "It's *no wonder* you feel that way, Mina. After all, you've been here for over seventy-two Earth hours."

"Seventy-two hours? How is that possible? I haven't slept or eaten the whole time I've been here!"

Captain Key's words scrolled quickly across the map. "Well, I sense you're starting to realize this on your own, but this place isn't much like Earth. We live within a different realm of existence here. Moon Travelers don't actually need food or water to survive on the Moon. They choose to eat because it keeps them from feeling out of sorts. You should go ahead and eat for the same reason. You'll adjust better if you do the things that help you feel normal."

The captain was right. Mina *had* begun to realize that

something was off about the Moon. Nothing felt the same. Time, hunger, and even temperature were now foreign concepts. They still existed but not in the way Mina recognized from home.

She asked, "But if the Moon Travelers don't need to eat, then why do Maude and the other sellers want to grow their own food?"

Captain Key replied, "Like I said, they eat for other reasons than to survive."

Mina wondered if there was more to this explanation, but there was something else she'd been dying to know, so she moved on. "Who're all those people in the market, and why do they seem so out of it?"

Captain Key answered, "Oh, you haven't guessed? How funny. I was sure you would have figured it out."

The captain's words bothered Mina. She felt as though she'd failed to solve an easy math equation. She asked, "Can I try to figure it out before you tell me?"

"Go ahead." The captain's answer scrolled across the map.

Mina thought for a second and then answered, "The people in the market are people who have traveled here from Earth. Is that correct?"

"Very good, Mina. And can you guess why the people seem so confused? Why they never leave the market?"

Mina had to think about this question for a while. It was difficult to know in a place like this what was probable and what was absurd. Finally, Mina landed on the simplest of all the ideas she could come up with. "Are they under a spell?" she asked.

"That's funny," replied the captain. "Yes, I guess it *is* kind of like a spell. Suffice to say, the Moon Travelers have been drinking water that they shouldn't be drinking. When the Travelers first arrived, there wasn't any water available to them and hardly any food. But that was okay. The lunar wolves were happy to share their food, which was very generous since the Travelers didn't need the food to live, and the wolves did. It was the wolves' way of helping the visitors feel more comfortable."

"Wow!" said Mina. "I didn't even know there were wolves on the Moon."

"Yes, although not as many as there used to be. But I will save that story for another time. For now, I will only tell you about the Moon Travelers. Maude and her husband, Bob, arrived on the Moon first. The others, who came later, needed help getting here.

"By the time Bob arrived, there were many Travelers trapped on the same platform where you found your wings. Bob traveled here using a rocket-pack and—"

Mina interrupted. "Oh, so that's what Maude was referring to. The shooting star? Bob was the man strapped to the rocket-pack, right?"

"Right, Mina," replied Captain Key. "When Bob flew here, he noticed a dark bridge hiding in outer space between the Earth and Moon. The bridge was so dark that the people on the platform couldn't differentiate between the bridge and the darkness around it. They had no idea it existed, even though it was right in front of them.

"Bob and Maude created a chemical compound to illuminate the bridge in blue neon light. It did the trick. Once the stranded Travelers could see the bridge, they used it to cross over to the Moon. And over time, thousands of Moon Travelers crossed that bridge.

"When I was young, my family and I would go to greet the Travelers whenever new ones arrived. We brought them food and gifts, just like the wolves had done for the first Moon Travelers. Everyone in the community pulled together to make the new Travelers feel welcomed and to help them find a purpose so they could enjoy their new home."

"So, what happened?" Mina asked. "Why do so many of the Travelers not know they're on the Moon then? Before meeting you, Maude, and Ruth, I'd begun to think that everyone up here was mad."

The captain responded, "They used to know, Mina. Almost everyone knew who they were and where they'd come from. The confusion started when Dale took over. People were tricked into believing things that weren't true. Sometimes things that didn't even make sense. But he isn't the only one to blame. There's more to the story, but I'm not going to go into it now."

Mina thought for a moment, and then a lightbulb turned on. "Dan! It was Dan too, wasn't it? Dale has a twin brother, and he's to blame too. Isn't he?" Mina smiled, excited that she had solved the puzzle.

The map was blank, and Mina's smile faded. "Am I right, captain?"

"Yes, that's right. Dale has a twin brother. How did you find out?"

Mina became excited again. "Ruth handed me a note before I left her booth. There was a poem written on it about Dale and Dan."

"I see," said Captain Key. "Ruth overstepped a bit when she gave you that note. Maude didn't want you to know about Dan."

"Why not?" Mina asked.

"Because he's a very dangerous man. He's the real reason everyone's trapped inside the market. He used Dale to convince the Moon Travelers that Maude and Bob had lied to them about not needing water. He told people that their lives would be better—like their lives on Earth—if they started drinking water again."

Mina interrupted. "But I thought there wasn't any water."

"There wasn't, but Dan found ice deep inside one of the

massive craters on the Darkside. So, once Dale had everyone convinced that they needed water to make their lives better, Dan swooped in and told them that he'd found a way to bring them water.

"People were so overjoyed by the news that they never questioned Dan's miraculous timing, even though they should have known better. A group of Travelers volunteered to install the pipes needed to run water from the Darkside to the market. People were told that they'd have running water in their homes too, but that was never actually part of Dan's plan.

"Dan had poisoned the water so that whenever someone drank it, they became an alternate version of themself. Their egos grew and their logic shrank. They no longer realized there was more to life than what was right in front of them, which in their case was the marketplace. They forgot about almost everything, except for shopping or selling. They forgot about their families, their community, and everything else that had once made the Moon a good place to live.

"But that wasn't enough for Dan. After he'd poisoned people's minds, he set fire to the entire city. Our beautiful, innovative, technologically advanced city. Nothing was spared. Everyone's home and property were burned to ashes. He didn't want there to be anything left to remind people of the way life had been before. He even set fire to the land surrounding the city's border just to make sure that every last park and garden was destroyed too.

"The neon bridge was the last remnant from our previous lives that Dan decided to scrub. He blew it to kingdom come and then returned to the Darkside for good."

"My god! He's a monster, isn't he?!" Mina exclaimed. "Did *everyone* drink the water?"

"No, not everyone. There were holdouts like Maude, Ruth, and Bob, but Dan knew there would be. He uses his guards to keep them in line. The men in the blue suits. They don't technically work for Dale, though it's obvious that he thinks they do.

"Eventually, Dale began drinking the water too, but it didn't do much to alter his personality. The water just made him even more intolerable than he already was. I think Dan must have known that Dale would give in to drinking it at some point. It would've been unlike him to resist the temptation of doing something that everyone else was doing. It didn't really make any difference anyway whether he drank it or not. He was always going to be under Dan's control no matter what he did; he has been since they were boys."

"But why did Dan go to all that effort?" Mina asked. "I don't understand how keeping everyone locked away in the market helps him."

Captain Key replied, "Because Dan wanted total control of the Moon, or Theia as many of us call it. Once his plan to contain everyone succeeded, he rewarded Dale for his efforts by making him the mayor. Dan's reward was that he finally got what he'd always wanted—to live alone so he could work on his experiments undisturbed."

"But I still don't get it. Couldn't Dan have worked on his experiments undisturbed without poisoning everyone?" Mina asked.

"Of course, but that's not the way Dan does things. He wouldn't be happy until he believed there was nobody left to challenge him."

Mina felt her blood boiling. She didn't understand how someone could so callously disregard other people's lives the way Dan had done. She wanted to do something to fix it. She wanted to fight. "Then what are you all doing, looking for a bunch of greenhouse blueprints? Why aren't you doing something to stop him?" she demanded.

"It's not as simple as you might imagine. Looking for the

blueprints is an important step, though. You're going to have to trust me about this," said the captain.

"There's no way it's more important than finding a way to stop Dan from poisoning everyone. He has destroyed lives and taken away everyone's freedom! And worst of all, the people back there don't even know it! They're all just hanging around the market indefinitely with no clue that they've lost their minds. How could it possibly have gotten this bad? Hasn't anyone ever tried to stop him?"

"As a matter of fact, yes. I did."

Mina instantly felt embarrassed. She realized she didn't know all the details of what had transpired and that she was letting her anger get the best of her. She took a deep breath. "Dan did this to you, didn't he? He trapped you inside of the map?" Mina asked.

"I'm sorry, but that's all I'm going to tell you for now. The less you know, the better off you'll be. Again, you're going to have to trust me."

Mina stayed quiet for a while, eating some celery and feeling incensed over what Dan and Dale had gotten away with. She thought about what the captain was asking from her —trust. She knew there were certain things she was being protected from, but she also worried that being kept in the dark might have an adverse effect on her safety.

Finding the blueprints was far more dangerous than she'd been led to believe, and she was positive that Captain Key wouldn't have even given her all this new information if it weren't for Ruth's poem. What other big secrets was the captain keeping from her, she wondered. She didn't know if she wanted to keep going. Risking so much over a set of blueprints without any obvious plan to stop Dan seemed rather foolish. On the other hand, Mina still had no idea how to get home, and it had become clear that her chances of finding anyone else to help her were slim to nil.

Finally, Mina said, "How about we make a deal? I won't ask any more questions about Dan if you tell me why I should believe that Maude can send me home?"

"Alright, Mina. It's a deal. It just so happens that Maude is the smartest of all the Moon Travelers. She's on a whole other level than everyone else. She has been a lunar chemist, or what someone on Earth might call an alchemist, almost her entire life. And she was self-taught. Plus, her husband, Bob, is an inventor. He made those wings you're wearing. If anyone on Theia can get you home, it's those two."

Mina believed the captain was telling the truth, but the answer raised another question. "But why did Bob make these wings in the first place? I wouldn't be here if he hadn't."

"That's right," said the captain. "You'd be stuck on the platform all alone. Is that what you'd prefer?"

Mina shook her head, even though she didn't feel that the captain's reply had settled the matter.

The captain continued, "Anyway, now that you've finished eating your celery, it's time to get a move on. If we don't stop too much, we should be there by the end of the day."

"But how can you even tell if it's the end or the beginning if it never gets dark?" Mina asked.

"I'm wearing a watch."

"You are? *Really*? And you can see it, even though it's invisible?"

"It's not invisible to me. Now, stand up and head in that direction."

The words on the map vanished, and a giant arrow appeared in their place. It was pointing to the top left of the map, so Mina walked in that direction. As she went, she thought about how the map worked. *It's like a compass made of paper, except it's operated by an invisible person instead of a magnet.*

Mina followed Captain Key's directions for what felt like hours. She climbed over gray hills, walked across dusty plains, and wound her way through narrow valleys. Near the first range of hills, she picked up a gravel path that crossed over large patches of charred dirt. When they reached the top of the range, Mina looked out over the landscape in the direction they'd come from.

Off in the distance, not far from the marketplace, she saw a series of black dots. There were hundreds of them in neat rows with smeared black lines that stretched between them. The patterns formed an eerie black web that reminded Mina of the inkblots psychiatrists showed their patients sometimes.

"Are those black spots what I think they are?" she asked.

The arrow on the map faded. "Yes, Mina. You're staring at the ashes of our once great city."

A wave of sadness poured over Mina, and she felt guilty for having pointed it out. "I'm sorry. I didn't…it's just we're so far away. I wasn't sure."

"It's okay, Mina. I know you didn't mean to." The words flashed across the map once before disappearing.

Mina worried she'd upset the captain and didn't want to let her mistake linger, so she blurted out, "I found these little pieces of metal spread around the market. There are personal notes written on them." Mina pulled the metal pieces from her pocket. "Do you know what they are?" she asked.

"Yes. Those notes were written before Dan and Dale took control. Back then, the market was much smaller, and it wasn't walled off. But I've already given you more information than I'd planned to. I'd like to walk in silence for a while if it's all the same to you."

Mina felt hurt, but without saying anything else, she nodded and let the map fall to her side.

CHAPTER 15

THE VANISHING, PART I

Tegelro was the strongest and bravest member of his pack. Though he hadn't reached the proper age to become a leader yet, he'd been given numerous other responsibilities due to his immense popularity and natural talents. By far, the most important of these responsibilities was one that occurred only once each cycle—to lead his pack safely to and from the Darkside during the annual pilgrimage.

The journey was challenging not just because it took them over steep, rocky terrain but also because the Darkside was known to test minds in the most terrifying ways. Once the wolves crossed the border, they had to huddle together to keep their wits about them. But they also needed someone to run ahead and pick the right path, the one that would be easiest for the entire pack to travel on. It was a great honor for Tegelro to be chosen for this job, and it practically guaranteed that he would someday become the leader of one of the ancient packs.

Not long after Tegelro led his first pilgrimage, he decided it was time to usher in a new stage of life, so he chose Tahissi, his longtime companion, to start a family with. A few months before the next pilgrimage was set to begin, Tegelro and

Tahissi became parents to three lunar pups: Sangue, a boy; Hotep, his brother; and Mawd, their sister.

The three siblings were exceptionally good natured from the moment they were born. Unlike other lunar wolf pups, the triplets never fussed or cried for anything at all. They were perfectly content with whatever they were given and weren't prone to getting into mischief, either. The other pack members remarked many times on how fortunate Tahissi and Tegelro were to have such well-behaved pups.

Surprisingly, the pack leader, Chatan, even showed an interest in the pup's maturity. Though it was a rule that lunar pups couldn't make the pilgrimage until age two, Chatan gave Tegelro special permission to bring his young family along on the journey.

But Tahissi's mother, Neriti, who was a healer, warned the new parents against making the trip with the little ones. "It is true the triplets have strong souls and favorable dispositions unmatched by their peers," she told them. "However, I received an omen before they were born. I have not shared it with you before because I didn't want you to worry, but it is important that you hear it now.

"In the vision, the pups were being chased by darkness. The darkness crossed over the border and grabbed at the pups with long, shadowy arms. Then once it caught the pups, it turned each of them into dust. The vision was a warning. The pups should remain within the borders of the sun as long as possible.

"Their destinies are linked together in ways that can never be broken. Though their hearts are good, I have seen that two of them will turn to evil deeds. And the third will have to fight hard to keep this evil from spreading. You cannot stop these things from happening. The events that are to come were set in motion long before any of us were put here by the Great Energy. All you can do is try to understand the essence of the three gifts you have been blessed with. Delaying the inevitable is the best we can hope for."

Tegelro and Tahissi listened to Neriti's counsel and thanked her for sharing her vision. Later, though, while they laid in their private den with the sleeping cubs, Tegelro let Tahissi know that he had strong doubts about the type of magic the healers practiced.

"It's not that I don't believe that your mother had a vision. I just don't think any of us are meant to know the future like the healers claim to. Maybe Neriti tapped into something, but I don't believe it was an omen."

Tahissi's eyes narrowed with disapproval. "I see now that you think the healers' ways are foolish. Has it ever occurred to you that maybe you just don't understand their practices?"

Tegelro snickered. "Oh, I *definitely* don't understand their practices."

Tahissi tsked. "You laugh, Tegelro, but really you're turning your back on one of the most important lessons the Moon Walkers shared before their transcension. You're fortunate you've always been healthy. What if on the journey to the Darkside you became ill? Where would you turn?"

Tegelro shook his head. "I understand your point, and I acknowledge that the healers are able to mend wounds and heal the sick. Those are things we see them do all the time. It's the other parts I have trouble believing. Talking to spirits and connecting to energy that can't be seen sounds too much like fantasy to me."

Tahissi laughed. "Well, you're right about one thing, Tegelro. You really don't understand."

Tegelro looked mad, but Tahissi snuggled up close to soothe him. "Haven't you ever wondered *how* the healers are able to cure ills? It's talking to those spirits and connecting to that fantastical energy that gives them the ability to do these things."

Tegelro frowned, and for a while, neither wolf spoke. Finally, Tegelro broke the silence. "I admit that maybe there's more to the healers' practices than I can grasp. But something I do understand is the pride I have for this family we've created together. Our young have already gotten the attention of the pack leader. I don't think Chatan even acknowledged my existence until I was ten.

"I know it's frightening to think about taking the pups on the pilgrimage, but I think that will always be true. No matter how old they are, we'll always want to protect them. Right now, we have the chance to show not just our pack but *all* the packs what amazing pups we have. There will be no limit to what the triplets can achieve after that. But it won't be the same if we wait until next year. They would blend in with all the other pups that are making their first pilgrimage."

Tahissi thought long and hard before she responded. She took her mother's vision seriously, but she also wanted to do what was best for her pups' future. She knew what Tegelro was saying was true. The pups would be by far the youngest of the lunar wolves to ever make the journey to Crystal Crater. It would distinguish them from their peers if everything went well. After much internal debate, Tahissi asked, "If they come with us, do you promise you'll do everything in your power to make sure that no harm comes to them?"

Tegelro smiled. "Of course. I'll run three times faster and make shorter journeys back and forth so I'm never far away. But you don't have to worry. They may be young, but they have strong minds like their father. The darkness has never affected me the way it does others."

Tahissi wasn't entirely reassured, but she relented. "Okay, Tegelro. We will take them to honor the Moon Walkers ways like our ancestors have done since ancient times. But you should open your mind to Theia's energy during this pilgrimage. It would grow your heart and help you to become a great leader one day."

Tegelro nuzzled his forehead against Tahissi's neck. "I'll become a great leader one day because I have you and the pups by my side."

ON THE MORNING the pilgrimage was set to begin, Tahissi was beside herself with worry. Tegelro had spent the last several weeks working to build his speed and endurance so he could spend as little time as possible away from the pack during their trek. Unfortunately, with Tegelro away training all the time, Tahissi had spent most of her time alone with the cubs, thinking of all the things that could go wrong on their journey.

As plans got underway that morning, Tahissi paced back and forth across their den, unable to free herself from the weight of the dark thoughts she'd been collecting for weeks.

"Okay, everyone! The pack's ready. It's time to get going," Tegelro announced as he came dashing into the den.

The triplets leapt for joy, but Tahissi continued pacing, as though she hadn't heard him. Tegelro looked at the pups. "How long has she been doing this for?" he asked.

Hotep stepped forward. "All morning, Papa. She talks to herself too. And when Sangue asked Mama for a snack earlier, she didn't even get him one."

Tegelro looked at Tahissi with concern. "Darling, it's time to go," Tegelro said. 'The pack is lined up, and they're waiting for you and the pups to come on."

Tahissi still didn't seem to hear. She walked back and forth across the den, lost in thought. Not knowing what else to do, Tegelro decided to try something drastic. He stepped into Tahissi's path and dug his feet into the ground firmly.

Tahissi kept walking and whispering to herself until she'd walked right into Tegelro. She looked at him as if she'd known he was there all along, but then, for no obvious reason, she collapsed on the ground. Shaking and sobbing, she yelled, "We can't go…we just can't…something bad is going to happen…I can *feel* it! Please, please! We have to stay here. Something is after us! PLEASE! NO!!"

Tahissi trembled violently and wailed at a high pitch. Tegelro turned to the triplets. "Run as fast as you can and tell Neriti to come quick. If anyone tries to stop you along the way, tell them your mama is feeling ill, but she'll be better soon. Now, go!"

The pups jumped into action and ran to get their grand-mother. When they returned a little while later, Tahissi's shaking had subsided, but she was still sobbing loudly. Neriti moved across the den to her daughter and stood over her. "Mama is here, Tahissi. Tell me what's wrong."

Like before, Tahissi didn't show any signs that she was aware of her mother's presence. Neriti looked at Tegelro. "This is very serious, Tegelro. If I didn't know better, I'd say she's been filled with Darkside poison. Tell me everything that's happened."

Tegelro explained how he'd found Tahissi in this state when he'd returned from preparing the pack for the pilgrimage and how she'd screamed and wailed when he stood in her path. Tegelro, however, left out the part about what Tahissi had said. He didn't want to give any credence to Neriti's earlier warning. Luckily, Mawd filled her grandmother in on the rest of the details. "Also, Granny, Mama said we can't go or something bad will happen."

"Thank you, my sweet Mawd," Neriti said as she glanced at Tegelro with a raised eyebrow. "You know you can't go now. Right, Tegelro?"

"Don't start that again, Neriti. I don't have a choice. I have to lead the pack across the Darkside," Tegelro insisted.

"No, you don't. Let someone else lead the journey this year. Tahissi *needs* you!"

Tegelro shook his head and stomped his feet several times. "No, Neriti. *You* can look after Tahissi. You're a healer, after all. I'll take the pups so Tahissi can get some rest while we're gone. I'm sure she'll feel better after she has a break for a few days."

Neriti's face had become stony. "You're not that stupid, Tegelro. You've never seen another wolf act like this unless they'd been lost on the Darkside first. And I *know* that's true because neither have I, and I've seen it all."

Deep down, Tegelro knew that Neriti was right, but it didn't change his mind. He only grew more defiant. "You're not making any sense," he said. "Tahissi hasn't been to the Darkside since the last pilgrimage, which means that whatever's going on with her has nothing to do with all that. I think she's just exhausted from pointless worry—worry *you* caused with that silly omen of yours."

Neriti snarled. "If the triplets weren't present, I'd tell you what I really think of all your so-called toughness, Tegelro. You aren't fooling me. I know why you really want to take the pups, and it's not for Tahissi's benefit or theirs either. Beyond that, all I'll say is that I truly hope for Tahissi and the pups' sake that you don't come to regret this foolish decision of yours."

Tegelro felt rage growing inside of him, but not wishing to waste any more time on the matter, he stomped his foot once more to signal that the conversation was over. Then he said to the three little ones, who were cuddled up around their mama, "Let's go pups! We're already late for our adventure. You don't need to worry about Mama. Grandma Neriti will look after her while we're gone."

Slowly, the triplets moved away from their mother and towards their father. Mawd hung back the longest, pressing her face into Tahissi's tear-soaked muzzle. "I love you, Mama," she whispered. "Gran will make you better, and we'll all be back together soon."

"Come on, Mawd. The pack leader won't be happy that we've taken so long," Tegelro called from the den's opening. Mawd pulled away from Tahissi and followed her father and brothers out of the den.

Before Mawd crossed the threshold, Neriti whispered so that only Mawd could hear, "Trust your instincts, little one. Theia has a plan for you. It will guide you in the right direction, and one day, when I'm very old, we'll meet again."

Neriti's words scared Mawd, but she didn't have time to ask questions. Her father and brothers had already hurried away to meet the pack. She thought for a second about staying behind but knew it would make her father angry. Mawd nodded at Neriti and then turned to catch up to the others.

It worried her that Gran didn't think they'd see each other again for a long time. On many occasions, Mawd had listened to her father dismiss much of Gran's knowledge, and at that moment, Mawd felt like doing the same. Yet something inside of her told her that what her grandmother said was true. It was a feeling that everything was about to change.

CHAPTER 16

THE SHEEP SPA

The journey dragged on. Mina spent most of her time checking the arrow to ensure that she hadn't veered off course. After she had crossed the first range of hills and walked a good distance into the plains, Mina began to notice a bunch of small holes spread out across the flat expanse. She was intrigued because they looked more like burrows than the tiny craters she'd grown accustomed to seeing.

She had just passed two narrow tunnels close to the trail when she heard a loud "yipping" cry coming from behind her. Mina looked back to catch a peek of what was making all the racket; however, as she turned, the yipping stopped, and all she saw were the tops of the vacant holes. She continued to walk, but soon a chorus of tiny barks rang out from behind her. Once more, Mina turned to look, but again, she found only quiet, empty holes. *Oh, it's a game,* she thought.

For a moment, she decided to forget about the map and focus her attention on tricking the elusive creatures. She walked away from the burrows until she heard the chorus of "yip!"

"yip!" "yip!" Then she spun around fast. But there was still nothing there. With a better plan in mind, she turned away once again. She took a step, but before there was time for the barking to begin, she jumped back to face the holes.

This time she caught them in action. Five brown rodents stood on their hind legs, halfway out of their tunnels. They had short hair, beady eyes, tiny ears, and plump bellies. When they saw Mina staring at them, they dove back inside their burrows.

"They're prairie dogs!" Mina exclaimed. "How in the world did prairie dogs make it all the way to the Moon?" She looked to the map for an answer.

Captain Key responded, "After the Travelers began to arrive, so did the animals. The prairie dogs crossed the bridge, just like everyone else."

"I see," said Mina. "I bet it took them a really long time to get here, though."

"Come on, Mina," the captain continued. "Let's keep moving. You'll see more animals at the Sheep Spa."

Mina nodded and pressed on. The arrow guided her over three more sets of hills, around several wide craters, and across waterless seas of gray dirt. As she reached the peak of a particularly tall hill, she felt the urge to eat again—not because she was hungry, but because she was longing to break up the monotony of the trip.

Holding the map in one hand, she reached into her bag and pulled out a potato. She stared at it, wondering what a raw potato would taste like. Not ready to fully commit, she took a tiny bite and chewed its starchy flesh while climbing ten more steps to the top of the hill. When she arrived, she was greeted by the view of a large factory below, situated a hundred yards from the base of the hill. She felt excitement rush through her. *This must be it,* she thought. *I've made it to the Sheep Spa!*

It was a huge metal structure with a pointed roof and outside walls that had a dull finish. There were half a dozen windows and three large doorways, but all of them looked dark on the inside. From Mina's vantage point, it was impossible to tell whether this was because the lights were off in the building, or if it was because there was a dark material covering the openings. From the way it appeared, though, she suspected it was the latter.

A long, silver cable ran from the far side of the factory up the other side of the hill that Mina stood on. The entire setup looked like a ski lift, except instead of chairs, there were several medium-sized crates that hung from the conveyer. They dangled above the hill, as if waiting their turn to be sent away or pulled back. It reminded Mina of what one of the guards had said while escorting her through the market, "…the cage is ready and waiting for shipment." The memory sent a chill down her spine.

On the opposite end of the factory, a three-sided rail fence jutted out from the building and cordoned off a sizable piece of land. Inside the enclosure there were dozens of farm animals: cows, horses, goats, and sheep. Lots and lots of sheep. The tallest of the factory's three doorways loomed at the back of the animal pen like a large, rectangular void rising all the way to the top of the two-story building.

Mina took a few more bites of the tangy potato, then stashed it back in her bag and raised the map to eye level. Words were flashing across it repeatedly, and Mina realized that the captain had been trying to get her attention. "Take the switchbacks over to your right, and follow the path through the orchard of tantrum cactuses."

The words disappeared and new ones began to scroll across the paper. "And watch out for cactus needles. They're razor sharp and their oils can cause temporary paralysis if they get into your blood stream. Also, be careful not to touch their flowers; they're lethal when ingested."

Mina didn't like the idea of any of this. She asked,

"Wouldn't it be better if I took the path I've been following? You know, the one right here that leads directly to the Sheep Spa and has zero spiky death cactuses on it?"

"No!" Captain Key replied in bold letters. "The other path is safer."

Mina blew a whiff of air towards her forehead and rolled her eyes in frustration. "How is taking the road covered in spiky death cactuses *safer?*" she asked.

The captain replied, "Because it's not the spiky death cactuses you have to worry about."

Even more exasperated than before, Mina raised her voice. "I thought we came here because it's safer than the market. Now you're telling me that there's something even scarier than death cactuses that I have to worry about?"

"Calm down. You've misunderstood. I'm trying to tell you that it would be better to approach the spa on the side where the animals are."

Mina looked up from the map towards the factory again. "Why?" she asked.

"Because we're here to see the animals, and it would be best to avoid everyone else. The workers don't like visitors, and since they work for Dan, they'll almost certainly alert him to your whereabouts as soon as they realize you're here. Just try to stay focused and move quickly. Otherwise, we won't have enough time to get what we need before we have to leave."

Mina couldn't believe it. "So the *safe place* you and Maude sent me to is a spooky-looking factory filled with workers who will immediately turn me in to one of the madmen I'm trying to avoid? That really doesn't sound good. Are you sure you're trying to help me?"

Captain Key was quick to reply. "Yes, Mina, but you're wasting time. Trust me! I'll keep you safe. This is how we're going to get you home."

"Fine. I'll go find the blueprints for you, but it would've been nice to have known beforehand that the Sheep Spa was going to be dangerous. With a name like 'Sheep Spa,' I was expecting it to be less haunted factory and more fleece robes and foot massages," Mina grumbled as she started down the narrow switchback path lined with cactuses.

She soon realized that there wasn't much room to hold the map without exposing her arms to the dangerous cactus thorns. So she pushed the ends of the map together slightly, allowing the middle of it to sag towards the ground. Then she asked, "Where should I look for the blueprints once we get there?"

It was hard to read Captain Key's response because of the way the map was angled, but Mina thought she saw: "Look for the three-headed sheep. They're the ones you need to talk to."

A three-headed sheep? That can't be right, Mina thought. She wondered if maybe she'd bunched the map up too much. She was about to ask Captain Key to repeat the answer when, suddenly, she was stopped in her tracks. Someone had grabbed her from behind and was pulling her backwards with a firm tug. She tried to tear herself away, but they had her tightly by the wings. She was trapped.

After struggling for a while, she was worn out. She leaned all of her weight forward, hoping to pull free. But then a new idea popped into her head. Instead of resisting, she would push herself backwards and catch her captor off guard. She lunged two steps back and *voila!* She was free! She turned around quickly to find her two would-be kidnappers standing right behind her—green and spiky and covered in feathers.

Oh my god! That was a close one, she thought as she eyed the tantrum cactuses. She realized that while she'd been leaning down over the map, her wings had opened out wide and become entangled with the cactuses.

It was all the warning she needed. She pulled her arms and shoulders in around her torso to keep them out of reach of these prickly foes. Then she leaned her head and shoulders back so that her wings wouldn't spread out again. And in this awkward position, she cautiously made her way down the switchbacks and through the orchard of tantrum cactuses until she reached the end of the trail.

A hundred yards ahead was the animal enclosure. Mina looked at the factory. She could see that the doorways and windows were, indeed, covered in a heavy black fabric like she'd suspected. They reminded her of some photographs her art teacher had shown in class one time. They were of several famous paintings that had been done mostly in black. Her teacher said that many people found the paintings beautiful because of the powerful feelings the absence of color evoked.

Mina finally understood now what her teacher had meant. Not because there was beauty in the dark curtains that hung ominously over the openings, but because they had conjured up a deep sense of dread inside of her. She worried the curtains were hiding something ghastly. A factory full of gruesome horrors, perhaps.

She remained frozen, staring at the gloomy building when, out of nowhere, came a loud scratching sound from a few feet away. Mina jumped back, accidentally dropping the map which had been flashing the words, "Mina! Pay attention!"

In front of her, a patch of gray dirt began to spin in a circle like a tornado inside the ground. The scratching became louder, and pieces of gravel flew from the swirling pit. Mina's heart beat faster. She thought about fleeing back up the hill, but as she moved a few steps away, the churning patch of dirt caved in, opening up a sinkhole in front of her.

A radiant, white wolf leapt from the hole. It was enormous. Much larger than Mina would have expected a wolf to be. She was alarmed at first sight, but immediately she saw that the wolf had kind eyes and a friendly countenance. It panted heavily as it shook specks of dirt from its thick coat. Then its breathing relaxed, and it trotted over to Mina and scooped the map up from the ground with its mouth, shoving it back into her hand. "Thank you," she said, making eye contact with the wolf before looking back down at the map.

"Mina! Pay attention!" ordered the captain.

"Oh! Sorry, Captain. But look! I found a lunar wolf. I think it wants to help."

"Yes, I see that," Captain Key responded. "His name is Axel. Unfortunately, we don't have time for longer introductions right now. You need to hurry to the enclosure. You've already spent too much time in plain view of the factory. Go and find the three-headed sheep. Quickly!"

Mina did as she was told and jogged towards the enclosure with Axel in tow. *So there is a three-headed sheep*, she thought. *How peculiar. I wonder which head I should talk to.*

She asked, "Does the three-headed sheep know where the blueprints are?"

"Possibly," replied the captain. "But there are a couple of things you should know to avoid a bad impression. One, the three-headed sheep are three separate sheep that share the same body. And two, they'll each insist on having their own turn to talk. You'll catch on. Just do your best to figure out what each of them knows, and do it fast! Most likely, the workers will discover you at some point, and if that happens, we'll have to leave right away."

Mina didn't like the idea of having to flee again, but she nodded her head anyway. There was no point in arguing about it while they were short on time. When they reached the fence that encircled the animals, Mina began to scan the pen for the three-headed sheep. As she searched, she noticed that every animal was wearing a fancy collar made of blue satin fabric with a pendant hanging from it in gold, silver, bronze, or black.

She walked along the outside of the pen. Soon she'd crossed the entire perimeter but still hadn't found the three-headed sheep. She decided she'd have to try something else, so she stepped up on the lowest rung of the fence to see over the animals. She grabbed hold of the top rail and stood on her tiptoes, searching back and forth.

A large brown horse with a bronze pendant pranced up to Mina and snorted with pride. Then he opened his mouth wide to show Mina his teeth. He seemed to be expecting something in return, but Mina didn't have the foggiest idea what it could be. "I'm sorry," she said, "but I don't speak horse. Do you speak human?"

Just then, from a short distance away, she heard someone say, "Don't be ridiculous! Horses never *have* and never *will* speak human."

Then someone else said, "They think they're too good for it, they do."

A third voice said, "Probably rather die, they would."

Mina looked in the direction of the voices and saw the tops of three wooly sheep heads, tucked behind a large bale of hay. *It's the three-headed sheep,* Mina thought. She moved to her left and saw that the three-headed sheep were lying on their stomachs behind the hay bale, enjoying a snack. *How interesting,* she mused. *I wonder why all three of them need to eat when they only have one body to feed. And not a very big body at that!* The head closest to Mina turned and looked at her while continuing to chew on a piece of straw. Mina thought she'd better say something fast to keep it from getting the impression that she was only there to gawk.

"I'm sorry I've caught you during a meal, but would it be possible to have a moment of your time? I've been sent here to speak to you."

The sheep that was farthest from Mina replied, "It's rude

to interrupt an animal during mealtime, but lucky for you we're almost full."

Then the sheep in the middle said, "Don't like being bothered while we eat. Almost done."

Last, the sheep closest to Mina announced, "I'm bloated. Here comes the gas!" And he let out a thundering belch.

Mina was repulsed, but she did her best not to show it. "It happens to the best of us, I suppose," she said in response to the third sheep's grotesque display of bad manners.

She continued, "I'll be quick about this if you don't mind—"

But before she could ask about the blueprints, she was interrupted by the first sheep. "You can be as quick as you'd like. I don't mind. I've got all day."

Then the second sheep looked over at her and said, "Go ahead. Tell us what you want. We've got all the time in the world as far as anyone knows."

The third sheep stared straight ahead in a daze and said, "It never gets dark here. In my dreams, I blow up the sun and bring back the night."

Mina had begun to realize that there was something wrong with the third sheep. She looked at the map to see if Captain Key had noticed it too, but all she saw were the words, "Hurry up!"

The sheep stood up and approached her from the other side of the fence. Mina thought they were the strangest looking creature she'd ever seen. Each head was attached to an unusually long neck, and all three necks pointed in different directions. The sheep in the center was the only one whose neck was aligned properly to the little, round body they shared; however, there was nothing else normal about any of them. All three had dark black circles around their eyes that stood in stark contrast to the rest of their curly, white fur, and it made them look a bit crazed.

Mina was surprised that they didn't fall forward, considering how top-heavy they were. Even the different colored pendants that hung from their necks looked as though they should've been enough to tip the sheep over, planting all three faces squarely in the dirt.

Mina spoke again. "Unfortunately, I'm the one who doesn't have much time left, so I'll need to hurry this along—"

Again, the first sheep didn't allow her to finish. "Come, come. No one knows for sure how much time they have left. It's life's greatest blessing and most terrifying curse."

Mina tried to interject. "No, that's not wh—"

But the second sheep wasn't going to allow Mina to interrupt his turn. "Everyone leaves this world eventually," he said. "Not having much time makes you no different than the rest."

Mina tried once more to speak. "Okay, but that's not—"

However, it was the third sheep's turn to talk, and in order to drown her out, he loudly proclaimed, "I saw a cat bite the head off a bird once. Its time was up, but it probably knew that since its insides were made of clock parts."

Mina stared at the third sheep, trying to decide if this could mean what she thought it did. She didn't want to humor him, but she was finding it hard to stop herself. She asked, "The bird was made of clock parts?"

The third sheep blinked at Mina like he didn't understand the question. Then after a few moments of silence, he looked over at the first sheep.

Mina gave up. She decided she better get right to the point if she didn't want to be interrupted again. "Do any of you know where to find the greenhouse blueprints?"

The first sheep baaed and shook its head back and forth. "No, but I'll tell you the same thing I told you last time you were here. Try the greenhouse! It would be much more logical to find them there." Mina thought the sheep had a reasonable point, although she wasn't sure why he thought he'd already told her this.

The second sheep, not to be outdone, baaed even louder than the first and shook his head. "You're making things too difficult. Just build yourself a regular house, and don't worry about what color it turns out to be!" Mina thought this was also an interesting analysis of the problem despite being completely unhelpful.

It was time for the third sheep to take his turn. Mina braced herself. Just as the first two had done, the third sheep baaed loudly and shook his head, but before he finished baaing, he hiccuped and began to choke. He coughed and hacked over and over until, abruptly, he stopped. His eyes bulged from their sockets, and Mina worried that he'd stopped breathing. She was about to jump over the fence to try and save him, but before she could, the sheep let out one more giant cough. A wad of chewed-up straw and hair shot out of his mouth like a giant, furry spitball of regurgitated food.

Mina recoiled in disgust. She looked for some indication that the sheep was going to forfeit his turn, but he seemed completely undeterred by the mishap. He cleared his throat and began to speak. "Labels are used to distract us from our better nature. Color labels are often the worst. Green and blue, black and white, silver and gold. They're all just different wavelengths of reflected light. Don't be fooled. You must see past the labels if you wish to achieve a higher purpose."

Mina was taken aback by the third sheep's sudden insight. She asked, "What higher purpose do you mean?"

It wasn't the third sheep's turn to talk, though, so instead, the first sheep exclaimed, "Ignore that dribble! He's just *jealous* that his medal isn't shiny like mine!" The first sheep lifted his head high to show off his silver medal.

The second sheep nodded in agreement. "Or like *mine*," he

boasted, raising his head to show his gold pendant. "He's quite a spoilsport about it, really," added the second sheep.

The third sheep looked sad and stared at the fence post in front of him. "Sometimes you can't help your lot in life. The third head of a three-headed sheep has no right to expect any better than a black medal. Probably, I have little more time left than a wind-up bird flying over the head of a barn cat."

"You mean you're going to die soon?" Mina asked.

The first sheep rolled his eyes and shook his head. "Oh, *please*. Don't encourage his self-pity. He's right that he shouldn't expect more than a black medal! Yet clearly, he does. If he truly accepted his lot in life, the rest of us wouldn't have to hear about it all the time!"

The second sheep agreed. "Everyone gets a medal when they're born, and certainly the herders aren't going to waste one of the good ones on something as ridiculous as the third head of a three-headed sheep."

In a sad whisper, the third sheep said, "I'm lucky I got to live at all."

Mina was upset and had forgotten all about the blueprints, though if she'd bothered to look at the map, she would have seen that the captain was giving her a stern reminder. She said, "I don't understand the system. Who're the herders? What do the different colored medals mean? And how is it determined which medal goes to which animal?"

As expected, the first sheep spoke first. "The herders are the ones who watch over us. They take us where we need to go. If we need to be fed, they take us to the trough. If we need to be groomed, they take us to the spa."

The second sheep picked up where the first one left off. "If we need medical attention, they lead us to the appropriate doctor for treatment."

The third sheep added, "And if we're worthless, they lead us to the butcher."

Mina felt ill. "But why do you let them determine your worth?" she asked.

The first sheep scoffed, "They do *not* determine our worth. Our medals do! A silver medal means you've been blessed. You get the most food, the best spa treatments, and the best doctors."

The second sheep continued, "If you're lucky enough to have a gold medal, your lot is the same, except you're afforded less food, spa treatments, and doctor visits. The lesser animals who have bronze medals get the same amount of everything as gold medal animals, but the quality is far worse."

The third sheep finished explaining, "And then there are black medal animals like myself. We get the least and worst of everything. Least amount and worst quality."

The first sheep quickly spoke again, but he sounded defensive this time. "Not everyone can have the best! There has to be some way to make allotments, and the medals are a fine system that do just that."

The second sheep said, "The system makes sure that everyone gets the share they deserve!"

The third sheep said dryly, "The system is a huge pile of moldy horse turds."

The other two sheep's mouths dropped open. Too dumbfounded to speak, they began to bleat incessantly in a dramatic show of outrage. While they worked on finding the right words to express themselves, the third sheep took the opportunity to continue. "These two have nothing to complain about, so they don't bother to look at the system objectively. It's easy to assume the system is perfect when it's working perfectly for *you*."

Mina nodded. She felt sorry for the third sheep. She reached her hand through the metal fence and patted him gently on the neck. His wool was warm and thick. She looked into his dark eyes and said, "It's not fair that you're treated differently than the others. How did you end up with a black medal when your brothers were given silver and gold?"

The third sheep glanced at his brothers to see if they would try to give their own replies, but they hadn't quite finished with their relentless baaing. "Nobody knows for sure why the medals are given out the way they are. For a long time, everyone thought it was based on which animals were the best looking and the strongest. But that theory went out the window when we came along.

"My theory is that the medals are distributed based on the amount of money we can make for the herders. After we're born, the herders decide how much they're willing to feed us and care for us by calculating how much they think we can produce for them. Then, once they figure this out, they assign us a medal. Giving the best medals to the healthiest looking animals."

Mina asked, "But what about you three? Why would they have given you each a different medal if you all have the same body?"

The third sheep nodded. "Yes, I've pondered on this a great deal, and I think it has to do with the fact that the herders knew only one head was needed to produce most of what they want from us. To them, two of us are only worth the skin on our heads and necks. Soon I'll be slaughtered for the sole purpose of being one less mouth to feed. Later, my brother next to me will be slaughtered for the same reason. Killing us one at a time like this will help prevent our last brother from going into shock. Too much stress causes an animal's meat to sour, you know.

"Of course, even further down the road, the last brother will be butchered too. Only then will our deaths be truly valuable to the herders. They make the most money by feeding us to someone else."

The first sheep found his voice again. "Utter nonsense!" he cried in revulsion.

"Complete rubbish!" the second yelled in dismay.

"It's the god's honest truth," the third stated bluntly.

Mina believed the third sheep and spoke directly to him. "This can't go on. We have to do something. I'll talk to the herders. I'll beg them to let the animals share equally."

Mina didn't even think about what she was saying. Being fair was instinctive to her, and this seemed like the easiest solution in the moment.

Right then, a young goat moseyed up next to the third sheep. It stuck its head through the fence towards Mina's leg. She looked down and saw that it was reaching for the map, ready to take a bite.

"No!" Mina scolded as she pulled the map away. She started to inspect it to make sure no damage had been done but then realized she was in trouble. Giant words whooshed and flashed across the map like an angry storm. "What do you think you're doing? We're going to have to leave soon, and you've hardly found out anything! You let those silly sheep dominate the entire conversation!"

Mina heard the first two sheep beginning their cycle of commentary again. The first sheep snapped, "Look at what you've done!" The second sheep grumbled, "You only think of yourself!"

Mina wanted to jump in to defend the third sheep, but she decided to deal with the captain first. She didn't like how she was being addressed. Before she had even finished reading, she began to respond heatedly. Her voice rose in volume with every word she spoke.

"Don't talk to me like that! I did what you asked! Besides, you should have warned me you were taking me to a slaughterhouse for intelligent animals!"

Suddenly, everything stopped. None of the animals in the

pen made a sound, which made it eerily quiet. Mina felt panic rising in her chest. Axel, who'd hung back while she talked to the sheep, started to whimper.

Mina glanced at him and then looked at the map again. "The animals didn't know, Mina. Only the third sheep had it figured out. The other two denied it because they didn't want to believe it was true. It's time to go. The herders are coming. Run!" Mina understood the captain, but her legs were frozen. She raised her head towards the animal pen. The animals seemed to be frozen too, staring back at her in disbelief.

Riiiip! The long, black cloth that hung over the doorway was torn apart, and two men wearing white lab coats emerged from inside, each holding a metal rod that resembled a shepherd's staff. The men had black, curly hair with beards that matched and long, sunken cheeks that highlighted their angry expressions. They stood in the doorway until they locked eyes on Mina.

One of them called to her as they moved in her direction. "You there, feathered girl! Stay where you are!" Mina didn't have a choice; she was paralyzed with fear. Axel began to bark ferociously. It broke the animals' spell, and all at once, the entire pen came roaring back to life.

The animals didn't resume their normal routines, however. Axel's barking had agitated them, and therefore, they went on the defensive. The horses formed herds and galloped along the inside of the fence while the cows, goats, and sheep huddled together in the center. Some of the goats did wild kicking routines with their hind legs. Some of the sheep bleated loudly and reared up on their back legs. All of the cows stood perfectly still, unable to hide their fear.

The pandemonium slowed the men down, but Mina still wasn't able to make her escape. She felt ashamed. She told herself to run, but the sensation of panic was like concrete inside her legs. Axel grabbed one of her wings and pulled it gently. Mina worried he might pull her over, but then a sound rang out that jolted her back to life. *ZAP!*

The noise rippled through the animal enclosure like a sharp crack of electricity slicing through the air around it. *ZAP! ZAP! ZAP!* Over and over the sound repeated. It spoke to something primal inside of Mina, telling her to "Get away!" and "Take cover!"

She stepped backward away from the pen and looked around, trying to make sense of what she was hearing. At first, she couldn't tell what was going on. Her view was blocked by the herd of galloping horses. But once the horses turned towards the back of the enclosure, Mina saw where the noise was coming from.

The herders were firing shiny bolts of electricity from the ends of their staffs, electrocuting the animals that got in their way. As they pushed through the enclosure, they waved the long poles in front of them. Whenever an animal got caught in the electrical current, the electricity would spread across their skin until they stiffened and fell over.

This created a faster path for the herders because they were able to quickly leap over all the lifeless animals on the ground. Mina seethed with anger. She wanted to pry the electric staffs from the men's hands and give them a taste of their own medicine, but she knew she had no way to defend herself. She had to run like the captain had ordered, and she had to do it now.

She lunged into a hard sprint away from the enclosure. Axel ran beside her. Mina didn't dare look back. She didn't have to. She knew how close the herders were from the sounds of electricity behind her. Soon the noise stopped, which meant the men had made it past the pen and were close behind. She wondered how long she'd be able to stay ahead of them. She was already breathing hard and didn't think she could sprint much longer.

Mina tried to think of a way out of her dilemma. But Axel

kept distracting her by pushing the side of his body into her as they ran. He was tall enough so that the top of his back butted into her waist, almost knocking her over a few times. Finally, Mina was fed up. If he kept it up, he was going to foil any chance she had to escape. "Stop it!" she yelled. "You're slowing me down!"

Axel responded by barking at her and then speeding ahead a few yards. Mina was amazed at how easy it was for him to run twice as fast as her. The lunar wolf glanced back over his shoulder. Then he burst ahead another three feet and jumped in front of her. He dug his paws into the thick gravel and came to a halt. Mina nearly toppled over him as she skidded to a stop.

She looked back and saw the herders rushing towards them. Their white coats flew open as they ran, revealing dark stained overalls underneath. One of them yelled, "We've got her now! You grab 'er, and I'll shock that dang beast so it don't bite us."

Just then, Mina felt Axel scooting backwards below her, pushing the top of his back underneath her. She looked down and realized what he was doing—what he'd been trying to do all along. She sat down on Axel's back and pulled her feet up, resting them on his sides. Then, at a speed she would never have imagined possible, the large wolf raced forward.

Mina laid her torso flat against Axel's back and wrapped her arms around his neck. She clutched the map and tote bag tightly in each hand, hoping she could hang on.

It was incredible. Only seconds earlier, she had thought Axel was going to get her killed, yet here he was saving her life. Mina felt guilty for doubting him, and for the first time since she'd arrived in this hopelessly strange realm, she fully surrendered to her emotions.

Axel whisked her across the rocky plains as tears of gratitude, tears of sadness, tears of relief and frustration flowed from her freely and blended with the dusty, gray air that swirled around them. The tears kept coming for a long time. And when they dried, the water and dust that had mixed together left streaks of plaster spread across her face. Like the withered branches of a dying tree.

CHAPTER 17

THE VANISHING, PART II

When Mawd caught up to her father and brothers, her father was speaking to the pack leader, Chatan.

"It won't be a problem, sir," her father said. "Neriti is watching over her, and I can take the pups on my back the whole way."

Chatan looked unhappy. He eyed the triplets. "I don't think this is a wise decision, Tegelro. But since Tahissi is sick, I'll allow it. You'll leave the pups with the pack, though. You mustn't get distracted; our safety rests on your shoulders."

Tegelro nodded. "Yes, sir. I understand."

The journey soon got underway. The triplets stuck together and ran around the outskirts of the pack, just like the other young wolves who were making the pilgrimage for their first time. The pups didn't speak to the other youngsters, however, because they were too shy. Instinctively, they sensed the unspoken hierarchy that exists among sentient creatures and knew that, as the youngest, they were at the very bottom.

After a while, the pups grew tired of walking such a long way. A few of the mothers, whom Chatan had tasked with watching the triplets, took turns carrying the pups while they rested. Once the pups' energy was restored, they were returned to play among the other young wolves. Unfortunately, it wasn't long before they realized that they'd become the subject of ridicule among some of the other young wolves while they were away.

It began when two of the older first-time travelers got within earshot of Hotep and Sangue and began to make a show out of their disdain for the little ones. The larger of the two boys snickered. "Can you believe they had to take a break this early in the trip? What newborns. It's ridiculous that they were allowed to come."

The smaller pup said, "I heard Chatan only allowed it because their father's the pack guide. They're probably dumb enough to think that makes him special. They don't realize what a terrible job their dad has. He's just a sacrifice in case the Darkside tries to kill us. The pack leader always chooses the most useless member of the pack. It's why Chatan let them come. He feels sorry for them."

That was all Sangue could take. He ran at the other two youngsters, growling. Hotep, who was just as upset as his brother, followed Sangue's lead. This caught Mawd's attention. She'd been walking ahead, staying close to the mothers who'd taken care of them, but when she heard her brothers growling, she fell back to see what was going on. When she reached her brothers, they were face-to-face with the other pups. "Take it back!" Hotep snapped at the larger of the two cubs.

"Or what?" asked the larger pup. "You'll tell your loser dad what we said? I'm sure he already knows," the pup said tauntingly.

"What's going on?" asked Mawd.

Her brothers didn't take their eyes off the bullies, but Sangue answered, "These brats said mean things about Dad. They said he has a terrible job and that he's useless."

Mawd looked at the two cubs who were tormenting her brothers. "Why do you care what these two think? They're just jealous that we got to go on the pilgrimage two years earlier than them. Now can we go? The pack is leaving us behind."

Hotep and Sangue relaxed a little at hearing their sister's words. Hotep laughed. "You're right, Mawd. These two aren't worth it. I bet both of their dads combined aren't as brave as our dad."

This made the smaller pup angry, but instead of attacking Hotep, he lunged at Mawd, pushing her to the ground hard. "Stupid girl! You shouldn't talk when boys are talking!"

Mawd yelped in pain, and Hotep and Sangue jumped on top of her attacker. Within seconds, the larger bully had joined in, and all four boy pups were rolling around, tearing at each other with their claws and teeth. Mawd yelled for them to stop, but it was no use.

Seconds later, the members of the pack who'd heard the commotion surrounded the five pups. Several adults jumped in and pulled the boys apart by their scruffs. The smaller cub's mom ran to him. "What's happened, Podo? Were those pups being mean to you?"

Podo's eyes grew big and sad, and he nodded his head at his mother. "Yes, Mama. They said that their father is better than the pack leader. I told them that wasn't true, but then they attacked me."

Sangue yipped and struggled to break free from the lunar wolf who was holding him by the back of the neck. "That's not true! That jerk said our dad was useless, and then he jumped on our sister!"

At that moment, Tegelro appeared in the crowd, pushing his way past the other lunar wolves who were circled around them. "Dad!" the triplets chimed in unison, but Tegelro didn't' look happy to see them. "You three are in big trouble!"

One by one the triplets were dropped in front of their

father. Hotep tried to explain their actions, "But, Dad, those pups said bad things about you. Then that little one hurt Mawd!"

Tegelro continued to frown. "There's no excuse for violence. You should have gone and told one of the elders if they hurt you or your sister. Outside of that, you shouldn't have paid attention to their teasing. You let the situation get out of hand by allowing their words to have power over you. By ignoring their words, you take away their power."

The triplets looked ashamed. "Come on. Let's go," Tegelro said. "The three of you will come with me until we reach the Darkside."

Chatan, who was standing nearby, nodded his head to give Tegelro permission. Tegelro bent down, and the triplets climbed onto their father's back while the other wolves returned to the line.

"Hold on tight," Tegelro told them as he dashed towards the front of the line. "We're going to go fast. We have to make it to the border before we sleep tonight."

Once Tegelro reached the front of the pack, he took off galloping. The triplets knew very well that they were still in trouble, but they couldn't help enjoying themselves. Over many miles, they rode in silence. Traveling back and forth as their father chose the best paths for the pack to follow.

Eventually, Tegelro broke the silence. "You three have disappointed me. I wanted the pack to see how well behaved you are, but now they have the wrong idea. When you join them again, you will do your best to right this wrong. Do you understand?"

One at a time, Sangue, Hotep, and Mawd replied, "Yes, Father."

"Good, and while I don't approve of what you did, I appreciate that you wanted to stick up for your old dad. But in the future, you must remember that I can fight my own battles."

The pups nodded, though their father couldn't see them. It had been an eventful day, and they were ready for a long sleep. Tegelro sensed this. "We'll check in one more time with the others. Then, we'll find a place for the pack to rest overnight. Those mountains you've seen growing bigger for the last few hours are what separate the light from the dark. We'll sleep near the base tonight. Then tomorrow we'll travel across the Darkside until we reach Crystal Crater near the top of the Moon."

Sangue yawned. "But how will the pack make it over such tall mountains, Papa? I don't think the older wolves can climb that high."

Tegelro laughed. "You're probably right, Sangue. Luckily, we don't have to climb any mountains. There's a special tunnel that runs underneath the mountain range and joins the two sides."

Hotep asked nervously, "Is it dark in the tunnel?"

Tegelro laughed again. "No...well, actually yes. But that's okay. There are lots of crystals to light the way. You will need to keep your eyes closed when you pass through the tunnel, though. There are things inside that I think it's best for you not to see yet."

Sangue protested, "What do you mean? I'm brave enough for *anything!*"

Hotep joined in with his brother. "Me too! We aren't scared of a tunnel. Right, Mawd?"

Mawd seemed more concerned than her brothers. She asked, "What are the things inside the tunnel, Father?"

"I think I better not tell you. Your mama would be upset with me if it gave you bad dreams."

Sangue pleaded, "Oh, come on, Papa! Pleeeease!"

Hotep added, "Yeah. Pleeeease!"

Tegelro didn't respond immediately, taking a moment to think it over. Then finally, he said, "You know if we hurry, I could show you right now. I think if I explain it to you first, and we all go together, then it won't seem that scary at all."

Sangue and Hotep celebrated by letting out a few loud "yips!"

Mawd, on the other hand, was too nervous to celebrate. "Are you sure it's okay for us to leave the pack for so long?" she asked, hoping to reason with her father.

Tegelro looked back over his shoulder with a teasing grin. "What's wrong? You don't think your old dad can run fast enough to get us there and back before we're missed?'

Mawd didn't smile back, though. "No. It's not that. It's just, do you think it's a good idea to get so close to the Darkside without the rest of the pack?"

Tegelro scoffed, "You're starting to sound just like your grandma. Don't worry so much, Mawd. I'm not affected by the Darkside the way others are. I can protect you without the pack."

Mawd tried to relax. She knew there was nothing more she could say without hurting her father's feelings, so she gave in. "Okay, Dad. Let's go."

Without another word, Tegelro took off. They were already so close to the mountains that Mawd was sure they'd reach them in only a matter of minutes. She yelled, "Dad, will you tell us what's in the cave now?" If Tegelro heard Mawd over the loud beating of his paws, he didn't let on.

Soon they were at the entrance to the tunnel. "I thought you said it wasn't dark in there," Hotep sighed anxiously as he eyed the dark hole that led into the tunnel.

Tegelro sat down, and the triplets slid off his back. "It won't be dark once we enter, but there's something I want to tell you first before we go in."

"Is it about the crystals?" asked Sangue.

"No," replied Tegelro.

"Is it about the scary things?" asked Sangue.

"No," Tegelro said again, more curtly this time.

"Well, what's it about then?" asked Hotep.

"You three are still very young. You need to listen more than talk. To listen is to learn."

The three pups looked up at their dad with wide-eyed curiosity. Tegelro continued, "This tunnel we're about to enter is sacred. That means that the lunar wolves believe it's special and that it should be treated as such."

Hotep asked, "But why, Papa?"

Tegelro gave him a hard stare. "Sorry," Hotep said as he shrank into the ground.

"Long ago, something very sad happened. A pack of lunar wolves were on their way to Crystal Crater when they were discovered by a large group of monsters that lived on the Darkside."

"Monsters?" Hotep asked in a quivering voice.

"Yes," confirmed Tegelro. "They were known as bryobane. They were giant, hoofed animals with large horns. Some wolves believe that the Moon Walkers created the bryobane before they created us, although nobody knows if that's true. What we do know, however, is that before the Moon Walkers departed, they warned us never to go near the bryobane.

"The bryobane lived only on the Darkside of Theia. Their weak hooves prevented them from climbing well, so they weren't able to reach the top of the mountains. And though the other parts of their bodies were strong, their minds were exceptionally weak.

"While the Moon Walkers were still here, we stayed on our side, and the bryobane stayed on theirs. But before the Moon Walkers left, we were forced to cross over to learn more about the ancient practices. This is because many of the practices the Moon Walkers taught us involve the use of crystals, which don't exist on the Dayside, except for underground."

Hotep asked, "But why didn't the wolves just bring the crystals over to the Dayside?"

Tegelro shook his head. "The crystals don't work in the light. I know it's hard to understand. Honestly, I'm not even sure I believe half of it. But Theia's energy does seem to be much stronger on the Darkside. And the crystals are a physical part of that energy. Meaning a part that we can touch.

"The Moon Walkers taught us that we should honor Theia's energy, or what some wolves call the Great Energy. The Walkers claimed that if we didn't honor the energy, then life would cease to exist on Theia. We loved and trusted the Moon Walkers deeply, so we practice their ways out of respect. It's why we travel to Crystal Crater—to honor the energy as well as our lost friends."

"What happened to the first Moon Walkers?" asked Mawd.

"I don't know. Only the pack leaders and top healers are told that story. Maybe someday you three will be pack leaders, and then you will know too."

Sangue leapt into the air and did a twist. "Oh yeah! I'm gonna be a pack leader someday! Then everyone will have to listen to me!"

Tegelro snorted. "First, you'll have to know something worth listening to."

Hotep rolled on his side with laughter, and Sangue glared at him. Mawd smiled at her father. "I want to be a healer so I can help people," she said.

Tegelro looked disappointed. "You know, Mawd. You get to help everyone when you're a pack leader. Not just the sick wolves."

Mawd looked at Tegelro shyly. "I know, Papa."

Sangue, who was doing his best to ignore his brother's laughter, asked, "Can we go inside yet?"

Tegelro grunted softly. "Yes. In a second. What I've been trying to tell you three is this. After the Moon Walkers left, the lunar wolves dug tunnels just below the surface of the Darkside so that they could travel safely to Crystal Crater. They didn't want the bryobane to know they existed. The bryobane were angry, ruthless monsters, and the lunar wolves knew it would be terrible if they were ever discovered.

"Unfortunately, one of the packs *was* discovered after they tried to create a faster route to Crystal Crater that ran right underneath where the bryobane lived. This might have been alright, except that the wolves weren't careful when they built the tunnel, and it collapsed while their entire pack was in it.

"The monsters captured the pack, and later many others were captured while trying to save them. It was a very dark time in our history that lasted for generations. It only ended because the enslaved wolves decided to give their lives in order to rid the Moon of the bryobane forever. And that sacrifice happened in this very tunnel we're about to enter."

The triplets were mesmerized. Hotep asked, "Are the wolves still in there?"

Tegelro looked towards the tunnel. "No, son. After the tragedy, all the packs came together to move the wolves' remains to Crystal Crater. The leaders decided that the best way to express our gratitude to these wolves would be to bury them in the most sacred of places. We honor them every time we pay homage to the Moon Walkers and the energy. It's all part of the pilgrimage we're on.

"Our ancestors would have destroyed the tunnel if it weren't for the significance of what happened here. However, the packs made the choice to leave the bryobane remains where they were. We show our contempt for the bryobane by stomping on their bones whenever we pass through the tunnel. Many of the bones have already been smashed into dust, but the bryobane skulls were incredibly solid, and most of them are still intact. The sight can be upsetting to little ones who've never seen them before. But you three are going to show me how tough you are, right?"

The triplets looked apprehensively at the entryway to the dark tunnel. Mawd was the first to speak. "I'm scared, Papa. I don't think we should go in there without the rest of the pack. I have a bad feeling."

Tegelro frowned. "You've spent too much time listening to your grandmother, little one. You need to remember that a lot of her so-called *magic* is just misplaced worry. Yes, the healers have an important role to play, but a lot of what they do focuses too much on doom and gloom. They talk to spirits that aren't there and deliver frightening messages about the future. If you ask me, they should spend more time appreciating what they have in the present."

Hotep spoke next. "I don't want to step on the bones, Papa. Can I ride on your back instead?"

Tegelro nodded. "Of course. All three of you, hop on quick. I'm sure the pack will be missing us soon if they don't already."

As soon as the pups had climbed on, Tegelro leapt forward, ordering them once again to hold on tight. Then he bounded into the dark tunnel, and they dropped a dozen feet before Tegelro's paws hit the ground below. The triplets held their breath in terror. It was pitch black. Hotep was about to point this out, but before he had the chance, Tegelro began to chant a deep, rhythmic tune.

Suddenly, the tunnel walls were aglow in dark, multicolored light. Hotep, Sangue, and Mawd stared at the thousands of sparkling crystals covering the ceilings and walls, captivated by the kaleidoscope of colors. It was the most extraordinary sight they had ever seen. "Wow," Sangue whispered in awe, and Tegelro looked back at him and smiled.

Tegelro ferried the pups through the underground corridor, up and down slopes and around sharp corners and leisurely turns. The rocking motion of their journey lulled the pups into a state of relaxation. They had almost drifted off to sleep when they arrived at a low spot in the tunnel where the lights grew dim, and the crystals thinned out. Heavy shadows fell across the walls. There was such little light that it was difficult to see much at all, but Mawd thought she detected dark smudges of ash smeared across the walls—hiding behind the eerie haze.

The air was thick, and Mawd's body tingled as the energy around them shifted. She knew her brothers felt it too because they huddled closer. Mawd shut her eyes. She could feel the darkness drawing near. Her father slowed his pace, and the sound of his paws changed from a soft thud to a reverberating crunch as they moved from dirt to bone.

Sangue gasped, and Mawd felt his body stiffen. She looked towards the wall closest to him and jumped. Three gray and white skulls were peering back at them from inside a hollowed-out section of the wall. The skulls were as large as an adult wolf's torso with horns like giant crooked swords and eye sockets so big they could have fit an entire wolf pup inside. However, the most frightening part was the skulls' extra wide jawbones and razor-sharp teeth. Mawd shuddered.

"See, children?" Tegelro asked as he continued to carry them through the dark lair of skulls. "They may look a little scary, but they can't hurt you. They're just remnants of a bygone era. A time better off forgotten, frankly."

Mawd didn't feel like the skulls were so harmless, though. It had become nearly impossible to tell what was real and what was only a shadow in the low light, and Mawd's head swam with images of dead bryobane coming back to life in the dark. Every fiber of her being told her there was something else lurking in the tunnel with them. Something primordial that was done biding its time.

"Shouldn't we go back, Papa?" Mawd asked in a trembling voice. But Tegelro didn't reply. He continued walking down the path. His low cadenced tune turned into a slow, haunting chant that echoed all around them.

Sangue tried next. "Papa, won't the pack get lost if we don't turn around soon?" Again, Tegelro didn't respond.

Suddenly, the crystals in the tunnel began to flicker rapidly, alternating between light and dark until, all at once, the lights went out. Hotep whimpered and pushed even harder against Mawd.

"What's happening?" Sangue whispered loudly.

Without a word, Tegelro sat down, and the pups were forced to cling to his fur to keep from falling off. A moment later, Tegelro said in a childish voice, "I thought I saw you there before, but I can see you better now. Come closer."

"Who're you talking to, Dad?" asked Mawd.

"That little orb up ahead," he replied. "Look! I think it has a gift for us!"

Sangue climbed up on his father's neck. "Where?" he asked.

"Right there, son. Don't you see it?"

Sangue didn't say anything at first. But then he exclaimed, "Oh, yeah! I see it! I see it!"

Hotep, who'd been shivering next to Mawd, pulled away and climbed up on the other side of Tegelro's neck. "I don't see anything. Where is it?" he asked.

Tegelro shouted with joy, "It's right there! Right there! It's so beautiful. Look! Look, everyone!"

Mawd didn't move. Everything felt wrong. "Please, Dad! We have to go back now!" she begged.

But Hotep talked over her, "Oh! I see it too! Oh, Dad! It's so pretty. We have to bring it back to show Mama!"

"Of course! Mama! We have to show Mama! Let's go get it!" Tegelro shouted through frenzied laughter. Then he took off like a rocket.

Mawd dug her claws into her father's back to hold on. She

had never dared use her claws like this before, but she was willing to do anything to stop the nightmare. "We have to go back!" she screamed. "We'll get lost in the dark!"

She couldn't see her brothers, but she could hear them laughing like crazy hyenas, and she imagined them hanging wildly from their father's neck. "Ha-ha! That ball of light might *think* it's fast, but it's not faster than your old dad!" Tegelro shrieked with delight.

Mawd closed her eyes. She felt the path beneath them smooth out as they moved away from the bumpy remains of the bryobane graveyard. Tegelro was galloping at full speed, yipping and giggling like a playful pup. He ran and ran until the path curved upward, and Mawd realized they had left the tunnel behind.

Tegelro stopped. Mawd opened her eyes and saw the void of light known as the Darkside just a few yards in front of them. The area right outside the tunnel was visible, however. She looked over her shoulder at the jagged rocks that were part of the steep mountain behind them. Tilting her head up, Mawd gazed towards the mountain's peak. She could see that most of the Dayside's light was being eclipsed by the massive structure, but some of the light still managed to spill over the top.

"I don't see it anymore." Sangue whined.

"Me neither!" Hotep agreed. "No fair!"

Tegelro didn't say anything, but his head jerked back and forth, searching. Mawd prayed that whatever they'd been chasing was gone. She knew her father had made a terrible mistake by bringing them so close to the Darkside alone.

Suddenly, Tegelro's neck straightened up. "There!" he yelled as he stared into the darkness. Mawd's heart sank, and the hair on her back stood straight up as she realized what was about to happen.

"*Nooo!*" she screamed, but it was no use. Tegelro lurched forward. "I'm going to catch you, you stinky rascal!"

"Yeah, Dad! Get it!" yelled Sangue. "Show it who's boss!"

Mawd watched in horror as they were lured across the Darkside's threshold. "We have to go back, Dad! It's not safe —" but she stopped mid-sentence. Out of the darkness she heard a deep voice singing a slow, transcendental tune:

Come with me to see the light.
It's the light that never ends.
It's a ripe time now to change your form.
It's a ripe time now to be reborn.
Open your eyes to the big disguise.
To its will, you will bend, and bend, and bend….

Tegelro, Sangue, and Hotep continued to laugh and whoop it up as they raced around in the dark. "Shh! Listen! Don't you hear that?" Mawd whispered, but they didn't seem to hear her.

"We're almost there!" Tegelro shouted. "Just a little farther, and…"

Bzzzz! A ball of hot, white light and high-pitched static exploded all around them. The light was so powerful that it burned the wolves' eyes and the sound so intense that it felt like needles digging into their eardrums. It was instantly unbearable, yet somehow, it got even worse. *Brighter. Louder. Hotter. Brighter. Louder. Hotter.*

Mawd shut her eyes, but she could still see the white light. The heat penetrated through her fur and warmed her skin. Quickly, the warmth turned into searing pain, and she began to panic as a terrible thought occurred to her—they were being burned alive.

Then, suddenly, they were falling as Tegelro collapsed to the ground, burying Hotep underneath him. Mawd heard Sangue's screams mix with the blaring sound of the sizzling heat. Then, with no warning, the light, sound, and heat vanished all at once.

Mawd felt sick and disoriented. She opened her eyes and saw her father lying unconscious on top of Hotep. She turned to Sangue. "Help! Dad's crushing Hotep! We have to move him!"

But Sangue didn't budge. Instead, he stared straight ahead, hypnotized. That's when a terrible realization struck Mawd like an arrow through the heart. Although it was faint, there was still light to see by.

Mawd turned in the direction of Sangue's gaze and let out a blood-curdling scream. For towering just above them was a rubbery-faced creature with large, bulging eyes covered in a white film. Its evil grin was full of dozens of spearlike teeth that pointed out in all directions. And from the demon's head hung two slimy antennas that were capped by orbs. One dark and cloudy, the other glowing bright white.

CHAPTER 18

THE EDGE

Axel sped faster and faster, and at times it felt like they were flying. In the beginning, Mina could tell they were moving in a straight line, but eventually she felt her weight shift whenever the large wolf leaned into a turn.

Carefully, she positioned her head to the side of Axel's neck to see where they were going. Up ahead, a weathered mountain loomed above the horizon like an ancient temple. The waning light that illuminated its faceted surface gave the mountain a rich, red hue and bestowed on it an aura of gravitas. Mina found comfort in its beauty and wondered if this would be their destination.

The answer came before too long. As they approached the base of the mountain, Axel slowed down. Mina thought he was getting ready to stop, but instead he took a flying leap into a dark hole that led under the mountain. Air rushed towards them as they fell. Mina tried to scream, but her throat felt like it was clamped shut. Axel's front paws hit the ground, and Mina's face smashed into the back of his neck. She sat up. Her nose throbbed from slamming against Axel's vertebrae, but she was thankful to be in one piece.

It was pitch black inside the tunnel, which made Mina nervous. "Are you sure this is a good idea?" she asked, even though she knew she would get no response.

Axel began to steer them through the dark, and Mina decided that he must have excellent night vision or else know his way by heart. Either way, he avoided running them into walls despite the many twists and turns along the path.

Mina continued to lean forward and hold tight to her new friend. She was no longer worried about falling off. Instead, she held on to Axel for comfort. She found that his presence made her feel safer. From the second they had entered the tunnel, Mina felt like they weren't alone. She knew it was probably just her imagination because Axel would certainly sense if someone was there with them. Yet no matter how ridiculous she told herself she was being, she couldn't get rid of the feeling that someone was watching them.

After a long and bumpy ride, they turned a corner and paused. Mina saw a dim light up ahead. It trickled in from the outside, making it possible for Mina to see the tunnel for the first time. She was astonished to discover that not only were the walls covered in breathtaking crystals of all shapes and sizes, but they were also much taller than what she'd expected. She had imagined that the passageway was just big enough for them to fit through. But in reality, the walls stood over fifteen feet tall in the highest spots.

The soft light that broke into the tunnel spilled into the crystals as well, refracting into hundreds of rainbows that covered every surface. Even Axel's pure white fur turned into a beautiful multicolored coat as it reflected the beams of light from the ancient, glimmering rocks. Mina sat up straight on Axel's back and nudged him along. "Okay, Axel. That's enough. It's beautiful and all, but I'll feel better once there's some distance between us and the dark tunnels back there. Let's go."

Axel began to walk forward, but then he suddenly lost his balance and shuffled sideways a few steps to regain his footing. Mina was thrown hard into the wall, and the back of her head collided with one of the crystals. She cried out in pain. Something warm oozed into her hair. Lightly, she dabbed her fingers at the warm spot and then looked at them to see how bad it was. She was bleeding. It wasn't a whole lot, but she was sure she had a medium-sized gash where the crystal had stabbed her.

Axel looked back and whimpered, which Mina took as an apology. "It's okay. I know you didn't mean to. Let's just get out of here, alright?"

Axel walked them to the end of the tunnel where the walkway narrowed and rose to meet the wide exit. He laid down at the bottom of the incline and turned his head to make eye contact. Then he let out a little sound like a chirping bird. Mina understood he was telling her that it was time for her to make her own way again. She stood up and walked towards the exit. After a short way, she stopped to wait for Axel, but he was still lying on the ground.

She continued to the exit and peeked her head out of the hole. Once again, they were at the base of the mountain but this time on the opposite side from where they'd begun. The sun was behind her. Before her lay a shadowy plain, and just beyond the low-lit plain was the Darkside, at a much closer distance than Mina would have preferred.

Axel brushed against Mina's legs. She pulled herself out of the hole and walked a few steps, waiting for him to join her. He stuck his head out of the tunnel and watched her but didn't follow. Mina was confused. She walked back to him, but Axel lowered himself into the hole and groaned.

"Aren't you coming with me?" she asked.

The kind wolf looked at her sadly with his big brown eyes, and Mina knew the answer. She knelt down in front of the tunnel and reached her hand down to caress the fur on the side of Axel's face. "Thank you," she whispered.

Axel responded by moving in closer and leaning his head into hers so that the top of his brow touched her own for a moment. Then he pulled away quickly and darted back into the tunnel and out of sight.

∽∽∽∽∽

BETSY WAS SWEEPING the floor at the front of the greenhouse when the sliding glass door whooshed open. She looked up, but there was no one there. "I know it's you, Dan," she said. "You better show yourself, or I'll scream like a banshee!"

Suddenly, a man appeared out of nowhere, mere inches from the old woman's face. He had bright red hair and white, crusty skin, and he was dressed in a canary yellow jumpsuit. In his raised right hand, he held a lit cigar.

"Boo!" he whispered in a creepy voice as he materialized into view, exhaling a long breath of cigar smoke.

"Cut it out!" Betsy said, pushing the end of the broom against Dan's chest. "You know I hate when you do that. You better not have come all this way just to scare me," she said seriously, though with a hint of flirtation.

"No. What a ridiculous waste of time *that* would be," he replied, showing no concern for the bruised expression his answer had left across Betsy's face. "I came to tell you there's another angel on the loose. She's already come and gone from the market and the Sheep Spa, and I happen to know that she's headed here next."

Betsy asked, "What is it with these angels showing up all of a sudden? I hadn't ever seen an angel in my whole life until that young man came snooping around here. I think he was looking to steal some of my English ivies. I noticed he was real interested in their singing."

Dan rolled his eyes. "Betsy, I've told you already that he didn't want any of your silly ivies. Remember? He said he was looking for the blueprints to the greenhouse."

"Well, yes. I know that's what he *said*, but I'm still not so sure that's what he actually wanted. And now there's two of them!? There's something fishy about it if you ask me, Dan," she said with a suspicious look.

"You know, Betsy. I don't think it's a coincidence we've had two angel visitors in such a short time. There's something fishy about it if you ask me."

"But I just said that, Dan!"

"No, I don't think so," Dan retorted. "Anyway, I didn't get what I wanted out of the last angel, but now I have a plan. If the person sending these angels over here is who I think it is, then I know just what to do, and I need your help."

Betsy's warty face brightened, making her look even more like a swollen pumpkin than she already did. "That's great news, old friend! How can I help?"

∞∞∞∞∞

THE LIGHT WAS dim and the shadows heavy at the edge of the void. *Why would Axel bring me here?* Mina wondered. Then, suddenly, the answer popped into her head. He had brought her to the next part of her journey. She hadn't found the blueprints at the Sheep Spa, and she couldn't return to the market without them. Therefore, to continue her mission, she'd been brought to the place she feared the most. The Darkside.

Mina hadn't acknowledged Captain Key since they'd left the Sheep Spa. However, she didn't think the captain would be happy that Axel had brought them here, so she decided to divert her eyes from the map a little longer. Besides, their last few exchanges had left Mina with a sour taste. The captain had given her barely any information to work with yet had expected a lot in return.

Mina felt used and tired. She sat with her back against a large boulder next to the mountain. She knew she'd have to talk to the captain before deciding what to do next, but she dreaded all the scolding words she was sure she'd find when she opened the map. Not ready to face it, she flung the sheet of paper into the dirt nearby. Then she pulled the tote bag close and reached all the way down to the bottom to pull out another potato. The taste of the tough vegetable hadn't grown on her but eating it made her feel better. Or at least better than anything else had.

She sat for a long time staring into the dark, chewing on the hard tuber, and waiting to feel recharged. Her mind wandered in and out of thought, and at times, she found herself surrendering to her dreams. The way ahead looked like it had been overtaken by a heavy fog. There was only about fifteen feet of visibility before the light faded entirely. Here, the light and dark mingled and Mina thought that perhaps the air particles were doing a dance, waltzing up and down, weaving in and out of sight.

In this waltz, Mina imagined it was the dimming beams of light that led the dance and the void that played the music. As her daydream took hold, she thought she heard the sounds of an orchestra flowing out of the darkness. *Come join the dance*, the music tempted. A faceless boy approached her. He took her by the hand and escorted her to a ballroom filled with starlight. Then he pulled her close, and they danced—gracefully bobbing and spinning their way into the night.

After a while, Mina woke again to reality. She didn't know how long she'd been dreaming, but it felt like it could've been hours. She grabbed the map, certain the captain would be furious and with good reason this time. However, when she unfolded the map there were no bold words zooming across the paper like she expected. The map was blank. It should've been a relief, but it actually made her feel worse. She had hurt the captain's feelings.

Mina looked into the darkness, trying to find the right words. "I'm sorry," she began. "I was tired and—" But before she had finished, she looked down and saw that there were words moving across the map.

"I'm sorry, Mina. I should never have spoken to you the way I did at the Sheep Spa. I was worried you were going to get caught by one of the herders, and then my entire plan would've been ruined."

Mina wasn't sure she understood, "You mean your plan to get the blueprints?"

Captain Key replied, "No, Mina. That was never the plan —mine or Maude's."

"I don't get it. I thought I was supposed to get the blueprints so that Maude and the vendors could try to grow their own food."

"No. I'm trying to tell you it was all a ploy to get you out of the market. Maude believed I was going to lead you to the Sheep Spa to try to trick the workers into following us back to the market, but that wasn't the real plan either."

Mina couldn't believe it. She had been lied to, *again*. "So why in the world did we go there?" she asked.

"Because it's part of the plan I created to stop my brothers."

Mina thought for a second. Then her eyes grew wide, and she blurted out, "Oh my god! Dan and Dale are your brothers!"

"Yes, they are. Which is how I know all too well what they're capable of. I want to tell you a story about what happened when I was growing up, but look, Mina, we can't stay here. My plan will only work if we keep going."

Mina nodded, although she hadn't fully digested everything the captain had told her. "What do we do now?"

The captain responded, "Well, if you agree to it, we'll head to the main greenhouse. It's operated by one of Dan's most loyal allies. It will take a while to get there, but on the way, I'll tell you my story. If you decide you want to turn around at any point, I'll understand."

Mina looked into the darkness again. And suddenly, a thought occurred to her. "The greenhouse is on the Darkside, isn't it? Despite defying all logic, Dan built the greenhouses on the Darkside. It's the reason Axel brought me here, isn't it?"

"Yes, Mina. Everything you said is true."

"But then how will I keep from getting lost in my thoughts? If you're telling me a story while we're traveling on the Darkside? Maude said I had to keep talking. She said you wouldn't be able to save me if I got trapped inside my head."

"Maude doesn't know everything I'm capable of, Mina. Sometimes mothers have a hard time acknowledging what their children can do."

"My god! Maude is your mother *too?* Does that mean Bob is your father?"

"Yes, Mina. I know it's shocking, but we really must go now if you're ready. We have a lot of ground to cover."

Mina stood up, feeling energized by all the big revelations. "Okay. I'm ready, Captain."

"Good, but one more thing. Captain Key is a pseudonym I chose at my mother's insistence. She thought it would be important for me to have an alias in case Dan ever discovered you or Fred carrying the map. You don't need to call me that anymore. My real name is Helen."

CHAPTER 19

THE VANISHING, PART III

Neriti knew what was coming before the messenger arrived to summon her. She'd dreamt it, felt it, and dreaded it for months. Knowing didn't lessen the blow, however.

Neriti hadn't left her daughter's side since Tegelro and the pups had departed on the pilgrimage. She slept next to her, fed her, and spoke to her in the ancient words that the Moon Walkers had taught them. But Tahissi hadn't regained her senses. Her mind was like a fish caught in a net. Blinded by fear, it swam the length of an entire ocean without ever breaking free from its trap. After a while, Neriti made the tough decision to sedate Tahissi so her mind and body could get the rest they needed.

Two days after the pilgrimage began, the messenger appeared in the doorway to Tahissi's den. Though Neriti's back was turned to the young wolf, she spoke to him before he could announce himself. "Who will stay with my daughter while I'm gone?" she asked.

The young wolf didn't answer. He was trying to figure out how Neriti had known his purpose for being there before he had told her. "Never mind," she continued. "Go and fetch my assistant, Axel. Tell him what's happened. Tell him he'll have to stay with Tahissi until I return from Crystal Crater."

The young wolf finally spoke, "But, Healer Neriti, the pack never made it to Crystal Crater. Tegelro and the triplets went missing. They found them only a little way beyond the tunnel. They were—" But the rest of the wolf's words caught in his throat.

Neriti nodded. "I know, young wolf. After you fetch Axel, you must run back to the others as fast as you can. Tell Leader Chatan to have Tegelro and the pups moved to Crystal Crater. It's the only chance we have to save them now."

The messenger nodded. "Yes, Neriti. I'll run as fast as a meteor." Then he turned and bolted from the den.

Neriti sighed. She was only middle-aged, but she already felt old and tired, as though her star had burned too brightly in its youth. She bent down and pressed her forehead to Tahissi's. "I'm sorry, my love. Our family was chosen but not in the way we might have hoped. I must go now. I promise I'll do everything in my power for Tegelro and the pups."

Tahissi's eyes fluttered open for a moment, as if she were acknowledging her mother's words. Then they shut again tightly and remained closed until it was all over.

CRYSTAL CRATER WAS A DEEP, wide hole at the top of the moon that was filled with crystals of all sizes. Some were as large as sixty feet tall while others were no bigger than a pebble. They stuck out from every surface in the crater and pointed in many different directions.

When Neriti arrived at the top of the crater, she saw there were only three members of her pack present, along with a few head healers from the other packs. She made her way down the crystal lit path to the bottom of the crater.

Chatan ran to meet Neriti when he saw her coming. "I'm glad you're here. The other packs were sent home, but I asked a few of the healers to stay behind. They've already begun preparing for the healing process." Chatan paused before continuing, "Neriti, I'm sorry to tell you this, but it's not going well. I haven't seen any change in their condition so far."

"What is their condition?" Neriti asked.

Chatan cleared his throat. "Tegelro and the boys have very weak heartbeats. We've lost them several times, but the healers were able to bring them back. Mawd's heartbeat has been inconsistent. It continues to alternate between weak and strong.

"There's something else, though. This isn't like any case of Darkside poisoning I've ever seen. When the search party found them, they thought they were already dead. They weren't talking to themselves or wandering aimlessly like we would've expected. Instead, they were laying on the ground with foam coming out of their mouths and a thick layer of film covering their eyes. You're going to need to prepare yourself, Neriti, because they still look this way."

Neriti nodded. "I'm not surprised, Chatan. As you already suspect, this wasn't Darkside poisoning. They didn't get lost. They were lured over."

"By what though? The bryobane have been gone for centuries, and nothing else lives over here."

Neriti looked at Chatan knowingly.

"Oh," he said in a startled tone. "Are you saying that—"

"Yes." Neriti replied in a hushed tone. They had almost reached the center of the crater where the other wolves were huddled.

Neriti continued, "The healers must work now. Please ask the rest of the pack to give us privacy. You should stay, Chatan. But you mustn't come any closer than the crater's edge until further notice."

"Yes, Neriti. Let me know if there's anything you need."

Chatan motioned to the other pack members to follow him up the path to the crater's rim.

HOURS PASSED. Chatan watched the ancient circling ritual from the top of the crater as Neriti had instructed. Fires that had been lit around the center of the crater flared and dimmed in sync to the large crystals that reacted to the healers' chants. The healers spun around and circled the bodies that were laid out next to each other. Then they sat and chanted, then circled and chanted, then took turns alternating between different combinations of the ritual. Chatan couldn't hear the ancient songs the healers sang, but he knew a little about how the ceremony would go.

The fires and crystals glowed brightest whenever the chants were recited. The songs were filled with praises to honor Theia. Some were likely the same songs that all the packs would have sung together if the pilgrimage had continued as planned. Chatan understood, also, that some of the verses the healers sang were ones that only they knew. Verses that had been passed down by the healers who came before them. Chatan assumed, though, that these verses would be humble pleas to the Great Energy. Pleas asking Theia for mercy, especially for the innocent pups.

Chatan rested on his stomach and watched the sparks rise high into the black sky before vanishing like ghosts into the darkness above. He'd always enjoyed seeing the crater lit up like this. Staring into the chasm of colorful crystals brought warmth to his heart. He only wished he knew some way to extend this feeling to Tegelro and the pups—a way to bring them back. On the other hand, if Neriti's suspicions were correct, Chatan doubted there was anything that could be done to save them now.

Many more hours passed before Chatan's worst fears were

realized; a large spiral of dark blue smoke arose from the area where the four bodies lay. Moments later, two smaller spirals drifted up from the same spot. With each new spiral, the fires and crystals grew so dim they looked as though they might go out.

Chatan could see Neriti take a seat inside the circle the healers had formed. The other healers continued to spin around the circle and chant. Chatan thought this meant that one of the pups was still alive. Probably the little girl. He sat up and watched, hoping that at least one of them could be saved for the mother's sake.

Then all of a sudden, the ground began to shake violently, and the crystals near the circle sent out strobing beams of light —pulsating in every color. Chatan backed away from the crater's edge, fearful he might fall in. Seconds later, a giant ray of white light burst out of the sky from high above the circle and crashed into the bottom of the crater. The beam was steady and strong for a moment, but then it disappeared, leaving the entire crater twinkling in golden white embers that hung in the air before fading to black.

The fierce tremor came to a halt, and Chatan heard screams echoing from below. Neriti rushed from the circle and sprinted up the long path towards the crater's rim. Chatan paced anxiously as he waited for her, not knowing if it was safe yet to descend past the crater's edge.

The steep climb stole Neriti's breath, and she was unable to speak by the time she reached Chatan. She sat down and took a few deep breaths in an effort to regain her voice. Chatan already assumed the worst and was impatient to hear the news. In his best attempt to sound sympathetic, he asked, "What's happened, Neriti? Is everyone okay"

Neriti bent her head towards the ground. "Tegelro and the boys are gone. It's hard to understand. I've never witnessed anything like this before. Our circle couldn't even reach their spirits to find out what happened. It's like they'd already vanished, even though their bodies and life energy were still present."

Chatan shook his head. "I'm so sorry, Neriti. Your family didn't deserve this. Those pups were so young, and Tegelro was so brave and unaffected by the dark. I never would have guessed this could happen. I thought surely he was destined to be a pack leader one day."

"Yes, Chatan. Tegelro was born with a strong heart, but his ego got in the way. He believed too much in himself without putting any faith in the Great Energy. I suspect it made him an easy target."

"I'm partly to blame then," Chatan said somberly. "I should've impressed upon him the danger in admiring one's own abilities. He seemed so natural as a leader, but I fear I gave him too much credit. Maybe none of this would have happened if I'd spent more time guiding him."

"No, Chatan. We both know there are larger forces at work here. I've felt the energy shifting for a long time. I'm sure you've sensed it too. Big changes are coming. This is only the beginning."

Chatan jerked his head as if struck by a thought. "Wait! What about the girl pup? Did she survive?"

Neriti didn't react to the question. She looked over the edge of the crater towards the huddled circle of healers down below. "Forgive me, Chatan," she said. "I don't know how to explain it. I've been trying to think of a way to fix it, but there's nothing in our teachings about magic that comes from the sky."

Chatan grew concerned. "Neriti, you're worrying me. What is it? What happened when the light came out of the sky?"

Neriti looked Chatan straight in the eye. "Come with me,"

she said before leaping over the edge, back onto the path that led to the center of the crater.

"Are you sure?" Chatan hesitated. "It doesn't seem like the healing is done. Do you think it wise to break the circle?"

Neriti turned back around. "You're right. The healing isn't done, but I don't believe it's possible now. Mawd's spirit was unreachable, just like the others. Whatever was sent to take its place…well, you will have to see for yourself." Chatan was intrigued by Neriti's cryptic explanation. He nodded, and they took off down the path.

As they hurried deeper and deeper into the crater, Chatan felt the temperature rising. At first, he thought it was the effects of the exercise and his nervousness over what he would find at the bottom. A little more than halfway down, though, the sensation of heat had intensified to the point where he began to feel lightheaded. "Something inside of me doesn't feel right, Neriti," he said. "My skin is starting to tingle. I think I might be sick."

Neriti kept walking without turning to check on her friend. "It's not sickness, Chatan. You're feeling the effects of the energy the healers have harnessed. The energy is powerful. We have used the ancient teachings to call on the energy to heal. It will not harm you here. Take deep breaths and remind yourself that you're going to be okay."

Chatan followed Neriti's advice, and for a while it helped. But as they passed by the giant crystals, Chatan started to unravel. Close up, the crystals' light pulsations made it look like the crystals were throbbing. It was too much. The movement seemed perfectly timed to the waves of angst that were sweeping across every single nerve in his body, and soon he became certain that the back of his head was going to split apart.

"Breathe, Chatan," Neriti spoke soothingly to him. He looked ahead to where she was walking, in-between the shadows of the throbbing crystals. But there was something different about her now. Her white fur looked darker, and Chatan wondered if his vision was faltering because of the intense pressure that had built up inside of his skull.

Everything began to spin, but Chatan continued to stumble awkwardly behind Neriti, too afraid to be left alone in his condition. They passed near one of the fires that bordered the center of the crater, and Chatan suddenly became aware that Neriti had, indeed, transformed. Not only had her fur turned brown, but her head looked about three times larger and had slender curved horns pointing out of both sides.

"Bryobane!" Chatan gasped in horror at Neriti's new form.

The giant head looked back at Chatan, and only then did he recognize it as something other than a bryobane. Possibly an Earth animal. "No, Chatan. No bryobane here," said the large head in a deep voice. "What you bear witness to before the circle's energy fades, you must never speak of again to anyone. As a pack leader, I know you're bound by the sacred oath, but I feel obliged to remind you that the healers' ways are protected by this oath too."

However, Chatan was too far gone to understand the words being spoken by the dark, bushy-haired bovine head. He'd lost control of his senses and was drowning in the unyielding heat. *I'm a leader*, he thought. *I shouldn't be following this monster. I need to find a way out.*

His thoughts swirled as he looked every which way. *I'm a leader. I'm a leader. A leader too old and wise to be tricked by some wild beast. I have to run before it slaughters me.*

Without knowing it, Chatan had reached the healer's circle. From behind, he caught sight of what he perceived to be more wild beasts. One of them turned its head and looked at him from the side of its face with a piercing green eye. It wasn't brown like the animal he'd been following, though. It had orange and black stripes on its head that ran across its muscular back and all the way down its tail. Its long whiskers pointed away from its face, and when it opened its mouth, Chatan could see its fangs.

The intimidating creature said, "Why did you bring him here, Neriti? His presence is interrupting the circle's energy."

Neriti responded, "Chatan is here because this thing that has happened to my granddaughter concerns us all, Imgu. Not just my pack but all of ours. You must realize we can't undo what's been done. On many occasions, we've spoken of the time we knew was coming. Be honest with yourself, and you will know that time is now."

Another animal that had a long face and neck and a beautiful mane of shiny hair spoke next. "Neriti's right. We have discussed this in the council countless times. We have all had the visions. Many saw the light falling from the sky before it happened today. We may not like that it's true, but pretending it's not happening won't make it go away."

All of a sudden, a very large animal rose up on its back legs from behind the others. It had a big, circular head; cute, rounded ears; a short snout; and thick, brown fur. The whole thing would have seemed cuddly if it hadn't been for the four-inch claws that stuck out from each of its paws. "Neriti!" it roared. "Chatan is running away, and it looks like he has Darkside poisoning!"

Neriti turned to see Chatan wobbling up the path that led to the top of the crater. "Quickly, everyone! We must break the circle around Mawd," she ordered.

Chatan didn't know which direction he was going. He only knew it was away from the frightening animals that he was certain were planning to skin him alive and eat him. He could hear chanting from somewhere off in the distance. The tune sounded like peaceful music he had heard before, but he couldn't place it. He wanted to lay down to rest and listen, but he was too scared.

Then, in the very next moment, an unseen barrier was lifted away from his rational, thinking mind. It was such an instant and complete unburdening that Chatan fell to the ground and wept as his heart swelled with gratitude, confusion, and the seeds of trauma. Seconds later, his friend was by his side. "You'll be okay, Chatan. The circle is broken. You're safe from the Darkside now. Just keep breathing."

"Please, Neriti. I don't remember how I got here. What happened?"

"You were poisoned by the Darkside because you didn't have the energy's permission to go near the circle. I allowed it to happen, just as you allowed my grandchildren to go on a journey they weren't ready for, even though I begged you not to."

Chatan continued to cry. "That's awful! How could I have known this would be the outcome?"

Neriti snapped at Chatan, "I *told* you about the visions the healers were having. I *told* you this wasn't just about my family going on the pilgrimage. We were given a chance to stop what was foretold, but we had to trust each other to do so. You chose not to trust me. You dismissed my pleas like I was a crazy, old healer. And now..." Neriti paused for a moment and sighed deeply before she continued. "And now it's too late."

Chatan broke into loud sobs, and Neriti didn't speak until he had become quiet again. Then she said, "I cannot forgive your role in this, but I can accept that it was only one of many. Tegelro and my daughter, Tahissi, also played a role. As did I. I knew those pups were doomed, but did I take them away to protect them? No, I did not. So, in the end, I sealed their fate too."

"What you did to me was wrong, Neriti. I could have died!"

"No, Chatan. Not with the healers right here. It's unbelievable that you still doubt our power after all of this. Look, we can both stay angry, but it would be best if we choose to find common ground now. The loss I've suffered is greater than what I took from you, and yet we are both very much to blame. But now it's time to look at the path that has been laid out due to our lack of action. It's one on which many good wolves will perish, but maybe there's still hope."

Chatan didn't pretend his feelings were mended. He stood and composed himself in order to reclaim what he understood best—his position as pack leader. He and Neriti walked in silence to where the healers sat in their normal wolf forms.

Imgu spoke directly to Neriti, "It's awake now, but—"

Before Imgu could finish, Chatan pushed himself in front of Neriti and demanded, "Let me by! I want to see it."

The healers looked at each other, which only angered Chatan further. He forced his way past them. Neriti followed right behind him and stood next to the creature that had once been her little granddaughter, Mawd.

It laid before them on the ground with its smooth, furless skin and its wide-open eyes. It took Chatan a moment, but when he finally spoke, all the anger in his voice had melted into awe. "My god, Neriti. It's an earthling, isn't it?"

Neriti nodded her head. "Yes, Chatan. It's an earthling."

"I thought they were only legends, but this one is *real*."

Neriti spoke in a sad yet amused voice. "Yes, it's real, and there are many more of them besides this one."

Chatan looked at Neriti perplexed. "But how did it get here?"

Neriti shook her head. "When the light hit the ground, Mawd's body changed into *this*."

Before Chatan could ask more questions, the earthling began thrashing around on the ground. Imgu walked to Neriti and stood by her side. "This is what I was trying to tell you. It's awake, but I don't think it's aware of what's going on. It's like it's trapped inside a dream."

Seconds later, the earthling spoke, although not in a language any of the wolves understood yet. "Help! Please help! I'm drowning! *HELP!*" Then it started to convulse again with even more intensity than before. When her shaking stopped the young woman coughed, and water poured from her mouth. She sat up weakly, looked around, and gasped—clearly frightened by the lunar wolves staring back at her.

"*Beasts!*" she screamed in a frail, childish voice, and her eyes rolled into the back of her head as she fell unconscious once more.

CHAPTER 20

THE HEADLESS BIRD

Bob walked nervously across the padded floor of his tent. He didn't understand why he hadn't heard anything yet. It shouldn't be taking this long unless something had gone wrong.

A silver bird from Maude had arrived two days earlier; the note inside confirmed that the girl had departed from the market with Helen and was on her way to the Sheep Spa. That meant the coup to overthrow Dale should be finished by now, and Helen and the girl should be returning to the market soon if they hadn't already. That was the plan.

They were supposed to journey to the Sheep Spa and then return with Axel to the market after luring the Sheep Spa workers into following them back to the market. Maude and her soldiers would have plenty of time to carry out the coup before Helen and the girl returned. Then, once Dan's henchmen from the Sheep Spa reached the market, Maude and the soldiers would be ready to round them up too.

As Bob paced, he thought about what actions he would need to take if another day passed with still no word from Maude. He considered how many troops he could afford to send all the way to Waldoff, which was a three-day journey at the very fastest.

Several minutes passed before he heard his top aide, Lucas, call to him from outside the tent. "General, sir. It's Lieutenant Lucas. May I enter?"

"Yes, Lieutenant," Bob replied. A tall man in his early thirties dressed in a dark uniform pushed his way through the tent flap and saluted Bob. Bob saluted back and asked, "What do you have for me, Lieutenant?"

"General, sir, a silver bird was intercepted twenty minutes ago at the lookout post on Canyon Top. The private who intercepted it has been relieved from his post and is on his way here now, sir."

Bob felt a huge weight lift from his shoulders, though he was careful not to show it. He knew the silver bird would be from Maude, letting him know the coup had been a success. "Good. When he gets here bring the silver bird to me alone. In the meantime, tell the troop leaders to prepare the soldiers to march. I want everyone ready to go by zero two hundred."

"Sir! Yes, sir!" replied Lt. Lucas, who was having trouble containing his excitement. Like a boiling pot about to rattle its lid, he turned and left.

Once Bob was alone again, he sat down on a folding chair and leaned over, resting his head in his hands. He wasn't comfortable wielding so much power. He'd had countless moments of doubt during the two years he'd spent building his army. He'd never been sure that force was the way to solve their problem, and when putting so many lives on the line, he desperately wanted to be sure.

In his previous life on Earth, he'd been a dreamer and a tinkerer. Two traits that seemed to disqualify him from being a natural leader. He'd served his time in the military, working as an army engineer, but even then, he was mostly taking orders and rarely giving them. The closest he'd come to being any type of leader was during a short stint as a university professor after the war. Bob had only been at the job for one semester when he decided to test out an invention he'd been working on over winter break.

He drove to the nearest beach. He'd built the rocket-pack not so much for going up, but as a controlled way to come back down. Like a parachute with the option to go up and down, and side to side. Working up the nerve to take off was the hardest thing Bob had ever done, but his bravery was rewarded when he found himself on a journey to the Moon.

He and Maude had been on the Moon longer than any of the other Travelers, and because of this, they were treated like leaders. Though Bob never understood why. As soon as the others began to arrive, the couple became like a mother and father figure who were frequently called on to solve all sorts of problems.

Over time, Maude became a master at lunar chemistry and was able to learn more about the Moon than anyone else. Bob, who was already an engineer, taught himself to build new inventions using the Moon's materials. Whenever he couldn't find what he needed, he created alternative materials or asked Maude to make them for him.

As Bob thought about Maude, a twinge of pain bubbled to the surface. It reminded him of all he'd lost. He pushed it back down before it could burst, although he was grateful for the reminder. It helped him refocus on why their mission was so important and why he continued to lead despite feeling like an imposter most of the time.

The lieutenant tore back into the tent without announcing himself. Bob stood up quickly, and Lt. Lucas realized his error. "Begging your pardon, General, sir. I didn't mean to intrude. I brought the silver bird as quickly as I could."

Lt. Lucas held out what looked like a silver bird, but Bob knew right away that it wasn't one he'd made, which was troubling because Bob had made them all. He took it from the lieutenant. It was identical to his silver birds in almost every way, except that its small, pointed head was missing, and its wings were not the right shape. Instead of the tiny slivers of metal that he'd bolted to it from the inside compartment, there were two golden, triangle-shaped wings sticking out of the bird. A chill crept down Bob's spine.

He pushed his fingers against each side of the headless bird's stomach. The round door popped open, and Bob pulled a piece of paper from inside. He could tell that it had come from his own stash of paper, given to him by the lunar wolves long ago.

Before Bob created the metal notes, the lunar wolves had helped Maude and Bob by offering them paper that had been left behind by the Moon's first inhabitants, the Moon Walkers. The papers were covered in mysterious symbols and writings from long ago, but Maude had concocted an acidic formula that nearly washed away all the ink, making the paper reusable.

Neither Bob nor Maude had felt right about erasing ancient artifacts, but as the Moon Travelers' population grew, they became desperate for a way to record different kinds of information. Still, Bob had invented the metal engraving pens and writing sheets that replaced their need for paper as quickly as he could.

He unfolded the little note and read:

I've discovered your game,
thanks to the help of a barn cat.
Poor Maude. Never quite as clever
as everyone thought.
But I suppose that doesn't matter now.

I know Helen is out there,
and I know where she's going.
Once I find her, there's nothing you or that
ridiculous army of yours will be able to do to stop me.

Your smarter son,
Dan

A wave of panic crashed down on top of Bob. He continued to stare at the note until Lucas finally pulled him from his trance. "Is everything okay, sir?"

Bob looked at the lieutenant like he had just seen a ghost. He nodded once. Then he said, "I have to go away for a little while, Lucas. Lt. General Goodman will be in charge while I'm gone. Tell everyone they'd better be ready to march by the time I return."

CHAPTER 21

INTO THE DARK

Helen and Mina made their journey into the dark. Once they were surrounded by total darkness, Mina was thankful to discover that the map could glow on its own. It was just enough light for Mina to read Helen's words and see the ground a few steps in front of her.

"Why's it called the Sheep Spa?" Mina asked soon after they'd crossed over to the Darkside.

"Because at first only sheep lived there," Helen replied. "Like I explained before, the animals didn't show up until people started crossing the neon bridge. And for a while, only sheep made the journey across. Eventually, lots of other animals made the trip too, but there have never been as many of them as there have been sheep."

Mina continued to press. "But why is it called a spa? The name seems misleading."

Helen's words scrolled across the map. "Yes, it does. But when the name first came about, it wasn't so misleading. The factory wasn't built until after Theia's human population had reached over two thousand. That's when people started demanding to eat the animals that came across the bridge, just like they'd done on Earth.

"Before that there was a small building where the Travelers could take their pet sheep to be groomed. There, people bathed and sheered their sheep so that they'd have clean wool to use for knitted wear. Jokingly, it was referred to as the 'Sheep Spa.'

"Later on, the first Sheep Spa factory was built where the little building had been, but it was used for housing animals until they could be slaughtered. The name 'Sheep Spa' stuck around, probably because nobody could stomach the idea of giving it a proper name like…what was it you called it again? The terrifying slaughterhouse for intelligent animals?

"Anyway, the first Sheep Spa factory was near the market, but Dan burned it down when he destroyed the rest of the city. The Sheep Spa that we visited was built later on when Dan realized that people still craved food after they were poisoned."

"My god. What a shame," Mina replied. "Those animals deserve better."

Helen asked, "What would you change if you could?"

Mina thought about it for a minute and then answered, "Well, I'd start by preventing the more intelligent animals from being butchered.

"Okay, that's a good start. But how'd you go about judging the animals' intelligence?" asked Helen.

Mina replied, "I guess you'd have to do it by figuring out which animals could understand you and which ones couldn't."

Helen asked, "You think that if an animal can understand you, then it means it's more intelligent?"

The question made Mina feel defensive. "Yes, I'd say that's a good benchmark. Wouldn't you?"

"I don't know. Most of the people I've met during my life have been able to understand me just fine, but I'm not sure half of them would qualify as intelligent."

"*Ha-ha*," said Mina sarcastically. "But those are people you're talking about. I'm talking about how to test animal intelligence, not human intelligence," she argued.

"Well then, if you think there's a difference between animal intellect and human intellect, why would you judge an animal's intelligence using a scale that's biased towards human intelligence?"

Mina had to think about this question for a while. She knew it might be a valid point, but she wanted to explore it further. "I just think that it's quite remarkable for an animal to be able to understand a human, and even more remarkable if the animal can communicate back like the sheep did. It seems obvious to me that you wouldn't want to eat an animal like that, any more than you'd want to eat a human."

Helen rebutted, "I concur that it's remarkable for an animal to talk like a human or even to understand a human. But it isn't something I'd take into consideration when making my dinner plans."

With a hint of frustration, Mina asked, "What would you consider then? Or would you just eat all the animals regardless of their intelligence?"

"No. Quite the contrary. I'd eat none of the animals irrespective of their intelligence. It seems to me that if you want to treat the animals fairly, you should let them live out their natural lives without the fear of being eaten. Certainly, if we're the creatures with the highest intelligence, it stands to reason that we should have enough smarts to find plenty of alternatives to eating living creatures."

"So then, you don't eat animals? Like at all?" Mina asked.

"No," Helen responded. "I don't. I find the notion of killing sentient beings for food outrageous. Eating another creature when my survival isn't at stake doesn't seem logical to me. To do so means to devalue another life to the point of feeling justified in its destruction, just to satisfy one's appetite.

And I've never found a system of measure that allows me to justly devalue another animal's life to that extent. It's fully aware, conscious life we're talking about after all."

Mina smiled out of the corner of her mouth. "Okay, but what if you were *really* hungry and couldn't get to a vegetable fast enough?"

"Not funny!" flashed across the map several times.

Mina giggled. "Everything you said is reasonable, but I think it's hard for people to change their minds about something that's so widely accepted as normal. Even natural, really."

"What does it mean to be normal or natural, though? Your normal and natural could be very different than someone else's normal and natural. And besides, being normal or natural doesn't mean being right. Anyway, I wasn't trying to change your mind. These things have a way of sorting themselves out over time."

Mina was ready to change the subject. "Will you tell me your story now? You know, as long as you think it's safe?"

"Yes, Mina. Focus on the map. I'll guide you with the arrow at the top while I share my story. Watch the arrow turn. Focus…focus."

Mina suddenly felt very lightheaded as she stared at the map. She did her best to pay attention, though. Helen continued, "Very few people know what I'm about to tell you, but I think it's important for you to see the whole picture. Our world has gotten to the state it's in because we didn't spend enough time trying to understand each other in the beginning. And not understanding each other made it easy to disrespect one another. I don't want us to make that same mistake."

Mina nodded for Helen to keep going, but she still felt funny. The back of her head was beginning to tingle where the crystal had cut her.

Helen went on, "When Maude arrived on Theia, she didn't

cross over the bridge like the others or fly over like you, Fred, and Father. When Mom arrived it was by a beam of light that transformed a little wolf pup named Mawd into my mother.

"None of the wolves had ever known such a thing to happen before. My mother didn't have any memory of where she'd come from, and therefore, some of the wolves believed that she was the little girl pup transformed into a human. Even the little pup's mother believed so in the beginning.

"The pup's mother, Tahissi, had lost her three children and their father to the same tragedy. She was blinded by grief. The children's grandmother, however, was a powerful healer who'd witnessed the transformation take place. Eventually, she was able to convince Tahissi that the human woman was not her daughter."

"That's very sad," said Mina, "but why did it happen? Why did the little pup transform into Maude?"

"Nobody knows for certain, Mina. Theia's will is too great for any of us to decipher. She lives by millennia while the rest of us live only by seconds."

"So you're saying that the Moon…I mean, Theia is actually alive?" Mina asked.

"Yes, but not like you, me, or anyone else. It's a separate type of consciousness. A moon or planet's existence is different than anything we could hope to fathom. Trying to understand Theia's plan is like expecting the smallest earth creature to understand its place in the solar system when it can't even see ten centimeters past the rock it lives under. It's too big a concept to grasp."

"I see," Mina replied, doing her best to put all the pieces together.

"Let me back up a bit further," Helen continued. "I think it would help if I shared more of Theia's history with you."

Helen proceeded to tell Mina all she knew about the Moon Walkers and their ways, the bryobane and their demise, and the circumstances leading up to her mother's arrival on the Moon. Mina felt like she was living inside of the stories Helen recounted to her. Not like she saw a movie of them playing in her head, but like she was actually there watching it all happen. When Helen finished, she said:

Now, I will tell you my story. After my parents had the twins, they believed they were through having children. Mom had struggled through a difficult pregnancy, and the delivery didn't go well either. Besides, the twins turned into quite a handful as you might imagine, and my parents were already very busy. When they weren't helping with city plans, they were solving problems for the Moon Travelers, who looked to my parents for guidance on everything from marital advice to technical know-how.

Then one day, Neriti—the old, powerful healer and grandmother of the deceased triplets—visited my parents as she often did, but this time she told them that soon they would have another child: a girl who would carry Theia's energy inside of her and who would restore balance to the Moon.

Maude and Bob didn't know what to think of this. The twins were nearly in their teens, and they didn't know if having another child would be right for them. Yet, nevertheless, along I came a few years later.

From the moment I was born, Neriti, Axel, and several other healers guarded me around the clock. In many ways it was a relief for my parents. They were exhausted from having a newborn, and the extra help was appreciated. The wolves' presence didn't sit well with Dan, however. He had never cared for the wolves because he thought they were lesser animals that shouldn't be allowed to live freely among humans. So when the prophecy about my birth came true, and the healers were in and out of our house all the time, it drove Dan crazy.

He spent less and less time at home and started to hold meetings with other Moon Travelers who didn't like the wolves either. At first, they met secretly, but once their numbers grew large enough, they began to meet publicly in the city square. Of course, Dale was part of it all too. But as usual, he was mostly following Dan's lead.

Then one day, I became very sick. I cried constantly for weeks on end, but nobody knew what was wrong with me. My parents and their friends did everything they could to calm me down, but nothing worked. Eventually, I grew so weak that I finally stopped crying, and my parents were sure they would lose me.

It was then, however, that my father finally noticed something unusual about my skin. It was slowly becoming translucent. Nobody had detected it before because whenever I cried, I turned bright red, which masked the condition. My parents figured out that I was losing the pigment in my skin, causing it to appear invisible. Soon it would be possible to see right through to my insides.

Nobody on the Moon knew how to treat my illness. At the time, there were four doctors, and my parents consulted them all. The doctors tried their best, but after a while, they each told my parents to prepare for the worst.

Despite feeling extremely helpless, my parents never stopped looking for ways to heal me. They wrapped me in blankets; they laid me in the sun; they invented a special breathing machine that pumped high levels of oxygen into my blood, in hopes it would boost the production of the melanin pigment. They tried every herbal cream and homemade remedy they could come up with, but it was to no avail. They were running out of ideas.

That's when Neriti and the other healers stepped in.

They asked for my parents' permission to take me to Crystal Crater so they could use Theia's energy to heal me. Not knowing what else to do, my parents agreed and tried to go too. The lunar wolves, however, wouldn't allow it. They explained that the healing could only take place if my parents were willing to trust them unconditionally.

After discussing it thoroughly, Mom and Dad realized they had no reason not to trust Neriti and the other lunar wolves. In a way, I think it was easier for them to trust the wolves at that point than it was to trust themselves. I had only gotten worse with every new experiment they tried, whereas the wolves were confident they could save me.

The healers took me to Crystal Crater with the intent to perform their ancient healing ritual. However, as soon as they reached the bottom of the crater, they were surprised to find that I was already healed. Years later, Neriti told me what she believed happened. She said that the energy the healers had created to save her granddaughter, Mawd, had lingered in the crater until they brought me there. She was convinced it was that same energy that saved me.

All the healers were amazed. They believed a miracle had occurred and immediately started celebrating. But Neriti told them they weren't finished. She insisted that they go ahead and perform the ritual because part of the practice is to find the root cause of the injury in order to properly heal it. They placed me in their circle, and just as Neriti had suspected, the root cause of my injury was Dan. He had poisoned me.

The wolves took me home to my parents, but they didn't tell them what they'd learned. I still don't understand why, but I think it was their fear of the unknown. They may have worried that my parents would react poorly to the accusation. Or that it would set off a chain of events that the wolves already believed to be inevitable but were still hoping to avoid.

Their solution instead was to increase their protection over me. Several of the wolves took turns sleeping next to my crib every night, and others watched me during the day. When it came to my well-being, my parents were always happy to give the wolves free rein. They were extremely grateful to Neriti and the others for saving me and even referred to them as my guardian angels.

When I was old enough, the wolves began taking me all over Theia with them. My earliest memories are of Neriti and Axel carrying me around on their backs and bringing me things that pups enjoy playing with, like rocks, and sticks, and little wiggly animals. As I continued to grow, they taught me the healers' ways and treated me just like I was one of their own. And in my heart, I believed I was.

Soon, Neriti began to prepare me for the dark time that was to come. She spoke of it relentlessly. She wanted me to start thinking as though it were already here so I wouldn't waste time dwelling on it once it arrived. She and Axel and many others worked with me in secret every day. They passed down knowledge and taught me how to solve complex problems. It was hard work, but secretly I loved it because their attention made me feel special.

Meanwhile, Dan was building a following. The twins continued to lead the meetings where they stoked the flames of hatred towards the lunar wolves. Between their rambling speeches, which were always meant to belittle, they allowed people to air their grievances. To an outsider the complaints would have seemed trivial, exaggerated, or even completely fabricated (as many of them were), but the twins' followers ate it up.

Over and over, the meetings were the same: the twins blew hot air, several people stood up and told how the wolves have wronged them *this* time, the twins blew more hot air, and then the meeting was adjourned. It went on like this for years. It should have gotten old, but the people who attended never seemed to lose interest. In fact, they usually came back even more riled up and with friends in tow.

Then one day, once the crowds had become massive and Dan's rhetoric had reached a boiling point, he let them all in on a *little secret*. The wolves had been hiding something from the humans since the beginning.

"Get a load of this," he said to them. "*Certain people* don't want you to know this, but I would never lie to you. As soon as I found out, I thought, *the people have to know this.* All this time we could never confirm our suspicions about the untimely demise of those poor souls we discovered in the tunnel. The founders of this beautiful Moon of ours. We believed it was the sickness that killed them, but it wasn't! It was the wolves!"

This misunderstood truth turned the people's blood cold. After all, it was no coincidence that Dan's followers were the same individuals who believed the fairytales about the bryobane remains. For decades, they'd created backstories and lore around the remains. They'd built statues and erected temples devoted to worshipping them. And all while ignoring the wolves' pleas to leave the matter alone.

Now it made sense to them why the wolves had never approved of their worshiping of the bones. The wolves had killed the first Moon people to usurp control. When these people were at their weakest—fighting the terrible disease that turned them into giant beasts—the wolves seized their opportunity to overpower and murder them. And once Dan had firmly established this altered version of the truth in his followers' heads, the next connection was an easy one to make. If the Travelers didn't immediately exterminate the wolves, they would befall the same fate as the Moon's first inhabitants.

The mob went wild. Every wolf they could get their hands on was murdered on the spot. No pack went unscathed. Almost the entire population of wolves was wiped out in a matter of weeks, including many of my friends. Just as she'd foreseen, Neriti was one of the first ones to be killed.

After it was done, Dan made off to Black Ice Glacier to a fort he'd been building at the top of Theia. Along the way, he captured over a dozen lunar wolves, who were fleeing the violence he'd incited. He imprisoned them in his fort, and ever since then has been doing experiments on them to learn more about the Great Energy.

It was devastating. The lunar wolves who survived went into hiding. Axel, of course, was one of them. Before he left, he warned my parents to watch me closely. He finally revealed that Dan had caused my illness when I was an infant. He told us that because of the prophecy Neriti had foretold, Dan would eventually return to kill me if possible.

My parents were horrified. They knew about Dan and Dale's meetings and had tried to counter my brothers' actions by speaking out against them. It did little good, though. By the time Dan and Dale had started openly having their meetings, the hatred towards the wolves had already grown too strong. The tide was against my parents and their allies.

When they learned that Dan had tried to kill me, however, they went ballistic. Dan had disappeared to the Darkside, so they confronted Dale to see how much he knew about Dan's early attempt on my life. I'm not sure what happened during the confrontation. But when it was over, they kicked Dale out of the house, and he went to live with Dan on the Darkside.

Afterward, Mom and Dad didn't' let me out of their sight. I began to feel like a prisoner. They were terrified that Dan would return in secret to harm me, but this wasn't the only reason they were worried. Everything changed after the lunar wolves were massacred. Nobody trusted anyone anymore. There were lots of people who didn't like what Dan's followers had done, but they were too scared to do anything about it after witnessing the kind of cruelty those people were capable of.

Sometimes, people would make comments that exposed their disdain for the violence that had occurred. This always led to terrible fights. There were even several instances when people were murdered over their objections to what had been done to the wolves.

The city continued to function as it always had, but everyone was on edge. The tension was palpable. My parents thought about moving us to another part of Theia, but they were afraid of becoming too isolated. It was a no-win situation. A few years went by when, out of the blue, Dale showed up and began holding meetings again, just like the old days. But this time, instead of talking about the wolves, he was talking about water.

We couldn't figure out what he was up to, but some of the people who'd gone to hear him speak reported back to my parents. It turned out he was telling everyone that my parents had purposely kept water out of the city since the beginning. Like I told you before, he was convincing them that water would solve all their problems. It seemed to be an endeavor to recruit even more people to their side.

When Dan reappeared shortly after with the solution for delivering water to the masses, my parents were determined to stop him. They knew he had to be planning something evil, and they talked endlessly about what they should do. Nothing they came up with was safe, though, and I grew nervous that one or both of them would do something foolish and get themselves killed.

It was then that I decided to take matters into my own hands. My entire childhood, the wolves had been preparing me to solve big problems, and Neriti had prophesized that I would one day restore balance to Theia. I was certain this meant I was supposed to stop Dan. I realize now how naïve it seems, but you have to understand. Not only did I feel empowered by what the wolves had taught me, but I also felt the need to avenge my friends.

Dan had already returned to the Darkside with the volunteers who signed up to install the water pipes. I crossed over, determined to find him. I'd made it almost all the way to Black Ice Glacier when Axel caught up to me. He begged me to turn around. He told me this wasn't the way to fight Dan, but I didn't believe I had a choice. When I wouldn't listen, he insisted on going with me. I didn't want him to because I worried it would put him in danger, but he wouldn't take no for an answer.

When we reached Dan's, we were met by dozens of bryobane skulls hanging from the outer wall of his fort. Dan had taken them from the tunnel and was using them as terrifying décor to deter trespassers, I guess. I wasn't scared, though. Only appalled.

I knocked on the huge door at the bottom of the fort. I was prepared to tell Dan that if he ever dared show his face in the city again, I'd tell everyone what he'd done to me as a poor, helpless baby and then send the rest of the wolves after him. Unfortunately, I never got the chance.

What nobody knew was that Dan had been keeping a very big secret for years. He'd discovered a way to make himself appear invisible by using ground up crystals that he turned into a formula. The formula allows him to connect to a part of Theia's energy that alters perception. Making himself invisible was how he learned the lunar wolves' secrets. He was there while the healers were teaching me their ways, only no one could see him. It's how he found out what really happened to the bryobane, which gave him the idea to use the wolves' truth against them. And, of course, this eventually led to their massacre.

I continued to knock on the door for a long time, but Dan never answered. I asked Axel to sniff around and see what he could find. He'd only gone a short distance when, suddenly, I felt a burning hot liquid pouring over me.

Dan appeared out of thin air right in front of my face as I screamed in agony. Axel came running back, but it was too late for him to do anything. Dan had finally found a way to get rid of me, using a formula he'd created to purge me from the world.

Hurting and in shock, I didn't realize the extent of my injury right away. I screamed at Axel to run back and tell my parents what had happened. And he ran, so I thought he could still hear me. I threatened Dan with everything I could think of and more, but he talked over me the entire time. Then finally, when I began to listen to what he was saying, I figured out what he'd done to me. He said he'd chosen to erase me so that I could suffer the pain of not being seen or heard. He believed it was a punishment worse than death, and since his goal was to get rid of me, this seemed like the cruelest way possible.

I was furious, but there was nothing I could do. He had turned me into a ghost. I couldn't even interact with objects like a real person. With nothing left to lose, I went inside the fort to explore, but it was just another gut punch. Inside, I found the sad, emaciated lunar wolves, as well as dozens of formulas and hundreds of piles of notes. I also found gruesome keepsakes and inventions, like the rooms filled with bones from different animals and all of Dan's many, many torture devices.

I couldn't stand being there for long, so I decided to go back to my parents. I knew there wasn't anything I could do to alert them to my presence, but I thought it would bring me some peace of mind to be home. It didn't.

Axel had, indeed, run back to tell them what he'd seen, and when they found out, they went straight to Dale and told him that all of this had to stop immediately. They told him he had to convince Dan to call everything off before things got even worse than they already were.

Their demands fell on deaf ears, though. If Dale had ever had any warm feelings towards our parents, those feelings were long gone by this point. He told them that I'd been foolish to confront Dan and get myself killed and that he would never make the same mistake. Besides, he said that Dan planned to give him full control over the city once the water lines were installed. And before our parents had time to reason with him, Dale ordered the guards to take them away.

When Dale informed Dan that Axel had shown up in the city again, Dan went into a mad rage. To punish Axel, he set off poisonous gas bombs in the tunnels that housed the surviving lunar wolves. The gas didn't kill them, though. Instead, it took away their ability to speak. I can't say for sure why he didn't just go ahead and kill the remainder of the free wolves then, but probably it's because he thinks he might need them someday. Like in case he impulsively kills the ones he already has.

This part of the story you know already. Almost everyone in the city began to drink the water and forget—eventually becoming the most obnoxious, self-involved versions of themselves. After that, Dan burned everything to the ground and left his guards in charge to make sure nobody ever left the market.

Many years later, Dan sent one last message to my parents via Dale. It was attached to a formula. It said that if my mom drank the formula, he'd allow Dale to tell them what had really happened to me. Clearly, Dan felt the urge to poke at them after being away for so long. He needed to show them he could still torment them whenever he pleased.

Mom chose to drink the formula. She knew it could've been a trick. She knew Dan was perfectly capable of poisoning his own mother, but I don't think she cared anymore. My parents had changed. They had been hopeless for years. In my invisible state, I had watched them go on living, but they, too, were just ghosts of their former selves.

Mom suffered terribly after drinking the liquid Dan sent her, but as you know, it didn't kill her. Surprisingly, Dale held true to Dan's word. He let my parents know I'd been alive all this time but that nobody would ever be able to hear or see me again. He also informed them that the formula Mom had ingested would cause her to begin aging again, just like her children. The only difference was that the formula forced Mom to age rapidly until she reached her true age.

It was funny in a way because evidently Dan saw aging as a terrible punishment that he could torture Mom with. Yet I think she was actually relieved to begin the aging process again. In a lot of ways, it was the surreal experience of living agelessly on Theia for so long that had been the real torture.

Dan's plan backfired in another way too. The knowledge that I was still alive didn't cause my parents to suffer; it gave them new life. They were full of hope for the first time in ages. They started to dream again and make plans. It was exhilarating to watch. Right away, they began running experiments in secret, trying to find a way to communicate with me. It took several inventions and a lot of tweaking, but ultimately, they got *the map* to work.

I felt reborn. I'd spent years in solitude, watching the remnants of the world I once knew pass me by. But now I had a voice again. Even if it were through written words and not sound, it was paradise compared to what I'd been through.

However, my parents were even more determined than ever to lock me away and never let me out of their presence again. This meant keeping the paper concealed as much as possible and calling me *the map*, instead of Helen. They began to build a secret resistance to protect the few things they had left: their hidden experiments, their clandestine meetings, their covert communications, and me. They called on old friends they knew they could trust. Ones who had never given in to drinking the water either.

What was unexpected was that once they started working to unite people again, their friends and acquaintances began pressuring them to put an even bigger plan into action. It turned out that these free-thinkers and holdouts had never lost hope (even in the worst of times) that someday they would overthrow the twins and take back Theia.

Mom and Dad were inspired by the spirit and determination of these other Moon Travelers. Soon, Dad had crafted a plan to escape the market and travel to the Darkside in order to establish an army base there. Mom, in the meantime, formulated a system to recruit soldiers, by healing people who had been consuming the poisonous water.

Other members of the resistance brought people to her that they knew had been cajoled into drinking the water by family or friends. These were people who had never been followers of Dan and Dale. They were just people who had been swept up into something that was bigger than they understood.

The plan worked. When Maude's patients regained their senses, they were happy to do whatever was needed to help the cause. The majority were sent to the Darkside to join Bob's army. There are about three hundred soldiers over there right now, ready to fight Dan. And Mom has likely succeeded at reclaiming the market with the soldiers who stayed behind to help her. She even managed to recruit several of Dan's guards to their side.

Unfortunately, what nobody realizes is that none of this is enough. Dan is as tricky as they come. There was never going to be a plan the resistance could create that would succeed at toppling him—whether it involved stealth, force, or both. The only way to outsmart him is to ensure that he has no way of knowing what's coming. And that's why you're here, Mina.

After the lunar wolf massacre, I had a very difficult time. I experienced what's known as survivor's guilt. In my head and heart, I always believed I was a lunar wolf, so when the wolves were attacked by people that looked like me on the outside, I felt ashamed.

I wanted to rip off my flesh and become a wolf so I could show Dan's followers that I was the same as those they sought to persecute. I wanted to die with Neriti, not for a cause, but because it was too painful to be alive when those I loved were being murdered in cold blood.

My mom's friend, Ruth, was the one who pulled me back from the brink. She had a close relationship with the wolves too. She'd reciprocated their original offering of gifts. She brought them food and other items she knew they'd enjoy, like metal toys for the pups and wool blankets to be used as ground coverings in their dens.

The pack leaders considered her an honorary wolf because of the many kindnesses she paid them. They bestowed on her a small crystal taken from Crystal Crater. It is the most special type of gift a wolf can give because they consider crystals sacred, especially the ones found inside of Crystal Crater.

Ruth has worn it ever since, although she does so now in secret. But here's the thing, Mina. When Maude and Bob were busy trying to connect me to the paper, I realized that I was able to use Ruth's crystal to take control of her thoughts.

It wasn't something I meant to do. I'd been trying to talk to her through the crystal when I discovered the power it had. Quickly, I came up with a plan. I knew I had to be the one to confront Dan. After all, Neriti's prophecy had predicted that I would be the one to restore balance. But my parents were never going to let me near Dan again, so I invented my *own* prophecy and used Ruth to make it seem real.

I took ahold of Ruth's thoughts and had her write down the made-up prophecy. It foretold that two Earth children would come to Theia with the help of wings invented by a Moon Traveler. The first would be a boy and the second a girl. The boy would pave the way for the girl to succeed, and then later the girl would save everyone with the help of a talking map."

I was terrified once I was finished. I knew if they didn't take the prophecy seriously that I might never have another chance to get past my parents. I left Ruth alone to discover what she'd written, but I truly didn't know if anyone would believe it. Luckily, Ruth showed my parents, and the three of them decided that it had to be a prophecy sent from Theia. They worried a little that it might be Dan's creation. However, they assumed that if he had the power to control minds, he would be using it for something far more devious than writing fake prophecies.

Immediately, Bob went to work on building the wings. When he was finished, he flew to the platform with the last bit of fuel he'd been saving from his rocket-pack. Then my mother and I thought of a plan to ensure that "Ruth's prophecy" actually worked. I would guide the first child to the Sheep Spa to try and divert Dan's attention away from what Bob was doing at the base. If we could make Dan think we were up to something else, then Bob's army would have a better chance of succeeding when they finally attacked.

The plan we made up for you was like I told you before. We were going to lure the rest of Dan's guards away from the Spa so that Maude's soldiers could round them up once they reached Waldoff Market.

But neither of these plans was my real plan. My real plan was to find a way out of the market so I could face Dan one last time. Fred was my test run…and look, Mina. I know this was wrong, but I used Fred as a decoy for my own purposes. I gave him information that I wanted Dan to know before sending him on an errand to get captured. Afterward, it was Axel who carried me back to the market.

You are the one I've been waiting for to help me complete the final portion of my plan. But what I'm going to ask you to do is extremely dangerous. In a moment, I will tell you the whole plan, but it has to be kept strictly between us for it to work. Once, I'm finished you can decide what you want to do. Does that sound fair?

Mina had been so engrossed in Helen's story that it was like she was coming out of a dream. Her mind felt cloudy the way her eyes normally did when she first woke up. She took a moment to think about what Helen was asking. There wasn't a single part of her that didn't ache to go home, but she decided to listen to Helen's plan. "Okay, go ahead," she said. "I can't promise there's much I can do to help, but I'll listen."

Helen continued by telling Mina all the details of the plan, and when she was finished, she said, "I've laid out all the risks in no uncertain terms. And you must know that if you die here, nobody knows what that would mean for you. You aren't tethered to this realm *or* your own anymore. But if we succeed, then you will have saved the Moon Travelers *and* the lunar wolves from a terrible, terrible fate. So what is your gut telling you to do, Mina?"

Mina knew her answer right away. "It doesn't seem like I have much of a choice, to be honest. However, I do have one condition. It will mean altering the plan, though."

"What's your condition?" Helen asked.

"To save Fred. No matter what happens to us, Fred has done his part. It's only fair that he be rescued."

Helen paused for a second and then answered, "You drive a tough bargain, Mina. But okay. We'll save Fred."

CHAPTER 22

THE GREENHOUSE

The greenhouse was four and a half stories tall with a slanted roof. It was made from thousands of glass panes that fit into a crisscrossed titanium frame. The tinted glass panes glowed dark green and were lit from within by a host of dim fluorescent bulbs.

Mina was nervous. She gripped the map tightly. "What should I do?" she asked.

"Go ahead and enter," the words appeared across the map. "Ask for the blueprints and see what you can find out about Fred. Then leave when I give you the signal."

Mina still wasn't sure what to expect. She stalled. "And why do I have to ask about the blueprints again?"

Helen replied, "Because it will alert Dan to our whereabouts. We're leaving him a trail to follow so he thinks he has the upper hand."

Mina felt like she had a million questions, but she knew it was just her mind's way of avoiding the inevitable. She took a few more steps towards the glass building. She looked down at the map one more time to see if Helen was giving her any last-minute information, but the paper was blank. She dropped it to her side, knowing she would have to navigate on her own now.

When she reached the front of the building, she heard a soft melody coming from inside, and for a moment Mina thought it was children singing. She walked closer and noticed a large pane of glass perfectly aligned with the center of the building. *Hopefully that's the door*, she thought. A split-second later, the glass slid open and released a warm gust of wind.

Mina looked through the entryway and saw the shadowy outlines of ropes hanging from the ceiling. It was an unsettling sight, but Mina steeled herself and went inside. The soft melody grew louder when she entered the gigantic room. She looked up at the ceiling and all around as her eyes adjusted to the lights. Much to her relief, she realized that it hadn't been ropes hanging from the ceiling, but vines. The entire greenhouse was covered in them. Just like the ones she'd seen back at the market.

There were tall vines that had ascended to the top of the greenhouse and curled around the grow lights. There were small vines in pots on tables, just beginning to bud. There were lush, leafy vines that had spread across the tables and some that had climbed partway up the glass walls. Something Mina found peculiar, though, was that many of the vines had books, upside down pots, or even bricks and clothes irons balanced on top of them, as was the case for some exceptionally thick vines. Mina had never seen anything like it before and couldn't think of a reason for such nonsense.

She walked towards a vine that was not much taller than herself when she heard a woman's crackly, old voice. "Hello, little girl. Are you lost?"

Mina looked around for the woman but didn't see her. The vines were so dense and the lights so dim that it was hard to see anything at all behind the vines. Mina responded, "No, ma'am. I'm not lost at all. I've come here on purpose."

Mina heard the soft spritzing of a spray bottle. "Oh, you think you have a purpose, do you?" asked the woman.

Mina was confused. "For being here? Well, yes. I know I do, actually. I need to find—"

But the woman cut her off. "Did you know that most people think exactly the same thing as you?"

Even more confused than before, Mina stuttered, "I-I'm sorry, but I don't understand. What exact same thing do most people think?"

The woman continued to spray the plants as she said, "That they have a purpose. That they're *special*. And I guess that means you think you're special too, doesn't it?"

Mina had no idea what the woman was getting at and wondered if the woman even knew. However, not wanting to get too far sidetracked, she said, "I *do* have a purpose for being here. I've come to ask for the blueprints to the greenhouse."

The woman didn't say anything, but Mina could hear her shuffling footsteps coming closer. A moment later, she emerged from behind a dense wall of vines, holding her spray bottle in front of her, as though it were a weapon. She was short and squatty with blotchy skin, and her hair was tied up on top of her head in a tight bun. She had warts on her face and crooked teeth, but she wore a nice, proper, long-sleeved dress with an ivory neck brooch that was pinned perfectly in the center of her high collar. *My god! She's the hybrid of an old schoolmarm and a witch*, Mina thought.

The old lady looked Mina over and then laughed. "You came here to find the greenhouse blueprints, did you? Out of the question! I didn't give them to that last winged child that came looking for them, and I won't be giving them to you either!"

Mina was surprised. She hadn't realized that Fred had made it all the way to the greenhouse. "Was the last winged child a boy?" she asked the woman.

The woman glared at Mina. "Yes, I suppose so. Why do you ask?"

Mina ignored the woman's question. "Do you know what happened to him?" she asked.

The woman eyed Mina suspiciously and then glanced down at where Mina was holding the map by her side. A knot tightened in Mina's stomach. It worried her that the woman had homed in on Helen, especially right after Mina had asked about Fred. She decided to change the subject. She asked, "Where's that melody coming from? It sounds like children singing."

"Hrmph," the woman groaned, continuing to look at Mina with suspicion. "That's the sound of my English ivies growing. They do that when they're healthy, you know."

"No, I didn't know *any* plants could sing. It's very lovely."

The woman shrugged. "Yes, it is. Anyway, if the blueprints are all you came for, then you can go ahead and leave now. Don't need you wasting anymore of my precious time. I've got too many plants to water and weeds to pull!" Then the woman turned around and disappeared into a tangled mess of vines.

Mina followed undeterred, though she felt a bit wary due to her previous vine experience. "You aren't growing any swelter vines in here, are you?" she asked.

The woman snickered. "Swelter vines? There's no such thing as *swelter vines*. Where did you learn such rubbish?"

Mina protested, "There is too such a thing! I was attacked by one. It wrapped itself around my entire body!"

"That's poppycock!" the old woman snapped. "If a vine did that to you, it's because someone sprinkled some sweltering formula on it. Vines can't just do that on their own. Don't you know *anything*?"

Mina's jaw dropped. She realized that if the woman was telling the truth, then someone had intended for Mina to get snatched by the vine. Mina tore herself from this thought, however, when she noticed the woman was getting away. She hurried to catch up. "Please, ma'am—"

Without stopping the woman barked, "Don't call me that! My name is Betsy, but you should address me only as 'Botanist,' seeing as how I don't like you."

"Fine," Mina complied. "Please, Botanist, tell me why you won't give me the blueprints."

Betsy answered, "I don't have time for this. Don't you see how many plants there are that depend on me? If I spent all my time helping you silly winged creatures, there'd be no time left to help all these dear plants."

Mina didn't know what to say, but she continued to follow the botanist through the maze of vines. There were all different sorts. There were ivies, honeysuckle, wisteria, and jasmine, just like she'd seen back on Earth, except that their flowers were much smaller. There were also vines that Mina had never seen before. Vines that were as large as trees with leaves the size of serving platters.

The botanist stopped abruptly. She squinted her eyes at a vine in front of her, held up her spray bottle, and pulled the trigger. A cloud of fine mist floated towards it.

Mina used the moment to ask, "Botanist, why are the flowers so tiny on all these vines?"

"Ha!" Betsy exclaimed as she began to walk again. "That's a very wrong question, indeed. The *right* question is why are there any flowers at all? Vines are better without flowers. Everyone knows that. Yet, I can't get these darned things to shrink out of sight no matter how much shrinking elixir I give them!"

"I see," said Mina, "but if that's what you're trying to accomplish, then wouldn't it make more sense to give them a vanishing elixir?"

"If only such a thing existed," sighed the old botanist. "Alas, there are only two elixirs to assist with flower rearing: the shrinking kind and the growing kind. Although the latter is a complete waste of a concoction, if you ask me. Who would ever want a flower to grow *more*? What a state of disarray *that* would be! Flowers taking over everything, no doubt. Can you imagine!?"

Amused over the botanist's outburst, Mina replied, "Dear me, no! How horribly pretty it would all be!"

Betsy didn't seem to be paying the least bit of attention to Mina, however. She stopped and spritzed a large entanglement of ivies. Then she turned in Mina's direction and looked at her with annoyance. "You're still here? Didn't you hear what I said? I don't have time to be diddle dawdling all day. Be gone! Or would you rather these plants all shrivel up and die while I'm tending to your ridiculous desires?" Betsy turned away and continued her stroll through the tangled mess of plants.

Mina was frustrated. It was proving more difficult to talk to the botanist than it had been to talk to the three-headed sheep. Nevertheless, she continued to follow her. With a deep groan, Mina replied, "No, of course that's not what I want. Though to be honest, I don't really understand why you're growing all these vines in the first place."

The botanist spun around. "Of course you don't. You're just a stupid, little bunny rabbit who doesn't understand anything at all. Just like you, these vines need someone to teach them how to grow properly. You can't expect them to grow big and strong all by themselves, you know?" The botanist paused and looked upward with exasperation. Then she looked at Mina again and shook her head. "No, I guess you don't know, do you?" The botanist kept walking.

Mina shook her head too. "I really don't. Where I come from, plants grow mostly outside in the sunlight and only need a little water and pruning to help them grow."

Betsy turned her face to Mina with a horrified expression.

"Pruning? *Pruning?* Where do you come from?! A world full of monsters?"

Mina giggled. She couldn't help it. The woman's outrage seemed like an absurd overreaction. "No, I come from a world full of people, and sometimes in order for plants to grow bigger, they have to be cut back a little."

"That's the most preposterous thing I've ever heard!" said the woman as she continued to make her way through the greenhouse.

Mina argued, "I don't see how that's any more preposterous than putting pots, books, bricks, and *clothes irons* on top of plants. That's not even helpful like pruning!"

The botanist was disgusted. "I'll have you know that 'stunting,' as we professionals call it, is actually very helpful. It allows the vines to grow at the same rate as all of the other vines of the same age. This way they don't get too big before they're ready to go to market."

"That's silly. Why not let the vines grow at their own pace and then send them to market when they're big enough?"

"No! No! No!" Betsy shook her head emphatically, throwing her hands in the air as she walked. "That's not how it's done! There has to be the right number of vines sent to market each time. It's the only way to create demand. It would be terrible if the vines went to waste!"

Mina was surprised by this statement. "Have you been to the market lately?" she asked.

Betsy rolled her eyes dramatically. "No," she replied. "*Why?*"

"Because I don't think your plan is working. The whole plant section is covered in vines."

The botanist stopped again. They had reached the back corner of the greenhouse, away from the tunnels of vines. There were rows of clay pots on the ground. Some were filled with soil while others sat empty by a large pile of dirt. Another dozen or so sat in the corner chipped and broken and covered in cobwebs.

Mina wondered if she'd upset the botanist. She was standing perfectly still and wasn't making a sound. Mina could see the botanist's reflection in the glass in front of them, but the image was too warped to make out her expression.

Suddenly, the squatty botanist turned and lunged at Mina, catching her off guard. She was shaking and crying, and she yelled in Mina's face, "Why are you still here? Do you think it's amusing to harass an old woman whose only desire is to perform an honest day's work? Leave here at once!"

Betsy dropped the spray bottle as she pressed her hands to her face. Then she ran behind a curtain of vines and started to sob. Mina felt guilty for upsetting the old botanist. She surmised that the woman's unpleasant demeanor was due to the fact that she had nothing else in her life except for her job at the greenhouse. Mina decided she would try to be more respectful, even if the woman refused to return the sentiment.

"I'm very sorry I hurt your feelings," she called. "But I really can't leave here until you give me the blueprints or tell me where they are. It shouldn't take more than a minute of your time, and then you can be rid of me forever. I promise!"

The botanist emerged from behind the curtain of vines. She pulled a handkerchief from her pocket to blow her nose and dab at her eyes. Then she took a seat on one of the over-turned pots in the corner. Something seemed different about the botanist, and Mina thought it might be that her eyes looked darker than before. She didn't think about it much, though, because she was trying to decide whether the botanist's reappearance was a sign that she was finally ready to cooperate. Copying the woman, Mina sat down on a pot nearby.

Betsy asked calmly, "Do you know what a weed is?"

It was a strange question, Mina thought. But she had

decided to be nice, so she answered, "It's a plant that harms the plants around it."

"Wrong!" the woman screamed at Mina. "It's a wild plant that grows where it's not wanted." Then she repeated with emphasis, *"Where it's not wanted."*

"I get it," Mina said.

"Do *you?*" asked the old botanist. "Let's see if that's true. Look over there at those disgusting weeds."

Mina looked to where the botanist pointed and saw several small pots that contained two different kinds of vines she'd never seen before. One was dark and shiny and looked sort of like a black, fuzzy caterpillar with beautiful, red petals like hibiscus flowers. The other type of vine was a brown, wooden one that had specks of white, blue, and violet covering its bark. Some of these were growing flowers that looked like orchid petals bursting with orange and yellow.

Mina looked back at the botanist and frowned. "Those vines? Right there?" she asked. "Why would you refer to those vines as weeds when they're even prettier than the ones you're trying to grow?"

Betsy smirked haughtily. "I call them weeds because I can. Did I plant them in those pots? You better believe I didn't. That makes them wild. Am I happy they're growing there? Absolutely not! Which means they're unwanted and therefore weeds. And do you know what happens to weeds?"

Mina shook her head.

"I rip them up by their necks and tear their little spines out of the pots. Pots they have no *right* to be in! Then I throw them in the trash so they can rot into dust."

Mina could see that the conversation had taken a dark turn. She asked gently, "You do know that those vines have no control over where they grow, right? And maybe even more importantly that they don't have necks or spines? I mean that just seems like Botany 101, to be honest. Not to be rude, of course. I'm just trying to tell you that it's not personal."

The botanist replied, "It *is* personal! Do you know how much work I have to do to keep those hideous things from growing in here? Those hideous plants that think they're entitled to a pot in *my* greenhouse!"

Mina couldn't stop herself from trying to talk sense into the old botanist. "Wouldn't it be easier if you just let them grow? Maybe people at the market would want to buy them, and then you could benefit from them instead of spending so much time destroying them. Certainly, people aren't rushing to buy the other types of vines. Seems like it's at least worth a shot."

"No! Nobody wants a black or brown vine. People are used to green vines, and they don't like change! What a *terrible* botanist you would make."

Mina was discouraged. She hadn't meant to get so sidetracked again. She attempted to pull the conversation back. "Well, like you said, it's your greenhouse. Now, if you don't mind, may I have the blueprints so I can be on my way?"

The botanist frowned at Mina and shook her head. "Absolutely not. I told you already, I'm not giving them to you."

"Ugh!" Mina grunted in frustration. She'd felt so close, and she was getting tired of trying so hard. She knew that getting the blueprints wasn't actually the point of this charade, but she felt oddly determined anyway. She didn't want to let this strange, little woman get the best of her. "Please, botanist. It's for a good cause. There are people out there who want to do the same work as you. They have great respect for your job, and they've sent me to bring back the greenhouse plans so they can nurture plants, just like you do."

The woman retorted with a shaky voice, "You mean so they can do it *better* than me. That's what everyone out there thinks. They don't like the plants I send to market, and they think my job's so easy that they can do it better themselves. Isn't that true?"

Mina shook her head. "No. That's not true at all. Besides, they don't even want to grow vines. They want to grow vegetables."

Betsy smiled a horrible, knowing grin. Full of angry, crooked teeth. "Of course that's what they want to grow. The ones who still have their senses have always wanted to grow their own vegetables. They think they can take away my power if they have their own vegetable garden. Do they really think if they build their own greenhouse that I won't find it? Ha! Well, here's what I want *you* to do. You go tell those dirty rats that I will never allow it! Never!"

The botanist was so worked up she was practically foaming at the mouth. Mina had become extremely worried. She glanced down at the map. It hung at the side of the pot she was perched on, facing away from the woman. "RUN NOW!" flashed across it in bold letters.

She was confused. Helen hadn't given the signal. Had the plan changed? Mina felt too nervous to run. She wasn't sure she could make it back through the maze of vines; there was no clear-cut path. She thought the best thing to do would be to keep her cool, to pretend she was only leaving because she'd finally given up hope of getting the blueprints.

"Well, I guess you told me. I'll return to the Dayside now and let those rats know it's never going to happen." Mina stood up and began to go, hoping to get away from the botanist as quickly as possible.

But Betsy followed her. "You know why Dan chose me to run the greenhouse for him?"

Mina didn't say anything but shook her head. She was barely listening as she tried to sort out which way to go. She did her best not to panic, but she realized she had no idea how to find her way out.

"It's because I'm loyal and smart. I've been friends with the twins almost since birth."

Mina didn't stop but muttered, "Oh, I didn't realize psychopaths were capable of making friends."

The botanist grew angrier. "He's out there, you know? Waiting! He knew you'd be hard to get rid of. Told old Betsy to lead you away from the door so you wouldn't know how to escape. Gotta give it to him. He's always right about these things. A true mastermind! *Nobody* can match his wits." Then she leaned over Mina's shoulder with a devilish grin and whispered, "Time for you to scamper along, little rabbit. It's bunny pie day, and Uncle Dan is waiting for you."

A wave of terror crashed into Mina. She hurried away, leaving Betsy behind. She ran past a wall of vines and through a tunnel of creepers. Then another wall, and another wall, and another tunnel. She had no idea if she was going the right way. She was running scared, certain that at any minute she would run directly into Dan.

She heard the botanist calling to her in a raspy voice. "If you can still hear me, little rabbit, I just thought you'd like to know that you're a fool who was sent on a fool's errand…not that it will matter soon." Betsy broke into a loud, sadistic cackle.

Mina didn't have time to think about what the botanist meant. She hurried around another long row of hanging vines and stopped. She looked down at the map to see if Helen had anything to say about their predicament. "You're on your own now, but you won't be for long. Fold the map up quickly, and put it inside your bag. Then eat the cucumber. There's no time to explain. Just do it!"

Mina yelled, "I thought we were in this together! What do you mean *eat the cucumber*?"

But Helen ignored Mina's protests. "Do it now, Mina! Hurry!"

Mina was confused and upset that Helen was deviating from the plan without any explanation. Plus, she had no idea why she was being ordered to eat a cucumber. Still, she shoved the map in the bag and grabbed the green, vegetable-like fruit. *Focus, Mina!* she told herself as she took a few bites of the sweet, watery gourd. *You've got to make your own plan now. Find the exit. Hold the bag behind your back. When you see Dan, run at him and hit him across the face with the bag. Then run away before he has time to react. You can do this!*

Mina believed in her plan. She played it on repeat in her head as she ran, bobbing and weaving between the vines. Every time, she imagined herself leveling the evil man-beast she believed Dan to be. Soon she forgot she was running at all. She could only see the dream and feel the power it gave her.

For the umpteenth time, she ran at Dan in her mind. This time, though, he was standing on top of a tall, shiny tower, and instead of running towards him, Mina was taking huge leaps through the air. She began to pull the tote bag from behind her back, just like she'd imagined before. She would use the momentum that she'd built up from her giant steps to swipe a mighty blow across the side of Dan's head. Her eyes grew narrow as she focused. However, when she pulled the bag from behind her back, she saw that she was actually holding a massive block of cheese, bigger than any she'd ever seen. Her fingers quivered under the weight of it.

A look of shock and surprise crossed Mina's face as the rotten smelling cheese hit Dan with such force that it clung to his head and began to melt. Then Dan's head melted too, followed by the rest of his body. Mina couldn't believe it. She'd turned the evil moon man into a puddle of goo.

Before she had time to celebrate, a blast of icy air struck her in the face, jolting her out of her dream. She was standing at the exit. The sliding door was wide open. She was still holding the tote bag firmly behind her back, but she had no memory of how she got there. Confused, she didn't know if she'd just awoken from a dream or fallen into one.

Dan wasn't there like she had expected him to be, but everything else was the way she remembered it from when she first arrived. It took a while for the fog to lift, but eventually she became confident that her present reality was, indeed, reality. Mina exited the glass building and walked a few steps forward. The sliding door whooshed shut behind her.

She turned her head left and right, looking to see if Dan was anywhere to be found. Her eyes hadn't adjusted to the dark again, but she was pretty sure she'd be able to detect someone moving if they were close by. She didn't see anything and decided she needed to get as far away from the greenhouse as possible. If Dan were out there, looking for her, it would be easy for him to see her against the backdrop of the glowing, green structure.

Mina walked back into the night. This time without the map's light to help her see. Her stomach rumbled. "How can you eat at a time like this when you haven't been hungry in days? Maybe even weeks? Besides, didn't I just feed you a cucumber?" she asked her stomach. Strangely, she couldn't remember the answer to this last question, but she chalked it up to the panicky state she'd been in while fleeing.

Her stomach kept making weird noises, so finally, she decided to eat the cucumber Ruth had told her to take. After all, Ruth said to bring it in case she got into a pickle, and wandering around in the dark with a madman on her tail certainly qualified as a pickle, she thought. The idea of this made her laugh. Then the sound of her own laughter caused her to laugh even harder until she was laughing hysterically. Finally, she got ahold of herself and looked down at the cucumber she was holding.

Mina had never cared much for cucumbers in salads or sandwiches, but she found it a good deal more refreshing to bite into than any of the other vegetables she'd tried so far. Plus, for reasons she couldn't fathom, the cucumber seemed to be calming her down. By the time she'd eaten half of it, her fears had completely subsided. She was happy. Gleeful, even. She knew it didn't make any sense, but she was too relieved and worry-free to care.

She took big, clownish steps and smiled goofily. Her legs were in such a relaxed state that she was unable to fully control them. But it didn't matter. She inhaled deeply and thought about what it would be like to skip in the dark. *Probably very exciting*, she thought. She imagined herself skipping on a sandy, white beach, and as her daydream unfolded, she looked out towards the ocean's horizon to see the tiny, reddish-orange sun slowly sinking below it.

But then something unexpected happened. The tiny sun dipped into the ocean below the water. Mina could see it hiding underneath the surface before it dimmed and disappeared altogether. She wondered if the ocean water had caused the sun to fizzle out and waited to see what would happen next. It was still daylight outside, so she figured the sun must be alive and well somewhere close by.

And she was right. Moments later the sun began to glow in the water, then steadily drift back into the sky—just as a proper sun *should* behave. However, the sun was a mix of orange and black now. But Mina figured the black parts were probably from where it had gotten too wet in the ocean. It rose high into the sky, and once it reached its peak, it ignited into a fiery, bright orange.

Watching the sun so intently made Mina feel ill, but then she heard her stomach gurgling and realized that it wasn't the sun that was making her feel sick. It was the cucumber she'd eaten. Her nausea rolled over her like a strong current, and the beach scene vanished, replaced again by the void. Except part of her daydream remained. She could still see the sun glowing some distance away in the dark as it bobbed up and down.

Mina froze. An unpleasant, thick cloud of smoke hovered into her space, and finally it dawned on her what she had been watching the whole time. During her dream, she'd been immune to the smell, but now she began to gag on the festering air that was all around her. It clogged her nostrils and stung her eyes. Her throat tickled, but she fought the urge to cough. She worried it might be the last thing she'd ever do, for standing a short distance away was Dan. Watching her as he smoked his cigar.

CHAPTER 23

SPINDLE WHEEL

Ruth and Maude walked through the center of Waldoff Market. They passed hundreds of people who sat on the ground, propped up against sparkling storefronts. Some sat calmly with vacant stares while others fidgeted and squirmed, clearly agitated by some unseen force. They'd been off the poison for several days and were in the throes of detoxification. The two women, along with a dozen helpers, were preparing to pass out vegetables soaked in an antidote that Maude had created.

In the early days of the resistance, the first recruits had sat around in Maude's booth for days, begging loudly for the water that had blinded them to reality for so long. Bob and Ruth had gone to great lengths to keep these first men and women quiet while Maude hurried to develop a formula that could counter the effects of Dan's poison. The antidote she came up with wasn't instantaneous, but it sped along the cycle of withdrawal so that it lasted only a matter of hours instead of days.

Unfortunately, there hadn't been a way to ramp up the production of the antidote until after Maude's soldiers had taken back the market. This meant that many of the Travelers who had drank the water were now having to suffer while the lucid Travelers worked tirelessly to produce enough antidote for the thousands who needed it.

The volunteers spread out and began passing the vegetables to anyone who was coherent enough to take one. Maude and Ruth stood back-to-back, working both sides of the row. "You're worried about her, aren't you?" Ruth asked as they began their work.

Maude bent down to give a yellow squash to a plump, blonde woman and motioned to her to eat it. "Yes, of course I am," Maude replied to Ruth. "She's been gone much longer than expected."

Ruth put her hand on her friend's shoulder. The blonde woman took the squash and bit into it cautiously. Maude stood up. "I don't know what else to think, except that they've gotten captured. We all know Helen's incapable of getting lost; she knows Theia better than any of us. I know what your prophecy said, but I should never have let them go out there alone."

Ruth frowned. "That angel is strong, Maude. I could feel it. She isn't like that boy that Helen took over there. She'll keep Helen safe."

Maude snickered. "You know she's not actually an angel. Right, Ruth?"

Ruth smiled. "Maybe not. But on the other hand, maybe you'll feel differently when this is all over."

Maude shrugged. "I just wish the lunar wolves would check in and let us know what they've seen out there. Surely, they can't *all* be helping Bob right now."

Ruth handed a small cabbage to a young man. "There, there, sugar. I know the waiting feels unbearable. But if there really was anything to worry about, I'm sure someone would let you know. In the meantime, try to remember that no news is good news."

"I can't say that makes me feel any better," Maude sighed sadly.

Ruth nodded. "I know, but under these circumstances it's the best I've got to offer. War takes all kinds of outrageous tolls. Some visible. Some not."

Just then, a young man with dark hair came dashing down the center of the row towards them. His eyes were laser focused on Maude, and he waved his hands frantically to get her attention. "He's demanding to see you, ma'am!" the young man called out before he'd reached her.

Maude responded, "I don't care what he's demanding, Max. He doesn't get to make demands anymore. The whole point of locking him up was so he can no longer tell anyone what to do."

Max nodded in agreement. "I know, ma'am, and I know you said not to bring you any information about Dale unless it was urgent, but this *seems* urgent. He says he can help you stop Dan from killing our entire army. He said to tell you it pertains to what Dan learned the day your shed burned down."

Maude was clearly upset by this statement. She shot back, "That shed didn't burn down! It was blown to smithereens!"

Max looked at Maude as if to say, *exactly.*

"Fine," she said, throwing a zucchini at the ground in frustration. "But I want to go on record as having said this would be a big waste of time." Maude took off her bag and passed it to Max. "Here!" she said. "Take this and keep passing out the vegetables while I'm gone."

Max saluted her. "Yes, ma'am!"

"I told you all to stop doing that!" Maude said with exasperation as she began to walk away.

Max didn't respond, but Ruth called after her with a little chuckle, "Oh, Maude, just let 'em do it. It's good for all these youngins, anyway!"

∞∞∞

Mɪɴᴀ ʜᴀᴅ ʙᴇᴇɴ ʀᴜɴɴɪɴɢ in the dark since she decided it was the only way to escape Dan's clutches. Her feet felt light, but she didn't know which way she was going. Helen had told her to put the map away, and as far as she was concerned that was where it was going to stay until she was told otherwise. After all, she had to follow *the plan*.

So she ran and ran. She didn't feel panicked or concerned for her well-being, though. If anything, she felt lost in a deep sleep. Then, suddenly, she saw a flash of bright blue light off to her side. She turned her head to look at it. A small spotlight was pointing out of the ground a hundred feet from where she stood. It was illuminating a wooden sign staked into the ground in front of it. Mina couldn't read the words, but there was a large arrow underneath them that pointed down a nearby slope.

Mina approached the sign, and as she got close, she could see that it read, "Spindle Wheel Ranch." Curious to see where the slope led, she walked all the way up to it. However, when she reached it, she realized that the spotlight wasn't casting enough light to see very far. She was about to turn around when a long trail of tiny lights appeared out of nowhere, outlining a path down the incline.

They seemed to be calling to her to follow them. *Ooh! Those are pretty*, she thought. *I bet they lead somewhere exciting. Probably I should go see.* And Mina started down the trail of lights, partly because she was curious to see where they would take her, but also because she couldn't seem to resist them. Each colorful light sent a wave of happiness through her, and every twinkle made her yearn to feast her eyes on a hundred more, only bigger and brighter. She felt euphoric. She pranced and laughed as she followed the endless path of glittering treasures.

But then her feelings changed. It was like a switch had

flipped inside of her head. She sensed something was wrong. A second later the realization manifested—she was no longer in control. *It's okay*, she told herself. *I'm sure everything will go back to normal once I stop looking at the lights.*

She continued down the path, basking in the optical siren song until something caught her eye again. Up ahead, two large spotlights flashed on. Through the bright light, Mina could see a long fence running hundreds of yards in both directions. A tiny part of her was relieved to know she was nearing the end of the trail. But another part of her was searching past the two spotlights, desperately hoping to find even more twinkling lights beyond. Mina didn't see any more, but she did notice a structure hiding in the darkness beyond the spotlights' reach. It was difficult to tell what it was, but Mina thought it looked like a two-story barn situated on a hill.

Unfortunately, she was too enamored with the lights to think clearly about what to do next. All she could get her mind to focus on was dreaming about the biggest, brightest light that had ever existed—one the size of a star. The idea lingered until she reached the fence. It was made from thick, wooden vines, and in-between where the two spotlights shone, there was a latched gate that blended into the rest of the fence.

Mina looked beyond it towards the ghostly barn. Now that she was closer, she could see that the entire front of the barn had survived a fire. There were black singe marks across the top that ran all the way down the face of the building. The barn's frame had remained mostly intact; however, there was a huge gap in the middle of it where there was no structure at all. The metal rooftop was shredded on both sides of this missing section. It bent away from the gap in the center and curled around on itself like giant mangled fingers. *There was an explosion,* Mina thought.

She tried to decide what to do next, but her mind turned back to the lights and how incredible they made her feel.

Nevertheless, the rational part of her brain knew she needed to escape the lights' pull and did everything it could to force her to move on. With great difficulty, Mina lifted the gate's latch, and it swung open. She climbed up the hill towards the barn, but with every step, she grew more anxious. Once she'd made it halfway up the slope, her teeth began to grind, and her skin grew clammy and started to itch. She knew she had to turn around. She *had* to get back to the lights' warm embrace.

Mina dashed back down to the fence. Then just as she reached the gate, she heard a woman call to her from the barn. "Why hello there, dear! I'm so glad you came for a visit. Please do come in and sit down. I have something that will help you get your mind off those pesky, little lights!"

Mina wasn't sure what was creepier, the fact that she had no control over herself around the lights or that a strange woman had appeared out of a blown-apart barn to greet her. She knew it was rude not to respond to the woman's welcome, but she refused to tear her eyes from the dazzling lights again. Finally, she decided to reply to the woman without turning around. "Thank you for the kind offer, ma'am," she shouted back, "but I'd really prefer to stay right here by the lights. Would you mind telling me what you have that you think could help?"

"Oh, you are in a miserable state, aren't you? Can't even take your eyes off them. I could certainly help you with that if you'd just come in and stay for a spell. Don't you trust me, dear child?" the woman asked.

"Should I?" asked Mina. She really wasn't sure in the state she was in.

The woman responded, "Well, there's nobody else here to trust. Come on in and warm your bones by the fire. I have some hot tea brewing that will settle your nerves and release you from your present condition."

Mina continued to stare at the pathway of sparkling lights.

The thought of leaving them was excruciating, even worse than when she'd left everyone she loved back on Earth.

Pop! Pop! Pop! Suddenly, Mina's treasured lights vanished one by one as the electrical, popping sound stole them away. "Nooooo!" she screamed, struggling to resist the urge to run into the darkness and coax them back to life.

"Oh, dear," said the woman. "Well, you see now, that tends to happen in these parts. You can't depend on much of anything way out here. 'Up is down and down is up,' as the old saying goes."

Mina didn't hear the woman. Her brain was frantically searching for a sign that the power was going to come back on. Nothing happened, though, and after a couple of seconds, she felt a small hand on her shoulder. Startled, she swung around to find the woman standing right next to her. She looked back at the barn, wondering how the woman could have possibly made it to her side so quickly.

She turned again to the woman and gazed at her for a moment. The woman was wearing a flowy, yellow sundress and a sweet smile. She had a kind face that reminded Mina of Maude's, only the woman was much younger. Maybe forty or so. She was tall and had tan skin, but there was something unusual about her eyes. They were dark and devoid of life, as if a smooth piece of obsidian had replaced each of her eyeballs. Mina was uncomfortable looking at them and decided to direct her attention to the woman's mouth instead.

"There, there," the woman spoke softly. "It's difficult to leave the lights behind at first, but I think you'll find it much more comfortable inside the old barn."

Mina looked once more at where the lights had been. She could feel her infatuation start to dwindle a bit, although she sensed that she wasn't done with it yet. She nodded. "Okay. I'll come inside for just a minute."

"Splendid!" exclaimed the woman, and she turned and

walked up the sloped path leading to the front of the barn. Mina followed. The doors to the front were wide open. She could see lights dancing around the entryway like the light from a fire. She didn't think it could be a fire, however, because the light was an electric blue instead of a warm yellow.

Before she stepped into the barn, she looked up. A large wheel that looked like it could belong to some type of machinery hung above the doorway. Mina guessed it was the spindle wheel the ranch was named after. Right below the wheel was a wooden sign with the words "Maude & Bob's Family Work Shed. All Imaginations Welcome" seared into it.

Upon entering the large, drafty room, Mina saw that there was, indeed, an electric blue fire burning inside of what looked to be a black crystal fireplace. A teakettle hung above the fire from a small, linked chain.

Mina turned her attention to the middle of the barn where the blue firelight was much dimmer. She could see the emptiness where the structure had been blasted apart. However, if she hadn't known better, she might have assumed that this part of the barn was hidden in darkness instead of missing altogether.

"Make yourself at home," the tall woman said to Mina as she motioned towards three high-back chairs that faced the fire. The chairs were made of metal, except for the seat and back cushions which were made from sheep's hide. They were very narrow and didn't look like they offered much in the way of comfort.

Mina asked, "Are you expecting another visitor?"

The woman had moved to a long wooden table at the side of the fireplace and was busy inspecting the inside of a couple of mugs. She blew into one of them and wiped it out with a bunched-up piece of her skirt. "No, no," she said in response to Mina's question. "It's just you and me, dear. But you never know when a third wheel might roll up. Might as well be prepared. I'd sure hate for anyone to feel unwelcome."

As the woman in yellow spoke, Mina thought she noticed her gaze shift to the tote bag for a second. Mina resisted the temptation to look at it too, out of fear that she'd give away Helen's hiding spot. To avoid making this mistake, she walked over to the middle chair and plopped down onto it. The curly, white wool that covered the seat was warm from the fire's heat. It would've seemed pleasant if Mina could've stopped herself from thinking about how alive it felt.

The woman took the newly cleaned mugs and placed them on the mantle above the fire. Then she reached into the fireplace without any protection for her hands and removed the teakettle from its chain. "Oh my! Doesn't that burn?" Mina asked with an equal dose of concern and amazement.

The woman took her time as she poured a dark, steamy liquid into both mugs and returned the kettle to its place above the fire. She picked up one of the mugs and handed it to Mina. Then she took her own mug and sat in the chair to Mina's right. "You're on Theia now, dear. Our fire is a warm-hot, not a burning-hot. Once you've spent some time getting used to it, you don't even notice it. I don't think I've noticed it for several decades, in fact."

"Several decades?" Mina asked. "Well, you must not have been very old when you stopped noticing it then."

"Oh, that's kind of you to say. I do try to stay out of the sun. Go ahead and take a sip of your tea now, dear. It should be the perfect temperature," said the woman as she lifted her own mug and wafted the rising puffs of steam towards her face. Then she took a deep breath in and exhaled a peaceful sigh.

Mina, who'd never been much of a tea drinker, stared at the dark concoction inside her cup. She sensed it would be impolite not to take a few sips, but she also had a nagging feeling that she shouldn't. Conflicted by these opposing thoughts, she continued to sit and stare at the fire, hoping the friendly woman wouldn't notice that she hadn't taken a sip.

However, the woman did notice, and after a while, she asked, "What's wrong? Don't you want to get rid of your craving? Surely, you haven't managed to forget about those pretty lights yet, have you? Or maybe you just need a spot of lemon and honey to get you going."

In truth, Mina was still wondering about the lights, although only about every third thought now. She kept thinking that at any moment she might find an excuse to go check and see if they had turned back on.

"I suppose I do want to get rid of my craving," Mina lied. She'd decided she better go ahead and try the tea. She didn't really believe it would be able to cure her of her obsession anyway, and if it did, then maybe it was for the best. "I guess it can't hurt, right?" she asked.

"Oh, no! Won't hurt a bit. It'll make you quite comfortable. Like you can barely feel a thing. Drink up!"

Mina took a sip and found it to be soothing. Having not had any liquid since leaving Earth, she thoroughly enjoyed the sensation of the warm tea running down the back of her throat. It radiated heat throughout her chest and poured gently into her stomach like a tiny kitten curling up into a cozy ball inside of her.

Mina smiled a droopy smile as her whole body relaxed. She couldn't remember why she'd been so worried. The woman was nice, and clearly, she knew how to make her guests feel welcome. The serene feeling was fleeting, however. After the sip of tea settled in her stomach, Mina realized that something didn't feel right. The sensation started as a tingle like a foot that had fallen asleep, but soon every part of Mina had gone numb.

She slumped in the chair, unable to move. Her mind tried to understand what was happening, but her brain felt numb too. She was moments away from falling to the floor like a rag doll when the woman stepped in and pulled her upright again. Then she tied Mina tightly to the back of the seat and propped her head against the top so that it was facing up. "Comfortable dear?" she asked sweetly.

Mina couldn't respond. She'd resigned herself to staring groggily at the dark ceiling when, out of nowhere, she heard another person talking to the woman in yellow—only, it sounded like the same voice. The second woman asked, "What do you think you're doing? She's just a child. Was this really necessary?"

"*Of course* it was," replied the woman in yellow. "She was acting weird. Who knows what she would've done if I hadn't drugged her."

"She was acting weird because you lured her here with those stupid lights of yours. You knew what effect they were going to have!"

"Well, who's to say if that's true or not. She was out there snooping around, so she was probably a weirdo before she saw the lights. I mean, just look at her. Does she look normal to you? She's drooling, for crying out loud!"

"Dear god! She's drooling because you *doped* her! There has to be a better way than this."

"Well, until you figure one out, I'm going to keep doing it my way."

Mina was quickly losing her grip on reality. Her mind was racing into an abyss at a hundred miles an hour, and there was nothing she could do to stop it. With her last bit of sanity still intact, she asked, "What's happening to me?" It was unclear if the women heard her or not because she never received an answer.

Mina's vision blurred. The ceiling disappeared from view, and all she could see were bright blue waves of light gently rolling over her. At first, it was peaceful, but then the waves grew bigger and came crashing down faster with greater intensity. It was nauseating. Right as Mina felt certain she would be sick, everything went black, and her mind dove deep into the abyss.

When she awoke, she was lying on the ground inside a giant cave, surrounded by a dozen one-foot tall, hairless creatures that looked like ashy, gray elves. None of them were wearing clothes, but all of them had very round stomachs that covered the part where their private areas would be if, indeed, they had those. They were talking feverishly to each other in squeaky gibberish and didn't seem to notice that Mina was laying there, watching them.

She listened closely to see if she could figure out anything that was being said, and much to her delight, she realized that she *was* picking up the meaning of the strange words they used. In fact, it seemed the more she listened, the more she understood. At the moment that Mina gained full fluency, she heard several of the elven creatures say at the same time, "We can't keep her! She's too big! She'll eat all of our vegetable-berries!" 'Vegetable-berries' was spoken as a word that didn't have an exact translation, but Mina understood it to be a berry that tasted like carrots, beets, tomatoes, and armpit hair.

She sat up and giggled. She was overjoyed at how wonderful it was to be able to understand these silly, little beings. The elves all stopped and looked at her. Then in unison, they cheered excitedly and ran to get as close to her as they could, pushing each other forward as they went. Mina looked down and discovered that she'd become an elf magnet. They spoke over each other, but Mina could somehow hear all of them at the same time.

One with particularly large ears shouted, "We're glad you're here! Do you enjoy dancing?"

While another one with sunken eyes yelled, "We have waterfalls of boiling sludge for you to bathe in! It will help you get rid of that smell!"

Another elf, who looked like it might be a girl, spoke softly, "Please help yourself to my collection of egotistical snails."

Yet another pushed its face right into Mina's and then moved around to her ear and screamed, "You smell like toe fungus and raindrops!"

And during all of this, a very small elf that could have been a child hopped into Mina's lap and sang, "We're so happy you're here! We're so happy you're here! We were hoping you'd visit! And now you are here!"

Mina felt like a celebrity. She wanted to calm them down, but since she couldn't speak their language, she held up her hands instead. The elves seemed to understand what she was asking them to do, although it took them a few seconds to get quiet. When they finally did, Mina saw that they were staring back at her expectantly. She could tell they were waiting for her to speak. Not wanting to disappoint, she decided she would greet them in her own language. She only hoped they would be able to understand her the same way she could understand them.

She started to say, "Thank you for your warm greeting." But before she could utter a word, she felt a strange burst of energy begin to burn inside her stomach. It quickly rose through her esophagus, and once it reached her mouth, a deep, squeaky voice she'd never heard before erupted from her lips. She was stunned. Somehow, she was speaking the elves' language. It felt like magic.

The colony of little, nude creatures went wild. Some of them began to weep happily while others shrieked in ecstasy. Again, Mina extended her hands in front of her to settle the crowd, but this time it didn't work. Instead, the elves took turns wrapping their arms around her and pressing their faces into her hands like children snuggling a beloved toy.

Mina spoke again in the elven language, raising her voice to be heard over all the fuss. It came out sounding like she'd inhaled a high concentration of helium. "You're all so kind to show me such warmth, but I don't think I've done anything to deserve this kind of welcome."

The elf with soft features asked her, "Why would you think you had to do something to deserve it?"

Mina was struck by this answer. It hadn't occurred to her that maybe there was nothing unusual about the way she was being treated. That maybe it was normal for these beings to give unconditional love to everyone they met. She allowed herself to relax as she was cuddled and caressed from all sides. Soon, all her worries melted away under the warm glow of the elves' tenderness, and she began to weep.

"Tears!" yelled the littlest elf. A larger one cried, "Someone get the tear catcher!"

A few elves scampered away from the group. They returned a minute later, carrying a metal bucket that was nearly as big as them. Attached to the inner rim of the container were six curly straws that stuck out from the top. The elves carried it over to Mina who was crying so much that she was having to use the back of her hands to wipe the tears from her cheeks. Two of the littler elves came shuffling up to her and pulled her hands away from her face. "No. Don't waste!" they said.

The other elves positioned the pail so it rested in Mina's lap. Then they began to move the six straws so that each eye had three straws positioned underneath it—one straw under the tear duct, one under the center of the eye, and another pressed into the outer corner. As the elves performed this delicate work, Mina noticed a tiny metal scoop at the end of each straw that looked like it was meant to catch whatever tears it came in contact with.

She looked out at the rest of the group, and they in turn stared back at her with hopeful expressions. Suddenly, Mina felt an enormous amount of pressure to deliver tears into the bucket. It was as if a huge weight had been dropped onto her shoulders. The emotions that had caused her to cry in the first place vanished—replaced by a cold, sterile feeling that dried up all her tears. Only a few more slipped from her eyelashes as she blinked.

She assumed the elves would be disappointed over the small quantity of tears she'd given them, but she thought they deserved to be a little upset after ruining a perfectly good cry with such an odd contraption. Unexpectedly, however, the elves began to clap with excitement. "Thank you!" several of them shouted over and over as they all began to dance and sing with loud, squeaky fervor.

"But I didn't do anything, really. I barely gave you any tears at all. See?" she said, pointing inside the mostly empty bucket.

One of the elves who was close enough to hear Mina over all of the commotion replied, "But we only needed one for a souvenir. All the others were a bonus!"

Upon hearing the word "bonus," several of the elves began to chant, "Bonus! Bonus! Bonus!"

"You only wanted my tears to have a souvenir of me?" Mina asked.

A big elf replied, "Yes! We don't want to forget you when you're gone, and this way we'll have something to remember you by."

"Oh, I see," said Mina, feeling ashamed of herself for having been annoyed before. "Well, if you'd like a souvenir that's easier to hang onto, you can have a strand of my hair to keep as well."

All the elves stopped dancing and stood in slack-jawed silence. "You would give us your hair?" asked one of the elves.

Mina shrugged. "Well, sure. Just a little bit if you want," she said, and she pulled one of her locks in front of her face, as if she were examining it.

"Get the ax!" screamed one of the elves.

"Wait, ax? What do you need an ax for?" Mina asked with growing concern. "You understand I'm only giving you my hair, right?"

The girl-like elf squeaked at her, "Yes, but we only have the ax to cut it with."

"Oh, well that does change things a bit then," Mina squeaked back, feeling uneasy at the thought of one of these silly, little creatures swinging an ax towards her head.

"Don't worry! Donovan is an expert with the ax. He uses it to pick vegetable-berries!" another elf blurted out excitedly.

Mina didn't know why it would ever be necessary to use an ax while picking berries, or how that could possibly make Donovan an expert axman, but she quickly figured out a way to solve the problem. "If you don't mind, I'd prefer to cut my own hair."

As Mina spoke the shrill words, the elf who'd gone to fetch the ax returned, dragging it behind him. It was at least a foot and a half taller than any of the little creatures. Mina asked, "Why do you have such a large ax?"

Two of the elves replied in sync, "We found it! Isn't it shiny?"

Mina studied the ax for a moment. It *was* shiny, especially the blade, which gleamed. Mina stood up and walked over to pick up the ax, careful not to step on any of the creatures as she did. She held the ax in her right hand, and with her left, she pulled a thick handful of hair taught across the blade. She moved the strand back and forth against the sharp edge until, little by little, she'd cut through every piece.

She lowered the ax to the ground again and sat back down. "Who would like to hang onto this?" she asked, holding the fistful of hair out in front of her.

Every hand shot up as the elves began to squeak and wiggle like impatient children waiting their turn for a treat. In order to be fair, Mina decided to divide up her hair among all of the elves. She handed about ten strands to each little creature, and when she was through, she watched as they celebrated. Some jiggled their bodies around in circles as they pressed Mina's hair to their heads and stomachs while others held her hair in both hands and bounced from side to side, singing.

Mina laughed cheerfully, enjoying the festive mood, when, suddenly, she lost her vision. She could still hear the happy elves reveling all around her, but her sight was completely gone. Panicking, she moved her head in every direction, hoping she would see something, *anything* at all. But there was only darkness.

Then, like the light from a train speeding through a dark tunnel, Mina's vision came racing towards her. It grew bigger and brighter until it snapped back into place, and she could see once more. It wasn't what she expected, however. A giant, yellow bird towered above her. It walked with its back to her, and somehow she was following along behind it. Her point of view was from the ground, though, which made it difficult to tell what was happening.

Forgetting about the happy elves, Mina asked herself, "What is this? Am I a snake chasing a giant chicken?"

With this, the elves stopped their celebration, and she heard them shout, "It's time to go! It's time to go!"

Then a few of them said, "Yes! Of course! She mustn't be late to meet the giant chicken!"

Several others ordered, "Send her away! She must go now!"

At that precise moment, Mina's vision disappeared again,

and she felt herself beginning to float above the ground. She couldn't see what was happening, but it seemed like the gravitational force had been turned off. She heard a few of the elves calling to her from below. "We'll miss you, large friend! Goodbye and farewell!"

Mina tried to tilt herself down so she could wave goodbye to her adoring fans. However, before she could get her bearings, her head smashed into the top of the cave, and her vision came speeding back with a vengeance. But this time, all she could see were stars.

CHAPTER 24
A TALE OF TWO EGOS

Maude was dreading her meeting with Dale. It had been a long time since they'd met face-to-face, and their last encounter had been tumultuous to say the least.

After Axel told Bob and Maude what he'd witnessed Dan do to Helen at the fort, they decided to approach Dale. They went to him after one of his meetings in the city center and begged him to help them stop Dan. Dale had always been easier to talk to than his brother, and they hoped they might be able to bring him to their side if they convinced Dale that Dan had become a danger to everyone.

Unfortunately, it was too late. Dale explained to them how he'd finally come to realize that he was the only one of their children they'd never cared about. "You were always chasing Dan to keep him out of trouble and doting on Helen because of how *special* she was. But did you ever spend any time paying attention to me? *Never!*"

Dale warned his parents that there were major changes in store for them once Dan put him in charge of the city. "You'll finally get to see what it's like to be unimportant!" he shouted at them. "Nobody will care who you are! You'll just be two washed up has-beens!"

Bob and Maude ignored Dale's threat and cautioned that Dan might be planning something even bigger than he'd let on. They begged Dale to help, but he dismissed their warning and their pleas.

"Neither of you fool me. It was incredibly stupid of Helen to confront Dan. She was begging to be killed. Clearly, you couldn't care less if I die, but I have no reason to make the same dumb mistake she did. Dan and I have already worked out our deal. He's free to kill or torture anyone he likes as long as he does it on the Darkside.

"Oh, and one last thing, *dear parents*. Don't ever come to me again. You can keep on acting like you only have two kids because, from here on out, I want nothing to do with either of you!"

Then before Maude or Bob could get a word in edgewise, Dale ordered the guards to drag them away. It was the last time Maude laid eyes on Dale. When Dan had sent the formula for Maude to drink, in exchange for information about Helen, Dale had assigned one of the guards from the market to handle it. The guard had acted as a courier between the two parties, passing messages back and forth so they never had to meet.

Over the years, there had been plenty of opportunities for Maude to see her son from close-up or far away, but she'd never had any interest in doing so. She didn't even think of Dale as her son anymore. Deep down, she'd always known what the twins were but had done her best to raise them right and love them despite her fears. However, once she saw the horror and devastation they were capable of, she finally allowed herself to grieve for what they could've been if their hearts had just been different. It was the only way she knew how to sever her emotional attachment to the once cute, little boys, who'd actually been monsters in disguise.

Maude was worn out from the walk to the charred city, the spot they'd chosen to imprison Dale before moving him to his new home. Her face lacked even a hint of feeling as she approached the two soldiers who were acting as guards. They stood in front of a metal crate which had been sliced open on the sides so that it looked like a miniature jail cell.

She knew what the men's orders were because she was the one who'd given them. They were not to respond to anything Dale said to them. They were not to stand down to anyone, except for her, and only when given the correct series of passwords. And finally, if they received word that the army had lost the war to Dan, they were to dispose of Dale immediately, no matter what the consequence of their actions might be.

The two men wore the same stony expression as Maude. She greeted them as a civilian and not as the leader that all her recruits knew her to be. "Mark. Alex," she acknowledged each of the soldiers as she spoke their names. Then she handed a piece of curved metal with the etched passwords to the man she'd called Alex.

Alex verified the passwords and handed them to Mark who did the same. Once they were finished, Maude said, "Please give us a few minutes. I'd like to talk to the prisoner privately."

The two men saluted Maude and proceeded to walk out of earshot. As they moved away from the crate, Maude could see Dale lying inside, curled up in a ball of purple and black stripes. He snickered, "I bet you love this, don't you? Everyone takes you so seriously now. Even more than they used to."

Maude replied coldly, "I don't. That was always *your* thing, not mine. I prefer to be treated as an equal."

Dale pulled himself up and faced Maude. She was surprised by how old he looked. Without thinking, she asked, "Has Dan been keeping the anti-aging pills from you?"

Dale rebuffed her, "No. Of course not! I take them from time to time, but I'm allowing myself to age to the point of looking dignified. Everyone knows that men age better than women, so I've always figured that my looks would peak around forty-five."

Maude couldn't resist the chance to take him down a peg. "Well, you've missed that mark by a lot. Your hair has thinned out way too much for you to be a believable forty-something anymore. They say that's a gene you inherit from your mother's father. Too bad we don't know who my father was to know if it's true."

Dale wanted to make Maude pay for her comments. "You've aged a great deal, too, since the last time I saw you, *Mother*. But I guess you had a lot of catching up to do, didn't you? Good thing you foiled me when you did. By the looks of it, you don't have much life left. Of course, I'm sure you'll start taking the anti-aging pills now that you're in control again. There's no beauty left to preserve, but at least you can keep clinging to that little sliver of life you have left, right?"

Maude shrugged. "No, Dale, I don't think I will take those pills. I think it might be time to stop fighting the clock once and for all."

Dale laughed at Maude. "Oh please! Don't go kidding a kidder. You'd never choose to die if it meant leaving behind my *precious* father and sister. You don't have it in you."

Maude cocked an eyebrow. "You know, it amazes me after all this time that you still have no clue what kind of fabric I'm woven from. You and your brother always thought you were so much smarter than everyone else that you never spent a moment's time trying to understand anyone besides yourselves. You did as you pleased and ignored everyone else because you were so sure you had it all figured out. Only you didn't, did you?"

Dale scoffed. "What didn't we figure out? We figured out *your* weakness. You and Bob never could say no to anyone with a problem. You spent all your time helping everyone, except your own family."

Maude frowned. "Your father and I did what we could to make you happy. We even broke our own rules when we saw that we weren't able to please you in a conventional way. We didn't want to believe you could be so unaffected by our love because we knew in our hearts what that would mean. We went to great lengths to prove to ourselves that you were normal children and not the little psychopaths we feared you to be.

"But in the end, you two did everything possible to show the whole Moon who you really are, and I won't *ever* let that happen again. Now tell me why you sent for me, or we're done here."

Dale scowled. "Maybe I don't want to anymore."

Maude smiled. "Good. Then I'll be on my way." She waved to the guards to return to their post.

Dale spoke angrily, "Just wait a second now. I'll tell you how Dan plans to defend the fort if you let me go."

Maude, who'd been holding her hand up to the guards like a stop sign, laughed and waved again for them to return. "No deal," she said.

Dale was flustered. "Stop doing that! Please!? I'm trying to make you a deal. You should be thanking me! I mean, people's lives could be saved. *Okay!?* Isn't that what you *want?*"

"I'm not giving you your freedom, Dale. You have one more shot at this, and then I'm walking away."

Dale resented being talked to like this, especially by his old mother. He despised old people and had never particularly cared for his mother either. Yet here she was, the complete embodiment of both. Normally, he would've told her exactly what he thought of her, but he knew he had to suppress his hatefulness to get his way.

"Fine, then. I overheard someone say that the workers are

building a cell inside the Sheep Spa to keep me in for the rest of my life. Let me have the entire Sheep Spa as my prison, and I'll tell you what Dan's going to do."

Maude shook her head. "No. You can have half the factory as your prison. The other half will be for Dan, but there will be a soundproof wall between the two sides. And of course, no anti-aging pills for either of you. That's my one and final offer. Take it or leave it."

Dale gritted his teeth. "Fine. It's a deal, but just so you know, that second half will sit empty. Dan will never be taken alive."

"What makes you so sure? *You* were," said Maude.

"Oh, poor naive Maude. Now who doesn't understand so much about the cloth of your own kin? Yes, it's true I was taken alive, but between your two little psychopaths, I'm the one who loves myself, and he's the one who loathes himself."

Maude rolled her eyes. "That's enough. Start talking if you want the deal. But understand this first, if any of the information you give me turns out to be even the slightest bit inaccurate, even if it's just the tiniest of lies, I'll tell the workers to stop building you a prison apartment and stick you in one of the sheep cages instead."

Maude waved the guards over again. They looked like they weren't sure whether they should obey, however, so she called to them, "Come on. I'm not going to stop you again."

The guards sped up. When they got closer, Maude asked, "Do either of you have a silver bird I could use?"

Both men shook their heads. Mark replied, "No, ma'am. We told Max to send us one in case we needed it, but he must have forgotten."

Maude sighed. "That's okay. But I'm going to need one of you to run back to the center of Waldoff and find Max or Ruth."

"I'll do it!" volunteered Alex.

"Good," said Maude. "Tell whichever one you find first to send back a silver bird as quick as possible."

Alex saluted. "Yes, ma'am!'"

"Okay, enough of that. Now go!" Maude ordered and pointed her finger in the direction of the market.

Alex hurried off, and Maude turned back to Dale, who was sitting hunched over in the barred crate with his lip stuck out like a pouting child. "Okay, I'm ready now," Maude told him.

Dale laid down on his back with his legs bent tightly at the knees so that his body could fit between the ends of his cage. He reached his hands behind his head and began to talk. "It all started the year before you and *Bobby-boy* built Spindle Wheel Ranch. You know, the year Dan blew up your work shed after sneaking in and messing around with your potions."

"They're called formulas, Dale. You know that. Now get to the point. I have no interest in revisiting this particular memory," she snapped.

"Well, you're going to have to if you want to hear what I have to say."

"Fine. Get on with it!" Maude ordered.

Dale grumbled but continued, "Dan blew up the shed, but the explosion wasn't the most exciting part. Before the explosion, Dan noticed that one of the potions he'd been playing with had become destabilized, and he panicked. We had to jump out the window above your work bench to save ourselves.

After the mixture blew a hole in the roof, a couple of lunar wolves came running from the other direction. They didn't see us on the other side of the shed. Dark green smoke was pouring from inside, and the wolves ran in to see if there was anyone that needed to be rescued.

"At that point, Dan, who was wearing your gas mask, went back in through the front of the shed. He found the two wolves dead, which in itself was surprising because there hadn't been enough time for them to suffocate. Even more intriguing, though, was that there were half a dozen glowing, green spheres hovering over your workbench, spewing gas.

"Dan was ecstatic over what he'd discovered, but he knew he had to cover his tracks fast. He poured willow's sap on top of the spheres to neutralize them. Then he grabbed every cinder-ash potion that hadn't been destroyed in the blast, except for one. He placed them in the center of the shed, and with the last cinder-ash potion in hand, he exited. He tore off a piece of his sleeve and hung it out of the top of the cinder-ash bottle. Then he lit the other end of his sleeve on fire, threw the bottle into the middle of the shed, and we took off running. The second blast was what ripped the entire shed apart.

"Dan knew he'd created the building blocks for a powerful weapon that day. He's never talked to anyone about it, except for me, and even I don't know what potions he mixed together to make it. He's been extremely secretive about all the work he's done to develop it, but I know he's done a lot. It's the main reason he built his fort all the way up there on top of Black Ice Glacier. He didn't want anyone living near him because he feared they might witness the effects of his experiments."

As Dale spoke, Maude's expression had slowly morphed from cold and uncaring to downright panicked. "Oh my god, Dale!" she exclaimed. "You should never have kept this to yourself! All these years! I mean, I know you're protective of him, but oh my god! What have you done!?" Maude exclaimed as her voice rose several octaves.

Dale sat up. "What are you talking about? You sound like a crazy, old woman."

"No, Dale. It's just like you said. The difference between the two of you is that you're a narcissist, and he's a self-loather. How could you have never pieced it together before?" Maude wrung her hands as she paced around Dale's crate.

In his entire life, Dale had never seen his mother lose her

cool, and the sight of her this frazzled had begun to make him feel unsettled.

"Mom, what is it?" Dale asked in a worried tone.

Maude shushed him. "Don't interrupt me! I'm trying to figure out our next move. I'm having to rethink our entire strategy."

"Just tell me why you're so worked up. You know you can stop Dan from attacking. All you have to do is back down. It's simple!"

Maude glared at him. "You don't know what you're talking about, Dale! The one way that your brother *isn't* like you is the one way that's going to get us all killed. You two had no problem poisoning everyone to keep them under your thumb all these years. *You* had no problem with it because you crave the attention of followers. But *he* craves the opposite. While you want admiration and praise, he wants suffering and death. You stupidly allowed *that* kind of a person to work alone for decades, advancing a weapon that already had the potential to kill instantly."

"So what if that's true? He's only going to use it if your army attacks him. That's why you have to stop them. So that he won't use it to defend himself."

"No Dale!" Maude practically screamed. "You're not allowing yourself to see the truth! This was always Dan's end game. You designed your tiny world to boost your fragile ego, and he gave you the means to do it. He didn't do it because he *loves* you! He did it so you wouldn't notice he was designing a way to destroy us all!"

Dale looked terrified as all the pieces fell into place. "Oh my god…what are we going to do?"

Maude turned around and headed for the market, hoping she could get to the silver bird she'd sent for even faster. Before she was out of Dale's earshot, though, she yelled, "I'm not sure yet, Dale, but from the way things look at present, you might want to start kissing that narcissistic ass of yours goodbye!"

∽∾∽∾∽

Bob had been traveling in the dark for half a day when he sensed he was being followed. He'd taken his time on the journey to Black Ice Fort because he was certain that Dan had set traps on all of the predictable paths leading there. He also knew how dangerous it would be if Dan spied his intrusion. Not only would he be risking his own life, but worse, he'd be putting the whole army in danger.

To ensure his approach was stealthy, Bob created a longer route using natural formations, like craters, hills, and heavily shrubbed areas. Two miles from the fort, he was just beginning to round the far side of a hill cluster when he heard rocks skimming across the dirt a few yards back.

Bob stopped dead in his tracks. He'd been using a tiny flashlight to help guide him through the dark. But now, he wondered if he'd been too careless leaving it on for long stretches of time when he thought he was hidden. He clicked off the light and tiptoed a few paces from the base of the hill. Then he stopped again to listen, frightened about what might come next.

He held his breath until he was able to identify his stalkers by the light pitter patter of footsteps in the dirt and the faint sniffing sounds that were drawing closer. "You almost gave me a heart attack, Axel. What are you all doing out here?" he asked.

Axel's pack consisted of only five lunar wolves, and although Axel was a trained healer, he was also the leader of his little pack. He moved forward, and Bob flicked his light back on as he reached into his backpack to pull out the lunar wolf speaker.

It was a device consisting of a microphone that fit on the tip of a wolf's tongue and a wire that ran from the mic to a small metal speaker with an amplifier. The microphone was sensitive and could capture a wolf's tongue movements and the light vibrations from their larynx. This made it possible for the speaker to play the wolf's voice despite the damage the gaseous poison had caused.

Bob connected the microphone to Axel's tongue. Then, once Axel was hooked up, Bob asked, "Why did you follow me here?"

Like his mentor, Neriti, Axel had never been one to mince words. He cut right to the chase. "We came to save you from yourself. What you're doing is selfish and will get everyone killed. You need to turn back now. An army, like a pack, cannot function properly without its leader."

Bob remained silent for a moment. He knew there was truth to what Axel was saying, but he also knew that Axel couldn't see the full picture. "I know the risk I'm taking by coming here alone, but there's something you don't understand. I got a message from Dan. I think he's planning to—"

"Capture Helen?" Axel interrupted.

Caught off guard, Bob stuttered, "W-well, yes. But how did you—"

"It's what I came to tell you before I found out that you'd made off into the dark by yourself. Helen has a plan. Before she left the market, Helen took control of Ruth's energy. She possessed Ruth in order to compose a message to you, pretending to be Maude. It laid out some of her plan: Helen would be traveling with the girl to the Sheep Spa and then on to the greenhouse to search for the blueprints. Once she was finished, she put the message into a silver bird and programed it to fly back and forth over the Sheep Spa until it was intercepted. It's all part of the actual plan."

Bob was stunned. "What are you talking about, Axel? What actual plan?"

"I'm sorry, Bob. I really am. But I can't give you that information. Helen asked me to tell you exactly what I'm telling you now when the time was right. She told me not to let you interfere."

"*Not to let me interfere!?* What does that even mean? She's doing it again, isn't she? She's gone to confront her brother. She thinks she can save us because of some stupid prophecy," Bob shouted, despite the danger. "You all did this, Axel! Neriti should never have burdened our family with that damn thing. It's done nothing but tear us apart!" Bob stared angrily at Axel through the dim light.

"No, Bob," Axel replied calmly. "I know it's hard for you to believe, but Neriti's prophecy was only a glimpse of things to come. Your children were sent here by something more powerful than any of us.

"Your boys were sent for a bad purpose; your daughter was sent to counter it. Sometimes it's difficult to understand the meaning of events until you see the end result. This is one of those times. I still don't understand why so many of my beloved had to die by your son's hand. But I accept there's a reason, though I can't see it yet."

Bob shook his head. "Then you're better than me because I don't accept any of this."

Axel continued, "I'm not better or worse because I see things differently. I just have an easier time because I do. Your duty now is to think like a commander, not like a father. Helen's journey is separate from your own. This is something you cannot change. She and Dan will have to fight their own battle. It's not their fate to let you do it for them.

"You must focus now on what you and Maude have spent so long preparing for. Think of the thousands of other men and women who're counting on you to return them to a better life. That is what you have the power to do now."

Bob looked in the direction of Black Ice Fort, even though he couldn't see it. Then he spoke again. "I don't know how to do it, old friend. I don't know how to let go of these feelings that are telling me to protect her."

"You don't need to let go," Axel replied. "You just need to trust that she can protect herself this time."

Bob stared into the void a little while longer. Then he nodded his head. "Okay, Axel. I'll try."

CHAPTER 25

THE CHICKEN MAN

Mina stared into the eternal stretch of space above. Her head felt light and cloudy like she wasn't fully in control of her mind. She tried to lift herself to a seated position but couldn't. She strained all of her muscles to pull herself up, but nothing happened. Then she tried to use her hands and feet but realized they weren't accessible. She was trapped.

She rocked back and forth, hoping to free herself, but the movement didn't seem to do anything, except make her feel dizzy. Then Mina heard a voice. It was a grumbly voice, free of joy. A great contrast to the elven creatures she'd just departed. The voice spoke to her. "If you hold still and don't struggle, I'll cut you free."

Mina smiled because she thought it sounded like a nice offer.

"Is it a deal?" asked the disembodied voice.

She nodded, and within a few seconds, she was able to sit up and move her arms and legs again. She looked back around to see what had been holding her captive. It appeared that she'd been tied up inside of a very large peanut shell that was cut lengthwise down the middle. Thick vines had been chopped apart to free her. They lay discarded, wrapped around the back of the shell.

Mina looked ahead and saw a bright blue campfire blazing in front of her. Off to the side was a large wolf that looked familiar, though Mina didn't know why. Everything that seemed familiar also seemed confusing. She wasn't cognizant enough to realize it, but she was having difficulty accessing her memories, which meant that recognizing things had become a maddening and pointless exercise.

She watched the wolf for a moment. It looked disgruntled. She didn't want to provoke it, so she looked away. "Thank you for freeing me," she said to the wolf while staring into the fire to avoid eye contact.

The wolf didn't respond. She heard someone behind her say, "Don't mention it." She looked around quickly, and there he was—a man dressed in a giant chicken costume.

"Oh, pardon me!" Mina exclaimed in surprise.

"Don't try to run," clucked the chicken man. "Roger will tear you apart if I give him the command."

"Who's Roger?" Mina asked.

"It's that disgusting waste of fur over there," he said, motioning towards the large animal.

"Isn't that a wolf?" she asked. Mina still didn't feel like herself and was confused about what was going on.

"Yes, of course it's a wolf. A mean, bloated wolf."

Finally, Mina couldn't help herself. She had to ask. "Why are you dressed like a chicken?"

The man looked down at his clothes and then back at Mina. He raised his right hand to his mouth and took a long puff on the cigar he was holding between his fingers. The ash glowed bright orange like Mina had seen before in her daydream, but this time she didn't see a sun *or* a lit cigar. She saw a bright orange beak.

"I'm not, in fact, dressed like a chicken as you seem to be imagining. I guess I should ask *you*, though, why you're dressed like an angel." He pointed his cigar at her wings. Mina looked around to where he was pointing, but in her confused state, she had no idea what she was looking at. She could see the individual feathers but couldn't understand what they belonged to.

The giant chicken continued to speak. "Please don't bore me with some ridiculous explanation. I get it. You think you're important now. You may have even started to suspect that you really *are* an angel. After all, a few people at the market thought it was true, so maybe it is, right?"

Mina stared with fascination at the yellow gentleman. Her mind was only able to interpret him as a giant chicken, although it couldn't decipher whether he was a man masquerading as a chicken or a chicken masquerading as a man. Either way, he was quite a spectacle to behold—a giant, talking chicken with a man's face.

"Well, I have news for you," the chicken went on. "You are not special. In fact, you're just like everyone else here. Maybe that will come as a relief to you. But maybe not?" the angry chicken asked, eyeing her carefully—looking for a reaction that didn't come. "Do you hear what I'm saying to you? You. Are. Not. Special. In fact, you're extraordinarily un-special. Just a stooge!"

Mina felt sleepy. She didn't really understand what this chicken was yammering on about, but she could tell that whatever it was, *he* certainly thought it was important. She crawled back inside the giant peanut shell and tried to do her best impression of someone who cares about what the other is saying.

The chicken was telling her a story about an apple cart

he'd once robbed while it was on its way from the greenhouse to the market. Apparently, the apples were being sent to the children in the market who didn't have families.

"I told the guy that he was wasting all those perfectly good apples, and let me tell you, I know a thing or two about apples. But I left him half his supply, which I think was more than generous. Those orphans probably got two apples each. Maybe more. I don't know. I have never understood much about orphans. I never was one, you know. I've just heard people say things about them here and there."

Mina remarked, "That's fascinating. I didn't even know chickens liked apples."

The man looked at Mina angrily. "I told you! I'm not a chicken. It's the yellow suit, isn't it? Look, kid, here's the thing you need to know about chickens…" he said as he went off on an entirely different tangent.

If Mina had been listening, she would've heard an impassioned lecture regarding the best uses for toothpaste that don't involve teeth, why aliens from other solar systems shouldn't be trusted, what an amazing chef the yellow chicken man would be if he ever tried to cook something, and how things would've been better if the wolves had been exterminated long ago.

This last one upset Roger. He growled at the chicken man through clenched teeth until the chicken yelled, "Can it, Roger, or I'll lock you up in the dark again!" Roger stopped growling and began to whimper.

Mina's eyes were still open, but she had slipped away into her subconscious. It was recalling a memory of a little chirpy bird with a terrible singing voice. The brown, splotchy bird had sat outside her window every morning for months, waking her up at the crack of dawn with its earsplitting songs.

The stress of sleepless dawns had caused Mina to imagine doing all types of wicked things to the annoying bird, though it wouldn't have been in her nature to harm a feather on its head. There had even been times when Mina felt almost sorry for the ugly, little thing, except that the bird didn't seem to realize how wretched it was.

She'd tried shooing it away on numerous occasions, but no matter how many times she did, it always came right back. It was impossible not to want to teach a lesson to the little bird that behaved in such a self-important fashion, but eventually she left it alone, becoming complicit in her own suffering. She hoped the bird would die a natural death or move away, but in the interim, the best solution she had come up with was to wear earplugs to bed.

Finally, after ignoring the bird for a few weeks, it flew away for good. Mina thought it must have found someone better to annoy; however, she'd always wondered if the bird had ended up at the mill down the way from her cottage. She knew if it had gone whistling its awful tunes there, it would surely be a goner. The mill folks went to extreme measures to keep birds from going near their grain.

"Cluck. Cluck. Cluck," Mina thought she heard the chicken man say as the memory faded. She couldn't believe he was still yapping. She looked around to see if any of her elven friends were there. They had been much more entertaining than this blowhard chicken and his grouchy canine companion. Unfortunately, there were no elves to be found.

She sat there watching the chicken man for a long time while he went on and on about nothing in particular, just some nonsense strewn together. Mina thought the words only seemed to form real sentences because they were delivered with pizazz. A flick of the wings. A well-timed shrug. A large grinning smirk like the cat that ate the canary.

She heard him say, "And that's why I say, 'Fine, they don't have to drink the water if they can be peaceful about it.' But I'll tell you something; they're not going to upend a perfectly good system by building their own greenhouse. If I didn't have bigger plans, I would have had them dragged from the market and hung upside-down inside the main greenhouse. Betsy could probably have used the company. That old bat has gotten a bit too involved with her vines if you ask me."

"Hold on! What did you just say?" Mina asked. Something about what the yellow chicken was saying finally seemed important.

"Don't speak to me when I'm in the middle of explaining something," he snapped at her.

Evidently, the chicken man didn't like to be interrupted, but then again, he had never once paused to give Mina an opportunity to speak.

"He mentioned something important about a greenhouse," she said, ignoring the man, though it seemed like she was talking more to herself than to him. "What was it? Something about a blue greenhouse. Was I looking for a blue greenhouse? No. That can't be right. That would be called a bluehouse probably."

The disgruntled chicken flapped his wings a couple of times. "For god's sake! You were looking for the greenhouse blueprints, remember!? That cucumber really messed you up, huh? I've never seen anybody eat a whole one that fast."

Mina started to remember everything. The teakettle in the fireplace, the blown apart barn, the twinkling lights, and THE MAP! Mina looked all around, but the map was nowhere in sight. Neither was the tote bag. She tried to remember what had happened. She could recall taking a sip of the tea, but was she still holding the bag then? Surely, she must've dropped it when she was paralyzed.

The chicken man laughed, but Mina could see now that it wasn't a man dressed like a chicken at all. It was so obvious that she wondered how she could have been so blind to it the whole time. The tall man in the yellow jumpsuit was Dan, of course. He looked just like Dale, except that he was fatter in the middle and had red hair. His eyes were different too—pure black like the woman's eyes at the barn but even more terrifying and filled with dark promises.

"That's Dan!" Mina said, completely stunned.

"I know, and you're the girl angel. Only, we both know that's not true. You're just some girl they're using to spy on my operation. They keep sending you dumb earthlings my way. They say, 'Oh, Dan would never hurt two unsuspecting rubes.' They think I'm too nice, and you know, maybe I am. But maybe I'm not," Dan said with a horrible, smug grin.

"Are you?" Mina asked. She thought Dan might be speaking in code, but she had no idea what any of it meant. It was easier just to cut to the chase.

"What do *you* think?" he asked.

"I have no idea. I just met you," she replied.

"Well, once people get to know me, they find that I'm a genius-level kind of person. The crème de la crème. Regular people like you just don't get me. They don't realize how smart I am. If they were smarter, they'd show me more respect."

Mina had already grown tired of hearing Dan talk about himself when she thought he was a chicken. She ignored him and looked around for the map again.

"What you looking for?" Dan asked in an arrogant tone.

Mina could see he already knew. "I've lost my bag. It was slung over my shoulder when the woman at the barn poisoned me."

"And which woman would that be?" Dan asked. Suddenly, something creepy started to happen. Dan's face began to twitch and vibrate. At first, Mina thought her eyes were playing tricks on her in the low light, but then Dan's face morphed into the woman's face from the barn. His body quickly followed, and soon his clothes had changed from a jumpsuit to a flowing, yellow dress. The woman asked, "You mean this one?"

The hair on the back of Mina's neck stood up, and she slid farther back inside the shell. The woman burst into evil laughter. Then her head, neck, and shoulders sunk down as the top of her body collapsed into her lower half, transforming the tall woman into the old botanist. "Or maybe this one?" Betsy cackled in a raspy voice.

Mina had never seen anything like it. "How are you doing that?" she asked, frightened yet amazed.

The old woman stretched out into a featureless, yellow blob. The blob spun and vibrated until it had woven itself back into Dan. "I didn't do anything. You only think I did. At first you probably thought your eyes were deceiving you before you realized that what you were seeing was real, right?"

Mina nodded.

"But it *wasn't* real. Your eyes *were* deceiving you because I told them to."

"How did you tell them to?" asked Mina.

Dan's grin transitioned from smug to wicked. "I altered Theia's energy," he said, and Mina noticed an eerie twinkle flash across his glassy, black eyes.

He continued, "I've been studying the energy my whole life. Normally, it spreads outward in waves like a frequency, but I figured out how to control those waves. I pull them towards me and act as their center. Then I send them out, using my will to alter people's perception any way I please. It's a brilliant scientific procedure, and I figured it out all on my own."

Mina didn't think it sounded like such a brilliant procedure. She asked, "And by doing this, you can make people think that you've turned into different women?"

"No! Well, *yes*. But it's *more* than that. I can make people see whatever I want them to. I can lure them in and distract them by making them think they're enamored with a bunch of silly lights. I can get inside the head of a little girl who ate too much cucumber and figure out what she knows." Dan's twisted grin looked more frightening than ever.

Mina tensed up. "You mean you got inside my head?"

"Don't act so alarmed. It's pretty dull in there. But yes, I figured out what I needed to know and managed to keep you asleep the whole time. It was a long walk back to the glacier, and it was better for you to be conked out while that dumb meat-sack, Roger, dragged you."

Mina was dismayed. She hadn't given any thought to where they were. She had just assumed they were still near the barn, although she was beginning to suspect that the barn didn't really exist. It troubled her that she'd been dragged all the way to Black Ice Glacier unconscious, but it was even more upsetting to know that Dan had read her mind. She had to find out what he'd discovered.

"I don't believe you! If you really read my mind, then what did you see?" she asked, hoping she could trick him into giving something away.

"I saw everything. A scared little girl far away from her home. She misses the cottage in the green clearing near the sea. She misses the ugly, earth dog with long ears. She misses the people she loves, the ones who take care of her. Like the old man who burdens her with his stupidity."

Mina hated Dan for this. "My grandfather isn't a burden! He can't help that he forgets!"

Dan enjoyed Mina's protest. It fueled him. "But the little lost girl is here now. She thinks she's found people who'll help her get home. She thinks that if she does what they want, they'll find a way to save her. She doesn't see that she's being used. She only sees what she wants because she doesn't want to know the truth—that there's no way back."

Mina yelled angrily, "You don't know that! Maybe there's just no way back with *you* in charge!"

Dan frowned. "No. I made sure there isn't, and they *know*

that. They watched the bridge between our two worlds burn and vanish. The neon bridge that ushered all those pathetic, lost souls across the space divide is no more. I bombed it into tiny particles right after I burned down the city."

"And why?!" Mina shouted. "Because you *knew* that people would hate your way so much that they'd never stop trying to escape your tyranny!"

"Ha! Such a big word for such a small child. This is hardly tyranny, my dear. *Tyranny* was being forced to share with those ingrates while acting like they were our equals, especially the wolves. It was having to share what little we had with those loser Travelers when all they ever did was complain and ask for help. They were lucky to be saved from their shipwrecks, floods, and riptides, and they were even luckier that my family was here to constantly wipe their bottoms and mend their sorry little lives.

"If it hadn't been for my parents, they'd all be living in a desolate hellscape. No food. No shelter. No mechanics of any kind."

"But if that's how you feel, then why do you act like you hate your family so much?" asked Mina.

"I don't have to *like* my family to realize that they're better than everyone else. If my parents had seen the Moon Travelers as the wretched beggars they are, then maybe everything could have been different. But they always put them first, consenting to every request. No matter how big or small. And what was the point? They felt some obligation because they were the first ones here? It's absurd! The Moon Travelers never did *anything* for us! Yet my parents spent every single moment helping them while getting nothing in return. It makes no sense!"

"Maybe they did it because they were hoping to make Theia a better place for everyone to live," Mina said, trying to reason with Dan.

"No! If that were true, then they would have spent more

time with *me!* They knew how smart I was. I could have invented amazing things for the city. But instead of teaching me, they made me figure out everything on my own. They wouldn't even let me use any of their tools or formulas to make it easier. They forced me to sneak behind their backs, and then they had the nerve to call me a bad child. But they were the ones who were being *bad!*"

"Maybe they were afraid of you," Mina said. "Afraid of what you were capable of. Like having the wolves massacred, making your sister disappear, and destroying a whole city. Not to mention poisoning its citizens. Oh! And kidnapping Fred and me!"

"Who's Fred?" Dan asked.

"He's the other angel. You know? The one you captured?"

"Oh, *Fred!* I know him! He was like a son to me. In fact, he called me 'Dan' all the time."

"But your name is Dan," Mina pointed out.

"Yes, but the way he said it, it sounded almost like 'dad.' Terrible thing that happened to Fred."

"What happened to Fred?" Mina asked. She wasn't entirely sure she wanted to know.

"Well, just like you, he went messing around where he didn't belong, so I took him to my fort and interrogated him. He didn't tell me much. Shame I had to drop him down such a deep hole. Used to be a well but it's all dried up now."

"You didn't *have* to do that. You could've let him go!" Mina objected.

"You really don't understand much, do you? If I'd let him go, then I wouldn't have been able to slowly starve him into telling me the truth."

Mina fired back. "You're lying! You can't starve Moon Travelers."

Dan smiled with glee. "Yes you can. I know how."

Mina asked grimly, "So you killed him then?"

"No," Dan replied. "He's still alive but very thin now. It's a terrible look on him. Much too bony."

Mina felt sick. Dan was so flippant about torturing people, which was especially disturbing since she still didn't know what his plans were for her.

Dan seemed to read her mind. "You look like you'd wear the thin look better. We'll find out eventually, though, won't we? After all, nobody's coming to save you, just like nobody came to save poor, emaciated Frank. It's Frank, right? Oh, never mind. Who cares?

"Anyway, I threw all your things into the fire so there'd be no trace of you. Except this old piece of paper." Dan beamed as he pulled the map from his pocket and held it up for Mina to see.

"What is it you were calling this? A map?" he asked with a laugh. "That's hilarious! I mean look at where it's brought you! You must be as stupid as that dopey, old man back on Earth."

"You're an ogre!" Mina jumped to her feet and ran at him. This caught Dan off guard, which gave Mina enough time to kick him in the shin before he could react. Dan leaned over and yelped in pain. He grabbed his leg below the left knee where Mina's foot had struck him.

"You'll pay for that, you stupid brat! No apples for you!" Then, he raised himself back to a standing position. His face was filled with malice. His eyebrows hung low above his dark black eyes. He grabbed Mina by the neck and shoved her at the large, shaggy lunar wolf that was still laying by the fire. Mina fell face first into Roger's side, and he raised his head and growled at her.

The blow knocked the wind out of her. She gasped for air as she heard Dan roar, "Drop her in the well, Roger. She'll starve to death if the fall doesn't kill her. I don't need her anymore anyway."

Roger snarled as he stood. Mina's chest ached, but she had

to push herself up to keep from being dropped face first. Before she could return to her feet, Roger lunged at the top of her head and grabbed her hair tightly in his jaws. Mina screamed in pain as he began dragging her slowly across the ground. She raised a hand above her head to try and pull her hair free of the wolf's strong jaws. With the other hand, she dug her palm into the dirt in a futile attempt to push herself off the ground.

Despite her terrible predicament, Dan couldn't resist one last chance to goad her. "You're a very stupid girl. They deceived you, you know? They made you think you could face off against *me!* Where are they now? Have *they* come all the way here to overthrow me? Were *they* brave enough to ask me for the phony blueprints themselves? Or for what they really want? To return them all to their fragile little realities.

"No! Of course not! They're too weak! This whole thing is pitiful! They send a child to do their bidding. It could have been different for you. You didn't have to come here. You didn't have to do what they asked."

Mina couldn't think straight. Her scalp burned, and she felt chunks of hair being ripped from her head. She begged Dan, "Make him stop! I'll tell you anything. Please! Just tell him to stop!"

Dan came closer and leaned into her face. "Why do they keep sending you? And don't tell me *the blueprints* again. What else do you know?"

Dan snapped his fingers, and Roger loosened his grip just enough to ease some of the pain. Mina was shaking. She opened her eyes. Dan was livid. The black glass that filled his eye sockets looked like dark, swirling whirlpools.

Mina knew what she had to do. "There was a prophecy that two children would come from Earth to help save everyone from you and Dale. It wasn't true, though. Helen made it up so she could leave the market and stop you herself.

She's *in* the map. Your parents found a way to connect her to it. Everyone who knows about it calls her Captain Key to protect her identity from you and Dale."

Dan laughed. "Well, look at that! What a little fink you are! I bet my sister didn't see that coming. Too bad for you I've known about that map for years. It was easier to let them have their fun than to get tangled up in more family drama. Plus, the idea of my sister having been reduced to a talking piece of paper is about the funniest thing I can think of.

"If that's the best you can do, then I suppose it's time for me and my dear sis to play catch up." Dan smiled and held up the map again. "Sadly, I've got some bad news for you, kid. You're light-years behind on what's really going on here. Time to go!" Dan bent down and grabbed Mina around the neck, releasing her from Roger's grip and pulling her into a standing position.

Mina didn't even think about struggling. Dan shoved her forward, away from the bright blue firelight and into the darkness. Mina was scared, but she kept talking. She asked, "What do you mean I'm light-years behind? What else is there to know?"

Dan tightened his hold around her neck. "Despite what I might seem like, I'm not your tutor. I don't have to explain anything to you."

Mina scoffed, "Despite what you might *think*, most tutors don't seem like raving lunatics. But I think you're bluffing. You don't know any more than what I've told you. Otherwise, why would you let Fred and me live? You're worried you might need us because you haven't figured everything out yet."

Dan pulled back on Mina's neck tightly to stop her. He grabbed her forearm and held it up, spinning her around so they were facing inches apart in the darkness. "What makes you think I'm going to let you live?" he whispered in her ear.

But before she could answer, he drew her in so that her

body was pushed against his for the briefest of moments. Then with a large shove, he pushed her backwards. She threw her hands down to catch herself, but the ground wasn't there. "Nooo!" she cried out, but all she could hear were the sounds of Dan's laughter as she fell into a deep, dark hole.

CHAPTER 26

SAVING FRED

Ruth was waiting for Maude when she reached the market, but Maude quickly blew past her old friend. In an angry tone, she asked, "Why didn't anyone send a silver bird? I ordered Alex to find you or Max and have one delivered to me immediately."

Ruth struggled to keep up with Maude, who was power walking towards her booth along the length of the market wall. "Maude, there's something I need to talk to you about," Ruth said breathlessly.

Maude shot back, "I don't have time now, Ruth. I have to grab a silver bird and get a message to Bob right away. You have no idea what we're up against."

Ruth responded, "This is important, though, and you're gonna need to hear it before you send Bob a message."

Maude stopped and turned to her friend. "Fine, but hurry!"

Ruth looked sheepish. She and Maude had been friends for a long time—since before most people had arrived on the Moon even. Maude was like a daughter to her. When they'd met, Maude was still coming into her own, still at the beginning of what would become an amazing career in chemistry. Ruth could see such potential in her young friend, but Maude wrestled with demons as a result of her amnesia. They stemmed from the trauma of not knowing where she came from.

Ruth had stepped in to help her friend tame this side of herself, and the two became close. She taught Maude how to cope with the emptiness she felt and gave her a dependable shoulder to lean on.

Standing there in front of Maude was agonizing. Ruth knew that what she had to tell her would change everything between them, yet it was too important to remain a secret any longer. "Helen knows about the rest of Neriti's prophecy, Maude. The part about Dan and Dale. Neriti told Helen everything before she died."

Maude was glancing all around, thinking about the silver bird she needed to find, and clearly not giving Ruth her full attention. "What are you saying, Ruth? We don't have time for this. Just spit it out!"

Ruth continued, "I'm so sorry, hon. I shoulda told you sooner, but Helen begged me not to. Helen was the one who made up that prophecy about the two Earth children. Theia didn't send me the message. It was Helen using my crystal to control me so that she could write it herself. She had me fooled at first too. But eventually, I caught on to what she was doing… and I let her do it anyway. Here, she wrote you this note." Ruth held out her hand, offering Maude a piece of folded paper she'd been clinging to. "I wasn't supposed to give it to you yet, but I think it's time. You just gotta know that Helen's doing what she thinks is right."

Maude suddenly became dizzy. She propped herself against the wall and took the paper from Ruth's hand. She unfolded it and began to read:

Dear Mom and Dad,

I'm sorry I deceived you, but hopefully by the time you read this, you'll understand why I had to do it…

Maude wailed as she crumpled the note in her hand. "Oh, Ruth! How could you!?" she cried. And she fell to her knees and sobbed.

∽∽∽∽∽

MINA PLUMMETED into the dried-up well, positioned in a backwards dive. She cradled her head with her arms, hoping to lessen the blow that she knew was coming. However, as she neared the bottom, a warm white light began to shine all around her. And suddenly, she was floating.

Like a sinking feather, Mina drifted back and forth until she reached the ground. The light dimmed, and she sat up. For a split second, she could see she was at the bottom of a very deep hole that was covered in beautiful, white crystals—the source of the fading light.

She heard a young man speak to her from somewhere close by. "Who are you?" he asked.

Mina moved her head in the direction of the voice. "I'm Mina, from Earth. Are you Fred?"

"They sent you, didn't they?" he asked. "That's why you have wings like I did before…before he took them."

"Did he hurt you?" Mina asked.

Fred replied, "Well, if you count the injuries from being thrown into the well, then yes. I don't know how you pulled off that landing, but that's not what mine looked like."

"I'm sorry. Didn't the crystals slow you down?"

"Slow me down? Heck no! They didn't do *anything*. There was no magical light show when I fell. I dropped until the back of my pants caught on one of the crystals. Then I hung there for what could've been a day, maybe three. There's no way to know.

"I was too scared to try to free myself. I didn't know how far down the ground was, but eventually my pants ripped, and I fell the rest of the way. I broke my leg and sprained both wrists."

"That's good, at least. Not that you broke your leg, of course, but it could've been a lot worse."

"It *was* a lot worse. When my pants ripped, the sharp crystal I'd been dangling from gashed me in the back. It left a long cut that most likely needed stitches.

"Oh," said Mina. "But you're okay now, right? I mean, you've healed?"

"I guess so, but it's hard to think of myself as healed after spending weeks, or months, or maybe even years down here by myself. I've completely lost my mind several times. I hallucinate a lot. In fact, I'm not really sure whether you're a hallucination," he said, sounding worried.

"I'm not a hallucination," Mina tried to reassure him.

"Okay, but then how did you make those crystals do that? I've never seen them do that before. I didn't even know they *could* do that."

"I see..." said Mina, pausing for a moment. Then she continued, "I think I must've gotten lucky. Maybe it's because I felt at peace with what was happening to me. That's the only explanation I can think of anyway."

"Really? That's the only explanation? That you got lucky? That sounds like something a hallucination would say."

"I'm not a hallucination. Really, I'm not. I came here to save you."

Fred laughed. "I hate to break it to you, but this has to be the worst rescue of all time. There's no way out of here. If you were going to save me, you should have done it from up there. Not down here."

Mina brushed off Fred's skepticism. "Technically, I'm not the one who's going to save you. I'm just the one who wanted to."

"Oh, is that right? Well, who's going to save me then?" Fred asked in a mocking tone.

"The lunar wolves," said Mina with confidence. "They're going to dig us out."

"Umm, no. That's *not* going to happen. For one, the lunar wolves don't like me, but even if they did, it's still impossible. They would never be able to get through the ice. We're surrounded by a glacier on all sides," Fred argued.

Mina responded, "I would have thought that too, but Helen told me the glacier doesn't run underneath the well. One of the oldest tunnels lies right below here. The wolves are digging through the bottom of the well as we speak."

"Who in the world is Helen?"

"Oh, right," Mina replied. "Helen's the map. I mean, she controls the map."

"I don't think we were using the same map. My map was controlled by someone named General Longitude," Fred insisted.

"Does 'General Longitude' sound like a real name to you?" Mina asked. "I promise it's the same map. She was calling herself Captain Key when I met her. They were aliases she used to hide her identity."

"But I thought General Longitude was a man," Fred protested.

"Easy mistake. Anyway, we're wasting time. We need to start making a lot of noise so the wolves know where to dig."

Mina cupped her hands over her mouth and took a deep breath in. Then she exhaled the low and high notes the way Helen had taught her. Fred didn't do or say anything, and

Mina carried on humming this way for a long time. Finally, Mina had to take a break. Fred snickered and said, "Told you it wasn't gonna happen."

Mina was frustrated with Fred's lack of faith. "Instead of acting so smug, why don't you do something useful and take over for a while?"

"Why should I?" asked Fred. "What you're doing is just a big waste of air. Sooner or later, you're going to have to accept that we're stuck down here for good. Don't worry, though. Dan drops apples sometimes. He calls them 'luxury apples' because they don't have any worms in them. Hopefully, he'll drop twice as many from now on. Usually, he only drops a couple at a time; it's barely enough to survive on."

Mina ignored the comments about the apples. Despite what Dan had said, she still felt confident that they didn't need the apples to survive. She said, "I know you've been down here a long time, and you feel hopeless, but I've risked a lot to come and save you. I'd appreciate it if you'd at least humor me so I can give my lungs a quick break."

"You can spend all the time you want giving your lungs a break. That tune was grating on my nerves anyway. I'm not going to humor you, though. It's a huge waste of time and energy."

Mina couldn't hide her frustration any longer. "Let me put it this way, Fred," she began. "What else are you planning to do with all this time we have left? Besides, if it turns out I'm right—and the lunar wolves *do* get us out of here—you won't get to claim any of the victory for yourself if you don't humor me. And then you'll have to tell everyone that a silly girl and her wolf friends saved you."

"Fine," Fred conceded in a huff. "But just so you know, I'm only doing this to get you to shut up about it."

"Fine!" Mina shouted. Her patience had worn thin from all the arguing, and she was ready not to speak for a while.

Fred didn't start right away, and Mina wondered if he was having to reconcile his pride before he began. After a few minutes, though, he started to hum. At first, the notes sounded screechy like nails on a chalkboard, and Mina cringed. Not only at the sound, but at the thought of having to correct him.

Thankfully, after a few rounds, Fred figured out what he was doing wrong and shifted to humming a more pleasant series of low and high notes. He went on and on, humming the short tune for much longer than Mina had expected. In fact, when he finally ran out of steam, she was pretty sure he'd hummed the melody even longer than she had.

Without missing a beat, Mina picked up the song where Fred left off. Feeling a bit competitive, she pushed herself to continue making the sounds long after her lungs had begun to burn from overuse. Eventually, she yielded to the worsening pain, but she was pleasantly surprised when Fred picked up the notes right as she stopped.

Sitting close together in the dark, the two young Earthlings spent hours passing the musical baton back and forth. They became unified in an unspoken understanding that spending their time like this was better than spending it in empty silence, or worse, angry squabbling. The time ticked away one melodic breath at a time. After what felt like it could've been an entire day, Mina and Fred stopped their relay. It was Fred who spoke the words they'd both been thinking. "We need to stop. Not forever. I know this is important to you, but I think we should break the loop for a while to keep from losing our wits."

Mina appreciated the compassionate tone Fred was taking and knew he was right. The action had lost all of its meaning, and the repetition was starting to have a damaging effect. Mina didn't respond to Fred but let out a slow sigh of relief. Her throat muscles had never ached so badly, even the one time she'd been sick with strep throat. She wondered if she'd be able to speak. After resting for a bit, she decided to try. "Where did you live before?" she asked.

Fred didn't respond right away, but Mina didn't mind. She thought maybe he didn't feel like talking after the grueling exercise they'd just gone through. She had started to think about something else entirely when Fred finally said, "It was the apples. I knew what was going to happen when I ate them. I tried to hold off as long as I could. I even thought it would be better to die than to eat the poison, but eventually I gave in to my hunger. It was like I didn't have a choice. My survival instincts overpowered the rest of me, and I...I just did it. Honestly, the worst part is that the poison didn't erase every-thing. It only erased the parts of me and my story that I didn't want to let go."

Mina choked up as she fought off the flood of emotion that was threatening to pour out. She whispered through the dark, "I'm so sorry, Fred." Then she scooted on her knees to where she imagined he was sitting. She reached her hand out once she was sure she was close enough and gently grazed his arm. She moved her hand down to find his and clutched it gently but was alarmed by how bony it felt. It was like holding hands with a skeleton.

Doing her best to hide her fear, she asked, "Fred, how often does Dan bring you apples?"

"I don't know," he replied. "I guess not that often, though," he said with a little laugh, as though he were trying to shrug off the gravity of the situation.

"You know you don't have to eat them, right? We don't need food here. I think Dan may have done more than poison your mind. I think he poisoned your body too. There's no reason you should be this thin."

Fred replied softly, "I know I don't have to eat them, but you don't know what it's like down here. Not yet, anyway. You don't always have control over yourself. You'll see."

Mina didn't know what she'd do if the lunar wolves didn't turn up soon. She thought of her parents and her grandfather and Bonkers. She thought of her little town and her friends at school. She didn't want to forget anything about her life before. Even if she never got to go home, she wanted to hold onto all her treasured memories. It was painful to think she might never see the people she cared about again. However, it was a great deal more painful to think about forgetting them entirely. She continued to hold Fred's hand.

A few moments later, Mina heard something high above their heads and off in the distance. It sounded like an explosion coming from somewhere far away. It was hard to tell how far away, though, from inside the well.

Mina squeezed Fred's hand and said, "Listen! Did you hear that?"

There was another loud explosion and then another. "Yeah," Fred replied. "What do you think it is?"

Mina shook her head, even though she knew Fred couldn't see her in the dark. "I don't know. Have you heard anything like it since you've been down here? Maybe Dan's doing some kind of experiment. I know for a fact that he creates formulas. It's how he poisoned the water and probably how he created those weird eye-skin covers.

"Oh yeah. Those were *creepy*," Fred said, shuddering.

"*Boom…Boom!*" It sounded like the explosions were getting closer.

Suddenly, Mina understood what they were hearing. "Fred! I know what that is! It's cannon fire. I think Bob's army is moving towards the glacier!"

"What army? Who's Bob?" Fred asked, confused.

Before Mina had a chance to explain, the ground beneath them began to rumble. It started slowly but then picked up force until it was shaking uncontrollably. Rocks and dirt flew up and pelted Fred and Mina in the face. Still holding onto Mina's hand, Fred leapt to his feet, pulling her with him. Swiftly, he moved them a few paces from where they'd been sitting. He grabbed Mina firmly and pushed her against part of the wall where there were less crystals. Then he squeezed himself into the same spot so that they were pressed together.

"What's happening?" Mina cried to Fred over the thundering sound.

Fred didn't respond. He and Mina were starting to sink as the dirt under their feet slid away towards the center of the well. Mina imagined herself standing on a beach again. She could feel the pull of the tide reaching beyond her towards land. She watched the water and the sand as they passed over her feet. Then, suddenly, the water turned into a blinding, white light. Her eyes burned, and she jerked her head to turn away from it. She felt something tugging at her hand and realized it was Fred yanking her out of her dream.

The light was real, though. The white crystals were shining, just like they had when she'd fallen into the well, only they seemed brighter now. Mina looked over to see Fred for the first time. He was much taller than she'd imagined and also much thinner. His clothes were loose and tattered, and judging by his height, Mina thought he was about sixteen, though it was hard to tell because of how horribly scrawny he was. It was obvious that Dan had come close to starving him to death with the poison he'd been feeding him. His face was hollowed out, and his eyes were sunken.

Fred met Mina's gaze nervously. "I think there's something bad down there. It sounds like rushing water or giant worms. Let's hope it's water. If the well begins to flood, we're going to lock arms from behind, back-to-back, and stand in the middle of the rising water. We'll kick our way out of here together just like we're swimming up. You do know how to swim, right? Please tell me you do."

Mina smiled and shook her head but then quickly

corrected herself. "Yes, I know how to swim, but I don't think it's water *or* worms. I've seen this before—"

Just then, the vibrating blur of dirt and rocks gave way in the middle of the well, and five gray and white lunar wolves leapt from the center of the sinking dirt. Mina thought they were the most beautiful creatures she'd ever seen, and her heart swelled with gratitude.

Axel was the first to approach them. Mina recognized him right away. She bent down and threw her arms around his neck but then pulled back and bowed her head, realizing it was the more respectful way to greet him. Axel bowed his head too. Then Mina turned to Fred and asked, "Have you met Axel?"

Fred didn't say anything. He looked frightened. "What's wrong?" she asked.

Fred was staring directly at Axel. She turned back to Axel and saw that he was baring his teeth at Fred. "Stop that! What's going on?" she demanded.

Fred spoke nervously, "We met before when I was traveling with the map, but I don't like wolves, and they kept getting too close. I told the General, or Helen, or *whoever* that I didn't want them getting so close, but they wouldn't stop meddling in everything I did. So I might have kicked one or two of them from behind. It was only to shoo them away, though."

Mina was appalled. "That's terrible, Fred! How could you do something like that?"

Fred looked at her incredulously and repeated, "I don't like *wolves!*"

Mina rolled her eyes. "They're trying to help us! Talk about looking a gift horse in the mouth. Or kicking a gift wolf in the tail…Wait! Is that why you didn't want to help me call them?"

Fred was obviously annoyed at Mina for taking the wolves' side. "*No.* I just didn't expect them to come is all. I knew they weren't going to help *me*, but I didn't realize they'd make allowances for you. Anyway, I don't have to prove anything. I hummed that stupid tune for hours. It's probably the only reason they're here!"

Mina relaxed a little. She knew Fred was right, even if she didn't approve of his abhorrent behavior. She turned towards the wolves again. "Can you get us out of here, Axel?"

Axel bowed his head to nod, and Mina copied the gesture to show her thanks. Then he turned and jumped into the large hole. The other wolves followed to the same spot and jumped in after him, one after another. Mina prepared to do the same. She looked over her shoulder at Fred and beckoned to him with her hand. "Come on, then. You may not like the wolves, but you have to admit that getting out of here is a million times better than holding a grudge."

"It's not a grudge!" Fred fired back. "I don't understand why nobody can respect the fact that I don't want them near me."

"Well, you'll have plenty of time to keep your distance from them once we're out of here. But for now, maybe you could at least pretend to be appreciative? I mean honestly, I'm not sure you could've made it many more days down here in your condition," Mina said with a sympathetic smile.

Fred didn't smile back, though, and Mina sighed. She turned and walked to the edge of the hole to get a better view of the steep slope the wolves had created. It looked to be as much as a thirty-foot drop if she lost her footing on the way down. Beyond the slope, the tunnel curved around on itself like a corkscrew that led even deeper into the ground.

Mina looked back and saw that Fred had come a little closer, though it was obvious that he still hadn't fully committed himself to their escape. "Come on," she coaxed him. "If you fall too far behind, I won't be able to tell you everything I know about Bob and Maude's army." Fred didn't reply, but Mina was certain he'd follow when he was ready. He knew he couldn't stay. Pretty soon, he'd have to choose his freedom over his pride.

Mina eased herself onto the barely angled slope. She thought about sliding down on her bottom like a forward moving crab-crawl. However, she didn't want to make the lunar wolves wait too long, now that the battle was underway. So she shuffled her feet down the steep path and out of Fred's sight.

Fred hated the idea of plunging into an even deeper hole. But the lights had started to dim, and his fear of being trapped in the dark came rushing back. He looked high above to the well's opening, not sure what he hoped to find. He was taken aback when he saw how much the glowing crystals resembled sparkling diamonds. Immediately, he began to calculate how much money he could make selling them back on Earth—if only it were possible.

"What a waste," he said to himself, moving quickly to catch up to Mina. "Dan should've figured out a way to profit off the crystals and mined the well instead of using it as a dungeon."

He leapt into the hole and surfed clumsily down the slope. "Wait up, Mina!" Fred called. "I want to know about the army."

MINA HAD BEEN GOING on for a while, telling Fred everything that had happened to her since she left the greenhouse. She thought it would be good to share as much as possible so that Fred would understand the full extent of what Bob's army was up against—what they were all up against.

She followed the pack through the tunnels. The bright crystals lit their surroundings in a fiery glow. Fred walked behind Mina. He stayed quiet as she spoke, yet he was only listening to parts of what she said. He was tense and distracted. He didn't like being confined to small spaces, and compared to the well, the tunnel felt like being inside of a soda straw. When they reached a narrow spot of the tunnel where they were forced to crawl on their hands and knees, Fred stopped her. "I can't do this, Mina. You'll have to go on without me. I can't handle tight spaces."

Mina heard the panic in Fred's voice. She had bent down to crawl through the narrow space but stood up again when she realized he needed her. She reached out for his hand. "It's going to be okay. I'm not going to leave you, and I *know* you can do this. I can follow you if you want. Just imagine that you're crawling across the ground, through a giant field."

"No. I can't. I'm telling you, I can't! Just go!" Fred insisted.

Mina began to worry. Fred had convinced himself he couldn't handle the small tunnel, but there was no way she was going to leave him behind. She was positive he'd die or—even worse—end up back in the well at Dan's mercy. Mina looked down the tunnel. She could see the wolves up ahead. They had stopped to wait for them. Suddenly, an idea popped into her head. "Take my hands and breathe deeply," she told Fred.

Fred looked at Mina skeptically but did as she instructed. They stood staring at each other for a while, holding hands and taking deep breaths. Then Mina said, "It's going to be just like before. We're going to close our eyes and pretend we're back in the well, but this time we'll hum our tune together. Can you do that for me?"

It was hard to sense emotion from Fred's hollowed features, but after a few more breaths he nodded in agreement. "Okay, good," Mina said, seizing the moment, worried he would change his mind. "Here we go." Mina closed her eyes and hummed. Then she bent down and felt her way along the constrictive dirt passage.

Seconds later, she heard Fred behind her, humming in harmony to her tune. The harmony surprised her and made her smile. She kept her eyes closed, just like she had promised, but from out of the darkness, came colorful shapes of shimmering light. They hovered at the upper and lower edges of her peripheral vision. They grew and shrank, spun and morphed. It seemed impossible to look at them directly, for they drifted away whenever Mina tried to focus on them. She gave up and relaxed. Instead of trying to look at the shapes, she imagined herself floating towards one.

She could hear the music that she and Fred had been humming, except it was no longer coming from them. It sounded like it was being performed by a grand orchestra. The transformation was beautiful, and Mina was overcome with joy. Then, suddenly, she was teleported. The unexpected change to her surroundings sent Mina into a daze, and it took her a moment to realize that she was back on Earth.

Fred was there too, but he wasn't the tall, withered version that she knew. He was almost the same height as Mina, and his face was fuller, though not plump. They were on a crowded street that was devoid of cars. Four and five-story buildings with narrow windows lined the street and provided shade, but Mina could still feel sweltering heat rising from the pavement beneath them.

Several other boys and girls stood with them. Mina looked at Fred who was next to her. He was smiling and talking to two of the boys close to them, but she couldn't hear what he was saying over the loud orchestral music. She saw the boys laugh at whatever Fred had told them, and she wondered how they could hear him.

She looked at Fred again. He was laughing too, but she realized for the first time that something was off. The boys didn't seem to be aware of her presence. She reached her hand out to touch Fred's, but before she could, she began to float away. Mina rose high above the street and hovered at the level of the rooftops. She kept her eyes locked on Fred from afar as the music played faster and faster. Fred disappeared into one of the buildings and then reappeared seconds later. He threw a soccer ball towards his friends, and the three of them took turns dribbling it down the street.

Mina liked her bird's eye view. She felt perfectly content to watch while the boys enjoyed their game. She'd forgotten all about her own reality—the wolves, the tunnel, the Moon army marching into battle. However, the forgetfulness didn't last long as she was soon teleported back.

Once she returned, it took her another moment to remember where she was. It wasn't until the orchestra faded away and she heard herself humming along with Fred that she realized what had happened. Somehow, Mina had gained access to Fred's memories when he began harmonizing their tune.

Shortly after this realization, the tunnel widened again. Mina stood up and turned to Fred. She reached out her hand to help him exit the narrow space, but just like in the vision, Fred didn't seem to know she was there.

"Are you okay?" she asked upon noticing how pale he looked.

Fred nodded but stared straight ahead like he was in shock. Mina thought it would be better not to press him. She knew it hadn't been easy for Fred to face his fear, and she was proud of him for doing it anyway. She squeezed his hand, and the gesture broke his trance.

"I had a dream. I guess it must've been a daydream, but it felt so real I could've sworn it was happening. I was trapped under water. It should've been horrible because I couldn't breathe. But it didn't hurt. It was like I was floating. I could see the light shining through the waves above me. I don't know how to describe it exactly. It wasn't scary, though. It was peaceful."

Mina smiled reassuringly at Fred, although the account of his daydream had made her feel a bit unsettled. "I'm really glad we made it through that together," she said, patting him on the shoulder.

Up ahead, Axel let out a long howl. She turned to him, but he wasn't looking back at her. He was standing with his legs planted wide, staring at the wall. His hair stood on end like porcupine quills as he bared his teeth and growled.

Mina walked towards him but didn't see anything unusual about the space he was growling at. It was merely a large gap between the crystals. Mina rubbed her eyes. The red and orange light had become so dim that she was having trouble seeing what was right in front of her. "What is it, Axel?" Mina asked.

She reached out to the dark space on the wall and ran her hand over it. It wasn't dirt or rock like she'd expected; it was rough metal. Mina leaned in closer, and the wolf pack hummed louder. The crystals around the area brightened just enough for Mina to realize what she was looking at. It was a manhole cover made of dark, hammered steel.

"We're here…" Mina whispered.

Fred pushed up against Mina's side to run his hand over the black plate. He dug out some loose dirt from behind the metal cover so he could squeeze his fingers around the rim and pry it loose. He pushed his foot against the wall for extra leverage and tugged at the metal disc a few times. On the fourth try, the metal plate came free, revealing a dark passageway that led up a sloped path.

Fred set the cover down against the wall, and he and Mina poked their heads through the large hole together. "That's odd," he said. "Why would anyone bother to hide a tunnel all the way down here. Unless…"

"Unless what?" Mina asked.

Fred backed away from the tunnel. "Think about it, Mina. We've been wandering below Black Ice Glacier this whole time. It's how these wolves are getting us out of here.

Through a tunnel below the ice. And who lives on top of the glacier?"

"Dan does," Mina replied.

"Right," continued Fred. "So, don't you see? This isn't just some random tunnel. It's a tunnel that Dan spent a great deal of effort building and *then* hiding."

"Why do you think he did that?" asked Mina.

"Who knows? But I'm sure it wasn't to add more complexity to the sub-glacier tunnel system. No doubt it has some nefarious purpose, and I don't think we should stick around to find out what that is. Here, help me put the cover back on."

Mina didn't move. "You're right, Fred. You should go now. Follow the pack until you catch up to Bob's army. Bob knows how much you've sacrificed. I'm sure he'll help you."

"What do you mean? Aren't you coming with us?" Fred asked.

Mina looked back up the passageway that ran through the ice and shook her head. "I made a promise I have to keep."

"You can't be *serious*. You're going to climb up a tunnel that leads to Dan's fort? While it's being fired on? And after everything we did to escape from the well? Do you have a death wish or something?"

Mina laughed uncomfortably. "No, I really don't. I just know this is what I have to do. I'm sorry. I wish I could go with you."

Fred scoffed, "You don't have to apologize to me. It's your funeral, after all."

Mina nodded at Fred sadly and then turned to Axel to say goodbye. Axel didn't acknowledge her, though. Instead, he looked towards his pack and whimpered. He walked away from Mina and stood in front of the wolves, bowing his head deeply to each one. The other wolves bowed to Axel in turn, and then, one by one, they took off down the tunnel without him. Axel jumped through the hole and climbed a few steps before sitting down to wait for Mina.

Fred rolled his eyes and turned halfway around like he was going to leave without saying goodbye. But he stopped and said, "You know, there's no way I'm joining Bob's army."

"What do you mean?" Mina asked.

"It's not my fight, Mina. And it's not yours either, for that matter. We don't belong in this place. We had nothing to do with the way things are here. We're basically just tourists who got dragged into a squabble between the locals."

"Seriously, Fred? A squabble? The twins *poisoned* them! And most of those 'locals' are just like us. They traveled here from Earth too, and probably they just wanted to live a free and happy existence once they got here. But Dan and Dale robbed them of that. The same way Dan tried to rob us of *our* freedom. Doesn't that mean anything to you? Don't you want to make sure he can never do that to anyone again?"

Fred shrugged, but he wouldn't look Mina in the eye. "I just don't want to be involved anymore. I've had enough."

"But if you help them win, they'll find a way to give you your memory back."

"But, Mina, if they win, they'll do that whether I help them or not. And if they don't win, then at least I won't go down with them. Either way, my help or lack of help wouldn't make any difference."

Mina hated that Fred was being so selfish. "You don't know that, Fred. Maybe your help would make *all* the difference."

Fred took Mina's hand in his and held it. "No, Mina. It won't. I have to go now. Take care of yourself," he said, squeezing her hand before he turned to leave. Then he stopped one last time and looked over his shoulder. "Oh, and I've been meaning to tell you—for a hallucination, you're not half bad." He smiled and then hurried down the path after the wolves.

CHAPTER 27

BLACK ICE FORT

Mina was exhausted. She'd been climbing through the dark tunnel for what seemed like ages. It was the first time that her wings had felt like an inescapable nuisance. They dragged against the top of the tunnel, creating friction that caused them to feel much heavier than before. She wished they'd do their job and help her take flight again. *Even if it was a wild ride,* she thought, *at least I wouldn't have to climb anymore.*

Axel, who she'd been thankful to have by her side at first, was beginning to irritate her with his seemingly effortless ability to climb. She told him to go on several times, hoping he would leave her to sulk in private, but he continued to slow his pace and wait for her each time he pulled ahead.

She knew she needed rest, but for some reason, her brain was telling her that she needed food. She kept picturing her tote bag. At that moment, she would have done anything for a raw potato or a squash. It made her think of Fred. It was clear now why he hadn't been able to resist the apples; the truth was that even when memories faded, instincts remained.

Suddenly, the air grew warm. It was a huge contrast to the

glacial temperatures they'd been climbing through for so long. Mina began to feel cozy like she'd been wrapped in a soft blanket. She wanted to lay down, but she knew she couldn't give in to her desire. The voice inside her told her to keep climbing.

It was what she needed to hear. It made her feel agitated again, and she knew this feeling would keep her awake. She focused on the irritating sound of Axel's tail swishing back and forth over the dirt. Then, abruptly, the swishing stopped, and Mina became very alert. "What's happening?" she whispered.

Axel moved aside. She could see a faint, yellow light shining from somewhere up the path. Axel moaned, but they continued to climb until they'd reached the source of the light. However, it was not what Mina had expected to find.

The tunnel opened up to an enormous, black and white tiled bathroom with a large clawfoot tub as the centerpiece to the grand room. The ceiling was high, the walls were cream colored, and sparkling metal shower heads of all shapes and sizes were positioned randomly throughout. Mina noticed that the tiles were angled slightly towards the middle of the room. She took a closer look and realized there was a drain hidden underneath the tub. The entire bathroom had been designed to function as one gigantic shower.

"This is Dan's bathroom?" she whispered as she stepped closer to the vanity table which was positioned like a barrier to the tunnel. She reached out to touch the back of it but jammed her fingers. A giant glass pane blocked the hole between the tunnel and the bathroom. It was perfectly transparent, though, so Mina hadn't realized it was there. She shook her hand in pain, and Axel let out a low growl.

Mina didn't understand what he was growling at until she heard a toilet flush off to their left. A door opened and out came Dan, wearing a yellow silk bathrobe. He stepped out from the toilet closet, which was located on the same side of the bathroom as the tunnel. Mina turned to duck back down the hill, but Axel jumped in front of her to block the way.

Mina quietly hissed, "What are you doing? Do you want to get us killed?!"

Axel let out a deep rumbling growl and flicked his head towards the bathroom behind her. Mina looked over her shoulder, terrified she'd find Dan standing there. But she didn't. Dan was seated at the vanity table, picking at his eyebrows while staring into the glass. Except that it wasn't glass. "It's a two-way mirror," Mina whispered to herself as it started to make sense.

Axel walked right up to the glass and sat down. Dan would have had a perfect view of the lunar wolf if he'd been able to see through the glass, but he didn't react. Mina joined Axel. She stood a few feet back from the glass and watched as Dan sat in his bathroom, fussing over himself in the mirror. She was relieved to find that his eyes were no longer obscured by the shiny, black coating. However, they still looked abnormal, as though they lacked any feeling.

Dan opened a drawer in his vanity and pulled out a plump cigar. He held up an ornate, silver dragon and cut off the end of the cigar with a guillotine inside its mouth. Then he fished around inside the waist pocket of his robe and took out a jade lighter. A bright blue flame ignited from the top as he spun the flint. He pressed the cigar to his lips and leaned into the flame, pulling a few short breaths that created an orange ember at the end of the fat cylinder.

White smoke drifted to the ceiling, and seconds later, Mina smelled the heavy scent of tobacco creeping through the air. Dan lowered his cigar and propped it on the side of a decorative ashtray. He picked up a large satchel from the back of his chair, opened the top, and pulled out a folded piece of paper. It was the map.

Mina looked at Axel. He was as close as he could get to the glass without touching it. He snarled as Dan unfolded the map.

Dan, who still seemed oblivious to Axel's presence, situated the large paper on the table in front of him and began to speak. "Oh sister, sister, sister of mine, you've never been so quiet with so much on your mind." Mina looked around. She could hear Dan, but it wasn't through the mirror. It sounded like there were vents, or possibly speakers, in the tunnel that were amplifying Dan's voice.

Dan smirked and looked into the mirror again but then frowned. He stretched out the skin on his forehead and lifted the skin around his eyes. "Hmm," he sighed while grabbing some tissues from a drawer. He dabbed at his face, and slowly, it began to transform into a grotesque sight.

Mina hadn't realized Dan was wearing make-up and was horrified to watch as a heavy, white layer of paint and powder was wiped away to reveal boiled and blistering skin underneath. It appeared that Dan had been badly burned at some point, but Mina wondered why he would bother covering up his scars when he lived all alone on the darkest part of the Moon.

Boom! Boom! Boom!

The sounds of cannon fire erupted again. They were the same sounds she and Fred had heard earlier in the well, only they were much closer now. The vibrations rippled through the ground as Dan wiped the crusty make-up from his neck and arms.

"You hear that, Helen? That's the Reaper's song. He's come to collect. Of course, there's not much left of you to collect, is there? I'm astonished our father didn't build you some type of mechanical body. All these years you've been forced to rely on others like an invalid. Please tell me you realize how worthless you've become. Tell me you finally resent our parents as much as I do, after they allowed you to live in this sub-human form despite their impeccable talents for chemistry and engineering."

Mina's eyes moved to the paper, but nothing happened.

"At least tell me you realize what fools they've been! Did you really think I didn't know about their plans to rise up against me? My god, I can't believe it took *this* long. I guess good old Mom and Dad didn't bounce back so well from having everything they worked for destroyed right in front of their eyes. Truly, I'd hoped for some better opponents, but then again, forcing Maude to drink that aging elixir probably didn't help matters. How old *does* she look now? A quarter past dead?" Dan roared with laughter.

Words raced across the map, but Mina couldn't read what they said because the map was angled at Dan. At first, Dan didn't notice, but then his laughter stopped as he caught sight of his sister's words. He scowled, and a fire ignited in his eyes.

Boom! Boom!

The walls rumbled. Dan continued to read Helen's words as his skin turned a solid shade of crimson. He banged his fist on the vanity. "Enough!" he yelled. "I gave you a gift when I made you invisible! If you had *half* my intelligence, you would've found a way to work it to your advantage. You would've found a way to become something great! But instead, you cry over people's *feelings*! Heaven, help us all! It's time I put you out of your misery!"

Dan grabbed his jade lighter and held it up to a corner of the map. He spun the flint and a bright blue flame burst out, catching the map on fire. "NO!" Mina screamed. She pounded her fists against the glass as Axel barked, growled, and jumped at it. Dan held the flaming piece of paper towards the mirror with a wicked grin. Suddenly, his eyes turned black again, and he looked just like the devil he was. Mina didn't care, though. She hated him so much for everything he'd done that she was unfazed by his appearance.

She forced herself to think of the plan. Helen had walked her through all the possible outcomes, and she knew what she had to do, even though it had become more obvious than ever that her survival wasn't guaranteed. She looked at Axel who was watching the burning pile of ashes. He let out a whimper that sounded like a low, sad howl.

Dan didn't waste any time returning to his routine. He picked up his cigar and puffed on it a few times, watching himself in the mirror. "It's time for the party, but what will I wear?" he asked.

Kaboom! Kaboom! Kaboom!

The army had begun to fire a steady stream of cannon-balls. The tremors shook the dirt and cracked the ice in the tunnel. Dan made his way over to the wall by the mirror on the opposite side of the toilet closet. He opened a door and stepped into the wall. Mina heard the sounds of hangers scraping along a metal rack. Then she heard Dan's muffled voice. "Oh, yes! My yellow suit, of course! I do look so charming in yellow."

Mina made eye contact with Axel and pointed down the tunnel, urging him to go ahead. But then, all of a sudden, Mina heard Dan's voice loud and clear right behind her. "Aren't you going to stay for the party?" he asked as he grabbed her by the neck. Axel barked loudly and tried to jump at Dan, but there wasn't enough space for him to get past Mina.

"Run!" Mina yelled at Axel. She tried to pry Dan's fingers from her neck, but it wasn't working. The harder she pulled, the tighter his grip became. She stopped struggling to keep herself from being choked. Axel, who'd refused to run, lunged into the narrow space between Mina and the wall. He sounded like a rabid animal, growling and snapping his jaws at Dan's leg.

Gripping Mina's neck harder than ever, Dan kicked at Axel's face repeatedly, but on his third attempt, he struck the back of Mina's knee instead. The blow caused her leg to give out from under her, and she fell forward. Dan's leg was still in the air, and he had to let go of her to keep from being dragged down with her. Axel seized the moment to leap on top of Dan.

Mina's leg was throbbing, but she stood up and turned around just in time to see Roger entering the tunnel through a black cloth that hid the entrance to Dan's closet. Mina yelled, "Watch out, Axel! It's the evil lunar wolf!"

Roger growled and bared his teeth at Mina, but Axel jumped off Dan and hurled himself at Roger. Roger stood up on his hind legs and the two wolves flew sideways into the closet as they collided. Through the glass, Mina watched as they tumbled out of the closet into the bathroom. They broke apart for a moment, but Mina didn't see what happened next because Dan was back on his feet.

Mina tried to limp away, but Dan shoved her from behind. She fell forward and landed on her stomach, slamming her lower jaw against the ground. Barely able to move, she tried with all her might to pull herself forward, away from Dan. Before she'd made it even two inches, though, Dan grabbed her feet and began to drag her back towards the bathroom.

Mina clawed at the dirt in front of her. She tried to sink her fingers into it, to keep Dan from dragging her. But it was no use. Soon Dan had pulled her to the entrance of his closet. He yanked her up by the arms into a seated position. "What a muddy mess you've made of yourself. I'd make you take a bath, but there's no time. We don't want to be late for the main event. It's going to be a *blast!*"

Mina spat back, "I'm not going *anywhere* with you!"

Dan laughed. "Oh, how wrong you are, but how funny too. I've always enjoyed watching stupid people be wrong, especially when they think they're right. It's like watching an animal chase its tail."

Mina tried not to look at Dan. Besides being frightened, she was repulsed by his shiny, red skin. He was still wearing his robe, and up close, she could see that his neck and chest were horribly disfigured from what looked like chemical burns. Dan picked her up and dragged her by her wings into the closet, and Mina was forced to hold on to the bottom of her shirt so that it didn't come flying off. Inside of Dan's closet, she was surprised to see a long line of yellow jumpsuits and shoes. Dan obviously didn't enjoy options, but she wondered why he needed so many identical suits.

He pulled her into the large bathroom and spun her around to face him. The lunar wolves were wrestling on the tile floor, but Dan didn't seem to care. He lifted Mina up and hung her by her shirt on one of the shower heads. "I need you to hang around while I finish getting dressed," he said as he grabbed a yellow suit from the closet and disappeared behind another door.

Mina had to hold onto her shirt even tighter than before to keep from falling out of it. She leaned forward and pushed her feet against the wall to help shove her body up into her shirt. The wolves continued to roll around on the floor below, viciously biting and clawing at each other. From her higher vantage point, Mina could see that Roger had a size advantage over Axel, although it didn't seem to be working in his favor. Axel had pinned Roger for the sixth time when Dan came walking back into the room, fully dressed.

"That's enough, Roger! Let him go." Dan yelled at Axel.

Mina corrected him. "Roger is the one on the ground. Can't you tell the difference between them?"

Dan scoffed. "No. Of course not. Why bother? They're all the same annoying pests."

"Annoying pests? Isn't Roger your bodyguard?" Mina asked.

"That loser? I don't think *so*. He's just the only one of 'em that ever listens. I caught him snooping around here a long time ago. Long before I captured the rest of them.

"Lots of them used to snoop around the fort while I was building it. Why? I don't know. I couldn't get rid of them, though, and I hate it when they get sneaky. You know what I'm talking about. They go nosing around places they don't belong. I had to make them stop, so I laid out the treats they like—the really juicy kind. They couldn't get enough of those. They *had* to have them.

"And it worked like a charm. Once I lured them in, I let the hammer drop. Bam! They got to be my test subjects for whatever I was working on. Formulas, booby traps, torture devices. Eventually, all the early ones were disposed of, except dumb, old Rog. All they're really useful for is doing experiments on, and I have done a great deal of experimenting. This bathroom was built for my experiments. It's why I installed the two-way mirror. So that I could watch. These shower heads can shoot out gas *or* water. Makes the clean-up job a lot easier afterward.

"Oh, and that tunnel you climbed? I made that too. It took me years to build the equipment to dig through the ice. But once I completed it, I was able to have Rog drop off my specially made gas bombs all over the wolves' tunnel system. Oh boy, you should see some of the results from the experiments I've done. It makes me kinda glad we didn't exterminate them all when we had the chance, although most of the experimentation has just been for fun."

Axel, who hadn't moved from his dominant position over Roger, suddenly flew at Dan. But Dan was ready for him. Mina had seen him gripping a vial in his right fist. As soon as Axel leapt, Dan raised it over Axel's head and began dumping it out on top of him. Axel landed on his side with a startled look. Mina wasn't sure what was happening to him, but she was terrified. She screamed at the top of her lungs. Axel tried to stand again, but his bright white fur was fading. Mina realized that it wasn't just his fur that was fading but his entire body. Axel was melting into thin air. He looked up at her with a frightened expression and then disappeared out of sight.

Mina shouted at Dan, "You're sick! You're not even human! You're a demon in a human body!"

Unaffected by her insults, Dan gave her a little shrug and scolded, "You're very foolish to get upset over a stupid animal, especially when there are much more important things to think about. Let's take a walk."

Dan moved towards Mina and unhooked her from the shower head before setting her on the ground. He wrapped his stubby fingers around her neck again and pushed her through a door. They entered a long, dark hallway lined with glowing, blue lanterns that hung from the walls.

"Where are you taking me?" Mina demanded.

"I told you *already!* We're going to the party! It's at the top of the fort, and you're going to be my very special guest." They took a right into a hallway that was identical to the one they'd just traveled down.

"Why? I thought you were a hermit living all alone way out here. Why do you want company now? Is it because I'm your hostage?" Mina asked.

"Hostage? Oh, that's *funny.* You really are the funniest wrong person I've ever known. No. No. You're actually my special guest. All I ask is that you don't hold anything back," said Dan.

"Why would I hold anything back?" Mina asked.

"Let's see. Bravery, stubbornness, acceptance of your own mortality, to name a few."

They turned right again into another identical hallway. A grim feeling was taking hold of Mina. She knew Dan had something horrible planned for his so-called *party,* so she tried to get him to talk about it more. "What kind of party is it?" she asked as they turned into yet another identical hallway.

"Oh, it's a party to end all parties. But I don't want to give too much away. I'll tell you more once we reach the top of the fort."

Mina wasn't sure what else to say to get Dan to talk. They turned another corner, and suddenly, it dawned on her that the hallways were becoming shorter in length. They were walking along a very long path where each hallway moved them a little bit closer to the center of the fort. When they finally arrived at a door, Dan let go of Mina's neck and moved past her to open it. Then he grabbed her by the arm and pulled her into a large room. It was a room with a desk, a few leather armchairs, a four-post bed, and several animal skin rugs that had been laid across the wooden floor.

Mina was surprised by how cozy it seemed. She wasn't sure what she would've expected Dan's bedroom to look like, but it certainly wasn't this. Something puzzled her, though. A fireplace made from black crystals sat in the center of the wall, across from the bed, exactly like the one Mina had seen at Spindle Wheel Ranch.

"I thought I'd dreamt the barn," she said, "but it had that exact same fireplace. How can that be?" Mina asked.

"Never mind!" Dan snapped at Mina. "Over here. We have to keep going." He directed Mina to another door and flung it open. On the other side was a spiral staircase made of black stones. It led up. "Forward climb! Those explosions are the ticking clock of war. There's no time to spare!"

Dan and Mina wound their way around and around the spiral staircase. It was impossible to know how high they'd climbed, however, since there were no landings or windows to judge their ascent by. As they reached the top, the staircase dead ended into the ceiling. Dan raised his hands above his head and pushed. A large stone above him moved upward, and Dan slid it to the side, revealing an exit. He climbed out on top of the roof and extended his hand to Mina. She took it and allowed herself to be pulled from the stairwell to the top of the tower.

She looked around. They were high above the walls of Black Ice Fort. The roof was wide, and in each of the four corners, there was a crackling, blue fire burning inside of a giant metal cauldron. Mina looked down at the fort's walls. They formed a hexagon, and all around the base there were large mounds of crystals glowing a deep red. They cast enough light so that Mina was able to see the dozens of huge bryobane skulls hanging from the walls.

Off in the distance, Mina saw white flashes along the dark horizon. It was a visual cue that the cannons were still firing on them. She could hear the heavy cannonballs pummeling whatever ice, rock, and dirt stood in their way. With each blow, the ground exploded into the air like tiny volcanoes spewing black pumice. Then came the plopping sounds of heavy debris raining down over the surface. The only good news was that it sounded as though the cannons were still a good distance away from striking the fort.

Mina turned her attention back to the tower. At the very center of the rooftop was a bronze, cone-shaped vat that was held upright by a sturdy ring which looped around the middle of it, connecting it to four metal legs. The tip of the cone dipped just below the rooftop, but the top of the cone was too tall for Mina to see inside.

Dan noticed Mina staring at it. "It's a beauty, but don't get too close."

Mina wanted to rip the evil smirk off of Dan's face. "You're going to let them kill us, aren't you?"

Dan ignored her question. "Did you know we weren't the first ones here?" he asked. "The first intelligent beings to live on the Moon? This has all happened before. I bet my sister didn't bother to tell you that, though. She was too busy feeding you lies about greenhouse blueprints and filling your head with ridiculous notions about going home."

"If that's true, then what happened to them?" Mina asked.

"They're dead, of course. It's a very taboo subject among the masses. Nobody wants to admit we're doomed, even when they can see the writing on the wall or in this case, the crystals in the cave."

Mina didn't understand what Dan meant. She asked, "How did they die?"

Dan laughed. "Have you looked around? This place isn't exactly dripping in life-sustaining qualities. Sure, we don't need to drink, sleep, or eat almost anything, but is that really life? All around us is desert. Flat desert, ice desert, mountain desert, crater desert. *Everywhere* is desert. And why, you ask? Because, obviously, Theia wasn't meant to host life.

"When my brother and sister and I were young, our dad invented telescopic binoculars that let us look all the way through Earth's atmosphere and down to sea level with the proper adjusting. It was the closest we ever got to going on vacation. We spent hours watching the green and blue planet, so full of life and energy. The contrast to our world was painfully apparent, yet I was the only one who seemed to get it.

"There's a reason the bridge only brought us the lost earthlings. They weren't being saved; they were being discarded. The Earth was telling them it had no place left for them. No life left to offer them. But Maude and Bob refused to see it. They thought they were *blessed* to have found each other in this faraway world. They let it blind them to how horrid it is up here. Then, as if that weren't bad enough, they went and sold all those desperate rejects on their vision for a new life full of *technology* and *wonder*. It was such a damn joke. Nobody would face the fact that our world wasn't meant to exist, that we were an unintentional anomaly to life."

Mina asked, "But why does that matter? Even if life here *is* a fluke, so what? Lots of people on Earth think *all* life is a fluke. Where else in the universe does a planet full of life exist? As far as anyone knows, the answer is nowhere. Does that mean we should all lay down and die then? The only thing that seems like a *joke* is the fact that you can't appreciate the life you have, especially considering how highly improbable it is. Or is it that you're just jealous you never got to experience what all the others did? A life in a better place? A life on Earth?" Mina asked defiantly.

Dan refused to let Mina have the upper hand. "Maybe it's true that all life is a fluke. The thought has crossed my mind. But you're wrong that I think Earth's better. I would destroy it too if I could. But since I haven't found the means to wipe out more than one world, I guess I'll just have to stick to my original plan."

Mina felt sick to her stomach. "What are you going to do?"

"Oh, I'm not going to do anything. Everything's already been done for *years*, just waiting on the inevitable uprising to occur. That vat you see there is filled with my special creation. Melted glacier water flows up through one pipe and mixes with the mind-erasing poison in the vat. Then it flows back down and crosses through a series of pipes until it reaches the market. Directly below the vat, in a heavily fortified room, is a tank of Shadow's Spine formula. It's made from a mixture of volatile metals and bark from the scraggily trees that don the hellish Theian landscape.

"Shadow's Spine was the first formula Maude ever invented. She used it to light the bridge in neon all those years ago. What she didn't realize until later is that the formula is highly unstable when mixed with any substance other than neon. I figured this out when I was just a kid. Maude kept a few droplets of it as sort of a token to honor her first successful formula—a very stupid practice, if you ask me.

"Most of my younger years were spent sneaking into her

work shed to play with all the colorful vials. I'd asked the woman many times to teach me her trade, but she refused. She said I was too young, but I knew the real reason she wouldn't teach me. It was because she knew I was smarter than her. She didn't want me to beat her at her own game.

"But then one day, I found the jar of Shadow's Spine hidden away, deep inside her work bench. I dropped several beads of water into the tiny jar of formula and presto! With just the tiniest bit of curiosity and experimentation, I had created a poisonous gas bomb that could kill instantly.

"And do you want to know the best part? It doesn't actually matter how much water you use. The size of the reaction is completely dependent on how much Shadow's Spine there is. And do you want to guess how much is in the tank below us?"

"Not really." Mina shrugged.

Dan looked hurt. "Oh, come on. Take a stab at it."

Mina rolled her eyes. "Fine. Is it a lot? My guess is *a lot.*"

Dan laughed and smiled again. "Yes. It's a *whole* lot. Enough to create a cloud that will cover the entire moon in a green smog, killing everything at first contact!"

"So, let me get this straight then," said Mina. "You've had a flowing supply of water sitting right above this poisonous formula for years? Didn't you worry your plan to kill everyone might happen by accident?"

"No. Of course I didn't worry! Part of the fun was knowing that it *could* happen at any moment. But I knew it would most likely all come down to this day. And now it's here, and all we have to do is wait just a little longer. Soon those stupid people down there will break through the last wall and then KABAM!

"No doubt they think they're fighting for some trite principle like their freedom. Lucky for them, I'm about to unleash freedom the likes of which none of them has ever seen!"

Mina corrected Dan. "That's *not* freedom. You can stand there all you want, soaking up every moment of your twisted plan, but don't confuse murder with freedom. And *don't* pretend you're giving those people something they actually want!"

Dan walked back to Mina and leaned down in her face. His eyes were still solid black, and his burned skin was scabby and oozing. "You know, I think watching you die will be one of my favorite things ever."

Mina scoffed, "Except you'll be *too dead* to see it."

"Oh no! Did I forget to mention the rest of my plan? Oh, you're going to love this! I bet my dear sis told you all about that wolf prophecy, didn't she? She has always loved believing that *she* was the chosen one. The one who would save the Moon one day. It made her a hero before she was even born.

"What she might have failed to mention was that the prophecy wasn't just about her. There were two parts. Yes, it was foretold that Helen would be able to restore the lunar balance…blah, blah, blah, but that's ONLY if she could keep her brothers from taking over Theia's energy *first*! And guess what? I've already learned how to control it. Once I kill all these losers, I'll be able to do whatever I want! I'll be a god!"

"A god of what? Gaseous fumes? There'll be nobody left to worship you!" Mina yelled.

"Oh yes there will be! Don't you see? After I wipe the slate clean, I'll force the energy to create whatever life I want. It has already gone to great lengths to bring life to the Moon's surface. Clearly, it's what the energy wants. It'll do it again, only this time, *I'll* be the one in control.

"I'll blanket the world in grass, and water, and whatever else I see fit. I can control the frequency, which means I'll be able to make the new lifeforms see whatever I want them to. It will be a world even more beautiful than anyone on Earth could ever imagine. I'll—"

Mina interrupted him. "Wait. So, you're not actually going to make a new world? You're just going to trick whatever puny lifeforms you create into thinking you have? That's so pathetic!" Mina taunted Dan.

"Shut up! You just aren't smart enough to see how genius it is! *Everything* will be under my control. I'll make up for what this world lacks. I'll create a world worth living in, and I'll be worshipped for it! And if I'm *not*, then I'll tear it all down and start again!"

"Okay. So why haven't you done it already? I mean, you said you've just been waiting all this time. Why didn't you do it years ago?" Mina asked.

Dan's face filled with anger. "Because something was holding me back from taking full control of the energy. For so long, I thought I hadn't created the right formula or found the right medium to access it. But then, I finally understood. I couldn't take control of the energy because of *her*!

"That ridiculous prophecy was haunting me. I thought if I erased her, I'd finally have full control, but it didn't work. I knew I had to get rid of her somehow, so I killed two birds with one stone. I tricked Maude into drinking that horrible aging elixir before allowing Dale to tell our parents what really happened to their beloved daughter, even though that's exactly what I wanted him to do.

"I was certain they would find a way to bring her back. I just never imagined it would be so absurd. I thought they'd restore her to some type of body, not tether her to a dumb piece of paper. I needed her to be tangible again! To have her entire energy confined to one vessel so I could destroy it!

"But I didn't know how to make it happen until one day when I got lucky. My workers at the Sheep Spa intercepted a silver bird sent from Maude to Bob. It laid out Helen's entire plan. And you're going to get a real kick out of this! Did you know that Helen got that filthy wolf to plant a crystal in your head? When that mutt took you for a ride through the tunnel, he knocked your head into the wall. Didn't he?"

Mina's face sunk, and Dan smiled. "Oh, you've gotta give it to my sister! She's almost as wicked as me! This whole time you've been her little human sacrifice, and you didn't even know it! She's been inside that crystal in your head, controlling your thoughts so that she could try to beat me one last time. My god! I bet she's shaking in there right now! She had no idea she was doing me a favor by putting her energy into a single, tangible form. And now that the map's gone, there's nowhere for her to hide anymore!" Dan giggled sadistically.

"It was absolute brilliance on my part," he continued. "All I had to do to test my theory was wait around to see if you'd show up again. I knew there was no way you were going to get out of that well and come here unless *she* was pulling the strings. And now that I know she's really in there, I'm going to pull her out of your skull and dispose of her like the parasite she is. Once and for all!" Dan roared before bursting into maniacal laughter.

Mina looked back at the hole they'd come through, but it was too late. Dan pulled a pair of sharp tweezers from his pocket and grabbed Mina in a chokehold. Mina struggled and screamed as Dan gripped a chunk of her scalp with his tweezers and ripped it off.

He let go of her, and she tumbled to the ground. Grasping her head with both hands, she looked up at Dan. He was holding a tiny, blood-soaked crystal from the end of his tweezers. "What do you think of my sister now? You came here prepared to die for her—to save her from 'big, bad Dan.' But she was manipulating you the entire time!"

Dan took out a vial filled with clear liquid and dropped the crystal into it. The crystal began to fizzle and disintegrate. "No! Please don't!" Mina reached her hand towards the vial, but Dan threw it to the ground in disgust. It shattered into bits of glass and simmering smoke.

"Seriously? After everything I've told you? How can you

still care for her after what she's done? If I'm a demon, then so is she! She's the only reason you're even here! She's the one who possessed your body, and she's the reason you're about to die. If it weren't for her, you'd probably be tucked into your happy, little bed with your long-eared, ugly, earth mongrel! *She* did all of this to you! By god! Why can't you see that!?"

"All I see is a demented troll with an inferiority complex!" Mina slammed back.

Dan went into a full-blown rage. "Is that so? Well, fine then! If you can't see your way to hating her, I'll show you the way! I'll give you the ending she knew you were destined for when she sent you to me!"

Dan hurried to the bronze vat and climbed a stool on the other side. He grabbed a ladle from the top of the rim and dunked it into the water. When the ladle was full, he strode back to where Mina sat. The black whirlpools swirled wildly in his dark eyes. He pulled a vial from his pocket. It was filled with dark purple beads.

"Congratulations! You're going to be the warm-up show before the big hurrah! Sayonara, angel!" he yelled as he sprinkled the purple beads into the dipping spoon.

Violet-gray smoke poured from the ladle, and purple sparks burst out of the liquid. Mina was sure that Dan had turned the formula into a lethal concoction, and she began to think about the life she'd lose if she were forced to drink the sparkling liquid. He grabbed her hair and pulled her head back, holding the ladle above it. She held her breath and waited to see what would happen.

Truly, it was the gravest of situations for Mina to find herself in. The stakes were as high as they could be, and though few might wager on the abilities of a young woman when faced with a sadistic madman, there's usually more to be considered than what's on the surface. And in this case, there was more to be considered, indeed.

CHAPTER 28

RETURN TO THE CHICKEN MAN

"Mina? Mina? *Mina!* Am I coming through? Nod if you can hear me…*Dang it!*"

"And that's why I say, 'Fine, they don't have to drink the water if they can be peaceful about it.' But I'll tell you something; they're not going to upend a perfectly good system by building their own greenhouse…"

As Dan continued to talk, Mina suddenly felt the fog around her lift. She realized that something the chicken man was saying finally made sense.

"Hold on! What did you just say?" Mina asked.

"He's talking about the blueprints I sent you to find. Remember, Mina? They were the first part of the plan—my ticket out of the market. Are you getting any of this?"

"Don't speak to me when I'm in the middle of explaining something," the man snapped at Mina.

"He mentioned something important about a greenhouse," Mina continued. "What was it? Something about a blue greenhouse. Was I looking for a blue greenhouse? No. That can't be right. That would be called a bluehouse probably."

"You're getting there, Mina. It was the blueprints for the greenhouse."

The disgruntled chicken flapped his wings a couple of times, "For god's sake! You were looking for the greenhouse blueprints, remember!? That cucumber really messed you up, huh? I've never seen anybody eat a whole one that fast."

"Well, he's not wrong about that. I didn't expect you to eat so much of it. But honestly, you've done great. We're just where we need to be now."

Mina started to remember everything. THE MAP! Mina looked all around, but the map was nowhere in sight. Neither was the tote bag.

The chicken man laughed, but Mina could see now that it wasn't a man dressed like a chicken at all. "That's Dan!" she said, completely stunned.

"Yes, Mina. That's right. You were dreaming before, and Dan was controlling your dreams. Please tell me if you can hear any of this. I think the cucumber has almost worn off now."

Finally, Mina realized she wasn't hearing her own voice inside her head, but Helen's. She responded using her thoughts. *Yes, I can hear you. I'd forgotten all about the plan. I think that cucumber really did a number on me. Why did I have to eat it again?*

"Oh, thank god!" Helen exclaimed. "I was worried this wasn't going to work. We probably should have tested it out more before we got to the greenhouse. You did an amazing job back there! I'm sorry I didn't give you the signal like we'd planned. I took you to the greenhouse because I knew Dan would be waiting for you somewhere close by. I didn't tell you before we got there because I was certain it would frighten you, and it's important that you stay calm around Dan. He's capable of anything.

"When we were at the back of the greenhouse, I realized that Dan had switched places with the botanist. Betsy went behind the vines to cry, but it was Dan who returned, wearing a disguise of sorts. There was no point in giving you the signal to leave after that. You were right where you needed to be. I knew Dan would capture you before you could escape. I told you to eat the cucumber so you wouldn't try to fight him. He was less likely to hurt you if you were asleep when he caught you," Helen explained.

Mina was upset that she'd been lied to again, although she understood Helen's reasoning. After all, she *had* planned to hit Dan across the face with her tote bag. Or had that all been a dream? She really wasn't sure anymore.

"…They think I'm too nice, and you know, maybe I am. But maybe I'm not," Dan said with a horrible, smug grin.

"Are you?" Mina asked, even though she was thinking more about what Helen had told her.

"What do *you* think?" he asked.

"I have no idea. I just met you," she replied, continuing to stall so she could think.

Helen interjected, "Good. Keep him talking as much as possible. We need to find out the extent of his plans. Maybe you can get him to slip up. Just remember to act surprised whenever he reveals something you're not supposed to know. He *feeds* off that."

"…Regular people like you just don't get me. They don't realize how smart I am. If they were smarter, they'd show me more respect."

"Look around for the map again," Helen instructed. "He'll be expecting you to wonder where it is." Mina did as she was told and began to look for the map.

"What you looking for?" Dan asked.

"I've lost my bag. It was slung over my shoulder when the woman at the barn poisoned me."

"And which woman would that be?" Suddenly, something creepy began to happen. Dan's face morphed into the woman's face from the barn. His body quickly followed, and his clothes changed from a jumpsuit to a flowing, yellow dress. The woman asked, "You mean this one?"

Then the woman burst out laughing as her head, neck, and shoulders sunk down, collapsing into the lower half of her body. The tall woman was transformed into the old botanist. "Or maybe this one?" Betsy cackled in a raspy voice.

Well, that was horrifying, Mina said to Helen.

"Yes, he's very impressed with himself over that little trick. Between these visual slights of hand and his disappearing act, he thinks he has the Great Energy all figured out. Just ask him about it. I'm sure you'll get an earful," said Helen.

"How are you doing that?" Mina asked.

Dan explained his trick and answered all the questions Mina could think of to keep him talking. Helen took a backseat to Mina's performance until things became heated between Dan and Mina, and she had to intervene to remind Mina of who she was dealing with.

Dan beamed as he pulled the map from his pocket and held it up for Mina to see. "What is it you were calling this? A map?" he asked. "That's hilarious! I mean look at where it's brought you! You must be as stupid as that dopey, old man back on Earth."

"You're an ogre!" Mina yelled as she jumped to her feet and ran at him.

"Wait, Mina! Don't do it!" Helen pleaded when she saw Mina wind up to kick Dan, but Mina didn't listen.

"You'll pay for that, you stupid brat! No apples for you!"

"That was a terrible mistake you just made, Mina. Dan's a killer. Ridiculous? Yes. But still a killer," Helen said, trying to make Mina understand the danger she was in. But soon, Mina understood well enough on her own.

Dan recovered from holding his aching shin and threw Mina on top of Roger. Roger grabbed Mina's hair in his jaws, and Helen could feel Mina's thoughts scramble as she reacted to the pain. She tried to talk Mina through what to do next, "Listen, you have to take it back. Tell him you'll give him the information he wants."

But Mina didn't respond. Her scalp burned, and she wasn't sure if the warm liquid pouring over her head was Roger's drool or her own blood. She could hear Dan taunting her, but she could barely understand him *or Helen* through the intense pain. Finally, she begged, "Make him stop! I'll tell you anything. Please! Just tell him to stop!"

Dan leaned into her face, "Why do they keep sending you? And don't tell me *the blueprints* again. What else do you know?"

Dan snapped his fingers, and Roger loosened his grip.

Quickly, Helen instructed, "Tell him what he thinks you already know. Tell him I'm in the map. Tell him about Captain Key."

Mina said to Dan, "There was a prophecy that two children would come from Earth to help save everyone from you and Dale. It wasn't true, though. Helen made it up so she could leave the market and stop you herself. She's *in* the map. Your parents found a way to connect her to it. Everyone who knows about it calls her Captain Key to protect her identity from you and Dale."

Dan laughed. "Well, look at that! What a little fink you are! I bet my sister didn't see that coming. Too bad for you I've known about that map for years. It was easier to let them have their fun than to get tangled up in more family drama. Plus, the idea of my sister having been reduced to a talking piece of paper is about the funniest thing I can think of.

"If that's the best you can do, then I suppose it's time for me and my dear sis to play catch up." Dan smiled and held up the map again. "Sadly, I've got some bad news for you, kid. You're light-years behind on what's really going on here. Time to go!" he said as he bent down and grabbed Mina.

"This is good," Helen told her. "He's going to throw you into the hole where he's keeping Fred. He's probably hoping I'll confront him alone, using the map. See if you can find out anything else. I think he's bluffing about how much he knows."

How is it good that he's about to throw me into a hole? Mina asked Helen.

"Hey, you're the one who wanted to save Fred! We could have just skipped this part of the plan."

Mina replied, *I still want to save Fred, but it would have been nice to know beforehand that I was going be thrown into a hole. You're really terrible at giving heads-ups. Do you know that?*

Helen comforted her. "It'll be fine. I promise. Just keep him talking. Maybe he'll tell us more."

Mina did her best to find out what she could, but to no avail. Dan was finished with her.

"…But I think you're bluffing. You don't know any more than what I've told you. Otherwise, why would you let Fred and me live? You're worried you might need us because you haven't figured everything out yet."

He grabbed her forearm and turned her around so they were only inches apart. "What makes you think I'm going to let you live?" he whispered in her ear before shoving her into the hole.

Mina screamed for her life. "Don't worry. I've got you," Helen said, and right then, all the crystals in the well began to glow in a radiant white light. Mina slowed to a stop and then floated the rest of the way down until she reached the bottom.

The light faded, and she heard someone speak to her through the darkness. "Who are you?" asked the young man.

She turned her head. "I'm Mina, from Earth. Are you Fred?"

Helen said, "Just to warn you, Fred can be difficult."

Difficult like a voice inside my head that won't shut up? Mina asked, annoyed with how close she'd come to a grizzly death at the bottom of the well.

"I would say even more difficult than that. But what do I know? I'm just a voice inside your head," Helen quipped.

Mina and Fred talked for a moment. "…I don't know how you pulled off that landing, but that's not what mine looked like."

"I'm sorry. Didn't the crystals slow you down?" Mina asked.

"*I* slowed you down!" Helen chided Mina. "And *you're welcome* by the way."

Oh yes, thank you for not letting me die a horrible death so that you didn't have to stay trapped inside my lifeless brain for the rest of eternity, Mina shot back sarcastically.

"I don't think you really mean that," said Helen. "And besides, that's not how it works. I actually—"

Stop talking! I'm trying to listen to Fred!

"Fine. But just in case you were wondering, Axel and his pack are on their way to save you two. They're digging a hole below the well at this very moment. One of the old tunnels runs right below where you're sitting. Follow the pack. They'll take you to another tunnel that leads to Dan's fort."

Mina gave Helen the cold shoulder as best she could. After all, she'd come to rescue Fred and wanted to focus on him for a moment. Plus, she wasn't quite ready to shake off the hard feelings she had about being jerked around so much. Helen may have saved her from the fall, but as far as Mina could tell, Helen was responsible for pretty much everything that had happened to her since she left Earth. It was all because Helen needed her help.

"Okay, but then how did you make those crystals do that?" Fred asked. "I've never seen them do that before. I didn't even know they *could* do that."

"I see…" Mina began, but Helen responded to Mina's

thoughts. "Don't do it. He'll hate you if he thinks I'm helping you. Remember, Fred probably isn't too wild about the ghost map that got him into this mess.

Yeah, I can relate, Mina sighed at Helen.

To Fred, Mina explained, "…I think I must've gotten lucky. Maybe it's because I felt at peace with what was happening to me. That's the only explanation I can think of anyway."

The two earthlings talked back and forth for a while. "I don't think we were using the same map," Fred insisted at one point. "My map was controlled by someone named General Longitude."

"Does General Longitude sound like a real name to you? I promise it's the same map. She was calling herself Captain Key when I met her. They were aliases she used to hide her identity."

"But I thought General Longitude was a man," Fred protested.

Helen laughed. "Of course he did. Listen, Mina, it would help if you could make some noise. It will make it easier for Axel and the others to find your exact location. Cup your hands over your mouth and hum high and low like this," Helen said as she proceeded to demonstrate how to call to the wolves.

"Easy mistake," Mina responded to Fred. "Anyway, we're wasting time. We need to start making a lot of noise so the wolves know where to dig."

Mina cupped her hands over her mouth and inhaled deeply. Then she exhaled, humming the low and high notes the way Helen had taught her. She gave it all she had like their lives depended on it, which they did.

Fred refused to help, and he and Mina had it out until he grudgingly gave in. However, if the wolves had never come, Fred would have been pleased to tell Mina how wrong she'd been for the rest of the time they had left. Unbeknownst to everyone, the poison running through Fred's veins had amplified his worst traits, just like the poisoned water had done to the Moon Travelers.

But despite all of Fred's stubbornness and negativity, Mina felt an attraction to the young man that she would never learn to reconcile—even though it would last the rest of her life.

∽∽∽∽∽

HELEN CONTINUED TO GUIDE MINA, although she stayed quiet whenever possible. She helped Mina get Fred through the narrow tunnel but then left her alone mostly while she climbed the glacial passageway to the fort. She didn't want to overwhelm Mina with her presence. Nevertheless, once they reached the outer wall of Dan's bathroom, Helen intervened again.

When Dan exited the toilet closet, Mina tried to drop out of sight until Axel blocked her way. Mina hissed, "What are you doing? Do you want to get us killed?!" Axel moved towards the glass to show her they were safe. "Dan can't see you," Helen informed her. "He can only see his own reflection."

"It's a two-way mirror," Mina whispered as it started to make sense.

They watched Dan from behind the glass. After a while, he brought out the map and began talking to it. "Oh sister, sister, sister of mine, you've never been so quiet with so much on your mind."

Helen clarified what was happening. "He's putting on a show for us, Mina. He knows we're here."

Boom! Boom! Boom!

The cannon fire rang out in the distance. "You hear that, Helen? That's the Reaper's song. He's come to collect. Of course, there's not much left of you to collect, is there? I'm astonished our father didn't build you some type of mechanical body. All these years you've been forced to rely on others…"

Helen spoke again, "He's trying to get me to jump back into the map. I'm going to give him what he wants. Make sure you react as if you really believe I'm trapped inside of it."

Mina's eyes moved to the paper, but nothing happened. "…Truly, I'd hoped for some better opponents, but then again, forcing Maude to drink that aging elixir probably didn't help matters. How old *does* she look now? A quarter past dead?"

Words raced across the map, but Mina couldn't see what they said.

Boom! Boom!

Dan banged his fist on the vanity and yelled at Helen, "Enough! I gave you a gift when I made you invisible! If you had *half* my intelligence, you would've found a way to work it to your advantage. You would've found a way to become something great! But instead, you cry over people's *feelings*! Heaven, help us all! It's time I put you out of your misery!" Dan reached for his lighter and set the map on fire. Then as it began to burn, he held it up for Mina and Axel to see.

"NO!" Mina screamed, pretending like Helen was being murdered right in front of her. She pounded her fists against the glass. Axel barked and growled. Then he jumped at the glass, and Mina wondered if he knew that Helen wasn't tied to the map anymore.

Dan's eyes turned black again, making him look even more diabolical than before.

Kaboom! Kaboom! Kaboom!

The army was getting closer. Dan chased after Mina and Axel, but Helen didn't reappear in Mina's thoughts right away. Dan captured Mina while Axel was locked in a battle of strength with Roger. He pulled Mina into his large bathroom and hung her on one of the shower heads. Then while Dan was changing, Helen showed up again. "I think I have most of his plan figured out," she announced. "Get him to talk more. Let's see what he tells us."

Like before, Mina was able to keep Dan talking without any problem. But then something horrible and unexpected happened. Axel flew at Dan in anger, but Dan knew it was coming. He poured one of his formulas on top of Axel, and the brave lunar wolf fell. Mina screamed as she watched Axel fade away before her eyes.

She shouted at Dan, "You're sick! You're not even human! You're a demon in a human body!"

Dan didn't care about Mina's insults, though. He had a schedule to keep, so he grabbed Mina and led her towards the tower.

"It's going to be okay. Axel's not dead. You've got to calm down," Helen implored her, but Mina could tell that Helen wasn't okay either. It was the first time she had sounded shaken.

What do you think he's planning? Mina asked.

"I'll let you know as soon as I'm sure, but be prepared to fight. It will most likely come to that."

"Where are you taking me?" Mina demanded.

"I told you *already!* We're going to the party! It's at the top of the fort, and you're going to be my very special guest," Dan replied as he continued escorting her down the hallways that shortened with every turn.

"Why? I thought you were a hermit living all alone way out here. Why do you want company now? Is it because I'm your hostage?" she asked.

"Hostage? Oh, that's *funny.* You really are the funniest wrong person I've ever known. No. No. You're actually my special guest. All I ask is that you don't hold anything back," he said.

"Why would I hold anything back?" she asked.

"Let's see. Bravery, stubbornness, acceptance of your own mortality, to name a few."

When they reached Dan's bedroom, Mina was surprised to

find the crystal fireplace that she'd seen in her dream. For a second, she forgot about the secret she was keeping and spoke to Helen out loud. "I thought I'd dreamt the barn, but it had that exact same fireplace. How can that be?" she asked.

Dan blew her off, but as he began to lead Mina up the winding steps, Helen explained, "You did dream it, but Dan and I were there in your dreams the whole time. Dan wanted to confirm the accuracy of the information I planted in the silver bird—the one that he thinks was sent from Mom to Dad. He wanted to find out if I'm inside your head, controlling you.

"The Spindle Ranch in your dream was a combination of our energies. The barn at the ranch was where my parents worked together for many years. They built it after Dan blew up Mom's shed. I tried to give you a nice place to rest while the cucumber wore off, but Dan was intent on meddling. His vision interfered, which resulted in the blown apart barn.

"I gave into his meddling and watched to see what I could figure out. The fireplace was his touch, along with the tea. He thought if he could make you believe you'd been poisoned in your dream, then you'd start giving things away. Obviously, that's not the effect it had."

But before the dream changed, I heard another woman's voice talking. Was that you? Mina asked.

"Yes. I didn't like that he was trying to make you feel even more drugged than you already were, so I manifested as another figure in the dream. It was also a way to tip him off to my presence. There was no way he could have known for sure whether the other woman was your imagination or me. It was enough of a clue, though, to keep him intrigued. And even more importantly, to keep you safe."

I see. Well, thank you then. I didn't realize you were there the whole time. I thought you'd abandoned me at the greenhouse.

"No, Mina. I know you feel used, but you're actually very important to me. We're in this together now."

Mina wasn't sure what to say, so she nodded her head. She had mixed feelings about everything that had happened, but there was no time to think about it right then. They had reached the roof.

"We have to make sure we know his *entire* plan," said Helen. "Ask him whatever you can think of. The only way he can beat us is if he keeps a crucial part of his scheme hidden. If that happens, it will be impossible to stop him."

"You're going to let them kill us, aren't you?" Mina asked Dan. But Dan evaded the question. For a while, Mina wondered if he was just toying with her, but eventually he got around to divulging his entire plan.

"…Yes, it was foretold that Helen would be able to restore the lunar balance…blah, blah, blah, but that's ONLY if she could keep her brothers from taking over Theia's energy *first*! And guess what? I've already learned how to control it. Once I kill all these losers, I'll be able to do whatever I want! I'll be a god!"

"A god of what? Gaseous fumes? There'll be nobody left to worship you!" Mina yelled back.

"Oh yes there will be! Don't you see? After I wipe the slate clean, I'll force the energy to create whatever life I want. It has already gone to great lengths to bring life to the Moon's surface. Clearly, it's what the energy wants. It'll do it again, only this time, *I'll* be the one in control.

"I'll blanket the world in grass, and water, and whatever else I see fit. I can control the frequency, which means I'll be able to make the new lifeforms see whatever I want them to. It will be a world even more beautiful than anyone on Earth could ever imagine. I'll—"

Mina interrupted him. "Wait. So, you're not actually going to make a new world? You're just going to trick whatever puny lifeforms you create into thinking you have? That's so pathetic!" Mina taunted.

"Shut up! You just aren't smart enough to see how genius it is! *Everything* will be under my control. I'll make up for what this world lacks. I'll create a world worth living in, and I'll be worshipped for it! And if I'm *not*, then I'll tear it all down and start again!"

"Okay. So why haven't you done it already? I mean, you said you've just been waiting all this time. Why didn't you do it years ago?" Mina asked.

"Because something was holding me back from taking full control of the energy. For so long, I thought I hadn't created the right formula or found the right medium to access it. But then, I finally understood. I couldn't take control of the energy because of *her*!

"That ridiculous prophecy was haunting me. I thought if I erased her, I'd finally have full control, but it didn't work. I knew I had to get rid of her somehow, so I killed two birds with one stone. I tricked Maude into drinking that horrible aging elixir before allowing Dale to tell our parents what really happened to their beloved daughter, even though that's exactly what I wanted him to do.

"I was certain they would find a way to bring her back. I just never imagined it would be so absurd. I thought they'd restore her to some type of body, not tether her to a dumb piece of paper. I needed her to be tangible again! To have her entire energy confined to one vessel so I could destroy it!

"But I didn't know how to make it happen until one day when I got lucky. My workers at the Sheep Spa intercepted a silver bird sent from Maude to Bob. It laid out Helen's entire plan. And you're going to get a real kick out of this! Did you know that Helen got that filthy wolf to plant a crystal in your head? When that mutt took you for a ride through the tunnel, he knocked your head into the wall. Didn't he?"

Helen chimed in, "Okay, Mina. Here we go. He's going to take the crystal out any second. Be brave!"

Mina's face sunk, and Dan smiled. "Oh, you've gotta give it to my sister! She's almost as wicked as me! This whole time you've been her little human sacrifice, and you didn't even know it! She's been inside that crystal in your head, controlling your thoughts so that she could try to beat me one last time. My god! I bet she's shaking in there right now! She had no idea she was doing me a favor by putting her energy into a single, tangible form. And now that the map's gone, there's nowhere for her to hide anymore!" Dan giggled sadistically.

"It was absolute brilliance on my part," he continued. "All I had to do to test my theory was wait around to see if you'd show up again. I knew there was no way you were going to get out of that well and come here unless *she* was pulling the strings. And now that I know she's really in there, I'm going to pull her out of your skull and dispose of her like the parasite she is. Once and for all!"

Mina tried to be brave, but she wanted to run. Dan was cackling like a madman, and she could tell that he was capable of anything at that moment. She looked behind her at the hole they'd come through, but it was too late. Dan pulled a pair of sharp tweezers from his pocket and grabbed Mina in a choke-hold. Mina struggled and screamed as Dan gripped a chunk of her scalp with his tweezers and ripped it off.

He let go of her, and she tumbled to the ground. Grasping her head with both hands, she looked up at Dan. He was holding a tiny, blood-soaked crystal from the end of his tweezers. "What do you think of my sister now? You came here prepared to die for her, to save her from 'big, bad Dan.' But she was manipulating you the entire time!"

Dan took out a vial filled with clear liquid and dropped the crystal into it. The crystal began to fizzle and disintegrate. "No! Please don't!" Mina reached her hand towards the vial, but Dan threw it to the ground in disgust. It shattered into bits of glass and simmering smoke.

"Seriously? After everything I've told you? How can you still care for her after what she's done? If I'm a demon, then so is she! She's the only reason you're even here! She's the one who possessed your body, and she's the reason you're about to die. If it weren't for her, you'd probably be tucked into your happy, little bed with your long-eared, ugly, earth mongrel! *She* did all of this to you! By god! Why can't you see that!?"

"All I see is a demented troll with an inferiority complex!" Mina slammed back.

Dan went into a full-blown rage. "Is that so? Well, fine then! If you can't see your way to hating her, I'll show you the way! I'll give you the ending she knew you were destined for when she sent you to me!"

Dan hurried to the bronze vat and climbed a stool on the other side. He grabbed a ladle from the top of the rim and dunked it into the water. Then, when the ladle was full, he strode back to where Mina sat. The black whirlpools swirled wildly in his dark eyes. He pulled a vial from his pocket. It was filled with dark purple beads.

"Congratulations! You're going to be the warm-up show before the big hurrah! Sayonara, angel!" he yelled as he sprinkled the purple beads into the dipping spoon.

Violet-gray smoke poured from the ladle, and purple sparks burst out of the liquid. Mina was sure that Dan had turned the formula into a lethal concoction, and she began to think about the life she'd lose if she were forced to drink the sparkling liquid. Dan grabbed her hair and pulled her head back, holding the ladle above it. She held her breath and waited to see what would happen as the cold liquid poured across her tongue.

Mina coughed, spat, and gasped for breath, which made Dan screech with delight. He let go of her hair and backed away. She bent over with her head hung down, leaning her weight into her clenched fists. Pushing them into the icy, stone rooftop.

Kaboom! Kaboom!

The outer wall of the fort crumbled as back-to-back cannonballs blew it apart. "Well look at that! Maybe you'll get to see the main event after all! Probably not, though. That poison only takes a minute to do its magic. You should feel your major organs melting into a fiery puddle of goo right about now. Do you feel it? Just give me a thumbs up if you do."

Dan waited for Mina to show signs of excruciating pain, but something strange happened before he could get his wish. Everything went silent. The nonstop sound of cannon fire ceased.

Baffled by the quiet, Dan ran to the tower's wall. "What's going on? Why did they stop? WHY DID THEY STOP?!" he shouted.

When he spun back around, he found Mina standing right in front of him. Her long hair hung in front of her face, and purple-gray sludge oozed out of her mouth and poured down her chin. She stared at Dan with a foreboding expression.

"How did you do that?" he asked in horror. Mina raised her right hand. She was clutching something sharp. Dan moved away, but Mina moved with him and jabbed a long needle into the side of his neck.

Dan grabbed his face and chest in a panic. "Nooo! I'm invisible. That's not possible! How did—" But before he could finish his sentence, he fell to his knees in front of Mina, no longer able to speak.

Mina gave Dan's shoulder a hard shove, and he fell to the ground on his back. She reached into her mouth and pulled out more of the sludge, scraping out every last particle she could. Dan laid motionless in front of her.

"Listen to that, Dan. That silence is the sound of your

sister beating you." Dan's lips twitched, as if he were trying to respond, but Mina just smiled and wiped her chin.

"This mud is a nasty, little trick I learned right after I first arrived. You were right. This place is all desert, but lucky for me, it means the dirt's so dry it steals every last drop of moisture that it comes into contact with. It's a handy thing to coat your mouth with if, say, a deranged lunatic is trying to feed you poison. When you dragged me out of the tunnel, I grabbed all the dirt I could and pocketed it just in case. Then I stuffed it in my mouth while you were getting the water. It might not be as fancy as one of your formulas, but it seems to have worked out okay.

"Oh, and if you're wondering about that thorn sticking out of your jugular—it's a needle from a tantrum cactus. I was told they work well for causing temporary paralysis. And after a frightful run-in with some of the cactuses near the Sheep Spa, I happened to have a couple of the thorns hidden inside my wings.

"Dear god, Dan! You were *so* sure of yourself. You made it *so* simple for us to undo your plan. We just had to wait for you to lay all your cards on the table."

The black coating over Dan's eyes dissolved, and Mina could see that he was staring daggers at her as she leaned over him.

Mina continued, "You thought your sister was keeping you from taking control of the energy because you could never see what was so obvious—that you were too conceited to figure out Neriti's prophecy.

"Anyway, I hope you don't feel too bad about getting beat by your sister and her sidekick. After all, Dan, you told me not to hold anything back, so really this is all *your* fault. Speaking of your sister, she's back from foiling your plan and would like a word. Oh! And just so you know, I think watching this will be one of *my* favorite things ever."

"Tsk, tsk, brother." Mina's voice deepened slightly into that of an older woman's. "Nobody would peg you as a Darkside hermit. You look like you've never missed a full day of sun in your life. But seriously, Dan. Didn't you ever wonder why your skin burned every time you used Theia's energy? It's because you'd never actually learned to control it.

"Theia is its own lifeforce. You were only harnessing a tiny part of it to pull off a few silly tricks. And clearly, by the looks of you, Theia did NOT appreciate being messed with.

"The wolves aren't magicians. They honor the energy and use its power for the purposes they were taught. Neriti's prophecy never said you and Dale were going to become lords and masters over the energy. It said that to restore the lunar balance, I had to stop you two from taking control of the energy. But taking control of the energy never meant taking control of Theia, Dan. Really, I would've thought your worsening, red skin would have tipped you off to that.

"The most astonishing part, however, is that you completely overlooked the main ingredient of the prophecy. Many lunar wolves believed that you and Dale might actually bring about the end of all life if you succeeded at bending Theia's energy to your will. But Neriti knew the type of child you were. It's why she told our parents to keep the part of the prophecy about you and Dale a secret. Neriti worried that if you found out, you'd devote the rest of your life to taking control of the energy. Fortunately, she knew you'd be blinded by jealousy if you believed I was the only special child. And, of course, she was right.

"It distracted you from everything. You pushed Dale aside and started working on your own to defeat me when I was just a baby. And even when you learned the whole prophecy, you never took into consideration that it speaks of *brothers*. Not just you! You didn't want to admit you needed anyone to help you thwart your little sister. And certainly, you never wanted to share what you believed the reward to be—full dominion over Theia. If you and Dale had actually teamed up, who knows what would've happened. But thanks to your idiotic ego, no one will *ever* have to find out!"

Using Mina's body, Helen leaned down close to Dan's face. Beads of sweat dripped from the sides of his brow, and his eyes rolled around in their sockets. "I want you to know one last secret, Dan. I didn't need some mechanical body to beat you. I've been using the crystals to spy on you since I was a child, and I've had you figured out my entire life. I listened to the wolves' stories, and I learned from others' mistakes. And most importantly, I learned to never underestimate you the way you did everyone else, which is why this moment has finally come."

With Mina's hand, Helen reached behind Dan's head and pulled back on his wispy, strands of red hair. His mouth opened slightly, and Helen raised the ladle above it. It still contained a few drops of the lethal formula that had been intended for Mina. Then as Dan watched in terror, Helen drained the remainder of the liquid into his mouth.

Finally, she grabbed Dan by the sides of his burnt red face and whispered in his ear, "Now, how did it go again? Oh, yes. I remember. Oh brother, brother, brother of mine, you've *never* been so quiet with so much on your mind."

CHAPTER 29

SHAPELESS

Bob was nervous. The army had been marching slowly towards Black Ice Fort, pushing the cannons along in front of them. But they had fired too early. They had never felt safe testing the cannons so close to Dan's domain. And therefore, they had been unaware of just how short the cannons' range would be. They had intended to give Dan enough time to surrender—not to escape.

They had almost reached the fort. The front of it was lit up by dozens of red crystal mounds. The mounds had no clear source of power, but Bob felt sure that Dan had found some sinister way to keep them aglow. He was doing his best not to think of Helen, but he couldn't stop himself. He wondered if Dan had captured her. He wondered what kind of fight the little winged girl had in her. He wondered if she or Helen were even still alive, although this thought was too painful to let linger for long.

Kaboom! Kaboom!

Two cannonballs hit the outer wall almost simultaneously. Bob looked on as the fort's outer wall collapsed into an avalanche of ice and stone. For the dozenth time, he thought about telling the troops to cease fire. He knew he couldn't, though. He had to be brave. There was no turning back from what they'd started; it was the only way to put an end to Dan's reign of terror.

Another series of cannonballs were loaded. He knew this round would take down parts of the inner fort. He held his breath, and his chest tightened. The fuses were about to be lit when, suddenly, out of thin air, an apparition appeared. Only, it wasn't just one. It was more than a dozen of the same apparition standing in front of each cannon.

Several soldiers cried out in fear, but Bob was too stunned to make a sound. He thought his eyes were deceiving him at first because the ghostly vision was a sight that he never expected to see again—his beautiful daughter, Helen. For the first time in years, Bob heard Helen's voice, but it was coming from inside his head.

"Call off the attack immediately!" she warned. "Mina has Dan right where we want him. He'll no longer be a threat soon, but one more cannonball through the wall could wipe out all the life on Theia!"

Bob was visibly shaken. He yelled to his soldiers, "Cease fire! Cease fire! Stand down and disarm your weapons! We have new orders!" And with that, the apparitions vanished.

∽∽∽∽

Mina kneeled atop the tower. She had allowed Helen to take control of her body after she returned from stopping the army, yet she'd been present the whole time, complicitly watching as Helen finished off Dan. Her emotions were raw. She'd never been involved in serious matters involving life and death in *any* realm, and she wasn't sure how to process it.

"Why didn't you tell him the whole truth?" she asked Helen.

"I don't know, Mina. I guess I didn't feel like he deserved to know everything after all the pain and suffering he caused."

There was a long pause, and then Mina asked, "What do we do now?"

"I think we get you to Bob," replied Helen. "I'm sure they've already sent a team to secure the fort. When we find them, they can take you to him. There's one last thing I need to ask you to do for me, though."

Mina was hesitant. "What is it?"

"I'd like to talk to my father face-to-face. Would you mind, one last time?"

The question broke Mina's heart. She was starting to understand the finality of what Helen was facing. "Sure, Helen," she replied. "One last time."

MINA CLIMBED down the spiral staircase until she reached the door to Dan's bedroom. She began to open it, but she heard footsteps on the other side. She paused for a moment, holding her breath. She wondered if it was Roger coming to check on his boss.

Then she heard someone shout, "All clear, sir!" She realized it was the team that had been sent to secure the fort. She opened the door to find three soldiers in black uniforms with guns drawn on the other side. Mina put her hands out in front of her the way she'd seen people do in films.

"It's just me," Mina said nervously. "Dan's on the roof, but he's dead. There's something else, though. There's a vat of poisoned water up there right above a room filled with Shadow's Spine. If the two were to mix, it would kill everyone."

The men rushed past her. Once they were out of the way, she was left facing a tall, thin man with tan skin and beautiful eyes. "Dad!" Helen cried out inside of Mina's thoughts.

"This is Bob?" Mina asked out loud.

"That's right, and you must be Mina, the angel everyone's been talking about," Bob said with a wink.

"Yes, sir," Mina replied. She suddenly felt very small in Bob's presence.

"That's okay," Bob said, "You don't have to do all of that 'sir' stuff with me. You can just call me Bob. Am I right to assume you're harboring a dangerous fugitive?" he asked with a smile.

Mina was puzzled at first, but she quickly realized his meaning and smiled back. She nodded her head, and Helen began to speak through her. "I'm so sorry, Dad. I didn't want for you and Mom to worry again, but I had to do this on my own. Neriti taught me—"

But Bob put his hand up to stop Helen. "You don't have to apologize, sweetheart. You saved us, just like Neriti's prophecy said you could. I'm proud of you for being so brave. I think you must get that from your mother's side." They both laughed as Bob wrapped his arms around Mina and kissed the top of her head.

"I don't think I can remember the last time you were short enough for me to kiss the top of your head," Bob said with sadness in his voice.

"Me neither," sighed Helen. "Dad, you have to send Mina back as soon as you can arrange for her to travel safely. I don't know that she'll be able to return if she stays much longer. I can tell that she's already adapted quite a bit to Theia, more than I would have expected."

"Don't worry. We'll find a way to help your friend. We owe her more than that even. I think you summoned a pretty good partner when you brought her here. She must be as brave as you to have come this far."

Helen nodded Mina's head. "You knew then? But how?"

Bob nodded. "I put it together after Axel gave me your message. I had suspected you were using the crystals for a long time; you always knew things you shouldn't have had any way of knowing. You spent so much time with the wolves. And not just any wolves, but the most powerful of all the healers. I know enough of their history to know that Neriti was special, even if I didn't see eye-to-eye with her always.

"Anyway, when the wolves gave Ruth that crystal, I wondered if there might be more to it. I knew the crystals weren't supposed to work on the Dayside, but you were the chosen one, right? Plus, it came from hallowed ground on the Darkside. It didn't take a rocket scientist to figure it out."

Helen laughed. "But you are a rocket scientist, Dad."

Bob laughed too. "Oh, that's right. I'd almost forgotten."

Helen's smile faded. "There's something I have to tell you."

Right then, the soldiers in black returned from the rooftop and lined up in front of Bob to address him. The largest soldier said, "Sir, the angel's information is correct. The target has been neutralized. However, we need more time to study the vat's structure before we attempt to drain it. It could be dangerous, sir!"

Bob nodded his head, "Thank you, lieutenant. I'll put a team together to work on the task. However, I need a little more time here first. Please let the other soldiers know that Dan is no longer alive. Then split into teams and search the rest of the fort. Let me know when you've located the prisoners. And be careful! I'm certain there will be traps."

"Yes, sir!" said the lieutenant. The three men saluted Bob and then left the room.

Bob turned again to his daughter, who was looking back at him anxiously through Mina's young eyes. "What did you need to tell me, pumpkin? Or do you want to wait until your mother is with us?"

Helen shook Mina's head. "No, it can't wait. It has to be now."

Bob nodded. Then he took Mina's hand and led her to one

of the leather armchairs, taking a seat in the adjacent one. "Go ahead. Whenever you're ready," he said encouragingly.

Helen waited a few seconds and then began:

Before I set out on my journey, I used Ruth to write a letter to you and Mom. I wasn't sure if I would survive long enough to talk to you again. But I'd like to share a little more than what I was able to write in the letter. It's important for you to know about the Moon's history so you can use it to help the other Travelers. They need to understand what they're a part of now.

When they traveled here across the glass and neon bridges, they were crossing over an inter-dimensional relic, left over from when Earth collided with Theia eons ago. Unbeknownst to the Travelers, that process changed them in ways that no one has ever completely understood. Theia is not passive like Earth. By crossing the bridges, the Moon Travelers were unconsciously renouncing Earth and swearing an oath to protect Theia. This may seem trivial, but Theia takes the oath seriously, and she views the Travelers as one entity. If one of you were to step out of line, she would see fit to retaliating against all of you.

One of the most important things to understand is that Theia was once her own planet full of beautiful, rich life. Much like what you knew on Earth but even more vivid and interlaced with the planet. When Earth collided with Theia, it did terrible things. It stole almost all of Theia's life-giving properties, so after the planets broke apart, Theia had very few of these properties left.

She wanted nothing to do with Earth ever again. The majority of her energy moved to the far side of the Moon, away from Earth. There she ignored the bridges that tethered her to her tormentor, even though she knew that she could use them to help restore life forms to her surface.

Instead, Theia chose to focus her attention on the crystals that had formed during the collision.

Like the amber on Earth that fossilized ancient insects, the crystals captured the remnants of life that once existed on Theia's surface. Theia was able to use the crystals to recreate some of the life she'd once had, but her energy was so weak that she was only able to bring about one life-form. The Moon Walkers.

The Moon Walkers were an agglomeration of all the life that had ever existed on Theia. They took many forms but never held any definite shape for long. They were more like ghosts than humans, wolves, or bryobane. At one time or another, the Moon Walkers embodied all the different life-forms that had previously existed on Theia. But there were also times when they held no solid shape at all and would fade in and out periodically.

In the early days of the Moon Walker's existence, Theia assigned them to building the tracks underneath the Moon's surface. As you know, Crystal Crater and Black Ice Glacier are on the track system that remains always in the dark, pointed away from Earth. This was *very* important to Theia.

The Moon Walkers' energy burned brightly for a time, but eventually it faded. The lunar wolves believe this occurred because Theia stretched herself too thin when she tried to create everything she'd lost with only a tiny fraction of the energy she once possessed. Soon the Walkers realized they didn't have enough energy to continue living on Theia's surface in *any* form, so they used their own life-giving abilities to create the lunar wolves and the bryobane.

The Moon Walkers believed that by creating the bryobane they could protect the crystals from any unwanted visitors that might one day make it to Theia's surface. The Walkers created the wolves for an even more important purpose, though. They were brought to life to continue the practice of honoring the Great Energy once the Walkers were gone. The Moon Walkers told them that by honoring Theia they were helping her rebuild her strength.

The wolves have always spoken of how the Moon Walkers departed, but this description was purposely vague so that it would be misinterpreted. The Moon Walkers didn't go anywhere. They were reabsorbed by Theia's energy. Before they disappeared, they told the wolves that they would visit them through dreams and visions whenever they had reason to do so. The Walkers also spoke of a time when they would return to the surface, after Theia's energy was fully restored.

For hundreds of years, the wolves practiced what the Moon Walkers taught them, and the bryobane and lunar wolves did what they were made to do. The balance that the Moon Walker's created remained strong, and most importantly, Theia's energy continued to grow, albeit very slowly. Everything changed, however, when the bryobane enslaved the wolves. The harmony that kept Theia growing stronger was thrown off kilter by the suffering and chaos that ensued. Yet even after the bryobane were defeated, Theia was unable to regain a harmonious balance.

The Darkside showed the most significant signs of this imbalance. With the bryobane gone, Theia grew paranoid. She gave the energy she was harnessing free rein to poison any minds that ventured to the Darkside. It was Theia's solution for protecting the crystals in absence of the bryobane. But it had unintended consequences since the most toxic minds were often the least affected by the poison—like Dan's.

Theia was still too weak to create new life or to return the Moon Walkers to the surface. Yet after the bryobane were destroyed, she feared that all Theian life would be lost forever if she didn't bring new life to the surface. So she did what had once been the unimaginable—she reached down to

Earth and began taking back some of the life that had once belonged to her.

Before this happened, the Moon Walkers sent many visions and dreams to the lunar wolves, especially the healers, to let them know what was going to transpire. This is when it became apparent that to establish a new form of life on Theia, the wolves were going to have to sacrifice. Again.

Mom was chosen to be the first Moon Traveler. Theia used great power and depleted much of her stored energy to bring Maude to the surface. Her blood was intentionally mixed with the wolves' blood as Theia transformed the girl pup's body into a human form. This was done to intertwine the two species' destinies. Three wolf pups were sacrificed the day the first human came to the surface, but later Theia sent all three of us back again to be reborn as humans—the children of the first Moon Travelers.

We were sent to warn of the dire situation the humans are facing. Going forward, the humans can choose to get along with the wolves and honor Theia so that she can grow stronger and provide for the lives that inhabit her. Or they can continue to dishonor her by fighting and turning their backs on the ways the Moon Walkers taught.

However, if the Moon Travelers don't adapt to Theia's expectations, then, ultimately, all life on Theia will suffer and perish. This is an easy choice to make but a hard one to practice. It's why Theia has gone to such great lengths to make her point, and it's necessary for you to understand that this is the only warning you will be given.

Bob was overcome by this huge revelation. He had listened to everything that his daughter said but was still trying to absorb it all. He knew that every word she spoke was the truth because he could feel it inside of him. But he didn't know quite what to make of it.

"So then you and your brothers? You were the—"

Helen nodded. "Yes, we were the wolf pups. Neriti knew the truth before we were even born. It's why she spent so many years teaching and protecting me."

"But the twins. Why were they born the way they were?" Bob asked.

"It was Theia's will. Their good traits were withheld on purpose, to show the Moon Travelers a glimpse of how bad life could be if the humans don't keep their egos in check. I'm sure if Theia deems it appropriate, their good traits will be restored to them once they've been reabsorbed."

Bob looked at his daughter through Mina's face. He started to ask another question, "So now what will happen…that is…I mean, what's going to…" But his voice trembled as he fought to ask the painful question that he already knew the answer to.

Helen understood what her father was trying to ask and helped him. "Most of my spirit has already rejoined the Great Energy. I began connecting to Theia when I created the prophecy about the two children who would come from Earth. I had to connect to be able to pull off my plan. I knew I was no longer meant for this world, no matter what happened, and it was a sacrifice I was willing to make.

"Once I connected to Theia, the reabsorption began, and I was given the power to do things I wouldn't have been able to do otherwise. Like summoning the Earth children, or talking to you and Mina through your thoughts, or preventing Dan from disappearing when he realized he'd been beat. I was also given access to the knowledge that I'm speaking to you now.

"These are greater powers than any of the creatures of this realm are meant to have. Even the Moon Walkers didn't have powers this strong. Theia bestowed them on me to do what was needed before I left. She only allowed me to stay a few moments longer so that I could stress her warning one last time. But now it's time to go."

Tears were streaming down Bob's face. He fell out of his chair and embraced Mina tightly, wishing he could reach through her to hold his own daughter. "I will love you always, my sweet, sweet Helen. With every fiber of my being. I promise I will live the rest of my life, ensuring that your sacrifice wasn't in vain."

Mina's arms were wrapped tightly around Bob, and Helen whispered back to her father, "Please tell Mom I'm sorry I didn't get to say goodbye one last time and that I love her. I am eternally grateful for the life you both gave me. And I love you, Dad. So much. To the ends of the universe and beyond." Then just as Helen finished speaking these words, Mina's arms fell limp, and all signs of Helen faded away. Forever.

CHAPTER 30

HOME AGAIN

It was almost time for Mina to go, and Fred was nowhere to be found. Mina had searched all over the market's center and nearby aisles, hoping to say goodbye. Once again, she went unnoticed by the crowds, but this time it was because she'd been given a change of clothes, some denim shorts and a blouse, but no wings.

Finally, she ran into Maude and Bob at Maude's old vine stand. They were putting the finishing touches on Mina's wings for her journey home. Bob noticed her first and greeted her with a wave. "They're almost ready to go, Mina. I think once they're coupled with the rocket-pack, you won't have any problems getting home. Oh, and we have some good news. An old friend of ours has solved the dilemma regarding your re-entry into Earth's atmosphere. But I'll let him explain all of that when you meet him at the launch site."

"Good heavens, Bob!" Maude exclaimed. "I think 'launch site' might be a bit extreme. She's a human girl, not a rocket."

Bob nodded his head and said, "Oh, right, dear. I didn't mean to imply that." Then with a twinkle in his eye he said to

Mina, "Of course you're a human girl. A human girl who's about to be *strapped* to a rocket." Bob laughed.

"Oh, don't listen to him," said Maude. "If he could make it all the way to the Moon using that silly pack, then you should be just fine getting home with all the upgrades we've made to it. Plus, you'll have your wings to help you in case anything unexpected happens."

"That's wonderful!" Mina said. "Quick question, though. Have either of you seen Fred lately? I wanted to say goodbye."

Maude and Bob looked at each other knowingly, waiting to see what the other one would do. Eventually, Bob responded, "He stayed on the Darkside, Mina. To tour the crystal mines. He said he has things he needs to think about, and he wants to start mapping the tunnel system underneath Black Ice Glacier."

Mina was hurt. She'd been looking forward to seeing him one more time. Maude walked over and held her hand. "I'm sorry, hon. Some people just aren't able to live up to our expectations. I'm sure Fred appreciates what you did for him. However, now that things are getting back to normal around here, I imagine he's the one we'll be needing to keep an eye on."

Mina was surprised. "You mean, you think he could be dangerous?"

Bob shook his head. "Not necessarily. But you have to admit, it's strange he wants to stay on the Darkside after everything he went through."

Mina knew Bob was right. Plus, Fred's lack of empathy had been unsettling. Even so, there was something about him she couldn't resist, a mysterious allure that drew her to him.

Maude chimed in, "Don't get too hung up on him, hon. You have your own path and your own people to get back to. The ticking clock solves all problems, even when we're not around to see them get solved." Mina nodded. She knew there was nothing left to say. She couldn't give up her chance to return to Earth, so she put it behind her as best she could.

"Have you made any progress bringing Axel back?" she asked, changing the subject.

Bob shook his head sadly, "Not yet. We're trying to find a way to give the lunar wolves their voices back first. Once Axel can speak again, we'll be able to talk to him the same way we talked to…" Bob's voice trailed off.

Mina felt guilty. She'd been so focused on Fred and going home that she'd allowed herself to overlook the grief that Maude and Bob were going through.

She smiled at them sympathetically. "I know that would make Helen really happy. She told me how gifted you both are at solving problems. When she saw Axel disappear, she didn't even panic. I'm sure she knew you'd find a way to bring him back."

Bob and Maude both nodded, but they seemed to be at a loss for words. After a moment, Bob picked up the wings they'd been working on and showed them to Mina. They were smaller now and looked like they would fit better. "What do you think?" he asked. "Want to try them on?"

Mina laughed. "If I do, will I be trapped in them forever?"

Bob smiled. "Only if you want to be. Look, I was able to give you an adjustable harness this time. All you have to do is pull here to tighten the straps and right here to loosen them," he said as he demonstrated how it worked.

Mina let Bob place the wings on her back, and she fastened the harness around her shoulders. "They feel good. Thank you both for helping me get home. It really means a lot to me."

Maude leaned her head against Bob's shoulder. "Mina, you've done more for our family than we would've ever expected. This is the very least we can do for you. If you wanted to stay, we'd—"

But Bob stopped her. He wrapped his arm around her

shoulder and squeezed it gently. "Don't Maude. I know it's hard, but this girl has a family of her own. We can't ask her to give that up. We'll lean on each other to mend our wounds. Okay?"

Maude nodded, but Mina could see her eyes flooding with tears.

Mina took Maude's hand. "I'm so sorry, Maude," she said. "Helen was a brave woman. I know she would've stayed with you if she could have."

Maude smiled a little, wiping the tears from her eyes. "Thank you, hon."

Mina paused to think about what she wanted to say next, and after some deliberation she went ahead. "I know it's not my place to say so, but I think Helen would want you to forgive Ruth. Plus, it would probably make it easier for you since she can help you keep Helen's memory alive."

Maude looked away from Mina at the mention of Ruth's name. "I know, Mina," she said, although it was plain to see that the subject upset her. She hesitated for a few moments and then looked back. "I'll think about it, okay?"

Bob took Maude's hand in his. "Alright, it's time to get you on your way. Let's head over to the launch…I mean, the *departure zone*," he said, laughing at his correction.

The three of them left Maude's booth and walked down the long aisle, passing several groups as they went. Suddenly, the people who hadn't been able to recognize Mina before knew who she was by the wings on her back. Some of them smiled, and others nodded. Many looked taken aback and only stared or whispered to each other. A few people, however, said "thank you" as Mina walked by. At first, Mina felt shy about the attention she was receiving, but after a while, she began to smile and give a friendly nod to each group she passed.

When they reached the inside of the market's wall, Bob

walked over and placed his hand against it. "This really needs to go," he said out loud, though not to anyone in particular.

Maude grabbed his hand again. "It will, dear. One step at a time. Remember, we still have to plan a whole new city and replace what was lost. Only this time, I was thinking we should make it so that every home is self-sustainable. Maybe we should even consider stopping the Dayside track. We could use stored up solar power to light the city when we're pointed away from the sun. Or we could—"

Bob gave Maude a look to remind her of what she'd just said to him. Maude grinned. "Right. Like I said, one step at a time."

They exited the market and walked across the dusty plain, out towards where Mina had first arrived. There were other people outside of the market too. Some strolled leisurely while others explored. Some walked together, holding hands. Others walked alone, looking as though they were getting reacquainted with the world around them. Mina thought it was a beautiful sight, all these people who were finally free from the confines of the market. Nobody seemed lost or uptight the way they had before.

Thirty yards ahead, Mina could see a man in a white coat, standing with his back to them and a large wheelbarrow by his side. "Is that the little Frenchman?" she asked in disbelief.

Maude and Bob looked surprised. "You know Jacques?" Maude asked.

"Yes," Mina replied. "I met him soon after I first arrived. He tried to interest me in his cheeses but ended up feeding me dirt."

Bob laughed, and Maude nudged him. "You'll have to forgive Jacques," she said to Mina. "He was under the influence of the poison when he did that. I never gave him the antidote because I was worried that he'd blow our cover. As I'm sure you witnessed, he's a passionate sort of fellow, and I wasn't sure I could count on him not to take matters into his own hands."

Mina agreed, "Yes, I could see why you'd be worried."

Bob interjected, "But you gotta give him credit for having a great sense of humor. He may be an odd duck, but he sure is funny."

Jacques turned around as the trio approached. "Bonjour! Bonjour! Although, I never know what time it is anymore. It is so good to see you, Maude and Bob! And what is this? The heroine de la jour!"

Then Jacques took out a pretend notebook and pen from his chef's coat and said, "Aww oui, oui! I will have the heroine du jour with a bowl of mushroom soup on the side! Bon Appètit!"

Then he reached out his arms to Mina and said, "Come here, mademoiselle! Let me hug you. I promise not to crush your wings." He wrapped his arms around Mina's neck and shoulders and squeezed her tightly, nearly pulling her off her feet. When he was finished, he let go and pushed her back into an upright standing position.

Mina looked back at Bob and Maude. They didn't say anything, but she could tell that Bob was trying not to laugh. Jacques said, "Oh how rude of me! I almost forgot. I have brought des cadeaux! Some gifts! Here! Come look inside my wheelbarrow."

Jacques leaned over the large three-wheeled cart and pulled out a shiny metal rocket-pack like Mina had seen in comic books. It looked way too big to fit her though, and she started to feel anxious about their plan. Bob stepped closer, sensing her worry. "Show her the other part, Jacques," he said.

Jacques put the rocket-pack down and clapped his hands together. "Bien sûr! Of course! This is the best part!" he said, and he pulled a lumpy blue and gray suit from the wheelbarrow, along with a matching helmet.

Mina wasn't sure what she was looking at. It appeared to be an astronaut's suit that was made of rubber, but the color was so strange and the texture so lumpy that she couldn't tell what it was actually made from. Then, suddenly, it dawned on her. "Did you make this out of cheese?!"

"Mais oui! Of course!" Jacques grinned from ear to ear. But then his expression changed, and he looked stern. "Well, no, no, no. You still do not get to call it cheese, ma chérie, but *yes*. It is made from my best fromage and a watery blend of dirt. I turned them into a kind of paste. It is magnifique, non?"

Mina didn't know what to say, but Jacques didn't give her time to respond anyway. "Look! I've created a delicious lining right here on the shoulders for you to slip the rocket-pack into. Once it is on, I will close the lining up with a thick coat of paste. That should keep the pack secured until all the cheese melts off as you reenter the Earth's atmosphere."

Mina was baffled. "Wait! The cheese is going to melt off of me?! Have you even thought about how that's going to work? If there's molten cheese pressed against my skin, won't my skin be melting too?"

Jacques responded, "Well, of course I've thought of this! Why else would I have brought so much cheese cloth?" Jacques said as he held up the end of a long piece of white fabric that was attached to a spool inside the wheelbarrow.

Mina turned to Maude and Bob in shock. Maude moved in and put her arm around Mina's shoulders. "I know it sounds a bit crazy, Mina, and I won't lie. There's a great deal of risk involved here. You're the first Moon Traveler to ever attempt to cross back over to Earth, which means we don't really know what's going to happen. However, we've done our best to make it as safe as possible. The cheese cloth has been doused with a heat repellent liquid I created long ago after Dan blew up my work shed. As the outside of the fabric heats up, the inside will begin to cool. This *should* prevent you from being burned."

Bob spoke up, "There's something else you ought to know too. The time you've spent here has had an effect on you. The good news, though, is that your body has nearly finished the process of becoming hyper-exothermic. This means that it can instantly adapt to the most extreme temperatures. The space-suit will catch fire and disintegrate during your descent through the mesosphere, but as long as it holds up until then, you should be fine regardless of how hot it gets."

Mina asked Jacques, "How do you know the suit will be strong enough to hold up until that part?"

Jacques replied, "Oh, my dear girl, my fromages are the most durable, delectable fromages ever created. They could handle three mesospheres of heat and fire! You will see! I am sending you with some crackers. You will have fondue with what is left of the melted suit after you make it past this flambé part of the atmosphere." Jacques reached back into his wheel-barrow and picked up a bundle of crackers that were tied neatly inside of a cloth napkin. He handed them to Mina.

Mina couldn't believe it had come down to this, that the safety of her trip home was dependent on the eccentric French chef and his cheese. She wasn't even sure she could trust anything he said—it was all so ridiculous. Yet Bob and Maude seemed to have confidence that it would turn out okay, and the only alternative to their plan was for her to stay on the Moon.

Maude patted Mina on the back. "If you're ready, we can start getting you dressed."

Mina shrugged. "I guess I'm as ready as I'll ever be."

"Bien!" said Jacques, and he grabbed hold of the cheese cloth and began wrapping it around Mina like a tailor working on a fine suit. He pinned the cloth around every part of her, including her feet, hands, and face. Then he cut two tiny slits for her to see out of. When he was finished, he proudly announced, "Fini!"

Next, Maude and Bob helped ease her into the heavy

bodysuit. Mina was surprised by how much give there was in the cheesy material despite being very thick. Even so, it was difficult to pull on without undoing the layers of cheesecloth that Jacques had worked on so meticulously. After a great deal of care and very slow dressing, Mina was fully encapsulated.

All that was left to do was to secure the rocket-pack and helmet. Bob, being the tallest, reached down and hoisted the large rocket-pack above Mina. Maude grabbed the metal straps at the front of the pack and guided them over Mina's shoulders, into the slots that Jacques had created to hold the pack in place. Mina could feel the weight of the pack pulling her backwards. To counter it, she leaned forward, as though she were fighting a strong gust of wind. Jacques, in turn, leaned backwards while standing in front of Mina, applying the cheesy dirt paste that sealed the slots in the suit's lining.

It was finally time for Mina to put her helmet on. Maude held it in front of her with both hands, but before she placed it over Mina's head, she smiled sweetly and said, "Archangel Mina of the great Theian sun." Maude gave Mina a wink. "We are eternally grateful for the journey you took to save us. It took immense courage and sacrifice to accomplish your quest. Therefore, we will proudly remember you and Helen as our heroines, henceforth."

Bob added, "Hear, hear! We'll erect statues of each of you in our new city square! Built with the finest organic materials."

Jacques added, "Oui, they will be made from the finest fromages!"

But both Maude and Bob looked at Jacques and shook their heads. "No, Jacques," said Maude. "They're not going to be made of fromage."

Jacques looked hurt and said, "Well, we shall have to discuss this, of course."

Mina giggled, but then, suddenly, her emotions caught up to her, and she began to cry. She couldn't stop. Her tears soaked through the cheese cloth, and Maude looked at Bob with a worried expression. "It'll be okay," he said and motioned to Jacques. "Quick! Grab what's left of the treated fabric. I'll remove the part that's damaged, and you can wrap her up again."

Jacques sprang into action as Bob took out a pocketknife and began to carefully cut away the wet cloth around Mina's face, starting at the back of her head. While the two men worked, Maude spoke to Mina again. "Everything will be okay, hon. But there's something else you need to know. It's like what Bob started to tell you earlier. Your body has undergone some major changes, and we don't know what those changes will mean for you after you return home. We've known for a long time that life on the Moon is not the same as it is on Earth. The people who traveled here didn't have anything to go back to."

Maude paused abruptly, looking a bit forlorn. "Mina, there's a possibility that all that's left of us…that we're…"

Mina stopped her. She knew what Maude was going to say, and she could see that it was causing her great distress. Mina said, "It's okay. I've known from the beginning what this place is. Dan thought of the Moon as a place for lost souls, but I can see that it's much more than that. It's a place for second chances, a place to start fresh and work towards a happy life."

"Yes, Mina. I think that's right," Maude said with a kind, knowing smile.

Jacques and Bob finished replacing the tear-stained cloth. Then Maude raised the thick, lumpy cheese helmet and lowered it over Mina's head. "Safe travels, dear angel," she said. But Mina could barely hear her through all the layers of cheese cloth and helmet.

She watched as Maude took her place next to Bob and Jacques a few yards away. Bob yelled at her, "Once the suit starts to melt, the rocket-pack will fall away! But the location-seeker we attached to your wings will continue to guide you home!"

Mina was pretty sure she'd heard everything Bob said, and she tried to give him a thumbs up. But her suit was too thick for her to move any of her fingers, so instead the gesture looked like a backwards wave.

She felt a pit forming in her stomach as the reality of what was about to happen sunk in. Clumsily, she twisted to look at the spinning ball she was about to return to. Only a tiny sliver of it was visible in the sky. The rest was hidden in shadow. She turned back. Bob was holding the remote control to the rocket-pack in both hands while Maude counted down on her fingers. Mina's heart raced faster.

When Maude had gotten to three, Mina did her best to wave goodbye. Jacques waved back, and then with a burst of energy, Mina was lifted off the ground. She rose straight up at a steady pace, higher and higher like she was riding an invisible elevator. Maude and Jacques walked to the spot right below her and waved. But Bob hung back with his eyes glued to her, holding the remote tightly.

The three of them grew smaller. Mina looked out across the Moon. She could see the market with all the tiny people walking around it and the ashes of the burned city just beyond. She could see the hills that she and Helen had crossed on their way to the Sheep Spa, and way off in the distance, she could see the border between day and night.

She looked in the other direction, to a part of the Moon she hadn't explored. There were dry, cracked flatlands that stretched on for miles and scraggily trees and cactuses that dotted the landscape. There was also a giant bowl-shaped crater with an enormous gear wheel at the bottom of it. Mina thought it had to be part of the mechanics that kept Waldoff on the Moon's Dayside.

As Mina approached thirty thousand feet, she could see a

huge section of the glowing, gray and white Moon below. It appeared tranquil and luminous once again, the way it had looked in the night sky back on Earth. She took a deep breath, and in her mind, she bid a final farewell to the strange world.

Mina felt like she was slowing down. She had experienced a sense of weightlessness as she rose high above the Moon's surface, but now her suit felt heavy again. She worried that something in the rocket-pack had malfunctioned when, suddenly, she stopped moving altogether.

Immediately, she began to plummet towards the Moon's surface. She reached her arms out to the sides like she thought she might use them to fly, but it was no use. She tumbled a hundred feet in a matter of seconds. Then once she'd rotated into a position where her back was to the ground and her head was pointed slightly up—*Pow*! She was launched towards the Earth with a great amount of force.

It took Mina a while to get used to the direction she was moving. She could see the Earth in front of her, but because of the awkward position she'd been in during launch, she perceived it to be upside down. It wasn't until much later that her brain was able to accept her destination as being right-side up.

Mina was excited to see the world in front of her growing bigger by the second. But she was apprehensive too. She didn't know if it had been wise to believe that an untested spacesuit made of cheese could keep her safe. However, the moment of truth arrived quicker than she'd hoped for as she breached the planet's dark blue atmosphere, leaving the vacuum of space behind.

Mina got the sense, soon after entering the thermosphere, that she was falling again—only this time, headfirst. She could see the expansiveness of her home planet laid out below, and her entire body rejoiced to behold all the signs of green, flour-ishing life. Never before had she experienced such gratitude for the wonder of nature.

Up ahead, she spotted a satellite orbiting the path just underneath her, but luckily, she beat it by a hair. She feared what was coming next—the flambé. A minute later, Mina was engulfed in a fiery cone of heat. The fire tested her resolve to return to her homeland, as though it were a homicidal border agent determined to keep her out. It was unlike anything she'd ever experienced. The cooling solution that the cheese cloth had been soaked in did nothing to dull the intensity of the flames that penetrated her flimsy suit.

She felt waves of scorching fire pulsating through the suit's layers. And suddenly, she became aware that this was how she was going to die. She tried to let her consciousness slip away into another part of her brain, a dark corner that was bliss-fully ignorant of the stratospheric soufflé she was about to become. It was no use, though. The pain was too severe. She tried to scream, but her mouth was pressed tightly against her helmet. She felt the rocket-pack rip away, and she knew there were only seconds remaining before the suit had completely melted.

She closed her eyes, hoping for the end. Her body began to spin, as if it were tied to a spit. Like a roasting pig being turned at hypersonic speed. With the little presence of mind she had left, she willed herself to faint. Her eyes rolled back into her head, and she thought she might be close to losing conscious-ness when, abruptly, everything stopped. The heat, the spin-ning, the hurtling towards Earth.

She had temporarily lost her vision, but when the darkness lifted, she could see that she was still high in the air above the planet. Her wings had stretched out on both sides, and she was gliding across an arctic sea of air. Mina raised her arms to look at them. There were patches of melted suit still covering parts of the cheese cloth, but there were also spots where the cloth had come unraveled, revealing Mina's bright red skin.

She was extremely thankful to be alive. She celebrated by letting out a scream of pure bliss and then continued the celebration by crying frozen tears of happiness. As she soared over the ocean, she could see a continent with its landmass curving down on both sides like giant arms waiting to welcome her home. She was flying through the troposphere, in and out of big fluffy clouds. To Mina's east, she could see a dark blue sky. To her west, the sun was sinking towards the horizon. *It will be dark soon*, she thought, and she hoped she could make it home before nighttime set in.

Mina's heart leapt for joy as she crossed over the gulf that bordered her home to the north. She was almost there. She soaked in the cleansing, cool air that rushed across her body. Seconds later, her feet touched down in the grass near her cottage as the last few rays of sunlight faded from the sky.

∽∽∽∽∽

MINA'S GRANDFATHER sat on the edge of the cliff at sunset, gazing at the moon, just like he did every night. He sensed that he had a good reason for being out there, though he could no longer remember what that reason was. Most of his memories had worn away long ago, so he'd learned to depend on his instincts for guidance instead.

Many nights he imagined how nice it would be to travel to the moon. He would journey across its craters and hills and meet all the nice people who were taking their own lunar vacations. He thought that the dark side might be a great place to go star gazing; there would be no light pollution or atmosphere to interfere with the experience.

The sun dipped below the horizon, and the moon's glow intensified. The old man began to whistle a tune. A love song, he thought. He didn't know where the song came from, but he felt sure he'd whistled it many times before. The melody made his heart feel full, as though it would burst. Suddenly, he heard something rustling in the grass behind him. He stood up and looked around to find a portly basset hound running his way. "Ruff! Ruff!" the dog barked excitedly when he saw the old man.

A moment later a young woman with dark hair came walking out of the shadows from behind the tall trees. She smiled lovingly at him. "Hello, Papa. Bonkers told me I might find you here."

The old man smiled back at the young woman while studying her face. After a moment, he spoke to her. "You're my granddaughter, aren't you?"

Mina nodded her head. "Yes, that's right. I'm your granddaughter, Mina. What have you been doing out here?"

Mina's grandfather looked back at the bright moon. "I've been waiting for something, I think, although I can't remember quite what it was. Do you know, Mina?"

Mina's eyes sparkled in the moonlight. "Were you waiting for me, Papa?"

Her grandfather shrugged his shoulders. "Maybe, but I feel like it had something to do with the moon."

"I bet you're right," she replied. "It looks beautiful tonight, doesn't it?"

The old man continued to stare at it. "You know, Mina. I think there are people up there, just like us."

Mina moved to her grandfather's side. "Maybe so. Hopefully, they have friends like Bonkers to keep them company. Life would be pretty sad otherwise, don't you think?"

Her grandfather said, "I think I'd like to visit the moon one day. Maybe I'll invent a machine that can fly me there, just like those boys on television did a long time ago."

Mina laughed. "I knew a man who did that once."

"Really?" her grandfather asked. "Did he have a big adventure?"

Mina sighed sweetly. "Oh, yes. He had a very big adventure, indeed."

The two generations stood for a while longer, staring into the sky. Finally, Mina took her grandfather's hand and said, "Come on, Papa. Let's go get ready for supper. We can talk about it some more then."

And Mina led him away from the cliff by the sea as Bonkers bounced happily along behind them.

EPILOGUE

The bespectacled professor sat behind his desk, reading a magazine as the students trudged in and found a seat. Mina sat alone at one of the long rows in the middle of the tiered classroom. She had made very few friends during the four years she'd spent studying at university, and the few that she'd made were studying subjects outside of her major.

The bell rang, and the lanky professor stood up. He stretched from side to side. Then without a word, he took a stack of papers from his satchel and dropped them in front of the student sitting at the end of the first row. The young man took one and passed them over to the next student.

The professor spoke. "Welcome everyone. For many of you, this is the first day of your last semester. As I'm sure you've heard, Quantum Mechanics will be the toughest course you ever take, even if you decide to pursue your doctorate in the subject. The reason for this is that you have to unlearn everything you know before you can learn anything I'm going to teach you. And I plan to teach you a *lot*. However, I promise I'll do my best not to fail you as long as you do your best not to make me." A few of the students laughed nervously.

The professor continued, "With that being said, please direct your attention to the syllabus in front of you. Take out a pen and circle my office hours. You *will* need to know them by heart."

Mina looked over as the stack of syllabi was passed her way. She took one and turned around to hand it to a student in the row behind her. The door to the classroom swung open with a loud crash. Out of the corner of her eye, Mina saw a tall, dark-haired man enter the room and make his way up towards her row. The professor laughed and said, "Well, I guess we have one more joining us today. Maybe our *spirited* friend could *close* the door next time also." Several of the students laughed, but Mina was too distracted to hear the professor's joke. The dark-haired man had sat down next to her in the previously empty row and was beginning to spread out, taking up a bunch of her space.

Mina was irritated but not surprised. Being one of the few females in most of her classes meant that she was used to having so-called *dominant* males try to push her buttons. She ignored the intrusion and focused again on what the professor was saying. "Causality, locality, and realism: three principles that make up the very heart of how we understand the world around us. Principles that are so fundamental to our observations of everyday life, we're practically married to them. Well, get ready to go through a bitter divorce, guys, because quantum physics defies all three of these principles. Let's start with Bell's Theorem. In 1964…"

Mina began to take notes when, suddenly, the man sitting next to her shoved a piece of paper in front of her. Mina didn't bother to read the words scribbled across it. Instead, she flicked the paper away, intent on ignoring the rude interruption while she continued to pay close attention to the professor's lecture.

A few seconds later, the paper appeared in front of Mina again, only this time the words were written in big, bold letters. "Do you think this guy really knows what he's talking about?" the note read. Mina rolled her eyes. It was worse than she'd thought. This guy wasn't just trying to show her he was dominant, he was hitting on her too.

Again, she pushed the piece of paper away and continued taking notes, trying to keep up with what the professor was saying. Another moment passed and, again, the paper showed up in front of her. This time it read, "This sounds like a bunch of mumbo jumbo if you ask me."

Mina was fed up. She picked up her notebook and pen and moved two seats down the row, away from the annoying alpha male, who was doing his best to distract her. Ten seconds later, the man scooted down the row and took the seat next to her. He wrote something down and then shoved the paper in front of her once more. "I'm serious. I think this guy is just making stuff up as he goes. I mean, really! Ghost particles? Back on Theia we just call them Moon Walkers."

Mina's eyes grew wide with surprise. For the first time since he'd sat down next to her, Mina looked directly at the man who was sitting to her side. He looked back at her with a big grin. His face was long, but his features were chiseled and handsome. He had a radiating smile and long, black eyelashes. It was hard to believe at first, but soon Mina's eyes convinced the rest of her that it was true. The entire time, the annoying jerk sitting next to her had been Fred, except that he wasn't the starving teenager she remembered. He was a full-grown, healthy-looking man. Mina gasped.

The professor asked, "Is everything okay, miss?"

Mina's head jerked towards her teacher. She'd almost forgotten where she was. Doing her best to contain her excitement, she bit her lip and nodded. Fred spoke to her. "It's good to see you, Mina. Sorry to surprise you like this, but I really need to talk to you. Preferably alone."

Mina whispered back, "I can't just leave in the middle of class. I need to take notes so I don't miss anything."

Fred shook his head. "No, it has to be now. This is important. You have no idea how hard it was to find you. Get the notes from one of these bozos," Fred insisted, pointing to Mina's classmates.

Mina shook her head too. She whispered again, "No, I can't walk out. The professor would torment me the rest of the semester. It's bad enough being the only woman in most of my classes. I already get the wrong kind of attention from practically everyone."

Fred looked up at the professor and then back at Mina. "Hey, I know. Why don't you tell him you're going to the moon? That'll get a big laugh from all these clowns, and then you won't have to worry anymore about what they think."

Mina sighed. "I'm not going to tell him I'm going to the Moon, Fred."

"Why not?" Fred asked.

Mina was getting frustrated and started to speak a little louder. "Because I can't just—"

But the professor interrupted, "Are you sure you're okay, miss? Do you need to be excused?

Mina was horrified. She glared at Fred but responded, "No…I mean, yes. I mean, I do need to be excused to go to the restmoon. I mean, the restroom! Sorry! It's been a weird day."

Some of the students snickered. "I see," said the professor with a raised eyebrow.

Mina stood up and motioned to Fred to follow her out of the room. Fred commented, "Well, that way worked too, I guess, but my way would've gotten a bigger laugh. Just saying."

Mina didn't speak again until they'd reached the hallway. She shut the door behind them and asked, "What are you doing here, Fred? You can't just barge into my class after all these years and expect me to drop what I'm doing."

Fred looked back at the class still going on behind Mina and said, "Actually, I think that's exactly what I just did. I thought you would be happier to see me, though."

Mina relaxed a little. She *was* happy to see Fred. After all, she had never forgotten about him or any of the other friends she'd made during her journey to the Moon. It's why she'd chosen to study astrophysics. She had spent years trying to make sense of what had happened to her and hoped she could learn enough about space travel and the universe to make contact with her friends again one day.

"You're right, Fred. I'm sorry. I was embarrassed back there, but I am happy to see you." She reached out to hug Fred, but he backed away.

Mina looked at him with a hurt expression. He quickly explained, "No, you don't understand. I'm not actually on Earth with you right now. I'm still on the Moon. Bob found a way to project me in a pseudo-physical form onto Earth. It means I can interact with objects, but we're not certain yet what effect it would have on people. Oh, and I should've mentioned. You're the only one on Earth who can interface with me."

Mina's jaw went slack. "Are you telling me that nobody else in that classroom could see or hear you?" she asked in disbelief.

Fred smiled. "Yeah, sorry about that."

"But the professor spoke to you when you came in!" Mina protested.

Fred shrugged. "He was just making a stupid joke. You know, like your 'restmoon' one."

Mina put her hand to her forehead. "Well, I guess I'm just going to have to drop this course now since I can *never* show my face in there again, which means I can forget about graduating altogether, I suppose!"

Fred nodded as though Mina were being perfectly reasonable. He said, "Sure, sure. Graduate. Don't graduate. None of that really matters right now, though."

Mina was furious. "And why is that?"

The light in Fred's face suddenly dimmed, and his eyes filled with tears. "Because Maude died last night, Mina. I've come to tell you—you have to come back."

ABOUT THE AUTHOR

K.E. spends most of her time with her family, including her husband, growing humans, and full-sized pets. When she is not dreaming, writing, or editing, she is asleep. Or she is possibly outside having an adventure with her growing humans and pets.

If you enjoyed reading *The Moon Travelers*, please consider leaving a review. Reviews are the backbone of an author's success, and it always means a great deal to get readers' feedback. Thank you for your support!

The Lunar Wolves & *The Gods of Time*, book two and three of The Moon Travelers Trilogy, are available now. K.E. also has a new series coming out in 2024 and a prequel to the Moon Travelers Trilogy planned for shortly after.

Follow K.E. on Facebook, Instagram, Twitter, and Threads @davenportwriter. Or visit her website to sign up for the monthly newsletter.

www.kedavenport.com

ACKNOWLEDGMENTS

Thank you to all of my friends and family who encouraged me through this process.

A very special thank you to Mom, Dad, and Sheila for all of your help (in many, many different forms). Dad, thank you for turning me into a writer before I could even write. Mom, thank you for always being excited about whatever I was working on. Sheila, thank you for being so good to all of us.

Sean, I continue to be impressed with you every day. Thank you for so many things but especially for believing in me and being my go-to person. I love you.

www.ingramcontent.com/pod-product-compliance
Lightning Source LLC
Chambersburg PA
CBHW060944190726

48286CB00005B/1412